OFF *the* CLOCK

RONI LOREN

BERKLEY BOOKS, NEW YORK

BERKLEY

An imprint of Penguin Random House
375 Hudson Street, New York, New York 10014

Library of Congress Cataloging-in-Publication Data

Loren, Roni.
Off the clock / Roni Loren. — Berkley trade paperback edition.
pages ; cm
ISBN 978-0-425-27854-3 (paperback)
I. Title.
PS3612.O764O34 2016
813'.6—dc23
2015031568

PUBLISHING HISTORY
Berkley trade paperback edition / January 2016

Cover art: Leisure Legs © Kichigan / Shutterstock.
Cover design by Diana Kolsky.
Text design by Kelly Lipovich.

Penguin
Random
House

To my family, always

Acknowledgments

There are so many people behind the scenes that help these books happen. I could never thank them enough.

Donnie, for your love and laughter and unflagging support.

Kidlet, for being awesome.

Mom, for listening to me ramble about writing problems even though most of the time I'm probably not making any sense at all.

De, for always having full confidence in me no matter what.

Julie Cross, Dawn Alexander, and Jamie Wesley, for being my "friends at the office" while I was writing this book. Thank you for the venting sessions, the celebrating, and the gossiping.

My agent, Sara Megibow, for always championing my books and for doing power reads when I'm having book panic attacks.

My editor, Kate Seaver, for being such a pleasure to work with and for loving these books.

Taylor Lunsford, for beta reading, being honest, and for saying, "What about Eli?" when I was brainstorming the short story.

And always, always, to my readers, for being fearless romantics, for reading my books, and for being the awesome people that you are.

Thank you!

*The Pleasure Principle: The human instinct
to seek pleasure and avoid pain.*

One is very crazy when in love.

—SIGMUND FREUD

1

Then

"*I'm going to wrap my fingers in your hair and slide my other hand up your thigh. You have to be quiet for me. We can't let anyone know.*"

Marin Rush paused in the dark hallway of Harker Hall, her tennis shoes going silent on the shiny linoleum and the green *Exit* signs humming softly in the background. She didn't dare move. She'd been on the way to grab a soda and a snack out of the vending machine. Her caffeine supply had run low and watching participants snore in the sleep lab wasn't exactly stimulating stuff. But that silk-smooth male voice had hit her like a thunderclap, waking up every sense that had gone dull with exhaustion.

She'd assumed she was the only one left in the psychology building at this hour besides the two study subjects in the sleep lab. It was spring break and the classrooms and labs were supposed to be locked up—all except the one she was working in. That's what the girl she was filling in for this week had told her. But there was no mistaking the male voice as it drifted into the hallway.

"I bet you'd like being fucked up against the wall. My cock pumping in you hard and fast."

Holy. Shit. Marin pressed her lips together. Obviously two other people thought they were alone, too. Had students snuck into the building to get it on? Or maybe it was one of the professors. *Oh, God, please don't let it be a professor.* She should turn around right now and go back to Professor Roberts's office. Last thing she needed was to see one of her teachers in some compromising position. She would die of mortification.

But instead of backing up, she found herself tilting her head to isolate where the voice was coming from, and her feet moved forward a few steps.

"Yeah, you like that. I know. I bet you're wet for me right now just thinking about how it would feel. Maybe I should check. Keep your hands against the wall."

A hot shiver zipped through Marin, making every part of her hyperaware.

"I'm so hard for you. Can you feel how much I want you?" That voice was like velvet against Marin's skin. She closed her eyes, imagining the picture the stranger was painting—some hot guy behind her, pinning her to the wall, his erection rubbing against her. She'd never been in that situation, but her body sure knew how to react to the idea. Her hand drifted up to her neck and pressed against her throat, her pulse beating like hummingbird wings beneath her fingertips.

She waited with held breath to hear the woman's response, but no voice answered the man's question. *Can you feel how much I want you?* he'd asked. And hell if Marin wasn't dying to know. She strained to hear.

"I tug your panties off and trail my hand up your thighs until I can feel your hot, slick . . ."

Marin braced her other hand against the wall and leaned so far forward that one more inch would've sent her toppling over. *Your hot . . .*

"Goddammit. Motherfucker."

The curse snapped Marin out of the spell she'd fallen into, and she straightened instantly, her face hot and her heartbeat pounding in places it shouldn't be. There was a groaning squeak of an office chair and another slew of colorful swearing.

Whoever had been saying the dirty things had changed his tone of voice and now sounded ten kinds of annoyed. A wadded-up ball of paper came flying out of an open doorway a few yards down. She followed the arc and watched the paper land on the floor. Only then did she notice there were three others like it already littering the hallway.

Lamplight shifted on the pale linoleum as if the person inside the office was moving around, and Marin flattened herself against the wall, trying to make herself one with it. *Please don't come out. Please don't come out.* The silent prayer whispered through her as she counted the doors between her and the mystery voice, mentally labeling each one. When she realized it was one of the offices they let the Ph.D. students use and not a professor's, she let out a breath.

Either way, she had no intention of alerting her hall mate that he wasn't alone. But at least she could stop worrying she'd gotten all fevered over one of her professors. Now she just had to figure out how to get past the damn door without letting him see her. She'd gotten used to skipping meals to save money since starting college a few months ago. But she wasn't going to make it through the next two hours of data entry and sleep monitoring if she didn't get some caffeine. No wonder none of the upperclassmen had wanted to fill in during break.

Marin's gaze slid over to the stairwell. If she stayed on the other side of the hall in the shadows, she could probably sneak by unnoticed. She moved to the right side wall and crept forward on quiet feet. But as soon as she got within a few steps of the shaft of light coming from the occupied room, a large shadow blotted it into darkness.

She'd been so focused on that beam of light that it took her a moment to register what had happened. She froze and her gaze hopped upward, landing on the guy who filled the doorway. No, not just any guy, a very familiar guy. Tall and lean and effortlessly disheveled. Everything inside her went on alert. *Oh, God, not him.*

He had his hand braced on the doorjamb, and his expression was as surprised as hers probably was. "What the hell?"

"I—" She could already feel her face heating and her throat closing—some bizarre, instant response she seemed to have to this man. She'd spent way too many hours in the back of her Intro to Human Sexuality class memorizing each little detail of Donovan West. Well, his profile, really. And his walk. And the way his shoulders filled out his T-shirts. As a teaching assistant, he usually only stopped in at the beginning of class to bring Professor Paxton papers or something. But each time he walked in now, it was like some bat signal for her body to go haywire.

It'd started with the day he'd had to take over the lecture when Professor Paxton was sick. He'd talked about arousal and the physical mechanics of that process. It was technical. He'd been wearing a T-shirt that read *Sometimes I Feel Like a Total Freud.* It shouldn't have been sexy. But Lord, it'd been one of the hottest experiences of her life. He'd talked with his hands a lot and had obviously been a little nervous to be in front of the class. But at the same time, he'd been so confident in the information, had answered questions with all this enthusiasm. Marin hadn't heard a word in the rest of her classes that day for all the fantasizing she'd been doing.

But now she was staring. And blushing. And generally looking like an idiot. Yay.

She turned fully toward him and cleared her throat, trying to form some kind of non-weird response. But when her gaze quickly traveled over him again, all semblance of language left her. *Oh, shit.* She tried to drag her focus back to his face and cement it there. His very handsome face—a shadow of stubble, bright blue eyes, hair that fell a little too long around the ears. Lips that she'd thought way too much about. All good. All great.

But despite the nice view, she couldn't ignore the thing in the bottom edge of her vision, the thing that had caught her attention on that quick once-over. The hard outline in his jeans screamed at her to stare—to analyze, to burn the picture into her brain. The need to look warred with embarrassment. The latter finally won and her cheeks flared even hotter. She adjusted her glasses. "Uh, yeah, hi. Sorry. I thought I was alone in the building. Didn't mean to interrupt . . . whatever."

He stared at her for a second, his brows knitting. "Interrupt?"

Goddammit, her gaze flicked there again. The view was like a siren song she couldn't ignore. *Massive erection, dead ahead!* She glanced away. But not quick enough for him not to notice.

"Ah, shit." He stepped behind the doorway and hid his bottom half. "Sorry. It's, uh . . . not what it looks like."

She snorted, an involuntary, nervous, half-choking noise that seemed to echo in the cavernous hallway. Really smooth. She tried to force some kind of wit past the awkwardness that was overtaking her. "Ohh-kay. If you say so."

He laughed, this deep chuckle that seemed to come straight out of his chest and fill the space between them with warmth. Lord, even his laugh was sexy. So not fair.

"Well, okay, it *is* that. But why it's there is just an occupational hazard."

His laugh and easy tone settled her some. Or maybe it was the fact that he was obviously feeling awkward, too. "Occupational hazard? Must be more interesting than the sleep lab."

He jabbed a thumb toward the office. "It is. Sexuality department. I'm working on my dissertation under Professor Paxton."

She could tell he didn't recognize her from class. Not surprising since she sat in the back of the large stadium-style room and tried to be as invisible as possible. Plus, she was wearing her glasses tonight. "I'm with Professor Roberts. I'm monitoring the sleep study tonight."

"Oh, right on. I didn't realize he'd taken on another grad student. I'm Donovan, by the way."

I know.

"Mari." The nickname rolled off her lips. No one called her that anymore. But she knew he probably graded her papers, and the name Marin wasn't all that common. She forced a small smile, not correcting him that she was about as far from a grad student as she could get. She wanted to be one. Would be one day if she could figure out how to afford it. She'd managed to test out of two semesters of classes, but high IQ or not, that dream was still a long way off—a point of light at the end of a very long, twisting tunnel.

Marin shifted on her feet. "I was heading to get a Coke so that I don't fall asleep from doing data entry and watching people snore. You need anything?"

"A Coke?" He glanced down the hall. "Don't waste a buck fifty on the vending machine. I've got a mini-fridge in here. You can come in and grab whatever you want."

Are you an option? I'd like to grab you. The errant thought made her bite her lips together so none of those words would accidentally slip out. She had no idea where this side of herself was coming from. Not that she'd really know what to do after she grabbed Donovan anyway. This was a twentysomething-year-old man, not one of the few boys she'd awkwardly made out with in high school. This was a guy who'd know how to do all those things she'd only read about in books.

"No, that's okay, I mean . . ." She shifted her gaze away, willing her face not to go red again.

He caught her meaning and laughed. "Oh, right. Sorry. Yes, you should probably avoid strange men with erections who invite you inside for a drink. Good safety plan, Mari." He lifted his hands and stepped back fully into the doorway, the pronounced outline in his pants gone. "But I promise, you're all good now. You just caught me at an . . . unfortunate moment. And now I'm going to bribe you with free soda so that you don't tell the other grads in the department about what you saw. I keep these late hours and work through holidays to avoid that kind of torture."

He gave her a tilted smile that made something flutter in her chest. She should probably head straight back to the office she was supposed to be working in. He was older. Kind of her teacher. If he found out she was one of Pax's students, he'd probably freak out that she'd seen him like this. But the chance to spend a few minutes with him was too tempting to pass up.

Plus, the way he was looking at her settled something inside her. Usually she shut down around guys. Being jerked around from school to school on her mom's whims hadn't left her with much time to develop savvy when it came to these things. But something about Donovan made her want to step forward instead of run away. "Yeah, okay. Free is good."

"Cool." His face brightened. Maybe he'd been as lonely and bored tonight as she had been. He bent over and picked up the papers he'd thrown into the hallway and then swept a hand in front of him. "Welcome to my personal hell. The fridge is in the back corner."

Marin stepped in first, finding his office a sharp contrast to the sterile sleep lab. His desk was stacked with photocopied articles and books, a Red Bull sat atop one of the piles, and a microphone was set up in the middle with a line going to the laptop. Along the back wall was a worn couch with a pillow and a blanket. More books were on the floor next to the makeshift napping quarters. Controlled chaos. She carefully made her way to the fridge and grabbed a Dr Pepper.

"Did you want me to get you something?" She peered back over her shoulder.

Donovan was busy gathering a pile of papers off the one other chair in the small office. "No, I'm good. Just opened my third Red Bull. I think my blood has officially been converted to rocket fuel. Don't light any matches."

She smiled and stepped back toward the door. "I hear ya. Well, thanks for the drink. I'll let you get back to—uh, whatever it was you were doing."

He pointed to the spot he'd cleared. "Or you could stay for a sec and take a break. God knows I need one."

She hesitated for a moment, knowing she was taking the I'm-a-fellow-grad-student charade too far, but then she thought about the endless boredom awaiting her in the sleep lab. She moved her way around the desk and sat. What could a few more minutes hurt? "Yeah, you sounded kind of pissed off when I walked by."

He stilled, and she cringed when she realized what she'd revealed.

He lowered himself to the chair behind his desk. "You can hear me in the hallway?"

"I— Sound travels. The hall echoes." She made some ridiculous swirling motion with her finger—as if he needed a visual interpretation of the word *echo*. She dropped her hand to her side and tucked it under her thigh to keep it from going rogue again.

"Good to know. So you heard . . ."

"Enough."

He laughed, all easy breezy, like they were discussing what they'd had for lunch today instead of X-rated talk and random erections in an institute of higher learning. "Well, then. Guess I should probably explain what I'm doing so I don't look like a total perv."

"It's fine. I mean, whatever." She wasn't sure if she sounded nonchalant or like she'd taken a few sucks off a helium tank. She guessed the latter.

He lifted a crumpled paper off his desk. "This is what you heard."

She leaned forward, trying to read the crinkled handwriting.

"Scripts," he explained. "I'm doing my dissertation on female sexual arousal in response to auditory stimuli. I'm recording scripts of fantasies that we may use in the study."

"Your study is about *dirty talk*?" she asked, surprised that the university was down with that. And if he was the one doing the dirty talking, where did she sign up to volunteer?

He smirked and there was a hint of mischief in that otherwise affable expression. "Yes, I guess that's one way to put it. If you want to be crass about it, Ms. Sleep Disorders."

"I'm no expert, but I know what I heard."

"Fair enough. But yeah, I'm focusing on the effect of scripted erotic talk on women who have arousal disorder. A lot of times, therapists suggest that these clients watch erotic movies to try to increase their libido. But in general, porn is produced for men. So even though that method can be somewhat effective, the films don't really tap into women's fantasies. They tap into men's. Erotic books have worked pretty well. But I want to test out another method to add to the arsenal—audio. It'd be cost effective to make, wouldn't send more money to the porn industry, and could be customized to a client's needs. Plus, it's easy to test in a lab."

Marin liked that he was talking to her like a peer, and his frankness about the topic saved her some of the weirdness that would normally surface when talking about sex. Academic talk soothed her. Plus, his passion was catching. That's what she loved about this environment. In high school, everyone acted like they were being forced to learn. She'd always been the odd one for actually enjoying school. Books and all that information had been her escape. Schools changed. The people around her changed. Books were one of the few things that stayed constant. But here at the university there were people like Donovan, people who seemed to be mainlining their education and getting high off what they learned. "So what were you so frustrated about?"

He grabbed his can of Red Bull and took a sip, keeping his eyes on her the whole time. "I'm discovering that women are complicated and that I'm having trouble thinking like one."

"Ah. And this is shocking news?"

"Well, no. I knew it was going to be tough, but the fantasies are turning out to be harder than I thought. We did a round of romantic ones in a small trial run, and they were a major fail. Women reported enjoying listening to them but the arousal was . . ." He gave an arcing thumbs-down. "My friend Alexis, one of the other grads working under Pax, told me that I needed to go more primal, tap into the forbidden type of fantasies, that sweet romance makes a girl warm and fuzzy but not necessarily hot and bothered."

Marin's neck prickled with awareness, but she tried to keep her expression smooth. "Makes sense."

"Does it?"

"I—uh, I mean . . ."

"Never mind. I retract the question." He leaned back in his chair and ran a hand through his dark hair, making it even messier. "I met you like five minutes ago, and I'm already asking you if taboo fantasies do it for you. Sorry. Hang out in this department too long, and you lose your filter for what is acceptable in normal conversation. I spent lunch yesterday discussing nocturnal penile tumescence with a sixty-five-year-old female professor, and it wasn't weird. This is my life."

Marin smiled and played with the tab on the top of her soda. "I'm clearly hanging out in the wrong department. My professor just talks about sleep apnea. Though I've been monitoring the sleep lab and can confirm that nocturnal penile tumescence is alive and well."

"Ha. I bet."

She wet her lips and, feeling brave, leaned forward to grab the script he'd left on his desk. He didn't make a move to stop her, and she squinted at the page, trying to decipher his handwriting. The fantasy looked to be one between a boss and subordinate. She saw the parts she'd heard him read aloud. *I'm so hard for you. I tug your panties off.*

She crossed her legs. The part he'd gotten hung up on had various crude names for the female anatomy listed and scratched out—like he couldn't decide which one would be most effective. She didn't have input to give him on that, but just seeing the fantasy on the page had her skin tingling with warmth, her blood stirring. She shifted in her chair. Kept reading.

"Okay, well that's a good sign," he said, his voice breaking through the quiet room.

Marin looked up. "What?"

He leaned his forearms against the desk, his blue eyes meeting hers. "You just made a sound."

"I did not."

"Yeah, you did. Like this breathy sound. And your neck is all flushed. That one's working for you."

She tossed the paper on his desk. "Oh my God, you really don't have a filter."

He smiled, something different flaring in his eyes, something that made her feel more flustered than those words on the page. "Sorry. It's all right, though. Seriously. You already saw me with a hard-on. Now we're even. But this is good information. I thought this one may be too geared toward the male side—a fantasy that'd appeal to me but not necessarily to a woman. You're telling me I'm wrong."

"I didn't say anything."

"You didn't have to. You're like . . ."

She could feel her nipples pushing against her bra, their presence obvious against her T-shirt, and fought the urge to clamp her hands over them, to hid her traitor body. She stood. "Okay, so I'm leaving now."

"No, no, come on, wait," he said, standing. He grabbed her hand before she could escape, and the touch radiated up her arm, trapping her breath in the back of her throat. "You can help. I've got a stack of these. I need to know which ones to test next week and which ones to trash. Or maybe you can offer suggestions? I promise to keep my eyes to myself. And I swear, if you help me, I'm yours for whatever you want. I can take a shift in the sleep lab for you or something."

She stared at him. He was kidding, right? He had to be kidding.

"You want me to read through fantasies and tell you which ones *turn me on*?" His hand was so warm against her cold one. And she'd said the words *turn me on* to him. Out loud. She might just die. "Can't you ask your friend who's in this department to do that?"

"She's a lesbian, so her fantasies don't quite line up with these. I need a straight girl's opinion. Wait—are you straight?"

She blinked. Were they actually having this conversation? "I— yes. But this is beyond embarrassing."

"Why? Because you get turned on by fantasy stuff? It's not embarrassing. It's human. You'd be shocked by how many people struggle to tap into that part of themselves. That kind of responsiveness is a good thing."

Responsiveness. Donovan West was talking about her sexual responsiveness. *Hello, alternate universe.* "Donovan, I don't know . . ."

He let go of her hand and opened a drawer. "Here. I have an idea. I'll give you some headphones and a thumb drive with the ones I've already recorded. You can take them back to your lab and listen to them while you do data entry. Then you can just tell me which ones you recommend when you're done. You won't have to feel self-conscious sitting with me. Plus, I need to record some more tonight, and I can't do that if someone's in here with me."

He held out the earbuds and a blue thumb drive. She eyed them like they would bite her, but on those files would be Donovan's voice in her ear, saying those explicit things, things she'd never had a guy whisper to her. Things she'd only imagined in the private quiet of her room when she gave her mind leave to go to those secret places. The temptation was a hot, pulsing thing low in her belly.

She needed to say no. Make some excuse. Stop this lie she'd started.

She took the items. "Okay."

His eyebrows lifted. "Yeah?"

"I'm not making any promises, but I'll let you know if I've listened to any before I leave tonight."

His grin was like a physical touch to her skin. "That would be amazing. I'll owe you big-time, Mari."

She got caught up in that smile like a fly in a web and wanted to linger, wanted to stay there all night and listen to him talk about his research, what made him passionate, what else made him smile like that. But if she stayed, she'd only risk embarrassing herself further, or worse—get herself in trouble. Because the thing blooming inside her with him looking at her like that, like her opinion mattered, was intoxicating and potent. She wanted to cling to it, to wrap herself up in that feeling and jump into the unknown without thinking about the consequences. Something she could never do.

She lived her life carefully, always making sure to stay between the lines on the road. No alcohol. No drugs. And definitely no risky behavior with boys. She'd learned from her mother that one foot off the path, one chased whim, could lead to chaos. She knew enough about her mom's disorder to know that those genes probably lingered in her, too, and this pulsing desire to flirt with Donovan, to push this charade further, could be a dangerous one.

She probably shouldn't listen to the tapes at all, shouldn't open that door. Things were safe right now, calm. She needed them to stay that way.

But Marin couldn't bring herself to hand the flash drive back. Not yet. She didn't want to do anything to erase that smile off of Donovan's face.

So she mumbled a quick good-bye and headed down the hall

with the thumb drive tucked in her pocket and the soda in her hand. She'd only told Donovan she'd try. She had an out. She needed to take it and focus on her job. Get those little numbers entered into the computer, get lost in the monotony, and forget about the sexy TA down the hall.

But it wasn't more than twenty minutes after she stepped back into Professor Roberts's lab that the temptation proved too great. Maybe she'd just listen to one, show Donovan a good faith effort, and be done. She cued up the recordings, and Donovan's voice filtered into her head.

"I spot you first across the bar. You look beautiful, and I know you've come here with someone else. I can see him getting you a drink. But I can feel your eyes on me, taste your desire, and I know that tonight, it's going to be my hands on you, my body moving over yours, and my name on your lips . . ."

Marin didn't get another lick of work done that night.

2

Then

Marin rolled her shoulders before she climbed out of her car, trying to shake off the guilt. She'd picked up her little brother from art camp this afternoon, where he'd been all week, and Nate had begged her to stay home and have movie night with him and Mom. She'd missed seeing him, but this was the last night she'd get Donovan alone. On Monday, classes would start back up again. He'd find out she was a fraud. An eighteen-year-old one at that.

So Marin had promised Nate she'd have an epic Mario Brothers battle with him tomorrow and watch whatever movie he wanted afterward. He'd pouted but had made the deal when she'd added cookie-baking to sweeten the pot. Her mother had also given her the guilt routine, complaining that Marin hadn't been home at night all week and that Marin should be more sympathetic about the breakup she'd just gone through with random-asshole-of-the-month. Her mom had tossed out the word *sad*, knowing that the word was one that would normally trigger Marin to do whatever it took to fix it. Her mom's manic episodes were hard to deal with;

the depressive ones were annihilating. It shredded Marin to see her mother suffer through them. And scared her.

But this time, Marin sensed her mom was saying it more to manipulate her than anything else and it had pissed her off. Normally, she could keep the frustration in check, be understanding and supportive. She knew her mom's condition was an illness, that her mother couldn't easily control her emotions or her actions. But in that moment, Marin had felt so damn exhausted by it all. Smothered. So she'd let the anger take over and had told her mom she had to go to work on a Saturday because the only grown-up in the house kept getting fired from jobs and they needed the money.

It'd been ugly and mean, but sometimes the pressure in the volcano was just too much. The crack had splintered and broken open. Her mother had called her selfish.

Maybe she was. Tonight she needed to be. Tomorrow she'd mend the fences, smooth things over. But this week was her break from it all, and she wasn't going to let the last day be stolen from her.

Each night she spent in that empty psychology building with Donovan West was like this sweet, private vacation from her life. There were no heavy burdens, no household to run, no eggshells to walk on. Here she could be that girl she wanted to be—a carefree college student who spent her time researching fascinating things and crushing on a hot guy.

The escape was like a drug. Each night she would tell herself that tonight would be the last time, that she'd tell him the truth. But then she'd see him again, and all her good intentions would fall by the wayside. His research was on forbidden fantasies. But this was hers. Stolen nights alone with a man who was older, funny, brilliant. *Beautiful.*

Part of her felt like this was payback for spending her high school years on the sidelines, watching other girls get asked on dates, watching other people go to the dances or sneak kisses in the hallway, watching normal life go by without her. She'd always been the new girl. The quiet one. The smart one. And even when she'd been asked to parties on occasion, she'd rarely been able to go. Her mom and brother had needed her at home. If she didn't show up, who would make sure dinner was on the table or that her brother had clean clothes for the next day? Who would make sure her mom took her meds?

This week had been a gift. She and Donovan had gotten into a routine. She'd drop off the notes she'd made about his tapes, and they'd hang out for a while. She'd learned that he expected to graduate with his doctorate next year, that he liked old movies, that he'd originally planned to study addictions but then switched after taking a class with Professor Paxton and falling in love with the field. And she'd found herself sharing stuff about herself that she never did with anyone else—that she'd lived in eight different states in ten years, that she still lived at home to help with the money because her mom was in between jobs, that she read at least three novels a week.

She liked that he didn't pry, that he took the information she gave about herself but didn't push for more. When she'd told him about living at home, instead of the normal nosy questions or empty sympathy, he'd simply nodded and said, "That's cool of you to live at home and help out. Not many people would sacrifice their party years like that."

Even without him knowing half of what she dealt with at home, the simple acknowledgment of that sacrifice had meant so much more than he'd probably realized. She was so used to people looking at her with pity—therapists, the teachers at Nate's school, the doctors. Donovan had looked at her with respect. Maybe if he'd known about her mom's disorder, some of that pity would've leaked out, but she had a feeling he wouldn't be that way. That was the night she'd stopped seeing him as just a really hot guy and had found herself wanting him for altogether new reasons.

But their chats couldn't last long since they both had work to do. So they'd go their separate ways. He'd give her more recordings—some based on her suggestions, some tweaked with her feedback—and she'd go to the lab.

The rest of the night would be spent wrapped up in his voice, her body growing hot and heavy, the place between her thighs left wet and wanting. She'd never felt so much sexual hunger in her life. She'd fantasized, sure. She'd had crushes on guys. She'd made out with a few when she'd had the chance—satisfying her curiosity more than her desire. But never had she been consumed by need for someone like this. On some level, she now understood why her mom so easily got herself in trouble with men. This rush was a powerful one.

Marin's world had quickly narrowed to this one thing, this one person, during the stretch of spring break. The stress at home with her mother had faded to a hum in the background. In the mornings when she'd gotten home from the overnight shift, Marin had walked past the obsessively neat kitchen and living room, knowing it could be a sign her mother was bordering on one of her manic states. But she hadn't let herself fall into anxiety over it like she normally did. She'd checked her mom's pill supply to make sure she was still taking her meds, made sure food was in the fridge, called her little brother to check on how he was doing at camp, then she'd let everything fall away. She'd go to her room, slide beneath the covers, and replay the copies she'd made of Donovan's recordings—her hands standing in for his as she brought herself relief in the tell-no-secrets dark of her room.

Then when she'd wake in the afternoon, she'd work on notes for Donovan. He liked her suggestions, and she found herself moving past editing his words and penning her own private fantasies instead, her versions of what she imagined doing with him. She now had a stack of pages with him in the starring role—pages for her eyes only that she'd keep long after this.

She knew it was ridiculous, that she was treading into obsessive territory, that it was dangerous to chase this rabbit down the hole. She'd watched her mother get fixated on projects, on jobs, on men. So many men. She knew that intensity could be an early sign of things going askew. But Marin couldn't let herself think about it too hard. Her shoulders bowed under the pressure of always wondering if she'd have to face the same monsters her mother fought every day. It was too much to think about. Too big. This interest in Donovan didn't have to mean that. Girls got crushes on boys. It was okay. She needed this.

Plus, she wasn't sure when she'd get this kind of chance again. After break, life would go back to her duct-taped version of normal. So maybe it was okay to take this little risk. She was in college now. She craved the same things that other people her age did. Experience. Adventure. Fun. Sex. She knew for Donovan it was just a random meet-up with a random girl in a probably exciting day-to-day life filled with friends and dates and family. Everyone else was on break. She was there. And she was helping him. This was a one-sided fantasy. And she could deal with that.

But on this last Saturday before spring break wrapped up, the end loomed like cold, gray rain clouds, the brief vacation from her life slipping away from her. On Monday, everyone would return to campus. She'd have to go back to class. Donovan would find out who she was. She wouldn't be some savvy fellow grad student to him. She'd just be one of the students whose paper he graded.

She'd thought about taking a chance tonight, attempting to flirt. A relationship with him wasn't possible, but imagining things taking an R-rated turn was like staring at some ripe fruit hanging on the vine. She'd listened to the girls around her in school whisper about what they did with their boyfriends. She'd read enough romance novels to know how sexy those things could be. And now she'd spent a week listening to Donovan's voice and the fantasies he'd penned. She'd never gotten a taste of that kind of physical connection with a guy and now she wanted a big bite.

But she'd be delusional to believe that he looked at her the same way. The guy was a man on a mission. His love was his work, and he was only interested in talking with her because she was helping with his research. She needed to keep that in her head.

She checked her phone for the time as she walked down the hall. Donovan's door was shut. She was here early. She'd been so ready to get out of the house after the argument with her mother that she hadn't even noticed. But seeing his door closed, it hit her that he might not even come in tonight. It was Saturday, after all, and they hadn't made firm plans. Why had she assumed he'd be here? Just because it was a big, exciting event in her mind didn't mean it'd even hit his radar. He was probably out on a date or at a party or having a beer with friends. Disappointment moved through her like a cold gust of wind. What if she'd gone through that whole drama at home just to sit here alone tonight?

She sighed. Par for the course. She could at least drop off her notes. And maybe he'd come in later.

She gave his door a little tap just in case and then turned the knob when there was no answer. The old heavy door creaked open, and the dark office greeted her. The scent of books and something faintly spicy filled her nose. She felt around for the light switch, but when she flipped it, nothing happened. She let out a frustrated breath and carefully made her way to the desk to find the lamp. When she grabbed hold of the chain and clicked it on, a startled noise sounded behind her.

Her hand flew to her chest and she yelped, banging into the desk and dropping her notebook and everything else she'd been carrying.

A groan. "Jesus, Mari. You scared the hell out of me."

Marin whirled around to find Donovan stretched out on the worn couch—his dark hair a mess, his eyes puffy, and his chest . . . bare. *Oh. My.* She wet her lips, trying not to stare. But that was like expecting the clock on the wall not to tick. He looked like hell. And gorgeous. And very, very male—all sprawled out and sleep rumpled. There was no way she was going to be able to convince her eyes to focus on something else. A bomb could go off behind her and not turn her gaze. "Shit. I'm sorry. I didn't realize you were here. I was just dropping off notes."

He gripped the blanket that covered him from the waist down. "What time is it?"

"I'm early. It's not quite ten."

"Fuck." He ran a hand over his face. "I didn't think you were coming in tonight."

Her gaze alighted on the folded clothes on the nearby chair, on the takeout container on top of the fridge, on the opened bottle of whiskey next to it. "Sorry, I didn't mean to wake you up from your . . . catnap?"

She didn't mean for it to come out as a question, but what she saw said something very different from a nap caught between too many hours of research. Now the fact that he was always here, always working late when no one else was made sense.

He sat up and reached out to grab his T-shirt without meeting her eyes. He pulled it over his head, covering all that lean, sinewy muscle. "I stay overnight here sometimes. Dr. Paxton knows."

"I— Okay." She clamped her lips shut. She wasn't going to be one of those people who asked questions that weren't her place to ask. She wasn't going to ask why he slept here even though he seemed to have money—designer jeans, fancy laptop. And she wasn't going to ask why it looked like he'd been crying. And drinking. Alone.

Donovan pushed the blanket away, revealing a pair of wrinkled jeans and bare feet. "I didn't think you'd be die-hard enough to work on a Saturday night. You've got to have some place more interesting to be."

She backed away to the other side of the desk to give him space—to give *her* space. Last thing she needed was for her blushing affliction to start up. "I, uh, still have a lot of stuff to wrap up before Professor Roberts gets back."

He frowned and slipped socks on. "I'm sorry. I'm sure helping me has put you behind. You need me to pitch in? I'm fast at data entry."

"Uh, it's okay. I'll be fine. You can get some rest. I won't bother you."

"You're not—" He grimaced and shook his head. "You're not bothering me. I just— I wasn't expecting company tonight."

"Are you okay?" The question slipped out before she could stop it.

"I'm fine." The words were like a whip snapped.

She winced at the stinging impact.

He blew out a breath and looked up at her, weariness in those blue eyes. "Sorry. I'm— It's just been a shit day."

She shifted on her feet, not sure what to do with this version of the normally upbeat guy she'd gotten to know. He looked like he could use a hug, but she didn't like random people giving her those, so she wouldn't assume that he'd be cool with that either. Plus, she'd probably pant or drool on him or something, being that close. "Anything I can do to help?"

"Distraction'd be good. Wanna get drunk with me?"

She glanced at the whiskey bottle. "I don't drink."

His brows went up. "Ever?"

"Not my thing." No way was she testing her genes with a big heaping dose of mood-altering substances. "Maybe another kind of distraction?"

"Wanna fuck?"

The question zipped right up her spine, making her straighten and almost taking her feet out from under her. She hadn't meant her question that way, but now she realized how what she'd said must've sounded. "Uh . . ."

Donovan turned away with a groan. "Shit. Just fucking ignore me. I might still be drunk. I didn't mean to say that."

Her mouth was dry, her heart knocking hard against her ribs. She ached to go to him, put her arms around him, make whatever had beat him down today go away. To say, *Yes, let's do that thing you said. Right now.* But all she could do was stand like a damn statue in the half-lit room and say, "It's all right."

"No, it isn't. It's the opposite of all right."

She should leave. Let him deal with whatever was bothering him in private. But she couldn't make her feet move. "Tell me what's going on."

Donovan went about folding the blanket he'd tossed on the couch, his movements tense. One. Two. Three. He folded sharp lines into the soft quilt. She thought he was going to ignore her completely, but then finally, he spoke. "My parents were killed in a home invasion last year."

Her heart plummeted into her stomach, making a gust of air pop out of her mouth.

"Today, the courts dropped the case against the guy who everyone thought did it." He tossed the folded blanket onto the back of the couch with more force than necessary. "New evidence cleared him. Now there's not a fucking lead to go on, and the case is cold. My parents are dead, my family is gone, and whoever did it is out there living his goddamned life like nothing ever happened."

She closed her eyes, the pain in his voice seeping into her and making her hurt for him. "I'm so sorry."

He turned around, his jaw set. "Yeah, well, life isn't fair, right? The good guys don't get to win just because they're good."

The bitterness in his voice made her want to cry for him. "Tell me what I can do to help."

He stepped toward the desk and put his hand on the notes she'd dropped onto it when she came in. "We can not talk any more about it and work. I've learned it's like running in freezing weather. You don't feel the cold until you stop moving. As long as I keep focused on the project and keep working, I can block out the rest." He swiped a hand over his face as if trying to erase all he'd revealed to her in the last few minutes. Mask back in place. "So I'll go through your notes, and I have some new stuff for you. I really liked your insights on the last one. Have you ever considered switching to this department? I can tell the sleep stuff isn't really doing it for you."

The tone of his voice had switched to all business, the emotions packed up tight behind the safety door, padlock clicked. She knew that mode. It was that place she went when her mom had one of her episodes. Like when she'd come home one day a few years ago and all the plates had been smashed because her mom had been fired from another job. Her mom had been sitting among the mess, hands and knees cut from the jagged glass. Nate had been left at kindergarten because her mom hadn't remembered to pick him up. Marin had been thirteen, but she'd learned that day to switch off the fear and to keep moving forward. She'd bandaged her mom up, called a neighbor to pick up Nate, and had spent the night cleaning the kitchen.

So she knew not to push Donovan for more and went along with the shift in conversation. She'd run along beside him in those sub-zero temperatures.

"I might consider it actually. I've really enjoyed digging into your research." And that was the truth. She'd always planned to specialize since she wanted to be a researcher not a practicing clinician. But she'd had yet to find the topic that lit her up. This hadn't just lit her up, it'd set her aflame. Sex was fascinating—this strange, foreign thing she wanted to unpack and analyze. And learning from Donovan this week about all the different avenues in the field had deepened her interest even more. When he didn't respond, she shifted and cleared her throat. "So what have you got for me tonight?"

He sank into his chair, moving aside her notes. He wouldn't look at her. "I've been working on a force scenario. Nothing violent, but it's going pretty far in the taboo direction."

"Force?"

He glanced up at her, his eyes clearer than they had been a moment before but still tired. "It's a pretty popular fantasy according to research—capture fantasies, things getting a little rough—especially for women who are held back by having guilty feelings about sex. But it can be a trigger for others, so you need to tell me now if you're uncomfortable with listening to that."

Marin wet her lips, images of Donovan taking charge and taking over filling her head. She could still feel the anger rolling off of him and wondered if he'd come up with the fantasy because that's what he needed right now—a little violence, someone he could exorcise those demons with, a release from all that ugly reality. "I can handle it."

"Okay, cool." He rocked forward in his chair and grabbed a thumb drive. "Remember, I'm looking for unedited feedback. If it sucks or is horrible, you need to tell me. Don't coddle me just because I had a bad day."

"I wouldn't do that."

He nodded. "Thanks."

"So did it work for you?" The question jumped out before she could stop it.

He peered up at that, surprise there at first but then something else flashed in those blue eyes—wariness. "Well, I have no interest in forcing myself on anyone, if that's what you mean."

"That's not what I asked." Marin didn't know where her boldness was coming from. Maybe knowing this was her last night with him was making her daring. Or maybe she was still thinking about the alternative he'd suggested to drinking the night away. "You want me to listen to it and tell you what I think. Obviously, I don't want some guy to rape me."

He coughed and ran a hand over the back of his neck. "Sorry, you're right. I'm asking for all this personal honesty from you and you've given it. I'd be an asshole if I'm not willing to do the same." He straightened the papers on his desk. "The scenario worked for me. Rape isn't a turn-on. Obviously. But a woman consenting to playing that game, to letting it get kind of rough? That could be hot."

Marin rolled her lips inward, need curling like vines, tangling with the images in her mind. "Yeah, I bet it would be. Cathartic, even."

His jaw twitched, and he seemed to be thinking hard on her

words. For a moment she thought maybe it would happen. Maybe he'd get up, grab her and kiss her, put his hands on her. Maybe he'd let her help him forget for a little while. Help her forget. But then he cleared his throat and rolled his desk chair forward under the desk. "Thanks, Mari."

Any hope she had burned into a pile of ashes at her feet. Of course he wasn't going to stroll across the room and ravage her like some old-school romance novel. He'd confided in her about his family, but that's just because he was hurting and she was there. They were just working on a project together. Friends. Hell, not even that. She picked up her backpack and hitched it onto her shoulder. "Yeah, no problem."

He rubbed fingers over his forehead. "And I'm sorry about what I said earlier. It was completely out of line."

"It's fine. Don't worry about it." She grabbed the thumb drive. "I'll check in with you when I'm done."

Donovan looked up like he was going to say something else, but then seemed to think better of it. He clamped his lips shut and nodded, effectively dismissing her.

She headed down the hallway to the sleep lab on shaky legs. When she reached the lab, she let out a breath she hadn't realized she'd been holding. The room was empty and quiet except for the hum of the computers. Tonight there'd be no study participants on the other side of the glass, so she'd have the place to herself. She'd never been more thankful for it. She needed time to put herself back together.

She couldn't get it out of her head about what Donovan had gone through. That sadness in his eyes when she'd first walked in. Then the swift heat that had filled her when he'd said, *Wanna fuck?* Right then she'd had a feeling that despite the alcohol involved, she was seeing some real part of Donovan, the unrefined part that lurked in there, the part she'd only glimpsed in some of the fantasies he'd recorded. She felt guilty about even having those kinds of feelings when he was going through such a hard thing, but her body seemed to be programmed to respond to him that way.

Marin sank into her chair and rubbed a hand over her brow. After the fight with her mom and the conversation with Donovan, she needed this night in the lab. Predictable. Safe. She could block out all the ugly stuff and just focus on his voice, on escaping into the fantasy. She turned on her terminal, slipped in the thumb drive, and put in her earbuds.

She would listen to Donovan and block out the real world for a while. The tape started.

"You don't see me behind you. I know you know who I am, but you don't know I've been watching you. You don't know how much I think about you, about all the dirty things I want to do to you. You have no idea how badly I need you and no idea that tonight's the night you're going to be mine. I want to hear you beg for your pleasure and for my mercy . . ."

The smooth, deep voice in her ear let everything else melt away. She closed her eyes and let the words take over, sinking into the fantasy and feeling her body go warm and liquid after only a few minutes. The words were explicit, the scene intense. The man captured the woman, tied her down in his hotel room, brought her to the edge of orgasm over and over and then took her roughly from behind. But there were hints in the narrative that showed the man was taking care of the woman, that she'd consented to this earlier, that this was a taboo fantasy shared by willing lovers.

And it was *so* working for Marin.

She found herself squeezing her thighs together, the throbbing ache between them almost unbearable. She'd gone through this night after night listening to these tapes, but this one seemed to be pushing her buttons even harder, the taboo topic and danger of it tapping into some reckless part of her. And all the emotion from earlier with Donovan channeled into the fantasy as she pictured him in the role of the man, her in the role of the captive.

Her body thrummed as the scene unfolded in her head, every part of her going sensitive, primed. Like one touch and she'd go off. She tried to stave off the desire, clamping her hands around the arms of the chair and breathing through the rush. But finally, as the man in the tape brought the woman to another orgasm using harsh fingers and filthy words, Marin couldn't take it anymore and parted her knees. There was so much tension in her—from the crappy day, from her conversation with Donovan, and from this unmet desire she'd been fighting with all week. She couldn't resist anymore. She needed the oblivion, some kind of release from it all. The air of the room felt cool on her inner thighs and she pressed a hand over the throbbing part of her through her shorts, giving just enough pressure to offer some relief.

She let out a soft gasp and slowly rocked her hand against herself, the simple move sending sharp, electric currents racing through her, making everything go heavy and tight. Her breasts felt fuller, her blood hotter, her pulse louder. Guilt weighed on her. Part of her knew she shouldn't be doing this. She didn't deserve this pleasure tonight. But the freight train was already chugging down the hill with no brakes. She dragged her fingers over the cotton of her shorts, trying to be discreet but not gentle.

Before long, she was so swept up in it and so close to falling over the edge that she didn't hear the knock on her door when it came. She didn't know she was no longer alone, that someone was watching. Then the earbuds were yanked out of her ears.

She nearly leapt out of her seat. Her hand flew away from her shorts and gripped the arm of the chair. The scent of clean soap and whiskey cascaded over her. Donovan.

"*Mari?*"

3

Then

M arin's fingers went white against the chair arm. *Please, please, don't let him have seen what I was doing.* The prayer was desperate, yearning. "Shit. You scared me half to death."

She couldn't turn around. Not yet. She was afraid the desire would show all over her face. She'd been seconds from orgasm. Her body screamed in protest, air soughing through her lungs as she tried to reel it all in and look cool and collected.

"I called your name and you didn't hear me." His voice was there again, close, but not on a recording this time. His breath was hot against her hair as he loomed behind her.

"Did you need something?" Her voice came out way too breathless, like rubber bands had been wrapped around her windpipe.

He was quiet for a few long seconds. "Are you . . ."

No. No. No. Her head started to shake.

"Mari . . . I saw." The words were simple. Final. A guillotine.

Hope shattered into little fragments at her feet, raining down into a pool of humiliation. She switched into offense mode.

"Look, I caught you turned on once. Now you caught me. The script works. Hurrah. Make a note. Can we be grown-ups about it now?" She hoped the words sounded confident and brash even though she was trembling inside.

He was silent behind her.

"Did. You. Need. Something?" Her question came out sharp, pointed.

"I was bringing you something to drink. You forgot to take a soda with you."

Be a grown-up, be a grown-up. She forced herself to swivel her chair around, to look unaffected. She took the Dr Pepper from him and set it on the desk. "Thanks. You didn't have to do that."

His gaze rolled over her, a slow, seeking perusal. Something dark and tense glinted in his eyes. "You didn't get to finish."

"I'm fine," she bit out.

"You're out of breath and . . ." His focus shifted down her body. "And wet."

She glanced down. Saw the telltale spot announcing how turned on she was through the thin cotton of her shorts. Oh, shit. Oh, God. Oh, *fuck.* Mortification like none she'd ever experienced bled through her. Her thighs snapped together. "Can you please not make this worse with your analytics? Just let me be embarrassed in peace."

His blue eyes met hers, the tired resignation from earlier gone and replaced with something she'd never seen before from him— intent. "Let me help."

"*What?*"

"I made you a promise to keep things professional. I'll keep that promise if you want me to." He reached down and took the hand she'd been using on herself in his. He traced his thumb over her fingertips, setting the sensitive pads on fire. "But I fucking want you."

Marin's lips parted. He could've punched her in the face and she would've been less shocked.

"This week has been like the slowest, most painful kind of torture." His voice was like a hypnotic song as he held her gaze. "When you drop off the files at the end of the night, you're flushed and glassy-eyed. I can see how keyed up you are. I can almost scent it in the air." His Adam's apple bobbed. "Do you know what that does to me? Knowing you're turned on by *my* words? *My* fantasies? And now to walk in and see you touching yourself over them? *Fuck.*"

Marin was too stunned to speak.

"I get hard every time I think about you."

And she could see that, right there in front of her. That thing between his thighs getting more and more obvious as they spoke. She swallowed, his words and the sight like a lit match to the fuel flowing through her. "Oh."

"Yeah. Oh." He pulled her up to her feet but didn't break eye contact. "All the fantasies I wrote this week, guess who I was casting in the role in my head? Guess whose face I imagined? Whose body? I can't get you out of my fucking head."

She had no idea what to say. She could barely believe the words coming out of his mouth.

"But I'm not going to pressure you. I'm just letting you know that if you want my help. If you'd rather it be me getting you off than your fingers, you just need to say the word."

Her head was exploding. Bombs going off. Rockets launching. Everything inside her activating at once. She tried to form some sort of cogent response. But nothing came out.

"So tell me to go away, Mari," he said softly.

She shook her head slowly. Once. Twice.

He stepped closer. "Tell me."

It didn't sound like a request. It sounded like a dare.

That's when she kissed him. She had no idea where the upswell of bravery came from, but she grabbed his face and pressed her mouth to his like she knew what the hell she was doing. He stiffened under her touch at first, his whole body going rigid, but then she let her tongue graze his lips—a plea—and he groaned into her mouth, opening to the kiss and grabbing her waist with those long-fingered hands.

The first touch of their tongues was like a lightning strike, loud and powerful and blinding. Her brain buzzed with the impact of it, and she almost lost her rhythm. But then he took control of the kiss with an urgent fervor that made her moan, like he was a dying man and she was the sole owner of the last oxygen on earth. His fingers curled into her sides and his tongue dipped deeper into her mouth, exploring and mapping and tasting. Goose bumps chased tingles over her skin and she pressed herself closer, feeling the heat of his body, the pounding of his heart, the desperation of it all.

She'd imagined this so many times—what'd he'd feel like, what he'd taste like, how'd he kiss. She'd spent hours putting those fantasies together. She hadn't even been close to matching the reality. There was an intensity she couldn't have conjured up in her own mind, this raging need. She half expected their clothes to light up and burn right off of their bodies. Everything was on fire. She couldn't stop. This was like a first taste of a drug, hooking her immediately and making her crave more. Her fingers slid into his hair. That luscious thick hair that she wanted to nuzzle and tug and feel against her naked body.

She made a needy sound, one she didn't even recognize, and the kiss went deeper, lewd in the best way. He yanked her fully against him. His erection notched right along the spot where she'd been touching a few minutes before and sparks skated over her skin. She rocked her hips, rubbing herself shamelessly against him, her body going on some version of erotic autopilot.

He groaned and backed her up against the desk. His mouth attacked her neck, planting hot, wet kisses there, sucking, nipping. "You taste so good. I've wanted . . ."

She tilted her head back, giving him better access and not caring that he didn't finish the sentence. She knew how he felt. She *wanted*, too.

"Tell me to slow down, baby," he said as he dragged the hard length of himself against her. "It's been a fucked-up day and you feel so good. But I don't want to push you too far."

"I don't want to slow down."

He pulled back for a second and took her face in his hands, his gaze fierce. "Tell me it's okay."

"It's okay. It's so okay."

He stared at her for a moment longer and then his hands slid back, his fingers catching in her hair, and he bent and kissed her again. She reached for him, latching on to his shirt like a desperate thing, and pulled him even closer to her. Her body was already revved up, but now she felt as if she would incinerate from the inside out if he didn't touch her soon.

A low rumble escaped him as she grappled for him, and he slid his other hand down her hip while deepening the kiss. Her butt was pressed hard against the edge of her desk and when he gripped the back of her thigh, she damn near melted into his hold. He lifted her onto the desk, various office supply jetsam going overboard along with the soft drink, and she wrapped her legs around him. His fingers on her bare legs sent another wave of heat rippling over her.

"Donovan." His name was a prayer between kisses. "Donovan. I need . . ."

"I know, baby. I know. Me, too." He kissed her throat. "I'll take care of you."

His hand slid up her shirt, his hot palm finding the curve of her breast. She arched when his thumb grazed her nipple, and she grabbed for the edge of the desk, sending a canister of paper clips tumbling to the floor. "God."

He made a hungry sound in the back of his throat as he unhooked the front latch on her bra and cupped her naked skin. "Is that what you need, beautiful? I can feel how on edge you are. It's so fucking sexy. Your whole body is trembling."

She arched her back, a riot of sensations tracking over her. "I've been listening to you talk dirty for the last twenty minutes. The last week. I can't help it."

"Mmm. I love that my voice got you off." He kissed the spot beneath her ear. "And I love that you're wet for me."

It was like one of the fantasies on the recording times about a thousand. His breath against her ear, his hands on her, that silken voice threading through her senses. She let herself slip into the fantasy version of herself, the one who wasn't scared, the one who knew what she wanted and could be bold about it. The one who was not a terrified virgin. "I've wanted this all week." *Longer.*

The sound he made was one of pained restraint. He leaned back and went for the button on her shorts. "I was going to take my time with you. I was going to be slow and gentle. But I'm not sure if I have it in me tonight."

"Sounds like one of those failed fantasies from your experiment."

He laughed and dragged the zipper down on her shorts. "You're right. Lose the shorts and spread your legs for me. Let me feel you."

The words ripped over her like an electric current. She lifted her hips and shimmied her shorts down. They fell to the ground among a pile of documents and data she'd been entering. Seeing them lying there was surreal. She was on top of her desk in her panties with Donovan West. Maybe she'd fallen asleep in class and was going to wake up any minute now.

But when Donovan pushed the thin fabric of her underwear aside and stroked nimble fingers through her slick cleft, she knew she wasn't dreaming. Her dreams had never felt like this, this whole body rush of sensation. She moaned against the touch.

"Jesus, baby, you're soaked." He dragged firm fingertips over her clit and she whimpered. "Have you been like this every night you've left me?"

She closed her eyes, embarrassment trying to take over, her cheeks going hot. "Donovan."

"Tell me."

She rolled her lips together and nodded.

"I'm such a stupid, stupid man. I've been keeping myself on a leash when we could've been doing this every night."

He found her entrance and pushed a finger inside. She gasped at the intrusion. She'd done this to herself before, but feeling the rough-tipped, thick finger inside her was an entirely different experience.

He pressed his forehead to hers as he worked his finger inside her. "Relax for me, baby. You feel amazing, but you're so tense. You don't have to worry. I've got you."

She tried to take a breath, knowing that what he was feeling wasn't completely due to tension, but when he worked a second finger inside her and pressed his thumb to her clit, her vision blurred around the edges. "Oh, God."

"That's it. Trust me to make you feel good." He leaned close to her ear. "I'm between your spread legs . . ."

She groaned loud. The recording voice. He was going to narrate for her. She'd never survive it.

"You're so wet for me and my fingers are deep in your pussy. You're clenching around me, begging for me to be inside you."

Sweat trickled down her back. She was aflame. "Donovan."

"My cock is hard for you, and I can't wait to fuck you across this desk. I've been thinking about this moment for a week now. I've stroked myself to thoughts of you. I've come in my hands in that office down the hall while you were in here working."

Holy shit. Visions of his fist around his cock flashed through her head like a pornographic montage.

"But I want to hear you go over first. I want you to take what you need. Come for me, Mari."

She didn't need the instruction. It was going to happen whether he wanted it to or not. Starbursts bloomed behind her eyelids and she fell forward, bracing herself with her head on his shoulder as the orgasm steamrolled her. She cried out, too far gone to form words.

He palmed the back of her head, holding her against him and whispering her name, as his other hand worked between her legs. She was spasming and shuddering and gasping, but she didn't have any room for embarrassment. There was safety in his hold, freedom.

And when he finally moved a hand away and she could drag in a breath, he cupped her face and lifted it to him so that he could kiss her again. All of his need poured into it. She could feel it flowing off of him and infiltrating every part of her. And even though she'd just had the most intense orgasm of her life, greedy desire demanded more. She needed him. Wanted him inside her, taking what she'd never given to anyone else.

She broke away from the kiss, panting. "Please, Donovan."

When his eyes met hers, there was so much heat there she was surprised he didn't leave burn scars on her. "Turn around and bend over the desk."

The look on her face must've shown her shock because he ran his thumb over her bottom lip. "If we had a bed, I'd want to watch your face when I slide into you. But right now this desk is going to be more comfortable for you this way." He smiled, a wicked edge to it. "Plus, I've been imagining bending you over mine for a week now."

A hard shudder went through her, and she turned around. He tugged down her panties, tossed them aside, and then put a hand to her back, guiding her down to the desk. The exposure made her want to take cover. She'd had guys touch her during make-out sessions but never had she been on blatant display like this. There was no place to hide. But when she heard his groan of appreciation, the fear of being seen so intimately melted away. He couldn't fake that kind of interest.

And she knew her first time was supposed to be sweet and romantic. That's what the books she'd read and the movies she'd watched told her. But this felt dirty and illicit in the best possible way. It's how she'd pictured things with him. Explicit. Taboo. Daring. She'd listened to Donovan's words at this desk, had simmered with unmet need for hours. Now he'd give her the real thing where she'd weaved so much fantasy.

She pressed her cheek to the cool surface of the desk, her heart-beat loud in her ears. Donovan coasted his hand over her hip and she froze. "Wait."

His hand instantly stilled. "What's wrong?"

"Condom."

He let out a breath. "Oh, thank God. I thought you wanted me to stop. I've got us covered. Or me covered as the case may be."

"Well, someone was sure of himself."

He dipped his hands between her thighs and stroked. "No, I keep them in my wallet like a good Boy Scout. I promise this wasn't the plan. The plan tonight was to drink the night away—not to fuck a smart, beautiful girl over her desk in the esteemed psychology department. This is a way better plan."

She shivered, anticipation and nerves washing over her. She wished she could see him behind her. She'd imagined him naked many times, and now she wasn't going to get the chance to see the real thing. But the second he parted her legs and nudged the head of his cock against her entrance, all other thoughts dissipated. Every molecule in her body centered on that one spot of connection.

Fear washed through her—cold and quick. This would probably hurt. She tried to brace for it.

But then he backed off and something hot and wet pressed against her instead. Her knees almost buckled. "Oh, God."

Donovan's mouth. Donovan's mouth was *on her.* The sensation of it was like nothing she'd ever experienced—every nerve ending in her body standing at attention and then sighing all at once. Her legs quivered as his tongue moved over her, coaxing and teasing her clitoris, making her loose and languid with the pleasure of it. Making her so wet she could die. Holy fuck. *This* is what oral sex felt like? She'd really been missing out. After a few more glorious licks from that masterful mouth, his fingers tucked inside her again. "That's it, beautiful. Just relax and feel everything."

He pressed another openmouthed kiss to her flesh and then

pulled away and positioned himself behind her again. Unlike before, she had trouble accessing the fear. Her body was throbbing with this distinct emptiness, this need to be filled. She didn't care if it hurt at this point. She just wanted it to happen. But when he pushed forward with a gentleness that belied his harsh grip on her, there wasn't the expected pain. Just pressure. Tightness. She gripped the edge of the desk as the head of his cock breached her. The stretching sensation was foreign and a little uncomfortable, but she was so slick and ready for him that it eased the way.

She was beginning to feel confident—until he reached resistance and stopped. His hold on her hips tightened. "Baby, you feel so good, but I feel like I could hurt you. Are you okay?"

She wasn't sure. The feel of him partially inside her was making her restless and edgy, like she needed more of him. But the anxiety over what would happen if he pushed forward had her muscles coiling. She licked her lips. "I'm okay."

He ran his hand over her side in a soothing motion. "You have to let me in. You're tensing on me. I don't want to hurt you."

She took a deep breath. "I'm trying but . . ." *Shit. Shit. Shit.* "Just go for it, okay? You won't hurt me."

She hoped.

He seemed to hesitate for a moment but then she reached back for him, gripping his arm. "Please."

He thrust forward and pain shot through her—one sharp, shining moment. Her teeth clacked together, but she managed to hold back the sound. He held there a moment, his length deep inside her, and she breathed through it. Soon the pain faded to a dull throb, and she was left with this new feeling of fullness. She let out a breath.

"You all right?" he asked, grit in his voice.

"Great."

"Mari . . ."

She heard the question in his voice, the concern.

"Please. Don't stop." She rocked back against him.

He groaned and pulled back to pump inside her again. This time there was no pain, just residual tenderness and the sweet glide of his body joining with hers. She let loose a sigh. He adjusted his position behind her and reached beneath her to find her clit. His fingers against that sensitive nub made any last remnants of discomfort fade into a memory.

"Fuck, Mari. You're . . ."

The words were lost in the rushing sound going through her ears. She let her grip loosen on the desk and melted into the position. Donovan was making his own noises now—these sexy grunts and groans that were the hottest soundtrack she'd ever heard. And the sound of the sex itself was driving her higher still—slick and lewd and raw. She'd imagined what this would be like, but she'd never realized how all-encompassing it was. The feel of his thighs bumping against hers, the scent of their exertion and arousal, his rough fingers stroking her soft flesh. Every part of her seemed alive with sensation, her senses dialed to eleven.

"I'm close, baby." His voice had gone hoarse, strained.

They were the simplest and sexiest three words she'd ever heard.

His hold went to her hips and he dragged her back on his cock now, his pace hard and intense, his need overriding all else. She could feel all that anger and hurt he'd been dealing with channeling through him, the jagged edges coming out, the need to wail on something. And it was glorious, cathartic in a way she didn't understand. She slid across the desk, a rag doll to his strength, and her mind begin to fuzz. The pressure on her clit from the edge of the desk was driving her up another mountain.

She let loose a choked cry when orgasm crashed over her again, and he yanked her roughly against him, burying himself deep over and over until he pulsed inside her, a string of curses falling off his lips as he found his release.

He called her name. She called his. And they stayed there together until finally all the starch left the two of them and he slid out, leaving her in a melted puddle on the desk.

She let herself stay there for a moment, panting and trying to get her bearings. Then, deciding she wouldn't test her legs and attempt to stand, she eased off the desk and sank to her knees. When she managed to turn around, she found him on the floor behind her, leaning against one of the other desks, gasping for breath along with her. Sweat dotted his forehead, his hair was in more disarray than normal, and the fly of his jeans was spread open.

She couldn't help but look. But he'd already taken care of the condom and tucked himself back into his boxers. All she could see was the trail of dark hair that led downward. Sexy. Spent. Beautiful. She wanted to lick that spot. But knew she'd never get the chance.

She couldn't bring herself to look at his face, but she could feel the weight of his stare.

"Tell me you're okay, Mari." There was something hard in his voice. Almost cold.

The shift in him sent warning bells going off in her head. She reached for her panties and tugged them on, suddenly feeling self-conscious sitting here naked from the waist down. "I'm okay."

"Look at me."

She forced her gaze upward.

Lines appeared around his mouth. "There was blood."

"I—" She couldn't get any words out.

He closed his eyes and leaned his head against the side of the desk. "Please, please don't tell me you were a virgin."

Fire blazed over her cheeks. She looked away and grabbed for her shorts. "Okay. I won't."

"Fuck." The word was harsh in the quiet room. "Why didn't you say something? I wouldn't have— Jesus."

Anger and embarrassment rose up in her like a high tide, taking her under. She tugged on her shorts. "It doesn't matter."

"Of course it matters!" He scrubbed a hand over his face. "Christ. How can you be a virgin? The stuff you wrote into the fantasies, the stuff we talked about . . ."

"Nonvirgins don't have the monopoly on dirty minds."

"God, Mari." He reached for her hand and tugged her toward him. Reluctantly, she let him guide her closer. He gathered her into his embrace, tucking her head beneath his chin. "That's something you should tell a guy. I could've hurt you. I would never have been so rough or done it that way. Your first time should be gentle and with someone who—"

"Who what? Who loves me?" The words came out flat. "I'm not that old-fashioned."

"I was going to say with someone who's worth the trouble." His tone was hollow. "Not with some guy who's so fucked up he can't even sleep at his own house without panicking about people breaking in. Or who has to work nonstop because he can't fucking function otherwise. You deserve more than what I'm capable of giving you. This is all I've got, Mari. A hookup."

The words sliced through her. He'd called it what it was. It wasn't anything she didn't know, but it stung to hear it just as well. "Believe me. I'm not expecting you to give me a ring or anything. I like you and wanted this to happen tonight. It doesn't have to be more complicated than that."

He blew out a long breath. "Let me at least take you out to dinner. There's a twenty-four-hour diner right off campus. I know neither of us is going to get any more work done tonight. We can talk."

The offer was so tempting. Everything inside her wanted to go out with Donovan, wanted to get to know him better, wanted to keep this night going. But she'd dug the hole too deep now. She'd taken the lie too far. And this was probably only a pity offer anyway—coddle the poor girl who'd lost her virginity so she didn't freak out over her big night being only a hookup.

She closed her eyes, the reality of the situation swamping her. "I can't."

"Why not?"

She scooted out of his hold and stood on shaky legs. "I just can't. I need to go."

She hooked her bra back together beneath her shirt and grabbed her backpack.

"What?" He scrambled to his feet as he zipped up his jeans. "Mari, hold up."

It wasn't even her real name. How fucking pathetic had she let this become? She walked over to him and pressed the thumb drive into his hand. "Thank you. This week has been . . ." *Everything.* "Great."

He frowned. "Please don't leave. You don't need to do that."

She gave him a sad smile. "I really do."

She walked past him and forced herself not to look back, not to let him see the truth on her face, not to let it hurt so much.

I could love you, Donovan West. Maybe she already did.

But she wasn't Mari the grad student and this wasn't her real life and she didn't get to have this kind of ending.

Marin managed to walk away and make it to the car before any tears escaped. She'd known this had a time limit from the start. She'd never expected it to go this far, but she refused to regret it. She'd taken a risk and it'd been okay. She hadn't tumbled into the mental spin her mom did when she got involved with men. She hadn't fallen apart. And she'd never forget this week or this night.

She hated that she'd lied, but maybe she could spare Donovan ever knowing that he'd slept with an eighteen-year-old student. She could be that mystery girl he once hooked up with, and go on with his life. No harm, no foul.

They'd both survive.

By the time she parked in her driveway, she'd pulled herself together enough to make a plan. She'd drop the sexuality class and stop subbing in the sleep department. She wouldn't see Donovan again. He'd never have to know. And she wouldn't have to feel the loss every time she laid eyes on him.

She was feeling resolute about the plan. It would all work out. But when she walked into her house a few minutes later and saw the trail of blood on the floor and the small, crumpled body in the corner, she found out the planning was for naught.

Because her whole world was about to fall apart around her.

And she wasn't going to have to worry about boy trouble for a very, very long time.

4

M arin woke up to the sound of hushed voices and the envelope of the overdue electric bill stuck to her face. She lifted
her head, peeling the envelope away, and blinked in the lamplight
of her bedroom, trying to get her bearings. Night still hummed
along outside her window, black and quiet, and her laptop was
silent beside her on the bed along with the king-sized bag of
M&M's she'd polished off in her stress-induced haze. But something had woken her up. Voices. She'd heard voices.

She cringed. Hearing voices was never a good sign in this family. Now would be a really inconvenient time for a mental break-
down. But when a thump and a muffled curse sounded down the
hall, she let out a breath. Nate must be home.

Marin rubbed her eyes and checked the clock. Two in the morning.
Way past curfew. He was trying to sneak in. Too bad he was such a
fail at stealth mode. She shoved the pile of bills to the side of her bed,
knocking a stack of research articles to the floor in the process, and
sat up. Her bones popped and protested as she climbed off the bed.

Ugh. She needed to stop falling asleep in weird positions. But she'd been trying to stay awake to make sure her brother got in. Now she'd have to have a talk with him about curfew. She let out a heavy sigh. Sometimes she hated having to be the grown-up. She should be the one sneaking in at two in the morning.

She pulled a sweatshirt over her tank top and headed down the hallway. Muted light spilled from beneath Nate's doorway, and she tapped lightly on the wood. But there was no response, just this other subtle sound. She leaned forward, straining. A raspy breath, almost a choking sound. *Shit.* Her heart jumped into her throat. Nathan was having an asthma attack.

"Nate." The word came out in a panic and she shoved open the door. "Are you okay?"

But she froze one step inside the room because instead of finding her younger brother struggling for breath from asthma, she found him gasping for breath from what the guy parked between his legs was doing to him.

Nate's eyes went wide and he grabbed at his quilt, trying to yank it up over himself and his boyfriend. "Oh my God, *get out*!"

"Shit. Oh, shit. Sorry." Marin swung the door shut, her heart hammering and her face going hot. She leaned against the wall in the hallway and put her hand over her eyes, trying to erase the image. But there were some things you couldn't unsee. Her younger brother getting a blow job—yeah, that she could've skipped. She wanted to scrub her eyeballs with bleach.

There was rustling behind the door, hurried voices as the boys apparently got themselves together, and Marin slipped back into her room to give them space. She'd need to address this with Nathan. He knew he wasn't supposed to have guys in his room. But she'd give him a minute to get Henry out the door and put himself back together. Hell, she needed a minute. Maybe a week. A year might be good.

But her brother didn't give her that long. After the front door slammed shut, Nate stormed back down the hallway and pushed her door open. It hit the wall with a bang. "What *the hell*, Marin?"

He looked so tall in the doorway, so adult. How was this the same kid who used to make her turn on four different night-lights in his room so he could go to sleep? At seventeen, he could pass for a grown man with those long limbs and broad shoulders—but he still had those innocent green eyes. His age showed there. And right now, those eyes were burning with annoyance.

"I thought you were having an asthma attack," she said. "I heard—"

His face flushed to his hairline.

"Well, never mind what I heard, but I thought you needed help. I wouldn't have been checking on you at all if you had been in by curfew and not broken the rules about bringing someone into your room," she said, forcing righteous indignation into her voice and trying to sound like she meant it.

"Okay, I broke the rules. I'm sorry. But you can't just walk into my room. I need privacy."

She held up a hand. "I know, I know. I'm sorry. I would've never walked in for any other reason."

He blew out a breath, his eyes flicking to the piles of books and paperwork on her bed. "And you don't need to wait up for me. I'm fine. I'm not out drinking or getting high or doing anything dangerous."

"Just having unprotected sex in your room."

He groaned and raked a hand over his face. "I'm not . . . We're not. I haven't. We were just fooling around. It wasn't going to go beyond that. And if it did, believe me, I know to be safe. You've already made us get tested. And it's not like I'm going to get him pregnant."

She stared at him for a moment and then picked up a pillow to throw at him.

He caught it and grinned as he dropped it to the floor. "Look, I know if I contracted some horrible STD that the irony of that would literally make your head explode. I wouldn't do that to you, Mar."

Marin sighed. The irony *would* be deadly. She'd spent the last two years of her Ph.D. program and this past year in her postdoc position creating and testing a sex education program for gay youth. If her own brother didn't know how to take care of his sexual health, she really would be a serious fail. "You wouldn't have to worry about the STD because *I* would kill you."

"I know. And I'm sorry you saw what you saw. But I wanted to celebrate tonight, so me and Henry went to a party. When it started getting kind of crazy, we bailed and came here instead. We weren't doing anything we haven't before. I just forgot how noisy . . . things can get."

Marin lifted a hand. "I really don't need to know the details. And don't want to hear about your noises. Believe me, I heard enough."

"Wait. Are *you* blushing?" He laughed. "Dude, I'm the one who got walked in on."

"And I'm the one who had to see."

He smirked. "Aw, Mar, how is it possible you're such a prude? You're like a doctor of sex, and you get all red at the thought that people are actually out there doing it. You realize how screwed up that is, right?"

"I'm not a sex doctor. I'm a researcher. And I don't get red over people doing it. I get red at the thought of my *baby brother* doing it. You're still supposed to be wearing Underoos and those caped pajamas you used to live in."

He tucked his hands in the pockets of his jeans. "Those Superman pajamas *were* pretty kickass, but I'm not a kid anymore, Mar. You're gonna have to learn to trust me at some point."

She sighed. "I know that. Of course I know that."

"Especially since I'm going to be living in New Orleans in the fall."

Marin stilled, the words a record scratch to her train of thought. "What?"

His smile went wide. "See. That's what I was celebrating. The Duplais Art College called me today. I got in."

She blinked, the words taking a second to register. "*Duplais?* Are you serious? You got in?"

He nodded and rocked onto his toes, his excitement bubbling out of him. "Totally did."

"Nate!" She hopped to her feet and went over to hug him. "They said it was next to impossible to get in there."

He squeezed her back. "Right? But they loved that I used street art style in the portraits and that I do mixed-media stuff, said I show a lot of potential."

Her head was whirling. "That's amazing. I'm so freaking proud of you!"

He leaned back, his smile going goofy and lopsided, making him look like the kid she loved. "Thanks. I can't even believe it. I'm sure I sounded like an idiot on the phone because I kept asking them to repeat themselves. It sounded too good to be true. But they said they'd send me an intro packet and email you the info about the financial package."

She released him. "You mean the scholarship?"

He shook his head. "No, they only award four of those and I didn't get one. But they said there's some financial aid available."

Marin's stomach flipped over. She'd already looked into financial aid for Nathan. There were loans and some help, but only enough to cover a state school—and that was already going to be a stretch. The exclusive private art college in Louisiana was painfully expensive. She hadn't worried about it too much when Nathan had said he wanted to apply there because she'd heard it was like getting into Juilliard or Harvard—near impossible. And she figured if he did manage to get in, he'd land a scholarship. But without that, there was no way. She'd been losing sleep over how she was going to pay for a state college, but now . . .

She needed to tell Nate that this wasn't going to happen, needed to be honest about the reality. But seeing his face lit up like this— all that hope and promise—she couldn't bear it. This was the kid who'd needed therapy since elementary school because of all he'd been through with their mother. A kid who still had scars on his body to remind him of it. A kid who'd been so depressed before he'd come out freshman year that she'd worried for his safety. And now he was here—proud, brilliantly talented, and confident. She couldn't tell him his dream school wasn't possible.

She'd barely been keeping them afloat with her modest postdoc pay, but they had made it work. Hell, she'd managed to keep a roof over their heads while she raised him, went to college, and worked night jobs for all those years. Maybe there was a way to figure this out, too.

She wouldn't break the news to him until she'd looked at every possibility. Maybe she could get a raise, apply for additional grants to help supplement her salary. Maybe there were extra resources that she hadn't tapped into when she'd gotten her own financial aid for school. She knew they were all long shots, but for now she was going to let him have his happy moment. She'd figure out the rest later.

She put her hands to his face, which required reaching up these days, and smiled. "I'm really proud of you, Nate. Seriously. No matter where you land, you're going to bring beautiful things to this world."

His smile went crooked. "Aw, don't get sappy on me now."

She lowered her hands and waved him off. "I can't help it."

But he gave her another quick hug. "Hey, this is good news for both of us. I know you've given up a lot all these years, having me here. Once I leave, you can get your life back, do your own thing. Act like a twenty-seven-year-old for a change. Maybe you can be the one sneaking guys in at two in the morning. Or girls. Whatever you're into. Just don't tell me about it."

He scrunched his face up in a grossed-out expression.

She laughed. Her brother didn't even know if she was gay or straight. That's how pathetic her love life was. Nice. "I like guys, for the record. And you're not out of the house yet, so rules still apply. Until that diploma's in your hand, midnight curfew, understood? I don't want to be up worrying."

He rolled his eyes. "Yes, Marin."

She crossed her arms over her chest. "And if you and Henry need alone time, and you swear you're going to be safe about it, then he can be in your room. But not on a school night. And make sure you have your inhaler in there, so I don't have to bust in and be traumatized again."

Nathan's eyebrows went up. "Yeah?"

"You're almost eighteen, and you and Henry have been together awhile. I trust you to make smart decisions. I'd rather you both be in a safe place than hooking up in the corner at some drunken party."

He looked down and rubbed the back of his head. Despite his earlier teasing about her prudishness, he was obviously just as uncomfortable discussing this with her. "All right. Cool."

"And learn how to put on the radio and lock your damn door. *I'm* going to need therapy now."

He snorted. "You and me both. Henry, too. He may never show his face around here again."

"I'm sure he'll get over it to see you and to eat my food." She put her hand on his shoulder and steered him toward the door. "Now get some sleep. I'm glad you had great news to celebrate tonight. But your punishment for getting in late is that you're making the weekly grocery run tomorrow *and* washing the car."

He groaned. "I hate you."

"Love you, too."

He dragged his feet as he headed to his room, but then stopped in the doorway and turned back to her, his eyes serious. "Thanks, Mar."

"For what?"

He gave a tight shrug. "You know why. For all of it. I'm not dumb. I know how bad things could've ended up if you hadn't fought to keep me when everything happened with Mom. You kept it all together. My dream is happening because of you."

Her ribs tightened, heavy weight descending on her chest. "Honey . . ."

"Night." He slipped into his room and shut the door, never one to stick around when things got emotional, and left her standing there.

She stood in the hallway, tears threatening, and then slunk back in her room and fell onto the bed, the unpaid bills littered around her. She grabbed her laptop and woke up the screen. She could do this. She just needed to figure out how to make three times her salary immediately. Easy peasy.

That left winning the lottery, selling organs on the black market, and . . .

Hmm, maybe she could become a stripper. She glanced down at her faded, oversized sweatshirt, the empty bag of M&M's, and the yoga pants she had yet to use for actual exercise. Yeah, probably not.

She was so damn screwed.

5

The frustrated look on Dr. Paxton's face told Marin everything she needed to know. He was in his office, which was neat as a pin as always, but his gray hair was sticking up on one side. His hair only got like that when a study wasn't coming together or a student had done something stupid . . . or he had bad news to deliver. She'd emailed him over the weekend, requesting this meeting and letting him know what was going on with Nathan. But she'd known it'd been a long shot.

When he saw her standing in the doorway, he waved her in. "Come on in, Marin. I've got Clint bringing us some coffee."

She stepped inside the small but stately room and took a seat. The ceilings arched high and a tall window that looked out onto the big trees in the quad let in a flood of dappled light. It was the most coveted office in the psych building, and Professor Paxton, head of the department, said he wasn't giving it up until they dragged his cold, dead body out of it. He also joked that Professor Englebreit in the neuropsychology department was plotting his demise to make that happen.

Marin's office, on the other hand, was tiny and windowless. She didn't mind it much since she spent most of her time in the university's library or in one of the bigger labs, but some days she did feel like the walls of that tiny room were closing in on her. She'd been hoping to stay here long enough to get a tenured position at the university so that she could work her way up, maybe teach a few courses in between her research. But she may not have time for that dream to come to fruition. She needed a raise now. Not in three years.

Dr. Pax folded his hands atop his desk. They were good hands, solid ones. During her Ph.D. program and this postdoc, she'd relished those times when his big paw had landed atop her shoulder to congratulate her or to convey how pleased he was with her work. She'd never known her real father, and in a lot of ways, Dr. Pax had filled some idolized version of that role for her. A mentor. A person she'd been able to go to when all the stress of raising Nathan on her own had gotten just a little too heavy to bear. He had a therapist's soul and a researcher's mind. She'd learned a lot from him. She'd also learned how to read him.

"There's no room for a raise, is there?" she asked, getting the hard part out of the way first. "I'm going to need to pick up a second job."

He frowned. "It's a little worse than that, I'm afraid."

Marin tensed, but before she could say anything Dr. Pax's student worker, Clint, tapped on the door and carried in two cups of coffee. He set one on the desk and handed Marin the other.

The paper cup seared her cold fingers. "Worse, sir?"

He sighed and leaned back in his creaking chair. "When I got your email, I decided to call and check on the grant status. I thought maybe if we had an idea how much we were going to get this year, then I could find some room to adjust your salary. But the news wasn't good. We landed two smaller grants, but we're not getting the Filmore this year."

The words didn't register in Marin's head for a second. "Wait, what?"

He wrapped his fingers around his coffee cup but didn't take a sip. "Apparently, they have a new board in charge of the foundation, and they didn't think your research warranted new funds. They said they are excited about the program you've created but that they feel it's ready to go. Now the challenge will be getting it into schools, not doing more research."

"But there's so much still to do, components we haven't tested and—" Panic was tapping her shoulder, ready to tackle her.

"I know, Marin. I understand where you're coming from. I always think more research can only lead to a better product. But I see their point, too. You've developed an amazing online program for an underserved population. The sooner we get it out there, the better. If we turn over your work to a company that can streamline the program, we can get kids access to it all the sooner. Start helping people now. And if all goes well, you'll eventually make money on it."

Eventually. That was the key word. Eventually didn't help her right now. Plus, she didn't have it in her to charge some exorbitant price to nonprofits and schools for that kind of program. She sat back in her chair and set her coffee to the side, her heart like thunder in her chest. The grant had fallen through. No more study. "But if I don't continue that project, what does it mean for me? What am I going to do without that grant?"

Dr. Pax swiped a hand over his mustache and beard, his expression sympathetic. "Marin, without the Filmore grant, we don't have the funds to keep you on for another year at the salary you're at. You'd have to take a significant cut in pay, and I know that's the opposite of what you need right now."

Her breakfast threatened to come up. No money? There was *no* money. And that meant no position. She couldn't work for less than she was already. She'd starve. Nathan would have nothing to live on. She put a hand to her forehead. "Oh, God."

Dr. Pax leaned forward on his forearms. "Take a breath, Marin. I know this is a shock, and I'm sorry for that. But I've been thinking through this over the last day or two, and I may have an option that could work out for you."

She lifted her head. "What do you mean?"

"I know you've expressed that you're not interested in a clinical career. I get that research is your passion. But the truth of the matter is, you need money and clinical work is where you can find it. If you can get yourself set up in a private practice one day, you won't ever have to have this type of conversation again."

She blinked. "Clinical work? Like actually *be* a sex therapist? I don't know how to do that. And I can't do private practice. I'd need to get licensed and that takes at least a year of supervised work, right?"

He gave her a small smile. "You do know how to provide therapy. You've done an internship. Your training has given you all the tools you need."

She shook her head. All she could think about was her disastrous internship at a local mental health center. She'd had to do it as part of her program. But she'd been awful at it—awkward and bumbling, never knowing what was the right or wrong thing to say. What if she said the wrong thing and messed someone up? What if she was as bad as some of the therapists who had failed her mom? Then, in her first week, a client had stormed out mid-session, threatening suicide. Marin had promptly had a panic attack. She'd had to pull the fire alarm to get the staff to catch up with him and stop him. It'd been a goddamned nightmare. After that, she'd asked to transfer to a school position where she'd be able to focus more on educating students on mental health topics rather than actually providing one-on-one therapy.

"I'm good in a lab. I'm not good with people."

He chuckled. "You're just fine with people. You work with your research volunteers well, and you're a good listener. But you're right, though you have the tools and the smarts, more experience is needed. You would need to work under a supervising psychologist for a year to qualify for your license. But after that, you could do what you want."

She took in a deep breath and tried to process his words. He was trying to help. She didn't have a lot of options right now and couldn't dismiss one out of hand. "I don't even know where I'd start looking. I can't imagine those types of positions pay much before you're licensed."

"Typically, no. But since your brother will be attending art school in New Orleans and I figured you might be open to moving there with him, I took the liberty of reaching out to Dr. Anala Suri at The Grove, a private institute in Louisiana. She'd called me recently, letting me know that she was down one clinician in their sex therapy department and wondered if I had any recommendations. They're a very exclusive operation and only grant interviews through direct referrals. I've had a couple of students do well there. So I called her yesterday and told her you might be interested."

"Exclusive? What do you mean?" She shifted in her chair, trying to keep her nerves from showing on her face.

He considered her as he took a sip of coffee. "Expensive. And experimental. Most insurance companies won't cover the services there because they do some cutting-edge treatments."

She frowned. "Who can afford treatment with no insurance help?"

"The wealthy. The famous. It's very private, tucked away right off the bayou, and clients can stay on the grounds when there for treatment or can drop in. It's off the beaten path, but it's popular with celebrities because they can avoid the press. Plus, from what Dr. Suri tells me, New Orleans is becoming Hollywood South with so many movies and TV shows filming there now. So there's a need to have something high-end and private nearby."

"There's that high of a demand for sex therapy?"

"They don't just do sex therapy. It's a complete operation— rehab facility, family counseling, individual and group therapy. It would give you lots of opportunities to work with professionals from all different kinds of specialties, and the salaries they offer will knock your socks off. I've been tempted more than once to leave all this tenure behind and take over a department out there."

Marin's nerves curled in her belly. "Why haven't you?"

He let out a soft laugh. "Because my wife would kill me if I tried to move her out of state and because I'm never giving up this office. I can't let Dr. Englebreit win."

She let out a little laugh even though anxiety had clamped her in its grip.

"But I think you should take the interview. Dr. Suri is tough, and she'll demand a lot of you if she hires you, but she's a good supervisor. She'll challenge you."

Marin looked away. She didn't want to seem ungrateful. But giving therapy to a bunch of spoiled celebrities and rich people wasn't just galaxies outside her comfort zone. It flat-out terrified her. She wasn't equipped for that. "I'm not sure—"

"You're a brilliant researcher, Marin. You've been an asset to this department, and I've enjoyed seeing how you've grown here. But I think you're limiting yourself. You shouldn't avoid clinical work because you're scared to be out in the real world. I worked in the field a number of years before I came back to academia, and the experience was invaluable. You can always come back to this, but for now the higher salary could support you and give you some left over to help your brother. And once you have your clinical license, you'll always have something to fall back on if you need it. The Grove is a big hitter to have on a resume."

Marin swallowed hard. She hated that he'd pinpointed her apprehension so easily. That thought of being out in the real world, trying to help people with their problems, had anxiety crawling over her like swarming ants. She hadn't been able to help her own mother, how the hell was she supposed to help anyone else? But what other options did she have? All the other local postdoc positions would be filled by now. And she didn't want to have to move to God knows where and be even farther from Nathan to find something else. She also couldn't go home unemployed, nearly broke, and with no prospects on the horizon. They wouldn't last two months without her paycheck coming in.

She rubbed her hands on her slacks, her palms clammy, and looked up at Dr. Paxton. "Well, I guess I better plan a visit to the bayou."

"Excellent." His smile lifted the lines in his face and he gave her a nod. "I'll tell them to give you a call and set something up."

She blew out a breath and stood.

Dr. Paxton rose from behind his desk and stepped around it.

Marin put out her hand. "Thanks, Dr. Pax. I can't tell you how much I appreciate you going to these lengths to help me find something. I know you didn't have to do that."

Dr. Paxton took her hand and instead of shaking it, stepped closer. Then the ever-professional professor pulled her into a hug. She stiffened with surprise at first but then relaxed into the gentle warmth of the gesture. She closed her eyes. He smelled like libraries and black coffee and her version of safety.

He leaned back, his hand clasped on her arm and a tenderness in his eyes, and gave her arm a gentle squeeze. "You're going to be just fine, Marin. You've survived much worse than this and have landed on your feet. I have nothing but full confidence in you that you'll make a brilliant therapist. The Grove would be lucky to have you."

Her eyes burned, tears threatening for some reason, and she gave a quick nod. "Thank you."

He gave her arm another pat and then stepped back. "Let me know how the interview goes, all right?"

She told him she would and headed out of the office. The hallway was buzzing with students and activity as she walked toward the quad, the familiar sounds making her want to cry even more. This wasn't going to be her place anymore. This wasn't her home.

She'd spent so many years here, learning, growing, finding who she wanted to be. She passed the door of the sleep lab and got an old, familiar pang of sadness. She'd even lost her innocence here and had her first heartbreak.

Now she'd have to face what was outside these walls. The world. Real life. She couldn't be a student any longer. She couldn't hide.

She pushed out into the spring sunshine and tried not to dissolve into tears.

6

Donovan woke up with a booming headache and the cloying scent of lavender filling his head. He grimaced and rolled his face into the pillow. The smell only got stronger, confirming it wasn't his pillow. Or his bed. *Fuck*.

He turned his head and forced his eyes open, the morning light piercing his brain like tiny knives. Eyelet curtains blew in the breeze of the open window, the sound of the ducks puttering around the pond nearby drifting in. Great. Not only had he fallen asleep in the wrong bed, but he was all the way across campus, late, and hungover. Dr. Suri would shit a brick if she found out. He reached for his phone, which he'd managed to leave on the side table but not set his alarm—brilliance in action—and hit the speed dial.

His assistant, Ysabel, answered on the first ring. "I've already rescheduled your eight o'clock and pushed the morning group back a half hour."

Donovan let his head fall back to the pillow. "I love you, Ysa. Marry me."

"You're not my type. I need more boobs and less penis."

"I could work on the first if you keep bringing in those beignets from the Morning Cup. But the penis has to stay."

"I'm out, then. What's your ETA?"

"An hour?"

"Be quicker. Dr. Suri called for you earlier. I told her you were on the phone. She didn't leave a message because she was walking into a meeting, but you know she'll call back when she gets out."

"Shit. All right. Got it. Thanks, Best Assistant Ever."

"Yeah, yeah. Kiss up. But you can't keep pulling this shit. Dr. Rhodes is never late. I want that bigger office. And I don't want him messing around on our wing."

He grimaced. Both he and Clinton Rhodes were up for the director position for the couples counseling building. The position would mean more money, a better office, extra support staff, and more time to devote to research in addition to the therapy. Donovan had stronger experience, but Clinton knew how to put on a good show and brownnose. And he showed up on time.

Fuck.

With a sigh, he let Ysabel go and braced himself for the conversation he had waiting for him outside of this room. He rubbed a hand over his face and sat up, his head pounding with a wine hangover and the need for coffee. Might as well face the firing squad and get it done with.

He climbed out of bed, made a quick trip to the bathroom, and then searched around the bedroom for his clothes. After he'd pulled on his boxers and slacks, he found his shirt in a ball on the floor. He shook it out and saw that half the buttons were missing and there were lipstick marks where the buttons used to be. Great. Someone had been aggressive last night. He tugged it on and had to leave it hanging open.

He found his way into the kitchen. Elle was sitting at the table with a big mug of coffee and her laptop open. She was already in her physician wear—gray slacks and a black top, all very conservative and to the point. She glanced over when she saw him walk in. "Good. You're up. I need you out of here. I have an appointment in fifteen minutes and the cleaning lady will be here any second."

"Fine. Is there more coffee? And do you have any T-shirts that would fit me? You demolished my buttons."

"No shirts." She frowned. "And I've already drank the pot I made."

She didn't offer to make more. He wasn't surprised or offended. Elle didn't make coffee for men on principal.

He went to the cupboard to get a glass and filled it with water from the sink. "Why didn't you wake me up? You know I didn't plan on sleeping here."

She barely glanced over. "I'm not your mother."

He sipped his water, evaluating her. Her blond hair was neatly tucked into a bun, her lips pursed as she typed away on her laptop. Dr. Elle McCray was a cool fortress of impenetrability ninety-nine percent of the time. Her patients and colleagues called her the Bitch, sometimes behind her back, much of the time to her face. But you had to have an ego of steel to work in the rehab wing, and Elle did. Handling pampered celebrities detoxing from drugs was like working in a daycare half the time and a war zone the other half. Addiction had an insidious way of bringing out the worst in people and smothering the good. And Elle was like the priest in *The Exorcist*, helping patients tackle the demons for what they were and fighting hard for the soul choking for air beneath. You couldn't go into that fight without a lot of armor, and Elle was armed to the teeth.

But he was beginning to wonder why Ms. Cool Customer had let him sleep over the last few times. That wasn't what this relationship was. They both knew it.

He needed to stop drinking when he came over here. Elle had grown up in Napa and had a penchant for a good, strong cabernet, but the stuff was too easy to drink. He couldn't let these lines get fuzzy. "Me sleeping here isn't a good idea."

Her jaw tightened. "*You* called *me*. *You* drank too much. It's not my fault you fell asleep. I didn't hold you down and make you stay."

No, he was usually the one doing the holding down. That's where they connected, despite barely being able to tolerate each other at work. Elle liked her sex like he did—unsentimental and without strings. Hate-fucking. They were good at it. They served a purpose for each other—two workaholics letting off steam. At least that's what it was supposed to be.

"Well, I've got to get going. Suri is hunting me down this morning."

Elle smirked. "Oh, poor Donovan."

"Don't mock. She loves you." He dumped his glass out and set it in the sink. "Must be nice."

She sent him an angelic smile. "I know how to play the game and follow protocol. You should learn it sometime."

"I'll take that into consideration, Dr. McCray." He strolled past her and grabbed his keys off the counter. They didn't kiss or hug. He'd tried that after their first night together, feeling like it was the right thing to do even if he hadn't been overly inspired to do it, but she'd shrugged him off. *I don't need empty gestures, Donovan,* she'd told him. *Just sex.*

Fine by him.

They exchanged a nod of good-bye, and he headed outside. He'd walked over to her place because it'd been a nice night, but now he regretted it. His house was on the other side of the expansive compound and making it across campus in his wrinkled clothes without being seen would be a challenge. He just had to hope that most of his co-workers were in sessions by now or at least in their offices.

The last thing he needed was Doc Suri finding out he was sleeping with a colleague. She already considered him the problem child since he liked doing things his way and couldn't keep staff for long on his floor. He'd probably already be gone if it were solely up to her. But he was good at what he did, well-known from getting a few national TV spots when his female arousal research went viral, and the elite clientele here asked for him because of it. The Orgasm Whisperer. That's the ridiculous name the media had given him. But it worked. The board of directors wanted him here because it brought in high-paying clients, and it let him get away with a few transgressions more than Dr. Suri would normally tolerate. But she had her limits, and he was close to pushing over them.

Donovan slipped around the north edge of the pond and avoided the tai chi class going on nearby. The ground was spongy from an overnight rain, and his dress shoes sank into the earth, making obscene sucking sounds as he skirted the edges of the surrounding trees. By the time he reached the main parking lot, his favorite shoes were a loss. Fantastic. Between his ruined shirt and muddy shoes, he was starting to resemble a hobo. But at least he was making good time and no one had seen him. The administrative building of the institute loomed in the distance, but this parking lot was quiet since this was the visitors zone and visiting hours didn't start until ten.

He was almost home free. His house was only a few hundred yards on the other side of the trees. But when he hurried around a large pickup truck to turn onto the walking path, someone ran smack into him.

He let out an *oof* and automatically put up his hands to block whoever or whatever it was, but when he did so, the person who'd run into him lost her balance and went sailing backward onto her ass. Papers flew in the air. A curse flew from her.

The wet sound of her butt hitting the earth alongside the path made Donovan cringe. Only then did he take in the sight. A woman in a business suit. Short dark hair. Horrified expression. He went to her side. "Shit. Are you okay?"

Ignoring him, she peered around at the scattered papers and the mud that had splashed onto her legs and skirt. "Oh, you've got to be kidding me."

He reached out his hand. "Here. Let me help you up."

She glanced up then, annoyance in every corner of her expression, but when her gaze met his, she froze. Her lips parted for one long second and she blinked rapidly.

Donovan stilled, his hand extended, and a little jolt of awareness went through him. He wasn't sure what it was, but something about her seemed familiar. He frowned, trying to place her. A former client, maybe? "Are you okay, miss?"

She broke the eye contact and took his offered hand. "I'll be fine."

He helped her to her feet, and then they both gathered her things. She pulled a tissue out of her purse and did her best to clean off some of the mud.

"Do you need me to get you anything? Paper towels?"

"It's okay." She glanced at him again, her gaze briefly tracking over his state, and only then did he remember how he must look. His shirt was hanging open with lipstick all over it, and he looked like he'd just rolled out of bed. Of course she didn't want help from him. She probably knew not to trust strangers wandering the grounds of a psychiatric institution.

"Are you here for an appointment?" he asked.

She tucked the tissue in her purse and gripped her stack of papers tightly. "Yes. And I need to get going or I'm going to be late. The guard already held me up forever at the main entrance."

He ran a hand over the back of his head, still trying to place her. She had that Demi Moore vibe, *Ghost* era, with her pixie cut and those big hazel eyes. Maybe that's what was poking at his brain. Or maybe she was some B-list actress that he'd seen in a movie. Lord knows there were enough of them who came here for treatment. But she didn't have that emaciated body that so many of the wannabe stars strived for. There were soft curves and gentle lines. His fingers flexed. "I'm really sorry about bumping into you."

"My fault. I was looking at my phone instead of up. I—" She pressed her lips together and shifted her gaze toward the main building. Nervous. "I've got to go."

"Need me to point you toward any place in particular?"

She had already started walking, her heels *click, click, clicking* on the pavement. She called back over her shoulder. "Nope. Thanks. I'm good."

She had a smear of mud on the back of her skirt from the fall, but she held her head high as she walked like it didn't bother her. Only the stiff set of her shoulders told him she was strung up tight. Huh. Maybe that's what she was coming in for—anxiety. At least it would mean she wouldn't be one of his clients. Thank God. Talk about awkward. *Hello, doctor. Oh yes, you were the one doing the walk of shame this morning. Nice to meet you. Now I will confess my deepest, darkest secrets and trust you with my mental health.*

Talk about breaking any semblance of professional credibility before even getting started.

Donovan jogged the rest of his way to his place and thanked the universe he hadn't run into anyone he knew. Now he just needed to make sure he was at his desk before Dr. Suri tracked him down again. Small miracles. He'd take what he could get.

7

The place used to be an asylum. Considering how crazy Marin felt for even taking this interview after what had happened in the parking lot, it seemed fitting. When she'd looked up and found Donovan West holding his hand out to her, she'd tumbled back in time for a second. Everything in her had fluttered like she was still some eighteen-year-old girl with a crush.

But when he hadn't recognized her, she'd slammed right back into reality. She was here for an interview, sitting in the mud, and the man she'd lost her virginity to didn't even know her name. She didn't blame him for not recognizing her. It'd been nine years. There was little left to resemble the girl she'd been. Her contacts were in, she'd chopped off her hair a few years ago, and she'd gained at least fifteen pounds since then. He looked different, too. Older. Broader. More of a man now, with his morning scruff and the faint lines of life around his eyes. And she wasn't going to think about the bare chest beneath his shirt or the dark hair that had curled down a body he obviously took very good care of. She would not think about that at all. Especially considering the very obvious pink lipstick that had been all over his ruined shirt. Someone had apparently not lost his penchant for hookups.

That wasn't a surprise. Perversely, she'd followed Donovan's career for a few years after they'd slept together. It'd been her secret, masochistic indulgence. Everything had been so chaotic then. She'd had to drop out of school for almost a year, had to fight for custody of Nate, had to figure out how to support a household on her own. Looking up Donovan had given her a brief escape.

She'd watched his research get published. She'd seen the buzz that had made it all the way into the mainstream media. And she'd seen him do interviews on the talk shows. She'd been happy for him, but after a while, seeing his success had begun to sting more than comfort. The sweet, sexy guy she'd gotten to know that spring break week had changed. She could see the shift in the interviews. The limelight had made him smug. Cocky. Soon, there were rumors that he was dating actresses and Hollywood elite. The media gave him a ridiculous nickname. Marin had stopped looking.

So she had no idea why the hell he was in nowhere Louisiana now. She would've assumed he was still riding his sliver of fame with some private practice in L.A. But nope, he was here. Half-dressed and helping her to her feet.

Maybe he was a client here. Ha. She wouldn't be so lucky. She should walk straight back to the rental car and get the hell out of here. She'd already ruined her outfit anyway. She was going to walk in looking ridiculous.

But she'd come this far, and she didn't have any other options that would give her a chance at the pay she needed. She needed this. Nate needed this. She took a few more steps forward.

The chalk-white building loomed in front of her, intimidating and grand with its three-story-high Greek columns and a grove of ancient oak trees surrounding it. Gnarled branches with snaking Spanish moss seemed to hold the historic structure in their grasp. Breathtaking, really. But a pervasive sense of dread filled her. She imagined the people who were committed here back when it was an asylum had found no comfort in it either. Beauty with bite. This place seemed too grand, too ancient, too everything. She felt like an intruder at the gates.

"Need help finding something?" someone asked from off to her left.

She turned to find a tall, dark-skinned woman in a white coat sending her a polite smile. "I—"

Her smile fell when she took in Marin's state. "Oh, Lord. What happened to you?"

Marin looked down at the splashes of mud on her skirt and her soggy papers. "I got in a fight with the lawn and lost."

The woman gave her a sympathetic laugh. "Oh, no. That bayou mud will get you after a rainstorm. I can show you where the bathrooms are if you want to wash out your skirt and can get you some scrubs to put on in the meantime."

"Thanks. I would, but I'm here for an interview with Dr. Suri, and I don't want to be late."

She cringed. "Oh, wow, yeah. Being late would be a bad idea. She's kind of stickler for time. Just tell her what happened with the fall. Why does that kind of thing only happen on job interviews? I got a flat tire when I came for mine."

"Guess you got the job anyway."

"That's because I'm so good." The woman brushed imaginary dust from her shoulder with playful confidence. "Two years and running. Hey, maybe bad luck before the interview is a good omen."

After the parking lot, Marin was thinking not. But she smiled anyway. "Maybe."

The woman stepped closer, her brown eyes flashing golden in the dappled sunlight that streamed through the branches of the surrounding oak trees. She stuck out her hand. "Oriana Wallace. Addiction wing."

She shook her hand. "Marin Rush. Interviewing for the sex therapy program."

Her eyebrow lifted. "Wow, the X-wing, huh? Interesting stuff."

"The X-wing?"

She shrugged. "It's what we call it around here. You know, rated X? All the departments end up with their own code names. My area is referred to as the R and R."

"Rest and relaxation?"

"No, rinse and repeat. My clients are the ones most likely to make repeat performances. Nature of the addiction beast, unfortunately. Come on, I'll lead you into the gauntlet and show you the quickest way to Suri's office. It's easy to get lost. They had to retrofit a lot of the offices and it can make you feel like a rat in a maze. I have yet to find cheese, though."

Marin smiled, thankful for the help and a friendly face. "That'd be great."

Oriana led Marin up the front stairs and into the building, which had been beautifully restored to period details of the nineteenth century with its wide baseboards and Greek Revival architecture, but there was a poshness to it that she doubted had been present back when it was an asylum. Expensive-looking artwork, a lobby area with fine antique furniture, and a chandelier that sent sparkling light over the marble floors. It was a lobby meant to impress. But when they went through the double doors to get to the offices, Marin understood what Oriana had been talking about. Signs pointing every which way demarcated the offices, but it was a twisting tangle of hallways and doors. She half-expected that little kid from *The Shining* to roll up on his Big Wheel.

They took the elevator to the top floor and Oriana dropped her off there. She put her hand out to keep the elevator door from closing. "Dr. Suri's office is the one at the end of the hall."

"Thanks so much," Marin said, her nerves bubbling up again and making her voice shake.

"No problem. Good luck with the interview. Just remember that if you managed to get an interview here, you're already great at what you do. She only talks to the best, so be confident."

"Ha. Sure, no problem. I'm just going to walk in with my muddy clothes and wet resume and wow her right out of her chair."

She laughed. "How about I be confident on your behalf? *When* not *if* you get the job, you owe me a cup of coffee for being your tour guide."

"Deal."

She tapped the side of the elevator. "Go get 'em, doctor. Lord knows the X-wing could use some estrogen."

"Oh?"

She smirked. "See ya."

The elevator doors shut, leaving Marin in the hallway alone. She took a deep breath and headed toward the office, the sound of her heels echoing off the floors with an ominous reverberation. She tried not to think about how little experience she had in clinical work. She tried to forget that the man she'd tried so hard to block out of her mind was somehow tied to this place. She tried to remember why she was doing this.

This was insane.

She walked into the office and gave the secretary her name.

The woman smiled. "You can go on in, Dr. Rush. She's waiting for you."

Welcome to the asylum, we're all crazy here.

8

"Do you think once a cheater, always a cheater? I mean, how am I supposed to trust him when he screwed that skinny bitch behind my back?"

Donovan hooked his ankle over his knee and leaned back in his chair, trying not to cringe at his client's shrill tone. He should've had more coffee and extra aspirin before this first appointment. "I think each situation is different. Rarely are things always or never."

Claire Daniels swept her long bangs away from her face with a huff, but tears glistened in her eyes. "This is such bullshit. I did the cover of *Maxim* last month. Men all over the world want me. And my jackass boyfriend fucked a wannabe catalog model." She leaned over and yanked something out of her purse. She held up a computer printout of a redhead in a bikini. "Look at her. She looks like a boy. Who would you rather sleep with?"

Donovan frowned. The truth was he had no interest in sleeping with either. He'd rather go celibate than hook up with another actress. He'd learned that lesson the hard way. But he wasn't going to answer that type of question in a session anyway. "Is that really what you want to know?"

Her gaze dropped down to her hands. "No."

"What would you like to ask, then?"

She closed her eyes, and two fat tears rolled down her cheeks. The reviews of her latest movie had called her a pretty crier. Donovan hadn't thought there was such a thing, but Claire did seem to make it look tragically elegant. She shook her head. "Am I that broken, doc? Would he rather be with someone like that because I'm just not worth the trouble?"

There it was. The real question. He was proud of her for being brave enough to voice it. In their early sessions, Claire had maintained a cool facade of the untouchable actress and had been combative when Donovan had tried to get her to open up. Finally, she was showing some trust in him. "I think we're all broken in some way, Claire. But no, I don't think you're unworthy or that you deserved to be cheated on. And blaming yourself for someone else's actions isn't going to help. Benny strayed. You're not responsible for his behavior."

"But if I was giving him what he needed, if I wasn't so fucked up . . ." She looked up and swiped at her tears. "What kind of woman can't enjoy sex?"

"Lots," he said, leaning forward and bracing his forearms on his thighs. "Especially ones who went through what you did as a teenager. Give yourself a break and some time. You're here and working on this. That's more than most can say. And I don't know exactly why Benny cheated without talking to him. People stray for all kinds of reasons. Sometimes it's a lack of impulse control, other times it's some kind of internal issue—insecurity, fear of aging, depression. Sometimes it's impaired judgment from drugs or alcohol. It could be a lot of different reasons."

She looked out the window at the sprawling oak trees that stood like sentries throughout The Grove. "Because the other person is sexier?"

Donovan let out a breath. This was one of Claire's issues. The people who watched her in movies and smiling on magazine covers would never suspect how deeply insecure she was, that she'd grown up hearing that she was ugly and dumb. It was one of the reasons she was attracted to shitty guys and jumped from relationship to relationship. She needed empty compliments filling the ever-draining well. "I think if you want to work through this with Benny, he's going to have to come in for a few sessions with you. You two need to decide whether or not this is a deal breaker."

She chewed her lip and looked away. "I'm not ready to leave him. I know you probably think I'm stupid. The press definitely does."

He glanced down at his steno pad and made a note. "I think decisions in life aren't as cut and dried as they appear from the outside looking in."

"Have you ever been cheated on?"

Donovan's gaze jumped back to her, his pen pressing hard into the paper.

She gave him a sheepish look and an apologetic shrug. "I heard you dated Selena St. Pierre. And she got together with Ryan Vickers right after that."

He held back the grimace that tried to surface. He hated that clients could so easily dig into his personal life. He was supposed to be this blank slate, a sounding board, a trained ear. But people could find dirt on him if they wanted it because he'd been stupid enough to date a TV actress. He'd been stupid in general. Luckily, the only thing that had made it to press had been the breakup and the rumored infidelity, not the . . . aftermath.

"Claire, my personal life has no bearing on yours. And every situation is going to be different."

"But is that why you two broke up?"

Yes. No. He'd tried the committed thing with Selena. After being in L.A. for a few years, riding the success of the arousal research and indulging in too many women who wanted their round with the Orgasm Whisperer, he'd given a relationship a shot. He'd been moving too fast for too long, trying to run from all that had happened in Texas, and was burned the fuck out. Selena was a beautiful and talented woman. They got along. And she'd had a big family and group of friends surrounding her. Part of him had been so drawn to that, that possibility of belonging somewhere after so many years on his own. He'd let himself take a breath.

It'd been a mistake.

After six months, they got engaged. She wanted the big diamond and the celebrity-grade wedding and the smiling couple cover of *People*. He didn't know what he wanted, but that train had been on greased rails. He'd gone along with it until he couldn't. When he told her he wasn't ready to set a date, instead of just getting mad or breaking it off, she hooked up with her co-star and timed it so that Donovan would find them together. Naked bodies twined up in his bed.

She'd wanted a reaction. A big declaration. A surge of possessiveness from him.

But it hadn't come. Instead, he'd just felt . . . nothing. Resigned. Like part of him had always known it would end. That Selena and her family and their group of friends were mere apparitions, players on a stage, and he was easily cut from the cast.

He'd been trying to be something he wasn't, and they'd found him out.

She called him heartless.

She was right.

"I'm sorry. I can't answer that." Donovan set aside his notes and gave the clock behind Claire a pointed look. "And unfortunately, we're out of time for today."

She sighed and shoved the photo of the women in the bikini into her purse. "Okay."

"This week, I want you to practice the relaxation exercises we talked about and try some self-stimulation when you feel ready." He stood and went to the cabinet behind his desk. He pulled out a small unmarked box and walked over to hand it to her. "This is the vibrator I mentioned to you earlier. It's a simple one meant for clitoral stimulation but has more focused power than what you've been trying to use. And I'll send over the file with the audio recording to your private email."

She stood and took the box from him. "Thank you."

"I also want you to see if Benny would be willing to come in with you for your next session."

She nodded. "He's on the road right now, but I'll let you know."

"Great." He opened the door to let her out. "Good work today."

She paused before stepping out. "Thanks, Dr. West. I thought you were going to spend the whole session telling me how I needed to leave him."

"That's not my call to make."

She gave a put-upon sigh. "I know I should probably cut the asshole loose, but I really have this gut feeling that he's the one, you know? He can be so sweet when he wants to be, and I think it's just hard for him to know he can't magically fix me."

Donovan gave her his sympathetic therapist smile. "Let's get him in here and see what happens."

She nodded, a glimmer of hope coming into her eyes, and then slipped out the door, gracing the hallway with a hip-swaying runway walk.

Donovan closed the door and shook his head.

The One. Right. It was such a crap concept. One that got a lot of people in trouble. So many of his clients had this fantastical notion about The One—this fated person who would make everything in their world click into place. The sun would look brighter. The sex would be amazing every time. Their lives would be perfect. Fa-la-fucking-la.

But it was such a damaging goal. People spent all this time trying to track down that elusive unicorn and trying to make their lovers fit into this mold of being that one imaginary person. But he'd done this long enough to know that the concept was just words in a fairy tale. The only two people he'd ever seen who had come close to the soul mate thing were his parents. And even then, there was no happily ever after. Why would fate have given his parents their one magical person only to have them murdered a few years after they found each other? It was bullshit.

Relationships were simply negotiated terms between people. Sometimes they worked. Sometimes they didn't. Even in the early stages with Selena, he'd never thought she was some predestined soul mate. They'd gotten along. They'd had chemistry in bed. They'd fit into each other's lives in a practical way. Then they hadn't. It was really that simple.

When couples came in for therapy, his job was like a mediator between businesses, making sure middle ground was found, needs were met. He was good at it. But when people brought up the mystical concepts of fate and The One, he kind of wanted to throw one of his psych textbooks at them. If people were convinced it was fate, why bother with therapy? They wouldn't hear anything he had to say that didn't fit into the story they'd already created for themselves.

Which is why he dreaded the next session with Claire and Benny. Couples therapy drained him. Give him someone with arousal disorder or sex addiction or a fetish any day. He'd much rather tackle those issues than deal with the should-we-or-shouldn't-we-stay-together situations.

But Zach, the guy who'd been hired to help take some of Donovan's caseload and handle those types of marital issues, had quit two months ago when he decided Donovan was "difficult" to work with and that the clients were too intense. Really, the guy had gotten chewed up and spit out by a particularly combative couple who'd threatened to sue when they blamed his treatment plan for making the marriage worse.

Amateur mistake.

Celebrities and the wealthy were their own breed. They were used to people catering to them, and a therapist's job was to help them see things about themselves in a way they didn't necessarily like. It didn't always go over well. People got pissed. They swung their power around. You couldn't let them. Zach was the second therapist they'd lost on this floor in eight months.

Donovan hadn't been surprised. The only way to deal with big egos was to make sure you had one, too. That's who survived here. And Zach just didn't have the backbone for it.

Of course, Donovan's boss had blamed him for the loss. Apparently, she'd seen it as a *failure to be an effective mentor*, and it'd ended up being a mark against him for the promotion. Another point to add to her list of grievances.

So now he had double the caseload and another hill to climb in Suri's eyes. He didn't mind the extra work. In fact, he preferred having the floor to himself. He liked the control of that and being busy. But too many couples sessions in a week could drive him to the brink. And if he ever wanted to add research to his plate again, he would need to get promoted and have someone else on this floor to ease the workload. Another therapist would be for the best. He just dreaded the process of dealing with someone else new.

The buzzer on his office phone went off, and Ysa's voice filled the office. "Dr. West?"

He leaned back in his chair and rubbed the spot between his eyes. "Yeah."

"Six people confirmed for the sex addiction group this afternoon. But Karina showed up early in an outfit that was, uh . . . quite revealing, so I ushered her to the private room across the hall so she wouldn't bring that distraction into group."

Donovan looked to the ceiling. "How revealing?"

Ysa sniffed. "She sat across from me in the waiting room. I can confirm that the carpet matches the drapes."

Donovan couldn't stop the chuckle at his assistant's deadpan tone. Ysa wasn't fazed by much these days. "Call the main building and have someone bring her a pair of scrubs. Tell her she's not allowed into group otherwise."

"Will do. Oh, and Dr. Suri just called. She wants you in her office in ten minutes."

Donovan sat forward, his chair squeaking in protest. "For what?"

"Didn't say. And you know I'm not asking. She had that tone."

He sighed. "Fantastic. I'm on my way."

Ysabel wished him luck, and he got up to head over to the main building, hoping Suri hadn't somehow found out that he'd shown up late again today. He greeted people as he made his way through the snaking hallways and jogged up the stairs. When he walked into the office, Agatha, Dr. Suri's assistant, gave him a broad smile. "Long time no see, Dr. West."

"I've missed your beautiful face, Aggie. But you know me, I try to avoid trips to the principal's office."

"Stop trying to charm an old woman. It won't work on me." But she gave him a wink from behind her glasses before picking up her phone. "Dr. Suri, Dr. West is here."

Aggie nodded and hung up the phone.

"You can go on in," she said.

"Am I in trouble?"

Aggie's smile went sly. "Aren't you always? But not the kind you're thinking."

He lifted a brow. "Now you've got me curious."

"Well, you know what they say about that."

Donovan frowned at the playful warning but walked over to the door and stepped inside of Doc Suri's office. Suri was at her desk, intimidating despite her diminutive height and the soft bun twisted atop her head. The president in her oval office. Her gaze slid to him with dark eyes that could go warm with friendliness or singe with disapproval. Well, at least he'd heard about the first one. He had yet to truly witness such an occurrence. She stood. "Dr. West, glad you could make it over here between appointments."

"Sure, no problem. What can I help . . ."

But his words drifted away from him when someone rose from the seat across from Suri's desk.

"I wanted you to meet someone," Dr. Suri said.

The woman whom he'd run into in the parking lot had turned toward him. She closed her eyes for the briefest of seconds, like she was pained, but then quickly hid it behind a tight, Mona Lisa smile.

Suri stepped around her desk. "Dr. West, this is Dr. Marin Rush. She's interviewing for the open position on your floor. Since you'd be training her if she's hired, I thought it was important for you to join in on the second part of the interview."

"I—" The name was ringing bells in his head—thick, reverberating sounds. *Marin. Marin.*

"Marin, this is Donovan West."

Marin's lips tilted into the barest of smirks, and that's when it came back to him, in one, scrolling memory. Late nights and long conversations. Teasing glances and longing looks. He'd kissed those lips. He'd touched this woman. But only once. *Mari.*

Fuck.

Mari—no, *Marin*—took a step forward and put out her hand formally. "Nice to meet you, Dr. West."

He took her hand. It was chilled, delicate, but the squeeze she gave him was firm and confident. He didn't want to let it go. "You can call me Donovan."

"Donovan, then."

He couldn't read her eyes. She was giving him a professional mask. A stranger's face. But the way she'd said his name and the slight flush in her cheeks told him she wasn't unaffected. This was why she'd been so freaked out when they'd collided outside. She'd recognized him. Now he felt like an ass for not placing her sooner. But she looked so different. No less striking but a much more refined version of the girl he'd shared spring break with all those years ago.

Dr. Suri smiled, which lit her normally stern face with a cheerfulness he hadn't seen before, and headed back behind her desk. "Marin attended Dallas University and worked under Dr. Paxton like you. You were probably there at the same time, though Marin just graduated last year, so I doubt you crossed paths."

"Last year?" He frowned.

Marin smiled. "Yes, I remember hearing about your success with your research after you graduated. I was a sophomore at the time. Congratulations on that, by the way."

Donovan blinked. "A soph—"

That would've meant . . . *Ah, hell.*

"Why don't we all sit down and chat?" Dr. Suri suggested. "Marin's research is very impressive, and she's come to us with the highest of recommendations from Dr. Paxton."

Donovan nodded and went to the other empty chair, his brain spinning. He'd looked for Mari after that night. Not just because he'd felt like a bastard for unceremoniously taking her virginity but also because he'd liked talking to her. He'd been so messed up back then, and she'd been this light in the dark, someone who had made him smile and want things and hope. A reprieve from the anxiety and crushing depression his parents' murder had brought on. He'd known it was a bad idea to get involved with anyone, but he hadn't been able to let it go that easily. He'd gone to the sleep department to find her, but no one had known a "Mary." After a few useless attempts to track her down, he'd stopped because he'd realized then that if Mari had wanted to be found, she would've come to him.

Now he realized why she'd bailed. She'd lied to him. He hadn't just taken her virginity. He'd fucked a goddamned teenager. His stomach flipped over.

Dr. Suri asked about Marin's accomplishments. The woman had an impressive research track record for only being a year out of her program. And when she spoke about it, she was as articulate and sharp as he remembered. Her passion was evident in every word, in the bright spark that lit her eyes when she got into the data. He got that. Research used to light him up like that, too. But he had to focus.

He could deal with whatever happened between them in the past later. Right now, she was being considered for a position on his floor. He'd be responsible for her training. If he failed again, he may as well hand the director position to Dr. Rhodes. He needed to forget about who she was and look at her with critical eyes. Do a real interview.

He sat back in his chair and considered her. "Dr. Rush, it's clear that you've excelled in your research and have a lot invested in it, but I haven't heard you speak about your clinical experience besides that internship at the high school, which sounded more education focused than therapy based."

Marin's gaze, which had been firmly on Suri, slid his way. Her lips thinned and worry flickered on her face. She cleared her throat. "My clinical experience is limited since my research took so much of my time, but I'm well-trained, a quick study, and am eager to work in the field under a strong supervisor."

He frowned. "No clinical internships with adults?"

She shook her head. "I worked a few weeks in a mental health center."

He tried not to groan. The girl was as green as spring grass. *No bueno.* "That definitely wouldn't have prepared you for this. Our clients have extremely high expectations and can be a lot to handle. We've lost two experienced therapists over the last year. The X-wing can be a gauntlet."

She sat up straighter. "I'm not scared of a challenge."

She was lying. He could tell. But he wasn't going to call her on it in front of Suri. "I'm not sure this is going to be the right fit for you."

Something fierce flashed in her eyes. "With all due respect, Dr. West, I think you're wrong. And if you give me a chance, I can prove that to you."

"This isn't—"

But Suri interrupted him. "Marin, I think that's an excellent idea, actually. I, too, am a bit concerned about your lack of field experience. But your background is impressive, and I take Dr. Paxton's recommendations very seriously. Skills can be learned if you have a solid foundation to work with and a *dedicated mentor* committed to your success." She cut a look Donovan's way, her warning landing like a grenade in his lap. "So why don't we start with a six-month probationary period?"

Marin's attention swung to Dr. Suri. "Probationary?"

"Yes. We'll set you up with temporary housing on campus. All of our therapists and doctors get the option of free housing on the grounds if they're willing to be on call a few days a month. Are you willing to do that?"

"Yes," Marin said without hesitation.

"And we'll pay you as if you're a permanent employee. But I want you to work with Dr. West for a few months. He's right. This position has been particularly hard to find the right person for. We'll have you shadow Donovan, gain some experience, and then we'll reevaluate at the end of the trial period—both to see if you think it's right for you and to determine if you're the right fit for us."

Donovan opened his mouth to protest.

But Dr. Suri nailed him with that gaze again. "Dr. West, I trust that you will work hard to mentor Dr. Rush and get her up to speed."

His lips flattened. Her message clear. *Her success is your success. Don't fuck up.* "Of course."

She turned to Marin and smiled. "I guess you have an official offer then, Dr. Rush. Do you have any questions for me?"

Marin's hands were twisting in her lap, the only sign of her nerves or excitement or whatever the hell she was feeling. He'd think it was cute if he wasn't so annoyed at being strong-armed into this hire. "Just one. I don't live alone. How does that work with housing?"

Donovan's neck muscles pulled tight. She didn't live alone. She had someone. Of course she did. Why wouldn't she? His gaze drifted back to her hands.

No ring.

Not that it mattered. This girl was off-fucking-limits. He was going to train her. No. He was going to make sure she was the best goddamned therapist she could be. And he was going to get his promotion. End of story.

Suri waved a dismissive hand. "Not a problem. Anything else? Do you need time to think over the decision?"

Donovan knew what the answer would be. Maybe Marin had a pile of other offers on the table. People who got interviews here usually did. They only hired the best. But they *were* the best. When you got an offer at The Grove, you didn't say no.

Marin smiled. "Not at all. When can I start?"

9

One month later

Marin tried to keep the giddy smile off her face as she and Nate unloaded the moving truck and carried their things into their new two-bedroom cottage. When Dr. Suri had offered her the job and told her that free housing was involved, she'd nearly spun around in a circle and broken into song.

In that moment, she hadn't cared that this was a probationary appointment or that Donovan West was burning a hole into the side of her head and clearly didn't want her here. She had a job, a place to stay, and would have enough money to send Nate to school as long as she got the permanent position. And there was no god-damned way she wasn't going to. She had six months to prove herself, and she would do whatever it took to make it happen. The salary they'd offered and this house were like winning a small lottery. She wasn't going to be rolling around in dollar bills on her bed or anything, but that ever-crushing stress of living paycheck to paycheck would go away. She'd be comfortable.

And this house . . . God. When they'd said they had housing, she'd expected something stark and dorm-like, but these cottages were posh. Gorgeous refinished wood floors, high ceilings, period details mixed with high-end appliances and furniture. They'd taken simple houses that had been built for staff when it was an asylum and decked them out. And the look on the outside was pure New Orleans with its pale pink clapboard and raised foundation. Marin imagined it had seen a lot in its years—survived floods and famines and hurricanes. Somehow she was comforted by that, made the place feel solid and dependable beneath her feet. And the view out the windows of the trees and gardens was stunning. It was a fairy-tale cottage. One that put every other place they'd ever lived in to shame.

But despite the nice digs, Nathan was less than thrilled about the arrangement, so Marin was trying to keep her enthusiasm in check. Nate had planned to spend his last summer before college with Henry and his high school friends, but Marin had told him that if he wanted to go to art school, this was the price. He'd have to live with her at The Grove for the summer before moving into the dorms at school. He'd agreed, but now she had a sulky, lovelorn teenager on her hands.

She understood where the angst was coming from, but he was going to have to get over it. She had her own angst to mull over. New job. New city. Donovan fucking West. She stacked a third box on a pile of two. "Lots of pretty scenery to paint around here. You can get some practice on landscapes."

Nate didn't look her way. "Uh-huh."

She frowned and tried again. "What time do I need to bring you into the city for your interviews?"

At her behest, he'd applied to a few jobs. She needed him occupied. Otherwise, he'd mope all summer. But instead of applying in Bellemeade, the small town that was a few miles outside The Grove, he'd applied to places in New Orleans—art galleries, coffee shops, photography studios. It was forty-five minutes away, which she didn't love, but she'd compromised. The kid was an artist. He craved the city. Maybe if he fell in love with New Orleans, it would ease the separation from his friends and boyfriend.

Nate shrugged. "You don't need to bring me. I can take the bike."

She scowled. Nate had saved up all his money from his after-school job for a used motorcycle. She hated the whole idea of it, but he'd reminded her that he'd turned eighteen last week and could make the call. She didn't give a shit about the age thing, but he'd also reminded her that they couldn't live on one car anymore. She'd be stranded every day when he went into the city to work. Plus, he'd need something once school started. She hadn't been able to win against the practical argument. But she didn't have to like it.

"Make sure you wear your helmet every time and don't speed. And always have your inhaler with you and—"

He lifted a hand. "I got it, all right? Don't do stupid shit that will get you killed."

"Yes. Good advice in all situations."

He shoved his hand in his pockets. "Do they have Internet here? I told Henry I'd Skype when we got here."

She headed to the kitchen where her welcome packet was and pulled out the card with the Internet code. "Campus-wide wireless."

He plucked the card from her fingers and grabbed his laptop. "I'll be in my room."

"Tell Henry I said hi."

He grunted.

She rolled her eyes and went back to unpacking. But just as she opened one of the kitchen boxes, there was a light knock on the back door. She'd left only the screen door closed, so when she looked up, she saw Oriana giving her a little wave. "Welcome wagon's here."

Marin smiled and abandoned the box. "Come on in. It's not locked."

Oriana swung open the door. Today she wasn't in her white coat but instead looked to be heading out for a summer stroll in pale yellow capris, big sunglasses, and a sleeveless white shirt. She had a potted plant in one hand and a wine bottle in the other. She lifted both toward Marin by way of greeting. "I come bearing gifts."

"Ooh, thanks." She took both from Oriana and gave the plant a sniff. "Mmm, basil."

"It's from the community garden we have near the children's building. Basil brings good luck to a new home. And wine brings good luck to everything." She leaned against the counter, glancing around. "You also may want to burn some sage to cleanse whatever bad energy is left from the last resident. He got fired for hooking up with a patient. Very scandalous."

Marin lifted a brow as she brought the plant to the sunny window over the sink and set it on the sill. She put the wine on the counter. "Cleansing bad energy? A doctor who believes in superstition?"

Her lips lifted at the corner. "I grew up in New Orleans. It's a requirement to have a healthy respect for otherworldly things. Plus, my grandmother was big into natural remedies and taught me a lot about them. Some work. Some don't. Some have a placebo effect. But the clients here like a holistic approach, so it's good to have some tricks up your sleeve." She gave a wistful sigh. "I'm still waiting for that love spell to kick in with that hot orderly on the inpatient ward, though."

Marin laughed. "I'm afraid to ask what's involved in that."

She sniffed. "Mostly longing looks from me as I pass him in the hallway. We're both too smart to risk our jobs over a hot interlude in the supply closet. Though, sometimes I wonder . . . May be worth it."

Marin scrubbed a hand through her hair, the humidity making it stick to her forehead. "So they're pretty strict about interoffice stuff here, huh?"

A picture of Donovan rumpled and covered with lipstick marks ran through her mind. She had no idea where he'd been coming from that morning, but it was pretty obvious it was from some woman's bed.

She shrugged. "I'm not going to say it never happens. With so many of us working long hours and living on-site, it can be a little like boarding school. But it's best not to get caught. The head honchos don't want the drama. The clients provide enough of that."

"I'm sure."

"Mar, have you seen the charger for my computer? I just lost the—" Nate stepped into the kitchen and stopped talking when he saw Oriana there. "Oh, sorry."

"Nate, this is Oriana. She's another psychologist who works here. Oriana, my brother, Nathan."

Oriana smiled and put her hand out. "You can call me Ori."

Nate gave her hand a quick shake. "Nice to meet you."

Marin was pleased to see that despite his pouty mood, he hadn't forgotten his manners. "I think the charger is in the backseat of the car."

"Cool. Thanks." He jogged out the back door, no doubt in a hurry to reconnect his call with Henry.

Ori watched him leave and sent Marin a questioning look. "He's staying with you?"

"Yeah, he starts art school in New Orleans in the fall, so he'll be here for the summer."

"He didn't want to stay with your family?"

"I am his family. Our mom passed away when he was nine, and no dad in the picture, so I've been raising him since then."

"Wow. I'm sorry about your mom."

"We've done all right."

"Yeah, he seems like a nice kid. Good looking, too. You better keep him away from east campus. We have a residential teen program, and those girls will fall on him like starving tigers."

Marin laughed. "He has a boyfriend, so I think he's safe."

"Ah, well keep him away from west campus then where the teen boys are. Same threats apply."

Marin smirked. "Noted. Hey, you want some coffee or something? I think I can find the coffeepot."

Ori waved a dismissive hand. "No, I'm heading into town to do some shopping. I'm on call tonight, so I have to get out while the getting's good. I just wanted to stop by and welcome you to the insanity since I know it can be a little intimidating to start here. The place can be kind of cliquey. So know you have at least one friend already."

Marin reached out and gave Ori's hand a squeeze. "Thanks. That means a lot. Believe me."

"We'll do coffee soon. I expect sordid stories from the X-wing."

"I'll do my best."

She gave one last wave and headed out the door. Marin let out a breath and sat down at the small dining table in the kitchen nook, the drive to Louisiana, the move, and all the transition over the last month catching up to her. She'd been so focused on the money and getting her and Nathan here that she hadn't let the reality of what was in front of her sink in.

Monday she was starting a job that she had no experience in. And the person responsible for training her didn't really want her here. Over the past few years, she'd walked into things with confidence because she could stuff her head with the knowledge she needed beforehand. She never had to be off the cuff. She had the tools in her pocket at all times when she went into a research environment. For her dissertation defense, she'd practiced so much that she could've recited the thick document by heart. There was no question they could've thrown at her that she hadn't prepared for. But there was no armor she could walk in with Monday.

People were going to want her to fix their sex lives.

Problem was: How was she supposed to do that when hers had started and ended on the same night, at eighteen with the very man she had to report to tomorrow?

She lowered her head to the table and tapped it lightly against the wood.

Time to give a whole new meaning to the term "faking it."

10

Donovan strode into the office on Monday morning with his second cup of coffee and his training plan already forming in his head. He'd thought long and hard about this over the weekend and had decided that he needed to get out ahead of this Marin thing right at the gate.

Dr. Suri expected him to fail. She expected him to run Marin off like he had the others. He hadn't successfully mentored a more experienced therapist, so she'd sent him a complete newbie—a bigger challenge—to prove her point. If he couldn't train Marin, Suri had a solid reason to tell the board why she'd gone in a different direction with the promotion. Hell, maybe it'd give her a solid reason to get rid of him altogether: *Does not play well with others.*

It'd be easier to defend himself if it weren't true.

He set a steaming latte on Ysa's desk. "Good morning, sunshine."

"Only fifteen minutes late. That's almost early for you." She took the offered coffee and sipped. "Mmm, the expensive stuff. This is why I put up with you."

"She here yet?"

Ysa tilted her head toward his closed office door. "She got here early. Brought pastries for us. I gave her a quick tour, showed her the office she'll be using, and then set her up in yours. Try not to scare her off, all right? I think I'm going to like this one."

"Because she brought you croissants and showed up on time?"

"That doesn't hurt." She sipped her latte. "I'm easily bribed. But I will deny that if you call me out on it."

"Noted."

"But no. I liked talking with her. Did you know she developed a sex ed program for LGBT kids?"

"Yeah, I read through her research over the weekend. Robust program. Good stuff."

"I would've killed to have that around when I was in high school." She shook her head ruefully and then shrugged. "I guess I like that she spent all that time fighting for the underdog. The clients here need someone like that."

He smiled. "I love that you see our wealthy, celebrity clients as underdogs."

"Hey, people here are fighting a lot of demons. That's David against Goliath if I've ever heard it. Money can't always save you from yourself."

"Ain't that the truth." He tossed his coffee cup in the trash. "Hold my calls for now. I need to get Dr. Rush up to speed on a few things, and then I'll have her shadow me for the rest of the day on my appointments. You may want to warn the clients that I'll have a second therapist in the room today."

"Got it."

He rolled his shoulders, trying to loosen the tension that was grabbing hold, and pushed open the door to his office. Today was going to be about training, but he had to get something out of the way first. He stepped inside his office and shut the door behind him.

Marin looked up from her spot on the couch, her hazel eyes

widening for a moment before she smoothed her expression into one of professional passivity. She had her phone in her hand and she dropped it into her bag. "Good morning, Dr. West."

"You only have to call me that in front of clients. I think we passed the formalities stage a long time ago. Don't you?"

She gave a curt nod. "All right. Donovan, then."

He tried not to focus on the way her pale pink gloss slid over her lips as she smoothed it. He'd sucked that bottom lip between his teeth. Tasted it. *Focus, West.* "So before we get started, how about we slay the elephant and get that out of the way first?"

Her hands were in her lap and they flattened against her thighs, like she was shoring herself up, preparing for impact. "Which elephant should we tackle first?"

He leaned against the edge of his desk and crossed his arms. "What do you mean?"

"Seems we have a herd. Or is it a parade of elephants? I can never remember." She shook her head as if admonishing herself for the tangent. "So which one are you talking about? The fact that once upon a time we slept together? Or how about that you don't want me here? Or is it the one where I ran into you half-dressed and covered in lipstick the day I interviewed?"

He cringed. "Yeah, sorry about that last one. I feel like a dick for not realizing who you were."

She lifted a shoulder. "It's been a long time. I wouldn't have expected you to recognize me. We were kids."

He frowned. "No, *you* were a kid."

She had the decency to look chagrined. "Yeah, sorry about leaving that part out."

He sighed. "Just please, please tell me you were at least eighteen."

"I'd turned eighteen a few months before that."

He tilted his head back and pinched the bridge of his nose. "Somehow, that doesn't make me feel any better. I can't believe you were that young. You seemed so smart and . . . poised."

"Poised? Ha. I hope you're a better read of people now than you were then. I was anything but. I was kind of a disaster."

He lowered his head and peered at her. He could still see the girl she used to be in the curves of her face, but everything was more refined now, polished—the look in her eye world-weary. "I looked for you the next week."

Her gaze slid away, refocusing on some invisible imperfection on her slacks. "I had to drop out for that semester. Family stuff. Long story."

"Oh." That wasn't what he'd expected to hear. But her shoulders had curved inward, her entire posture closing off—*don't push*. If they were in a session, he'd chase that rabbit. But she wasn't his client. She wasn't even his friend. It wasn't his business. He leaned back on his hands. "As for that other elephant—that I don't want you here—you're wrong."

Her attention flicked up at that, a don't-bullshit-me look on her face. "You tried to talk Dr. Suri out of hiring me. I was sitting right there."

"I wanted a more experienced therapist, yes. But that was nothing personal. I have a busy schedule and was hoping to have someone who could hit the ground running. I know what it's like walking out of a research environment into a clinical one. It's not an easy transition. The lab is all about facts and numbers and structure. Therapy is almost all feel and instinct and thinking on your feet."

She uncrossed and recrossed her legs, meeting his gaze levelly though he could sense her nerves in the way she was holding her posture so rigidly. "I'm not going to pretend this isn't new for me or that I don't have a lot to learn. But I promise I'm more motivated than anyone to make this work. I work hard and learn fast. You tell me what you need me to do or learn or improve, and I'm going to do it."

Donovan ignored the ping that went through him at her words. It'd been a long time since they'd shared those few days together, but he'd never forgotten the fantasies she'd helped him with, how she'd gotten turned on by the kinky ones. How willingly she'd melted under his touch. *Tell me what to do, and I'm going to do it.* He could think of more than a few things to put on that list. Starting with . . .

He pushed off the desk and put his back to her. *Fuck.* He couldn't let his thoughts drift in that direction. He couldn't make a move on her. She was going to be his trainee. His colleague. Beyond risking her feeling harassed, if he didn't train her well, he'd lose the promotion, maybe even his job. And he couldn't lose this goddamned job. He liked stretching the rules around here because he knew exactly how much he could get away with, but he never wanted to push over that danger line. And messing around with someone in his own department was past that line. This job was too important. Like the clients who came here, this place kept him sane, stable. The packed schedule. The challenge of it. The puzzle of figuring out how to help someone. It was his medicine. The rope that kept him tethered.

He stared out the window at the grounds and tucked his hands in his pockets, centering himself and bringing the focus back to the task at hand. "I want you to succeed here, Marin. Don't doubt that. I'm going to train you to the best of my ability, and I have full confidence that you'll catch on quickly. As for our past, I think we're both grown-ups and can leave that where it is." He paused, trying to let go of his dour thoughts and channel some levity. He smiled at his reflection in the window. "Unless you need to profess some undying love that's been burning for me since you let me divest you of your virginity?"

Marin's whirling work-related thoughts skidded to a halt, all of them falling off the edge at Donovan's comment. Her lips parted.

But Donovan spun around, a devilish smile on his handsome face and his hands still tucked in his pockets. "That's how it's supposed to go, right? The guy who takes the V-card always has a special place. Research has proven it." He put his hand on his chest.

"Come on, did you write my name in your notebooks with a heart around it? You can tell me. I'm a doctor."

A choked laugh escaped her. "Research doesn't say any such thing. Plus, your name would be too long to fit in a heart. And if you recall, *I* walked away from *you* that night, *doctor*. So you were probably the one pining over your misguided night with a teenager."

He chuckled, the sound as rich and warm as she remembered. It softened some of those hard edges he'd acquired in the years since she'd known him, gentled the icy blue in his eyes. "Of course I was. There was bad poetry written. Sad songs played. I went through this weird emo/goth phase. It wasn't pretty."

"I'm sure," she said dryly but let out an internal sigh of relief at his shift in mood. This was the Donovan she remembered. He was still in there somewhere. She could work with that guy. She wasn't so sure about the other one.

He grinned, unrepentant. "See? You're going to do just fine. There are two important requirements to work in this field: shamelessness and a sense of humor." He raised a finger. "Oh, and the ability to keep a straight face no matter what."

He gave her a super-serious therapist face.

She tried to give her own back to him, but she lost the staring contest and laughed.

He pointed at her. "All right. Elephants slain?"

He still hadn't told her what he'd been doing in the parking lot in that half-dressed state, but it really wasn't any of her business. "Sure. Bleeding on the floor."

"Aw, poor elephants."

He slipped off his suit jacket, hooked it around the back of his chair, and sat behind his desk in one gracefully executed maneuver—all confidence and swagger. The accomplished doctor. The ridiculously beautiful man. Donovan West was pure impact.

She had a feeling he was probably loved or hated around here, not much in between. He was a man who inspired reaction. He'd sure as hell always inspired one in her. Just not one that had any place at work.

Stop it. She sat up straighter, studiously ignoring how well his shoulders filled out that dress shirt, how the blue of his tie matched his eyes, and how his dark hair looked thick enough for her fingers to get lost in. Nope. Totally wasn't going to pay attention to any of that.

He spread his fingers over the papers on his desk. "Okay, so I'm a big believer in learning by doing. You can read textbooks and academic journals until your brain explodes, but none of that is going to prepare you for when a client is there with you, asking for help. So most of this training is going to be you sitting in on sessions with me."

Marin laced her hands together, trying to keep them still. She knew that experiential learning would be involved but anxiety still fizzed in her veins. "Okay."

"And I don't want you to feel like you have to stay silent. I'll take the lead at first, but if you have something to add or a question to ask the client, go for it. I want you to participate. You may think of something I missed, which is always helpful. But it also makes people more comfortable if you're part of the conversation and not just this stranger listening to them. If you go off track, I'll help guide you back. Don't be afraid to mess up. I've got your back."

I've got your back. Images of being bent over that desk in the sleep lab, his hands on her hips, his body pumping into her, flashed through her mind. Heat crawled through her. Damn, she had to stop doing that. Why did he still have that effect on her? She was a grown woman, not some teenager with a crush. She really should've tried harder to find a guy in the last few years. It was screwing with her head that her only associations with actual sex involved this man. It was her only reference point. And it didn't help that he was still so fucking attractive. Even more so now, if she was honest.

She cleared her throat, hoping her makeup covered the warmth that had rushed to her cheeks. "Telling a perfectionist not to be afraid to mess up is like telling the grass to stop being green."

He gave her a half-smile. "Seeking perfection is the surest way to drive yourself crazy. Believe me. We're an imperfect species. Good thing—since you and I would be out of jobs otherwise." He leaned on his forearms, those blue eyes impossible to look away from. "But you're not going to learn if you don't take some risks. You're not going to get in trouble for a mistake. I'm not your boss, and I'm not looking for reasons to mark off points. This is a team effort. Our goal is the same: Help the clients and keep Dr. Suri happy. That's it."

The sustained eye contact was almost too much. She released a breath and nodded. "Okay."

"And you'll learn quickly that we're not very by-the-book around here anyway. People pay a lot of money to come to The Grove because we do take risks. We're not afraid to try out experimental techniques or go about things from a different angle. The only rules you need to remember are that we're here to diagnose and treat, not judge, that there has to be consent for every treatment we try, and that you have to keep your boundaries crystal clear with your clients. If you have those three things covered, you're golden."

"Got it." She sat up straighter. "So what's on the agenda today?"

Donovan checked his watch and stood. "An appointment in ten minutes."

Her ribs cinched tight. "Right into the fire, huh?"

He smirked. "Is there any better place to be?"

She stood, smoothing her slacks just to give her fidgeting hands something to do. "Should I read the client's chart first? Or maybe see the treatment plan? Are they going to be okay with me being in there? I don't want to throw anyone off or compromise—"

"Whoa, there. Slow down." He stepped around his desk.

She nodded, a quick, jerky gesture and her fists balled. *Dammit. Dammit. Dammit.* So much for calm, cool, collected Marin. She'd lose all freaking credibility if she had some kind of panic attack in his office before they even got started. "Okay. Right. Yes. Slow down. Sorry. I think I had too much coffee this morning."

He stepped in front of her and took one of her clenched hands, smoothing it out and sandwiching her cold fingers between his warm palms. "Look at me."

She did.

"Take a breath, Dr. Rush. You've got this." He squeezed her hand, his attention not wavering from her face. "And even when you don't, you've got me."

His voice had lowered since he was close, and it reminded her of the long-ago voice on those private recordings, that sinful voice whispering filthy things in her ear. She closed her eyes and inhaled deeply, trying to ignore the way his touch zinged up her arm, the way her heart went from jog to sprint. "I'm good. I'll be fine. I just like to be prepared."

"You're as prepared as you're ever going to be." He let go of her hand, offering some relief from that electric sensation, but then he put his palm against the small of her back instead. Oh, that was so much worse. So. Much. Worse. Warmth curled up her spine. "Come on. You can get settled in the room before anyone shows up. Get your game face on."

She let him lead her to the space next door, her heartbeat like a pulsing fist in her throat. She could do this. She had to.

He opened the door for her. Inside was a room much bigger than his office but matching the general decor she'd seen on the rest of the floor—modern touches tastefully mixed with a few antique pieces. Elegant but welcoming. Like a posh hotel. There were two heather-blue Victorian couches with curving wooden legs, a cushy armchair, and a pair of high-end desk chairs that rolled. Large black-and-white photos of various landscapes decorated the walls. And on one side of the room was a large plate-glass window that looked out onto the grounds, providing a gorgeous view. The desk was tucked in the corner—unobtrusive and simple, a place to take quick notes after a session.

"Nice setup."

He let her step inside first and his hand slipped away, making her feel both relieved and adrift. "Yeah, they don't cut corners here. Lots of space to use on this floor. And we can use our individual offices for sessions, but I prefer this one because of the view. It gives clients the option of facing us or going Freudian on the couch and putting their back to us while they talk."

"Right." Marin walked over to a long panoramic photograph of a beach. It was a stunning landscape. Pristine sand and churning water, big sky. But instead of appearing serene, it seemed lonely, desolate. Maybe it was the black-and-white tones, but she found herself wishing it had been photographed in color. She turned back to Donovan. "So you're not going to tell me anything about who we're seeing?"

"Not enough time. But you'll catch up easily enough." He headed over to the desk and grabbed two steno pads. He handed her one along with a pen. "Just relax. The first time is always the hardest. Best to get it out of the way quick and dirty like."

She snorted and quickly tried to block the noise with her hand.

The corner of his mouth curved. "Yeah, okay, I walked right into that one. *That's what he said*, right?"

She feigned an innocent look. "I didn't say a word."

"Uh-huh. Maybe that's what I would've said back then if I had known the state of things. But *someone* was good at keeping secrets." He sent her a playfully admonishing look. "But this time— no running away, all right? I know where you live, woman. I will hunt you down."

She laughed, her nerves making her a little giddy, and took the notepad from him. "Got it. No running."

Not like she had anywhere else to go.

There was a knock at the door, and she turned to look that way. A blond man with football-player shoulders and a leading man face was leaning in the doorway with an easy smile. "Ready for me, doc?"

Marin took a deep breath. *Here we go . . .*

11

Donovan waved the man in. "Come on in, Lane. I'd like you to meet Dr. Marin Rush. She's going to be braving the X-wing with me and sitting in on the session today."

The man's smile was affable, dimples slashing his cheeks, as he walked over to Marin and put out his hand. "Lane Cannon. Nice to meet you, Dr. Rush."

"As well," she said, shaking his hand. Lane had bright green eyes, the hint of a Southern accent she couldn't pin down, and a hand that was big and warm around hers. She could imagine him to be a firefighter or something—some job where you needed to be big and tough but reassuring at the same time. Or more likely with the cost of The Grove, a guy who played a firefighter on TV. She knew she'd find out his background in the session, but she'd always had a habit of guessing who and what people were on first impression. It was a game she liked to play. She was right a good part of the time.

Donovan tucked his hands in his pockets. "Lane is one of the surrogates who assists us when we have clients who need that kind of intensive help."

"Surrogate?" Marin blinked, the word not registering for a second. How could he be—then it clicked. "Oh. *Oh*."

Her cheeks felt warm all of a sudden.

Lane smiled like he was used to that type of reaction. "Yeah, that kind."

She heard a buzzer sound in her head, like a game show contestant getting something wrong. *Bzzt!* Wrong answer. Not a firefighter. Not an actor. Not even close. "A sexual surrogate."

He released her hand. "We use the term *therapeutic assistant* around here, but yes. I'm certified in California for what I do, but Louisiana's laws are a little knotted about it, so we're more careful about terminology."

"I can imagine."

Donovan indicated they should take their seats. Lane claimed the couch, and Marin found her way to the office chair next to Donovan. She kept her expression neutral, but her mind was reeling. She knew the history of sexual surrogacy. It'd been around since Masters and Johnson, but she had no idea it was a method still in active use or that there was a certification.

Donovan hooked his ankle over his knee and leaned back in his chair. "Lane's assisting me with a client who has crippling social anxiety about dating. Bianca will be coming in shortly to join us, but I usually chat with Lane first to get an update."

Marin nodded and straightened her spine, trying to find her professional self again. "What's the background?"

"Bianca was scarred in a car accident when she was young and has avoided intimate relationships because of how she looks. But now she's in an online relationship and is hoping to bring it to the in-person level. She's gotten to the point of video-chatting with this guy, which has been a major step. But even after that progress, she was still a thirty-two-year-old with no sexual experience and was terrified at the thought of navigating an adult relationship. That's why we brought Lane in originally."

Marin took notes. "How long have you two been working with her?"

"Six months with me. I brought Lane in about three months ago. He's been doing one-on-one intimacy training sessions, taking it very slowly. But Bianca has made a lot of progress in the last month. They moved onto full intercourse last week, and last night the plan was to try again since they had the normal discomfort associated with first times during the previous session."

Marin's attention flicked up at that, the question falling out of her mouth before she could halt it. "You can have sex with the clients?"

Lane's lips curved upward, and he stretched his arm over the back of the couch, completely relaxed. "If it's a part of the treatment plan, sure. Of course, both parties have to agree to move forward in that way. Not all of my clients need it taken that far. A lot of my work is getting people used to touching and being touched. But it was important for Bianca to take that step. She didn't want the pressure of having her first time be with someone she actually had feelings for."

"Understandable thought process for an older virgin," Donovan said, almost to himself. "Especially for someone like Bianca who likes to get everything just right."

Marin's gaze flicked over to Donovan. He was looking down at his notes, but his mouth twitched into a wry expression as if he'd sensed her looking at him.

Is that what he thought? That she'd used him like a surrogate? For practice?

Donovan tapped his pen along the edge of his notepad and gave her a quick knowing glance before addressing Lane again. "So how'd it go?"

Marin's attention swung back to Lane.

His expression went serious, businesslike. "She handled it pretty well. We took it very slowly again. But she panicked when she got close to orgasm. She thought she was going to look silly and got self-conscious. So I backed off, and we talked it through. I reminded her that a good lover wants to please her. They're not going to be turned off by how she looks when she comes. They'll be excited. Plus, I assured her we all look a little ridiculous when we orgasm anyway."

Donovan chuckled. "True enough."

Marin peered his way. Was it? She had a hard time believing he'd look ridiculous in that situation. She imagined that firm mouth going lax, those sharp blue eyes going unfocused, the muscles in his neck tightening. Would that cool mask fall away completely? Would fire burn there instead? She'd never gotten a chance to see that.

Ugh. Stop. She gave herself a mental punch in the face. She was sinking into stupid land. He was her co-worker now. They were not together. She should not give a shit what he was like in private, personal moments. She didn't.

She totally didn't. Her pen poked a hole in her paper.

"How'd she respond to that?" Donovan asked, blessedly oblivious to Marin's R-rated train of thought.

"She was really good with openly talking about her feelings. Eventually I got her to sit in front of a mirror with me, and she let me bring her to orgasm with a small vibrator. She admitted afterward that she thought she'd looked kind of sexy."

"Wow. Excellent." Donovan sounded genuinely pleased as he made a note. "That's huge progress."

"Yeah, I thought so. But I think I've brought her as far as I can get her at this point. The variable is going to be this guy. He's going to have to be patient with her. And she's going to have to be prepared for it to go a number of ways."

Donovan made a sound of agreement. "That's what we're going to be working on today. Both the separation from you and how to have coping strategies if the guy turns out to be a dud." He looked to Marin. "One of the issues with surrogate therapy is that someone gets used to having a partner who is sensitive and focused on their needs and issues. It's a safe place. Not to mention a heady experience having all that focused attention. Then they try a real relationship."

"And are jumping off a cliff into a sea of imperfect people," she filled in.

Donovan met her gaze, mouth in a flat line. "Exactly. Not just imperfect people. Imperfect is expected. The assholes are the problem. They're good at finding the vulnerable, and one shitty experience can undo a hell of a lot of work."

Lane groaned and tipped his head back against the couch. "God, I hope this guy isn't a dick. Bianca deserves someone who's going to be good to her. She's worked so hard."

"Agreed. But there's no way we can predict how this is going to go. We'll need to prepare her to not accept anything less than a great guy. No settling. She can't get The One Syndrome."

Marin paused in her note-taking. "The One Syndrome?"

Donovan checked his watch and then peered her way. "It's a disease you'll see a lot around here—that belief that there is one person for everyone, that you're fated in some way. Or, in this case, that this is Bianca's one chance at love. There is no One. But I've seen the notion keep people who should be divorced together way too long. I've seen people cling to damaging partners over it. And I've seen people fall into despair when they think they've lost their one chance."

Lane smirked. "Didn't work out so well for Romeo and Juliet either."

"Exactly," Donovan agreed. "The One got them killed."

Marin lifted her eyebrows. "Well, aren't you two a couple of romantics. Remind me not to invite either of you over for my annual marathon of Nora Ephron movies."

Donovan groaned. "Just work here for a couple of weeks. You'll lose your taste for fated love stories."

She smirked but didn't say anything more. She knew it was

probably a silly thing to hold on to that kind of magical thinking. But watching those kinds of movies had kept her going through the past few years as she watched friends and co-workers fall in love and pair off while she remained alone. The movies and books were fantasy, sure, but part of her still wanted to believe that there were Harrys and Sallys, and Sams and Annies, and Empire State Buildings on Valentine's Day.

"Bianca will be here any minute," Donovan said, breaking her from her thoughts. "Let's see how she's feeling about taking the next step and meeting this guy. Then we'll go from there."

Marin nodded. "Sounds good."

Bianca showed up a few minutes later—tall, graceful, and dark-haired. One side of her jaw and neck had burn scars, which apparently continued down her body. But her brown eyes were big and bright, her smile genuine, and her clothes chic. When Marin complimented her blouse, Donovan informed her that Bianca was a very successful fashion designer.

Bianca wasn't what Marin had expected. She was quiet, but she clearly had developed a comfort level with Donovan and Lane. If Marin hadn't known Bianca's history, she would've never guessed the woman had issues dating.

Bianca sat next to Lane, and they talked with each other like business partners instead of people who had slept together the night before—mutual respect and a friendship there. Marin sat fascinated as she watched Donovan work with the two of them.

She didn't feel confident enough yet to interject much, but she took notes at a rapid pace and tried to absorb everything she could. She couldn't get over how brave it had been for Bianca to be open to surrogate therapy. Lane was a big, intimidating guy. Attractive. Very experienced. That was like plunging into the deep end of the pool for someone so inexperienced.

Though, Marin realized with an internal cringe that the woman sitting before her actually had more sexual experience than she did now. And this woman was in therapy for it. Nice. Marin was here trying to help other people with their sex lives and hers was non-existent. Maybe she should be the one in therapy.

"Marin, do you have anything to add?" Donovan asked, breaking her from her ruminating.

Everyone looked her way. She froze for a second, feeling like the kid in the back of class caught daydreaming by the teacher. But she cleared her throat and tried to gather thoughts that had scattered. "Uh, yes. All I'd add is that I think you're a lot stronger than you give yourself credit for, Bianca. You're not alone in your fears. There are many women and men who are inexperienced and anxious about it, who let that insecurity lock them up for good. Most never have the guts to ask for help and tackle the issue head-on like you have. So no matter what happens with this guy, know that you've gotten over one of the biggest hurdles. You're armed and dangerous now."

Bianca broke into small smile. "I do feel kind of like a warrior these days." She reached over and patted Lane's knee. "And this guy has set a high standard, so I promise I'm not going to put up with some man being a jackass to me. Though, I really, really hope that Cal doesn't turn out to be one of those."

Donovan stood, the chair creaking beneath him. "We'll keep our fingers crossed for you. And you know what to do if things don't go like you hoped."

Bianca nodded and they all stood. She gave Lane a hug and then put her hand out to Donovan to give his a quick press. "Thanks, Dr. West. I'll see you next week."

Everyone filed out, and Marin stayed behind until Donovan came back into the office. He lifted his arms above his head touchdown-style. "You survived!"

"I didn't do anything but sit here."

He lowered his arms to his sides. "Not true. You had encouraging words at the end, which showed Bianca you'd been listening closely. And you asked some solid questions."

"I guess."

He considered her. "Don't be too hard on yourself. That was only your first one. We have a booked schedule today, so you'll get lots more practice. And after we're done, we can sit down and talk it through. Good points and stuff to work on."

"There's already stuff to work on, isn't there?"

He unbuttoned his cuffs and rolled his sleeves to his elbows, revealing strong forearms with a dusting of dark hair. "There's always stuff to work on. This is a journey, not a destination."

"Thank you, Aerosmith," she said, deadpan. Sarcasm would keep her safe. Sarcasm would make sure she didn't focus too much on those hands or forearms or anything else on his body for that matter. "Any quick tips for the next one?"

He reached up and tapped her cheek, a featherlight touch that sent a shiver working through her. "Work on not wearing your feelings on your face or I'm going to start calling you Dr. Blush."

She straightened. "Crap. I blushed?"

"When Lane told you about his job, your reaction was pretty much an open book. You looked scandalized and your cheeks got all flushed."

"Shit." She brushed her bangs out of her eyes. "I was surprised. I wasn't judging or anything. I think it's fascinating."

"It's okay. Just something to practice."

"Got it." She rubbed her lips together, trying to find the right words to address the other thing that had bothered her during the session. "And . . ."

When she didn't finish, he lifted a brow. "And what?"

"What you said in the session . . ." She glanced toward the window, feeling all kinds of awkward. "I didn't use you back then, just so you know. It wasn't like some older-virgin plan of attack or anything. What happened just . . . happened."

He sniffed, the amusement evident in the simple sound. "Elephant still wandering around, huh?"

She looked back to him. "Wounded but strong, apparently."

"Let's find a more effective weapon, shall we?" He leaned forward, his voice conspiratorial as he put his mouth right next to her ear. "Once upon a time, I hung out with this hot girl who was way too young for me. She was smart and funny and kept me distracted during a really shitty time in my life. We flirted, we laughed, and we had sex. I have fond memories of all three."

Marin bit the inside of her lip, a tingling awareness weaving through her, his breath on her neck warm and silky.

"But that girl and that boy are not in this room." Donovan straightened to his full height, his expression going grave. "The memories are just that. Life has happened in between, and we're nothing but strangers now. I don't think any differently about you than I would've if this were the first time we'd met. This is an absolutely fresh beginning. There is no angst, regret, or assumptions. Feel free to pretend it never happened if that makes it more comfortable for you."

Pretend it never happened. Sure. That was probably a cinch for him. God knows how many women had made their way through his bed since. He'd been engaged to a celebrity for God's sake. But how was she supposed to forget the one guy who'd ever taken her to that place? She nodded anyway, hoping her professional mask was intact. "Okay. I can do that. Consider it forgotten."

His eyes creased at the corner, some strange tension there, but he simply nodded. "Good."

She shifted in her heels and cleared her throat. "So what do we have next?"

"What don't we have? It's going to be a busy day."

Fantastic. Anything that would get her mind off the past, off the way her body was feeling right now, and off Donovan West sounded like a great plan. A vital one.

"Bring it on."

12

"I wrote her an email." Lawrence chewed the corner of his thumbnail as he stared out the window in the therapy room. "I wanted to send her pictures."

Donovan kept his sigh to himself but couldn't contain the frown. "What kind of pictures did you send?"

Lawrence's gaze shifted over to Marin, who was sitting prim and poised at Donovan's left, taking notes. She'd taken out her contacts after lunch and put on her glasses. The sight of her was driving Donovan to distraction. He'd told her this morning that he saw her as a stranger because he could tell their past was making her feel off-balance, but he was so full of shit. Sure, she was a stranger in many ways, but the ways in which she was familiar were far too vivid in his mind. He'd had to fight all day to keep his focus on his clients. And apparently it was taking Lawrence's focus as well, but for different reasons.

Lawrence gnawed harder on his hangnail and looked back to Donovan. "Personal photos."

Which meant dick pics, or worse. Great.

Lawrence had been obsessed with a particular porn star for the last year, and Donovan had been trying to help him detach from that fantasy, to go out in the world and date real women, but Lawrence was regressing.

"What did you think the email and pictures would accomplish?" The question came from Marin.

Donovan looked her way, pleased that she'd jumped in. He'd sensed Marin's nerves and her hesitation in sessions today. She was confident when talking with him in between appointments, and her assessments of the clients were pretty spot-on. But once she was face-to-face with them, that confidence collapsed.

Plus, she was way too easy to read. Even when her poker face was in place, her body language and tendency to blush were giving her away. On one level, he thought it was sexy as hell. He could imagine the things he could do or say to her to coax that kind of reaction from her. But for work purposes, she wasn't going to make it long if she didn't loosen up and relax in the sessions. Her blushing was the equivalent of an M.D. grimacing or saying *Oh, gross* when a patient revealed some medical issue.

Lawrence shifted in his chair, looking uncomfortable that Marin had spoken at all. Not surprising. Lawrence knew how to objectify fantasy women, not speak to real ones. "I thought maybe if I tried to talk to her and sent her pics, she'd email me back. I . . ." His jaw twitched and his gaze flicked toward the window again. "I've got a big cock, you know, so I thought she'd be into that."

Marin's lips pressed together as she obviously tried to temper her reaction and not roll her eyes or something. "I see."

Donovan was proud of how mild and unaffected she sounded. He made a note. "Did she respond to the email?"

A secret smile touched Lawrence's lips. "She did. She said I was hot and that she was sorry she couldn't be there with me, but she sent me a code to get a discount off of her body mold so I could, you know, fuck her. I ordered one."

Fan-frigging-tastic. Donovan wanted to tap his head against the wall. All the progress from previous sessions was unraveling before his eyes.

Marin's eyebrows lifted in question as she looked Donovan's way.

He could tell she didn't want to ask and seem uninformed, so he threw her a rope. "So when you say body mold, you mean the sex toy that's specifically shaped like Rebecca Bling's anatomy."

"Yeah, pussy *and* ass." The pleasure in Lawrence's voice was bordering on giddy. He'd slipped into fixation mode. He wasn't looking at either of them anymore. He'd gone into his head. "I don't know why I didn't get one before now. It's like fucking the real thing, especially with that lube that heats up. I rubbed my dick raw this weekend."

He grinned, but then he lifted his head, apparently remembering that there was a woman in the room, and winced. "Why the hell does she have to be here again?"

Marin sat there stoically, but her fair skin took on that telltale shade of pink again. Donovan couldn't tell if it was embarrassment or anger. Either way it was not going to go over well.

Donovan put down his pen. "Because Dr. Rush is training with me and is here to help."

"Look at her. She's fucking judging me is what she's doing," Lawrence said, his voice going snide, the spoiled-rich-kid side coming out. "How am I supposed to talk about this stuff when some chick is staring at me like I'm a pervert? I want her to leave."

Marin blinked, her spine going poker straight, and she looked to Donovan, clearly unsure on how to proceed.

Donovan lifted a finger, silently asking her to give him a second. "You have the right to not have her observe, Lawrence, but maybe we should think through this for a moment. It seems like you're getting angry because Dr. Rush's presence has triggered some reaction in you. She's not looking at you like you're a pervert, but maybe that's a fear you're having. That this behavior makes you a pervert?"

"Fuck that noise. I'm just doing what everyone else does and doesn't have the balls to say out loud." He sent daggers Marin's way. "Dr. Proper over there probably has a big fake cock at her house to shove inside her. I don't see what's the difference."

Marin's face went full red now, and Donovan had to wrestle back his own flash of anger. He sat forward. "The way you're talking to Dr. Rush is beyond inappropriate, Lawrence, and you know it. I'm going to ask you to apologize to her, and we're going to end things early today and schedule another session for next week. I expect you to come back then and be ready to work instead of lashing out."

"You want me to *leave*? I'm paying for this fucking session." Defiance sparked in Lawrence's eyes.

Donovan almost pointed out that no, his parents actually were, but that would've been petty and would've risked Lawrence giving up on treatment altogether. Lawrence stared at him like he expected an answer, used to getting his way when he threw a man tantrum. But when Donovan didn't budge or say anything more, Lawrence launched himself off the couch and stalked toward the door, throwing out a *whatever*. When he passed Marin, he mumbled a *sorry* but didn't look her way or slow his stride.

The door slammed behind him, and the pictures rattled on the walls. Silence ensued for a few long seconds until Marin sagged in her seat and groaned. "Well, that went great. Gold star, Dr. Rush!"

Donovan smirked, tossed his notepad onto the nearby desk, and then stretched his neck from side to side. "Nah, it wasn't that bad."

She looked over at him like he'd told her turtles could fly. "Now I know you're bullshitting me. The guy just walked out because of me."

"No, he walked out because of him. Lawrence's biggest issue is that he objectifies women and fixates on them as tools for his pleasure. He got himself in trouble in high school because he got obsessed with a girl and started following her home and peeking in her windows. That's when his parents originally started him in therapy."

She frowned.

"He's moved on to a safer target in the porn star but not healthier. I mean, how apropos that he literally has a piece of a woman to use now? No face, no brain, no words." He ran his hand over the back of his head. "He's taken a big step back. It's frustrating. But having to deal with your reactions today—a real woman who has thoughts and opinions—could be therapeutic."

She rubbed her fingers over her forehead. "I don't know. That felt like a disaster. We had to end the session early."

He shrugged. "Clients are going to get pissed. You expose the vulnerable spots, and people are going to react like wounded animals. It's part of the deal. You use that anger to get to the stuff you need if you have to. And you always, always keep your cool."

"So *was* I looking at him a certain way?"

Donovan leaned forward, clasping his hands between his knees. "You weren't looking at him like he was a pervert. That was him projecting his feelings about himself onto you. But you did blush again, and that can be a problem in sessions. You've done it a few times today and most of the time it went unnoticed. But if they see it, it can make clients feel like they should be ashamed if you're embarrassed."

She pinched the bridge of her nose. "Shit."

"Don't stress. You can train yourself out of it."

She peered over at him. "Right. And how would I do that? It's not like I want to blush. I've been fighting that particular affliction since grade school."

"Easy. You have to learn how to be unshockable."

She sniffed. "The nature of shock is that you're surprised by something you don't see coming. How the hell can I prepare for what I don't know will shock me?"

"Oh, don't give me that, Rush. You have a good idea of what will do it." He rolled his chair over to hers so that he was facing her, their knees almost touching. This wasn't an issue he'd ever come across with another trainee, but it was one they were going to have to fix. Starting now. "Okay. What if I said, 'I like to cut my thighs with a razor when I'm having a hard day'?"

He said it with a straight face. Truth usually came out that way. Even if this one was a past truth not a current one.

A wrinkle appeared between her brows. "I'd say we need to talk about the dangers of self-harm and work on finding alternative ways to release stress or emotion."

He nodded. "Good. Now what if I said, 'I like to dig my nails into my thigh when I masturbate'?"

Sometimes true.

Sure enough, her cheeks stained pink. She licked her lips. "I'd say if that works for you, go for it."

The soft cadence of her voice and the sight of her tongue slipping over her lips distracted him for a second. If he wasn't careful, he was going to be the one getting too warm. He reached over and touched her hot cheek. "There's your answer, Marin."

She seemed startled for a second, something unreadable flickering in her gaze, and then she turned her face away with a grimace.

He lowered his hand to his side, knowing he shouldn't have allowed himself that touch in the first place. He dragged his focus back, trying to remind his brain that this was work and he was training her. "Society teaches us to react that way when people talk about sex. It's not your fault. But in this job, you have to lose that or it will be your downfall."

Her jaw flexed. "Believe me, I get that. But I'm not sure how to get past it—beyond time and a lot of sessions. I don't want to be screwing up with clients in the meantime."

Annoyance filled her tone. Annoyance at herself. He loved that she was so determined to get everything right. To be perfect right out of the gate. It was an impossible goal, but he admired that she set it for herself anyway.

Donovan leaned back in his chair and considered her. He should probably leave it at that, just let her work it out over time. That'd be the prudent course. Eventually, she'd get to the been-there-heard-that stage. But that could take a while, and he knew it would drive her crazy. She was a perfectionist. She was going to beat herself up over any mistake. And if she didn't fix it quickly enough, she'd fall victim to the dark side of perfectionism. Quitting. She'd bail because imperfection was too uncomfortable. He'd have failed her. And lost his promotion and maybe his job in the process. No way could he let any of that happen.

He clasped the back of his neck and rubbed the tension gathering there. He'd told Elle that he'd stop by after work for a chat. He hadn't gone over to her place since the morning he'd had to sneak out half-dressed. They needed to talk, cut the ties. But the whole idea of seeing her tonight had dread curling through him. He checked his watch. "What are you doing later tonight?"

Marin looked up at the shift in subject, brows scrunched. "Unpacking more boxes, why?"

"I've got an idea. There may be a way to tackle this issue guerrilla style."

"Uh . . ."

His phone vibrated in his pocket and he checked the screen. An appointment reminder for his weekly call with the private investigator he'd hired to work on his parents' case. He stood to get his things. "Look, I've got a few things to take care of this afternoon but can you meet me by the east side fountains around seven? I'll explain more then."

"Explain more about what?"

He headed toward the door, his mind already formulating a plan. A risky one. But a plan nonetheless. "Just trust me, okay? I think I have a way to help."

She frowned for a moment, and he thought she was going to refuse, but then she stood and shrugged. "Sure, whatever you say, boss."

"I'm not your boss." The words came out sharper than he intended them to.

Her brows arched. "O-kay, mentor. Does it matter?"

"Yeah. It does." He stopped in the doorway, his hand braced on it and peered back at her. "I can't be your boss. Because if what I have in mind is going to work, it's going to have to be strictly off the clock and off the record."

Her eyes widened. "Donovan . . ."

He tapped the doorframe. "See you at seven, Rush."

13

Off the clock. Marin wiped down the kitchen counter, trying to channel her nervous energy into something productive, but she ended up cleaning the same spot three times. Since she'd gotten home, she hadn't been able to get her impending meeting with Donovan out of her mind. She had no idea what he had planned or why they had to meet after hours to accomplish it, but it had her thoughts drifting down all kinds of curving paths. Dangerous paths with *Keep Out* signs and flashing barricades across them. What could be so covert?

It's not like he'd made a pass at her. He'd been nothing but professional today. And the way he'd raced out this afternoon after their last session, she was pretty sure he'd been heading out to meet up with someone—probably a woman. The thought niggled. But she told herself that if he had a girlfriend, that'd be a good thing. That would help her keep all stray thoughts about him out of her head. The last thing she needed was a resurgence of her crush on Donovan West. It'd gotten her in trouble last time. This time it could mean her job. Or his.

No thanks.

At least Nathan had been in a better mood when he'd gotten home. He'd landed a job at a late-night cafe that featured musicians and sold local art. It didn't pay much, but he said the place was "cool" and that he wouldn't have to wake up early. Apparently, these two things were of vital importance. The free coffee he'd get was a bonus.

She'd thrown together some dinner, and they'd eaten while he rattled on about what he'd seen in the city today. He was polite enough to ask her how her day went, but she had no idea what to tell him. How had it gone? The whole day had been fascinating but also stressful and strange. She hated feeling so damn incompetent. For the last few years at the university, her role had been like a second skin. People came to her for advice. She was the expert. The girl with the answers. Or at least the girl who knew how to find the answers. Now she was the novice in the corner, the interloper the clients didn't want in the room. The girl who felt awkward anytime someone started talking about sex.

So she'd told Nate that the day had been "fine." Sure. Whatever.

After dinner, she informed him she was going to meet with a few new colleagues. She almost wanted him to talk her out of it or make her feel guilty for leaving him alone. Then she'd have a good excuse to cancel on Donovan. But Nate had shrugged and said he planned to play Halo with Henry for the night and that he'd see her in the morning.

With no other excuses to hold her back, she changed into more casual clothes, slipped on her shoes, and headed out. *Here goes nothing.*

By the time she found her way to the large fountain, the sun was on its way to setting and the cicadas were playing their distinct songs, like a stiff wind rattling through reeds. Donovan was already there, flipping through a stack of stapled papers. He'd changed from his slacks and dress shirt into jeans and a pale blue T-shirt. Without the formal clothing and with his dark hair mussed from the breeze, he looked so close to the boy she used to obsess over that it took her breath for a second. She found herself standing there for too long just taking him in.

Donovan looked up after a while, apparently sensing he was no longer alone, and smiled when he saw her. "I didn't hear you walk up."

She raised a finger toward the trees. "The quiet night is not so quiet."

He tucked his papers into a bag by his feet. "Yeah, the cicadas are in mating season. It can get deafening at this time of night. But one of the groundskeepers told me that this species only comes out from underground every thirteen years, so we're witnessing a rare event."

"One big bug orgy, huh?"

"So it seems." He patted the bench. "I find it calming. Makes me want to sit on a porch and drink sweet tea while whittling wood or something."

She laughed and took the spot on the other end of the bench, turning her body slightly toward him. "Sorry. No wood to whittle and I forgot to bring the sweet tea."

"No worries." He reached down and dipped his hand into his bag. He pulled out a bottle of red wine. "I brought reinforcements."

She lifted a brow. "A little stronger than tea."

"I figured this would be more fitting after a first day at work."

She took the bottle from him and shook her head. "Oriana dropped a bottle off the other day, too. Guess she had the same idea."

"Yeah. We've all had a first day here." He pulled two red plastic cups out of the bag. "Wanna do it college-style?"

Her gaze snapped to his and she bit her lip. They'd only done one thing together college-style and it hadn't involved Solo cups.

He stared at her for a second, obviously confused, and then he let out a strained laugh. "Damn, I keep walking right into those."

She grinned and took one of the cups. "Yeah, you do."

"Sorry." Donovan twisted the top off of the wine and poured

them each a healthy dose. He set the bottle aside and lifted his cup. "To surviving your first day."

She touched her cup to his and then took a sip of the wine. "I'm not sure I totally survived. I may be slightly traumatized knowing that they make molds of porn stars' vaginas."

"And anuses," he said with mock seriousness. "Lawrence made sure to point that out. Can't forget the celebrity assholes."

She blanched. "I really don't want to know the process of how they take the imprint of the original."

"Yeah, sounds pretty uncomfortable. That's probably why those toys are expensive as hell. They work hard to make them lifelike."

"You sound like you know far too much about this device."

He sniffed. "Well, I haven't personally taken a test drive, if that's what you're getting at. But it's our job to know what's out there, so I've done research. I keep a closet full of toys at the office. They can be an important part of treatment, so I like to keep up with what's new. Though, I won't be stocking any porn star parts anytime soon."

"You actually give clients the toys? Don't most therapists just recommend stuff?"

"People here want full service. They don't want to have to hunt down something themselves. Plus, there's a lot of crap products out there. I curate what I've seen to be most effective. You'll need to do the same."

She shook her head and sighed. "I feel so completely out of my depth with this."

He gave her a sympathetic smile. "You don't need to know everything day one. Just tackle one hill at a time. Or one vibrator at a time as the case may be. Imagine how fun that research will be."

She laughed and looked down at her cup.

He reached out and tapped her wrist. "You're blushing again."

She touched her cheek, feeling the heat. "Oh, Jesus Christ. I'm hopeless. I should just get a spray tan and call it a day. No one will be able to see the pink beneath the glowing orange."

He huffed a laugh. "I don't think a spray tan is going to do it."

"No?"

"No. Blushing is only a symptom, not the underlying issue. Get rid of the blushing without tackling the root and another symptom will just replace it."

She groaned. "That is such a shrinky thing to say."

"Guilty. But seriously, I think the only way you're going to fix this is to figure out how to dig past this stuff and tap into that shamelessness I talked about. Let nothing shock you. Get comfortable with sex as just another topic to discuss in an open forum."

"I thought I was," she said, unable to hide the frustration in her voice. "It's not like I'm a prude or anything. When it came time to give my little brother the sex talk, it was like a targeted missile strike with how efficient and angst-free it was. And I never balked when I interviewed teens for my research. But I guess there's a big difference between discussing the basics of sex and health with beginners and hearing the kinds of things I'll hear in sessions here."

"Wow, you got stuck giving the sex talk to *your brother*? How'd you end up with that duty?"

"Long story." She looked over to him, not wanting to get into the tragic history. "Did you go through this kind of awkwardness in the beginning?"

He shrugged and sipped his wine. "I think I got inoculated to it when I did my research. I had to talk to people about sexual fantasies. I read erotica for ideas. I watched all kinds of porn. Then I had to put some of my own personal fantasies on recordings that everyone, including my professors and fellow grad students, heard. And once upon a time, I had this perfectly nice girl catch me with a hard-on while I recorded a kinky scenario. Once you get past that kind of embarrassment, you're pretty set for anything else."

She gave him a wry smile. "Yeah, that's pretty good exposure therapy. I'm just not sure how I could re-create that in a short time."

He cocked his head, watching her, and drummed his fingers on the back of the bench. "Mind if I get all shrinky on you for a second again?"

She took a big gulp of the wine, already feeling the tingly buzz working through her system. Maybe this is why he'd brought the wine. He had to counsel her like a client on day one. Wonderful. "Lay it on me, doc. Shrink me."

"All right. Total honesty?"

She waved her hand in a bring-it-on motion.

"Usually when we feel embarrassed or awkward about what other people say regarding their sex lives, it's because we're carrying that natural shame about our own sexuality—the shame that society teaches us to have. Acknowledging theirs is like outwardly acknowledging that we're sexual, too. That we have those kinds of thoughts, do those kinds of things.

"It's why you reacted when Lawrence suggested you had a toy at home. Whether it was true or not, he was outing you as being sexual. We all know that it's a part of being human, of course, but we walk around pretending that it's this other outside thing that we're not a part of. It's why no one wants to hear their parents talk about sex. We like our heads to stay firmly in the sand." His eyes traced over her face. "So when you blush, it's because your head was yanked out of the sand and that veil was lifted. You saw that secret part of the person or they saw that part of you. Like when Lane told you what he did for a living. He said it and then he was naked in your head, sleeping with some stranger, right?"

She straightened. "No, I—"

"Come on. It's a natural reaction. We're visual creatures. Someone says, 'I sleep with strangers for my job,' your thoughts are going to go there. The key is not being scandalized by where your mind goes. Just let it happen and then let it roll off you."

"But how do you do that?"

He shrugged. "Once you're exposed to those images enough times or do some of those things yourself, it becomes old news. I've observed Lane's sessions on occasion. I know what that kind of therapy looks like. I've researched the sex toys, so I wasn't shocked by what Lawrence said."

"I promise I will never be purchasing a porn star faux vagina."

He smirked. "Well, no, probably not. But remember how scandalous and exciting everything seemed when you were young, before you had any experience under your belt? When I was in middle school, I remember having this intense reaction to seeing the girl who sat in front of me's bra strap exposed. My face got hot. I got all sweaty and nervous." He shook his head. "Man, I jerked off to that image of her for months."

Marin rolled her lips together, biting down on the smile. "Must've been some bra strap."

He grinned. "It was pink, and it was spectacular."

The wine was taking effect, and she had to swallow down a laugh. "I once wrote a whole poem about the sliver of lower back this football player in high school used to expose when he bent down to get stuff out of his locker. It was so tan and muscular . . ."

He raised his cup. "Ha, see, exactly. But that tells you something. Now if you saw that, your eyes would just skim over it. You wouldn't blush or feel awkward. It would just roll off you. So you need to figure out a way to see everyone as a sexual being without being embarrassed or affected by it. Just have it be a simple fact. A part of life. Everyone's doing it."

"A companion piece to *Everyone Poops*," she joked.

"Yep. *Everyone Fucks*."

His frankness set her off balance for a second, and she glanced away, focusing on the grass. He was wrong. *Not everyone.*

"It doesn't have to be that hard." He put his hand to his chest. "You've seen me naked, and we're having this conversation without any awkwardness."

She watched him out of the side of her eye. "Actually I never did, but I understand what you're saying."

He frowned. "What do you mean?"

She waved a hand. "You were behind—I was—never mind. Let's not go there."

I will not picture how he must've looked behind me that night. Will not picture open jeans shoved to hips and straining muscles. Will. Not.

She set aside the wine.

"Now you're getting red."

She groaned. "Stop pointing it out."

He touched his shoulder. "Is my bra strap showing?"

"Shut the hell up," she said, smiling despite herself. "It's just embarrassing that the guy I'm now working with has seen me the way you have."

"What? Masturbating at work and then bent over a desk for me?"

"Donovan!"

But, of course, he didn't look ashamed at all. He waved a dismissive hand and took another sip of his wine. "No, no, this is good. This is part of the idea I had. I know I told you we could pretend the past never happened. But maybe instead, our former . . . knowledge of each other can be to our benefit. There's already a built-in comfort level here." He bent his knee, turning more toward her. "So you can practice with me."

She stared at him. "Practice what?"

"Immunizing yourself to sex talk. I'll try to get you to blush or get flustered, and you work on fighting that reaction." He grabbed the bottle of wine and poured a little more in each of their cups. "Alcohol will help for this intro session."

"Donovan. Seriously. We're so not doing this."

"Better with me than reacting badly to a client. And we know more about each other than we should already. This could be helpful."

"This is a bad idea."

He leaned back, mischief in his gaze.

Uh-oh. She could sense him loading his slingshot.

"I was fifteen minutes late this morning because I had a hot dream and jerked off in the shower."

"Oh my God." She closed her eyes. "You can't say stuff—"

Of course before she could even put her words together, her head filled with the image of him in the shower, naked, stroking himself, making those sounds she remembered. Her face flamed.

"Look at me." He voice was soft but firm.

"No way."

"Come on. No need to hide. Be bold."

She forced her gaze upward, her jaw clenching. "I hate you so much right now."

His eyes met hers, clear and unaffected. "Give me statistics about masturbation, Rush."

She blinked, her thoughts faltering. "What?"

"I know you know them. I saw them in your sex ed program."

She ground out a frustrated breath and pushed her hair off her forehead, grasping for the figures she knew were already in her head. "Uh, ninety-five percent of men admit to doing it, more than half do it weekly. For women, the numbers are only a few points less—eight-nine percent."

"I love that you can quote statistics even buzzed on wine. It's kind of awesome. We should do shots and try to quote studies."

She rolled her eyes. Though, she'd totally play and win that game.

"But my point is that you already know that, statistically speaking, masturbation in normal. It's healthy. It's natural. It'd be odd if I didn't do it. So why should it embarrass you to know that about me? Or anyone. Lane does it. The clients we saw today do it. I'm sure my assistant does, my boss, the guy who sold me coffee this morning."

"Yeah, but there's a difference between knowing something in theory and knowing it in reality."

"Sure there is, but that's the point. You have to break down the wall between the two, take the taboo factor out of it." He tilted his head. "Do you masturbate, Marin?"

"We are really, really not having this conversation."

He lifted a brow in challenge.

"Ugh. You use that brow lift on your clients. I saw you do it today. It's not going to work, West. I am immune."

He didn't relent. The brow only went higher.

"Goddammit." She looked to the sky. "Of course I do it. You know that. You've seen me."

He tapped her cheek. "Look at you. An admission to something personal and no blush. Progress."

She ignored him and took another sip of wine. She had a feeling she was going to need all the alcohol-laced fortitude she could get.

"Here's let's try another," he said. "Those fantasies you helped me with in college? Many were personal ones of mine. I like playing games of control in the bedroom and enjoy kinky sex. It's what drew me to this field in the first place. I wanted to know why I gravitated to that."

Marin's belly tightened. Her free hand curled around the edge of the bench as she remembered those fantasies she'd listened to, his voice narrating, how so many of those fantasies had intertwined with hers. "Donovan . . ."

"Now. Ask me a question. Pretend I'm a client telling you that."

Marin couldn't look his way. The pictures in her head were too much. Too loud. And the last thing she felt was embarrassment. But she took a breath, steeling herself, and let it out. "So does that mean you're a dominant?"

"Good question. I wouldn't label myself that. I work closely with a BDSM group in New Orleans and offer reduced rates for their members since it's hard for people to find kink-friendly therapists. So I have clients in the lifestyle and have studied it. But in my personal life, I don't really take it to that level. I'm more flexible about the dynamics. I enjoy games, role-plays, power exchange for the thrill of it. A lot less formal than D/s."

She cleared her throat and shifted on the bench. "Okay."

"Now, it's your turn. Claim something of your own. No shame. What do you like, Marin?"

The question slid through her, making her want to run. "I don't know."

He lifted his cup and nodded at her in a you-can-do-it motion. "You don't have to be scared. Think of all the things I've heard in this job. I'm unshockable."

"I doubt that."

His lips lifted at the corner, bordering on smug. "You really think you have something that scandalous?"

The wine and the conversation were making her nerves edgy but her thoughts slower. "Maybe."

"Well, now you've got me intrigued, Rush."

She shook her head. This was not a conversation they should be having. She would never have done this with any other co-worker, but somehow from the very beginning, Donovan always had this truth serum effect on her. He'd gotten her to talk about fantasies when she'd barely been able to say them aloud to herself. And now she found herself wanting to confess again. She didn't want to carry this around every day that she was training on this job. She didn't want to blush and feel uncomfortable every time someone said something surprising.

"All right." She downed the rest of her wine and then looked out toward the dark silhouettes of the gnarled oak trees. The cicadas had gone full throttle now, and the sky had turned from orange to silvery purple. Night in the bayou reclaiming its land. An otherworldly place where secrets almost seemed safe. She forced the words out. "I don't know what I like because since you last saw me, I've been raising my little brother and trying to graduate and keep a roof over our heads. There was no time for anything else.

No time for dating and certainly no time for sex. Bianca has more experience than I do."

The words drifted on the night air, mixing in with the bubbling of the fountain and the thick breeze. Donovan didn't say anything, and Marin couldn't bring herself to look his way. She kept her hands clasped around her cup and her eyes on the changing horizon.

The silence stretched on too long, and unease curled around her like choking vines, her throat tightening. The crush of anxiety sent her to her feet. "I told you this was a bad idea. I've gotta get going."

Donovan's hand shot out like a striking snake and grasped her arm, urging her back down. "No, please, don't. I'm sorry. I'm just . . . taking that in."

Her butt hit the bench again, and she ventured a peek his way. "Looks like I shocked Mr. Unshockable."

He stared at her, his gaze searching. "Are you telling me you haven't—"

"No. Not since you."

Deep lines appeared in his forehead, like he couldn't understand her words. "I— It's been *nine years*, Marin. You're saying . . ."

"Yep."

Wonder filled his face, like she'd revealed she was really a life-form from another planet, but concern quickly replaced it. "What the hell happened?"

She set her cup aside with a sigh. She hadn't wanted to get into this with him—ever. But she knew there was no backing off of it now.

"The short version is that everything in my life exploded that night we were together. My mom had suffered from severe bipolar disorder for most of my life, but that night she had a psychotic break. She'd been recovering from a bad breakup with a guy and had been faking taking her meds. I thought she was stable, but she was on the verge and something triggered her that night." She stared at her hands, worked the ring she wore on her right index finger off and on. "Probably me. I was supposed to stay home, but we got in an argument, and I spent the night with you instead. Nate said that after I left she started drinking and got paranoid, talking about everyone leaving her, that she was going to die alone." Marin looked out into the night, not seeing it, the horrible scene vivid in her imagination even though she hadn't been there. Hearing her little brother describe it had imprinted the images on her brain like it was her own memory. "So she decided she wouldn't die alone. She'd take someone with her." She peered over at Donovan. "By the time I got home, she'd attacked my brother with a kitchen knife and had slit her wrists."

Donovan's lips parted with soundless shock.

"Nate was bleeding out when I got there, but the paramedics arrived in time to save him. He had to have transfusions. Surgery. Nothing could be done for my mom." Marin still had nightmares where she stayed longer with Donovan, where she took that offer to go to the diner with him and got home too late to save Nathan. "I had to drop out of school for a while to put our lives back together and figure out how to keep Nate with me instead of losing him to foster care."

"Christ, Marin." There was no filter on his expression now, no therapist face. He looked . . . stripped. "I had no idea. I'm so sorry."

She rubbed her hands on her thighs, trying to get them to stop trembling. "Yeah, it sucked." *Understatement of the century.* "But Nathan and I have made out all right. He's about to start art school and I'm here"—she sent him a half-smile, trying to lighten the somber tone the conversation had taken—"embarrassing clients because I've managed to become the most inexperienced sex therapist ever."

He reached out and put a hand on her shoulder, his palm warm through the thin cotton of her shirt. The naked empathy in his eyes made something twist in her gut. "That last part's a minor blip on the radar. Look at you. It's a damn miracle you're here at all. When I lost my parents, I fell completely the fuck apart. And I was in my twenties, had a trust fund, and didn't have anyone else to take care of. You were a kid, had no help, and became a doctor while raising another human being on your own? That's superhero quality, Marin."

She looked down, the praise and his awed tone winding through her, nudging things she didn't want nudged.

He released her shoulder. "Don't be so hard on yourself. You can catch up on the experience thing. That's easy."

She laughed, though the humor felt forced. "Right, so easy. I just need it done in time for tomorrow's sessions. No biggie. Maybe I'll just run into town and pick up a guy who could show me a few things. Have him give me some kinky CliffsNotes. Or maybe I could call Lane. That's what he does, right? Teaches."

Frown lines bracketed Donovan's mouth. "You don't need Lane."

His sudden shift in tone caught her off guard. She tilted her head, matching his frown. "I was kidding."

Mostly. Lane was a tempting proposition. A good-looking guy who seemed nice enough, who could teach her a few things with no pressure or expectations, and who could keep it businesslike? It sounded ideal. Safe.

Donovan's gaze turned shrewd. "You're not going to go from novice to unshakable in one day. And bedding some random dude isn't going to do much good. You're not embarrassed by the basics of sex. And that's all most guys are going to give you—the blandest version of vanilla. And at least half have no idea what the hell they're doing anyway."

She smirked. "I love that you say that like obviously you know better. Humble, much?"

He shrugged, not denying it. "You spend your career focused on sex, you learn a few things."

"Obviously I missed that bullet point," she said wryly.

"You did just fine from what I remember." His eyes met hers, those blue eyes piercing her. "And believe me. I remember it all, Marin. Every. Damn. Second."

The words crackled through her like heat lightning. Donovan had kept things casual tonight, but something in his demeanor had shifted, letting her see a flash of what was beyond what he'd been showing her. That bad boy she'd heard about, that doctor who'd gone to L.A. and worked his way through actresses—that guy was in there twining with the brilliant boy she used to know and making her thoughts scamper in ten different directions. She shifted against the bench, long-dormant nerve endings waking up and paying attention.

Donovan peered toward the trees, tension that wasn't there before rolling off him. "I should stop talking now."

Yes, he should. He totally should. Her mouth opened before she could stop it. "Why?"

A muscle in his jaw ticked. "Because hearing you say you want someone to teach you about sex, that you need more exposure to taboo stuff, is making me want to offer things I shouldn't, making me remember how intense that week with you was, how hot things were when we finally gave in to it. And I'm not noble enough to play it off."

"Donovan." She inhaled a shaky breath, and her mind immediately jumped to what he wasn't saying. Donovan mentoring her in an altogether different way. Naked bodies. Skin pressing against skin. Forbidden fantasies springing to life in the dark. She ran her hand over the back of her neck, finding it damp and burning hot. "I—"

"Please don't say anything." He turned to her and frowned. "You shouldn't have to respond to that. I'm sorry. I promised myself I wouldn't cross the line with you. I owe you that. Just ignore me."

She blinked, off balance from his words, the wine, and the fact that she wasn't entirely sure she would've turned him down if he hadn't cut her off first. She closed her eyes, trying to regain some semblance of sanity. "Maybe I could do some online research on the areas I'm unfamiliar with."

The suggestion was lame, like throwing a deflated balloon in the air and expecting it to float, but she needed something to get them off this dangerous track. They were tiptoeing over splintered ice right now. One wrong move and they'd both be taken under. She couldn't go there. Her body wanted him. There was no doubt about that. But blurring their roles had disaster written all over it. She needed to stay focused on the job not her starving libido.

Donovan cleared his throat and seemed to drag himself back from the brink, too. He gave a brisk nod. "Sure. That may help some since exposure is what you need. There's a video for everything." He rolled his shoulders as if shaking off the previous conversation and regaining business mode. "I'll send you some from the X-wing collection if you want. You need to watch them anyway so you know which to suggest to people. But that kind of research just covers the knowledge factor, not the embarrassment or awkwardness. I doubt you'll get embarrassed watching porn alone in the privacy of your own home."

She took a breath, relieved they were backtracking into safe territory. "I honestly have no idea. I'm more of a book girl than a video one. Though I did find a DVD Nate tried to hide once. I didn't know what it was but watched more than I needed to once I put it in the player."

Her attempt at levity earned her a halfhearted smile from Donovan. "Teen boys usually pick the worst. What was it?"

"Well, Nate's gay, so . . ."

"Ah, gay porn. A fan favorite with my female clients. I recommend it often for those having arousal trouble."

"Really?"

"Yeah. I usually try the audiotapes first with female clients, but if they need something visual, that's the direction I go. Women say the guys are better looking, and there's no girl with fake reactions and too much makeup to distract them."

"Huh. Never thought about it that way, but it makes sense. It was pretty compelling until I remembered that it was my little brother's wanking material." She wrinkled her nose.

He huffed a quiet laugh. "Yeah, that could be a mood killer."

He was silent for a while, and she traced a finger around the edge of her cup. "I guess I at least have a place to start now. I like having a plan of attack. Although, I'm not sure which topics to tackle first."

He pulled out his phone and started typing, still not looking at her. "This will help. I'll email you our sexual history intake form we use for clients. It covers the gamut of sexual activities. Go through it tonight and familiarize yourself with it. If you don't know what something is, Google it. If something triggers a strong reaction in you, star it so that you know it's a potential stumbling block you need to work on. And maybe that will mean watching videos on the topic or delving deeper into it."

"Delving deeper?"

He tucked his phone in his pocket and finally met her eyes. "Yeah. Talking with me about it, asking questions, setting up observation if we need to. Lane is okay with therapists observing his sessions if the client feels comfortable with that. And I have an open invite to that kink club in New Orleans. I could take you there and let you watch some of the public scenes and talk to members. They'd be happy to help."

She nodded. The thought of remaining professional with Donovan at her side while watching people have sex sounded like a hundred levels of torture, but she could be a grown-up about this. "Okay."

Donovan's gaze held hers, something pained there. "And I'm sorry that I crossed the line tonight with what I said. I want you to feel safe and respected in this position. And I want you to be able to come to me with questions and learn without any other kind of pressure on you. The fact that we slept together before or that I'm still attracted to you now are moot points. I'm sorry those things invaded tonight. The wine was probably a bad idea."

She swallowed past the dryness in her throat. Part of her wanted to shout at the heavens in frustration. It'd been so long. She'd been on the shelf for *so goddamned long*. And now this gorgeous, intelligent man was saying he wanted to sleep with her and she couldn't act on it. She had to be responsible. Practical. Do the right thing.

She was so fucking tired of doing the right thing. "It's fine. No big deal."

Donovan reached for her hand and captured it between his warm palms. "And I've had too much to drink and am probably not expressing it well, but I really am sorry about what happened with your mom. I know what it's like to lose a parent. And I know what it's like to show up too late, to wonder what if, to worry that you're partly to blame. The night my parents were killed, I was the one who forgot to set the house alarm. I wouldn't wish that kind of guilt on anyone."

She rolled her lips inward and nodded, his words hitting her right in the gut and making her chest hurt not just for herself but for him, too.

He held on to her hand and with his other, reached out and cupped the side of her face, sending trailing warmth down her spine. "I'm so sorry if I contributed to that horrible night for you. I was selfish. I shouldn't have—"

"No." She closed her eyes, wanting to lean into his touch but holding the urge in check. "Please don't take it back. For a long time, those days with you were the only good I could hold on to, the only normal I could remember. Everything else was such a disaster. Of course, I wish I could go back in time and see the things I missed with my mom, intervene before it was too late. I regret not being home that night. But I never regretted what happened between us."

"Not even now?" he asked softly.

She opened her eyes, meeting his stare. His touch felt so right, and the way he was looking at her transported her back in time. He got it. Like no one else could, he got what it was like to have those big, looming specters in your life—what-ifs, blame, loss. His thumb ran along her cheek, and he wasn't moving away. Something swirled between them, sparked. She wanted to kiss him more than she'd wanted anything in a long damn time. Needed it. She licked her lips.

"Oh, I'm sorry." A loud, exaggerated voice broke through the private space Marin and Donovan had weaved between them. "I didn't notice you there."

Donovan jerked back, dropping his hand to his side, and turning his head. Marin immediately looked toward the intruder as well and found a blond woman in a tracksuit giving them a chilly smile.

Fuck. Fuck. Fuck. Marin had forgotten where they were.

A muscle in Donovan's cheek flexed. "Hi there, Dr. McCray. Out for a run?"

"Yep." She eyed the cups they were holding. "Out for . . . a drink?"

"Just a quick celebratory drink in honor of Dr. Rush surviving her first day on the X-wing. It's tradition."

Marin frowned. She had no idea if it was tradition or not, but she got the distinct sense that Donovan was lying. She also knew this woman had seen way more than them drinking. You don't cup the face of your co-worker. She cleared her throat, stood, and held out her hand. "Marin Rush."

The woman gave Marin's hand an overly firm shake. "Elle McCray."

"Elle's the head physician in the addiction wing," Donovan offered. "She's also one of your go-to's if you have a client who needs to be evaluated for a medical condition or needs a prescription."

Marin offered the most professional smile she could muster. "Great. Look forward to working with you, then."

Dr. McCray didn't respond. Instead, she sent Donovan a look, one edged with something sharp and deadly.

That's when Marin knew. These two had something between them. She didn't know exactly what, but she suddenly felt ridiculous for sitting there and entertaining lustful thoughts about Donovan. He'd said he was attracted to her, that he was tempted to teach her some things, not that he was available. Of course he had someone.

That's why he was fighting to hold himself back with her. She'd seen him with lipstick marks. The moment that had passed between them was just old stuff kicking up and too much alcohol, nothing more.

Marin shifted on her feet. "Well, I better get going. It's been a long day, and I have some things to catch up on before bed."

"Oh, don't leave on my account," Elle said with a flat tone.

"Marin—" Donovan stood as well.

She held up her hand in a quick wave. "I'll see you tomorrow, Dr. West. Thanks for the pointers and the drink."

He frowned, consternation in his eyes, but he didn't stop her from going. She turned too fast, making her head spin from the alcohol, but she kept her back straight and strode off, trying to look casual and unaffected. She hoped she pulled it off. But she couldn't resist one last look. So when she got far enough away to peek back over her shoulder without being too obvious, she saw that Dr. McCray had taken Marin's spot on the bench next to Donovan and was sitting way too close.

Something ugly rolled through Marin. Ugly and vicious and acidic.

But this was what she should want, right? There was no risk now. She could focus on the job at hand and not worry about Donovan or getting in trouble with her boss or screwing this all up over a misguided libido.

Great. Perfect. Shoot a fucking confetti gun!

She stepped into her house, the world swaying a bit in her vision, and slammed the door behind her.

Nathan looked up from his spot on the couch, computer on his lap, bottle of soda halfway to his mouth. "Whoa, what's wrong with you?"

She tossed her house key toward the entryway table but missed. "Nothing. I'm going to my room. I'll see you in the morning."

Had her words slurred? Maybe. She couldn't tell.

He frowned. "Are you . . . drunk?"

"No. I've got work to do." She grabbed the key from the floor, which took more concentration than it should've. "Which reminds me, if I needed to find the best porn sites, which would you suggest?"

Nate, who'd been staring at her with suspicious eyes, went slack-jawed. "*What?*"

She waved her hand in an out-with-it motion. "Come on. Best porn sites. Go."

"Oh my God, you *are* drunk."

"Are you going to tell me or what?"

Nate shifted on the couch and gave her a look like he would like to request an immediate transfer to another family. "Uh, not that I'm admitting to anything, but we aren't exactly in the same target audience, Mar."

"Doesn't matter. It's for work. And let's not pretend you're that innocent."

He cringed and leaned his head back against the couch, beseeching the universe. "What is my life?"

"Nate," she said impatiently.

He groaned and rocked forward to grab his phone from the coffee table. He set aside his computer and soda, and started typing on his phone. "I swear to God, I better not get bitched at for this when you sober up."

"What are you doing?"

"I'm texting you my sign-in information for a site. The good ones require a subscription. This one has . . . a variety of stuff."

"You have a *subscription* to a porn site?"

He gave her the side-eye. "Shut it, Mar. You asked for help. That gives me immunity. And please, God, do not save favorites or anything once you're in there. A guy can only handle so much trauma."

Marin's phone buzzed in her pocket with his text message. She titled her chin upward. "Fine. We'll both be adults about it."

"At least one of us will," he muttered and then looked her way again. "You sure you're all right?"

The little waver in his voice cut through some of the fuzz in her brain. Nate had rarely seen her drink. And he'd definitely never seen her tipsy. Their mom had liked alcohol way too much, and she'd been drinking the night she'd died, so Marin had avoided it for most of her life. Only in the last year had she allowed herself an occasional beer or glass of wine. But alcohol still meant scary, ugly things for Nate. He never touched the stuff. And she hated that she was making him worry for even a second.

She took a deep breath, centering herself and trying to clear her head of the buzz to focus. "I'm fine, kiddo. I met with a co-worker and had a few glasses of wine to celebrate getting through the first day. Obviously, my tolerance sucks. This won't be a regular thing. And the porn site really is for work research."

The glimmer of tension in Nate's expression softened. He gave a quick nod. "All right."

She lifted her phone. "Thanks for the info."

He gave her a wry smile. "I would say have fun, but then I might vomit."

She laughed. "Love you."

"Love you, too."

She trudged to her room and collapsed onto her bed.

In one day, she'd managed to piss off a client, almost kiss her co-worker in front of his girlfriend, and get porn recommendations from her little brother.

She might not survive day two.

14

Donovan was thinking about Marin. About almost kisses and soulful hazel eyes. About cicada songs and secrets shared in the dark. About all the things he wanted to do with her, *to* her. The fantasy was great. But he vaguely registered that Marin wasn't the one who was currently kissing down his neck.

He tried to fit the disjointed pieces of the current state of affairs together, tried to make sense of what was happening. Everything felt wrong. Why did it feel wrong? He concentrated. *Elle.* He was on Elle's couch. How the fuck had he gotten here again? Like hillbillies on moonshine, his thoughts were stumbling around and bumping into each other, slow and sloppy. *Focus.* He tried to will his mind to orient itself. Memories came back in wisps. Elle had asked to talk to him back at her place since he'd canceled on her earlier in the night.

He hadn't wanted to follow her here. He'd been knotted up with all that had transpired with Marin. But Marin had walked off, and he'd known Elle was pissed about finding the two of them together. So even though he and Elle didn't have any kind of exclusive arrangement and he hadn't touched her in a month, he'd felt like a dick anyhow and had agreed to come over to talk.

But while they were talking and he was trying to explain how this arrangement was no longer a good idea, Elle had served sangria. Lots and lots of sangria. And now Elle had crawled over to his side of the couch and was straddling him. She was taking control this time. But his head was muzzy, and though his dick was half-interested beneath her grinding movements, his mind was on someone else. He was getting turned on by images of a woman with short, dark hair who smelled like cotton candy and had cheeks that blushed at the slightest provocation. Had lips that wanted to be kissed . . .

Fuck.

He tugged away. "Elle, we need to—"

"Go to the bedroom. I know." She pushed her long hair away from her face. "But I thought a change of scenery might be nice. You can fight to be on top."

She pulled her T-shirt over her head, revealing lace-encased breasts, and took his hand, placing it over her and squeezing for him.

He winced and moved his hand away. His equilibrium whirled. "I'm fucking drunk, Elle."

"Well, I can stay on top, then." She slid her hand between them and stroked his now softening cock. "I don't mind doing the work tonight. Just stay hard for me and we're good."

He grabbed her wrist to stop her, his movements imprecise and delayed. "Goddammit, can you slow down for a second? I said I was drunk."

She rolled her eyes and sat back on his thighs to look down at him. "Are we seriously having a consent conversation right now? It's not like you don't know what we're doing. This is nothing new. You're drunk every time we fuck, Donovan. It's your thing."

The words rolled off her lips like it was no big deal, but they hit him like a freight truck. "*My thing?*"

She shrugged as if it was the most obvious thing ever.

"What? Now I'm an alcoholic?"

"Don't be stupid. You know as well as I do that you're not. But you never fuck sober. You drink and get to play a role. Saves you from that real inconvenient shit like intimacy and relationships and conversation." She gave him a brittle smile. "Which is why I know you were trying to fuck your new trainee tonight."

Donovan blinked, the accusation making it through the alcohol haze like a fiery arrow. It hit the target and sent a wave of anger rushing through him, clearing his head enough to act. He took Elle by the arms, lifted her off his lap, and stood. "I'm not trying to do anything with Marin. We're friends. We knew each other in school."

"Right," Elle said from behind him, sarcasm oozing off her tone. "Just a celebratory drink and a little face stroking between friends. A few more glasses of wine, and you would've been parked between her legs giving her a big welcome to the neighborhood."

He whirled around. "We were talking about our dead parents, Elle. It was a gesture of comfort. Jesus Christ."

She tilted her head, surprise morphing her features. "Your parents are dead?"

He stared at her, realizing that they'd fucked for all these months, and he hadn't told her a damn thing about himself. Not that she'd asked. They'd always been . . . drinking and playing the game. He looked away and raked a hand through his hair. "I can't do this anymore."

She groaned and stepped up behind him, wrapping her arms around his waist. "Oh, come on, don't be a baby and pout. Use that anger on me. You know that's what I like. I like you when you're pissed."

He gritted his teeth. He thought of all the times she'd invited him over, how she'd always had bottles of wine at the ready, how she'd purposely try to goad him so he'd get rougher in bed. And though his limits were pretty far outside the norm, her craving for the violent stuff surpassed some of his boundaries. So he'd hold his line, and she'd try to push him past it. It was a dance they danced. But apparently it'd gone far beyond what he'd thought.

She'd figured out why he drank and had encouraged it, had used it to get what she wanted. His stomach turned. *Fuck.* He thought they played games of control—and they had—he'd just never realized he'd been the one getting played.

He took her hands and unwound himself from her grip. He met her gaze. "We're done here, Elle."

Her eyes narrowed. "What? Because of the new girl?"

"Because this, us"—he pointed between the two of them—"was fucked up from the start. Just took me until now to see exactly how much."

She crossed her arms. "Oh, come off that high horse. This works because we're both screwed up. We get a fix from each other. You've known that all along."

He sighed and ran a hand over the back of his head. "Maybe I did. But I'm done making it worse. We can be fucked up alone."

She stared at him for a second and then shook her head. "Go to hell, Donovan."

Her voice was quieter and when she blinked, her eyes went shiny. Donovan couldn't believe what he was seeing. This woman never cried, never showed her poker hand. He didn't know what in her life had made her so hard, but seeing her about to cry made him feel like a world-class asshole. She'd used him, sure. But he'd used her right back. There were no saints here.

He walked over to her and put his hands on her shoulders. "Don't waste tears on me, Elle. You're a smart, beautiful woman. You can do better than this."

Her jaw tightened. "I'm not fucking crying. Get over yourself. I know I can do better than you. You're a prick. I don't even *like* you."

He sighed as he lowered his arms and then walked over to her kitchen counter to grab a sticky note and pen she'd left by the phone. He scribbled down an address, his handwriting more messy than usual with the lingering effects of the alcohol. "There's a BDSM club in the city. It's a well-run place with a good membership. I bet you can find what you need there." He held out the slip of paper to her. "I'm not it."

"Don't try to psychoanalyze me, you asshole," she said, not making any move to take the note from him. "You have no idea what I want or need."

"Okay. You're probably right. All the more reason for me to leave." He left the note on the counter and turned toward the door. "Good luck, Elle."

"So that's it?" Her tone was a knifepoint, poking him with sharp, stiff jabs.

He kept his back to her, this sense of calm coming over him. "Yep. That's it."

He walked out the door and didn't look back.

15

Donovan showed up to work late and hungover. Marin tried to keep her annoyance at bay while Donovan greeted Ysabel and got his messages, but it spilled over when he strolled into her office, set a cup of coffee on her desk, and sank into the chair across from her without apology. He flipped through a file he had in his hands. "Got a busy docket today."

"You're late."

His gaze flicked up briefly. "I overslept. I didn't miss any appointments."

Nope. He hadn't. He'd just missed the show. "Ysa says you're late a lot."

His jaw flexed but he didn't look up again. "So how'd the research go last night?"

So that's how he was going to play it? Just ignore that things had gotten weird last night? Fine.

"It went okay. I made a list from the intake form. Skimmed through a few videos." A lie. She'd done those things, but it had been anything but okay. She'd already been keyed up after her talk with Donovan. Two hours of going through a list of sexual acts and clicking through sexy videos had not helped. But she hadn't allowed herself to relieve the tension. Not when she knew she would've been picturing Donovan during it. No way was she stooping to getting off to thoughts of someone else's boyfriend. So she'd gone to sleep frustrated. And then she'd walked into a minefield this morning alone because Donovan had been sleeping it off. Fucker.

"Do you have the list? I can make suggestions if I know which areas you feel need the most attention."

"Yeah." She flipped open a folder and flicked the list his way, her irritation hard to contain. Then, she grabbed the coffee and sipped, burning her tongue. "Goddammit, do they have to make it *this* hot?"

Donovan glanced up, wincing a bit at her raised voice. He rubbed two fingers over his brow and then took the paper in his hands to scan over it.

"Headache?" she asked, not lowering her voice.

"Uh-huh."

She lifted her massive diagnostic manual out of her drawer and dropped it on the desk. It made a pleasingly loud sound. *Smack!*

Donovan jumped, almost dropping the paper from his hands. "Jesus, Rush, what the hell?"

She pretended to be searching for a certain page. *Flip. Flip. Flip.* "Guess who stopped by this morning to have a chat?"

Flip. Flip.

He groaned. "Please tell me it wasn't Suri."

"Nope." She glanced toward the door to make sure it was shut and then reached back into her drawer and tossed his wallet onto the desk between them. "Your friend Dr. McCray. She said you left this at her place last night. She also told me that she now understands how a complete novice got a job here. She implied that I must've been quite *generous* in college, doing special favors for the graduate students."

"She *what*?" Donovan's voice boomed in the quiet office.

Marin's fingers curled against the desk, the rage she'd felt earlier this morning seeping back into her veins. McCray had looked so damn smug. Like she was talking to a child. Marin had wanted to punch that expression right off her face. Beyond the accusation just being straight-up insulting, didn't women have enough trouble getting professional respect without throwing the you-slept-your-way-to-the-top allegation at each other? "I can't believe you told her—"

"I didn't!" Donovan said, lifting his palms. "I would never tell anyone that. I mentioned we were friends in school. She must've looked up what years we graduated and made assumptions."

"Did you also mention that you almost offered to mentor me in your bed last night?"

His teeth clamped together.

"No, I'm sure you didn't. She probably wouldn't appreciate that much." Marin straightened in her chair, refusing to show how much getting blindsided by McCray had affected her. "Look, I don't give a shit what you're doing with whom. It's not my business. But this job is important to me, and I need this position. I cannot and *will not* get dragged into some petty bullshit because your girlfriend is insecure and you play fast and loose with commitment."

"She's not my girlfriend."

"Whatever. Girlfriend. Sex buddy. I don't care." Okay, she did. She totally did. But she couldn't let him know that. "I've got enough on my plate already with this job. I don't need rumors or marks on my reputation to add to the stress."

He scraped his hands through his hair and then laced his fingers behind his neck. "I don't even know what to— *Fuck*. I can't believe she went there. I'm sorry. This is my fault."

"Yes. It is. Did you cancel on her to meet with me last night?"

Something fierce flashed in his eyes. "It doesn't matter. Like I said, she's not my girlfriend and there's no commitment. Never has been. And whatever we did have going on is done anyway. She has no right to dictate what I do with my time."

"I don't think she knows that."

"She knows."

"Right. She also told me she was just here to give me a friendly girl-to-girl warning. That I was too *naive* to mess around with someone like you. That you'd just break my tender little heart." Marin gritted her teeth. "I swear to God, Donovan. I was ready to throw down with her. No one gets to talk to me like I'm a toddler. And if she tries it again, I'm going to get myself in trouble. You need to fix this."

Donovan lifted a hand in surrender. "I promise. I will. She thinks me ending things with her has something to do with you because of what she walked up on last night. And she assumes you're an easier target for her wrath than I am."

"That is a seriously misguided notion on her part."

He rubbed his brow again. "I need more coffee for this kind of morning."

"You and me both. But there's no time. We've got a session in a few minutes." She pushed her chair back and stood. "And if you need aspirin, I have some in my purse."

A long breath gusted out of him, and he got to his feet, tucking her list into the inside pocket of his jacket. But when she walked past him, he grabbed her hand, halting her. "Wait."

She stiffened. Why did he have to touch her? Always with the touching. Touching was dangerous. His hand on her never failed to jolt her system, to make wires cross where they shouldn't. She tipped up her chin. "What?"

His eyes met hers, something unreadable there. "I really am sorry. Sorry that you had to deal with that this morning and that I wasn't here on time to intervene." His fingers tightened around hers. "And she was wrong to approach you like that but right to warn you away from me. I'm good at my job, and I'm going to train you with everything I have. But I'm an asshole most of the time and a fuck-up at most everything else. I didn't mean for you to get hit with any of my shrapnel."

She frowned. "You're not a fuck-up, Donovan."

"Yeah, when it comes to this kind of thing, I am," he said, his voice tired. "Scary to think people trust me to give them relationship advice, right? The only relationship I managed not to screw up was with my parents and that's because they died before I had the chance."

Marin's chest constricted. "Donovan . . ."

"It's fine. Those who can't do, teach—isn't that what they say?" He gave her a tight smile. "Regardless, I'll talk to Elle and make sure she directs her anger toward the right person. I won't let my shit mess anything up for you. I promise."

Her shoulders sagged, any residual anger slipping away at his weary tone. "I don't understand why you'd even get involved with someone like her. She seems so harsh and . . . cold."

His expression darkened and he released her hand. "Because I'm not any better."

"Of course you are," she said without hesitation. Sure, a lot of time had passed, but people didn't change their core personality, and the Donovan she'd known had never been cold. Lost and a little lonely, maybe, but not cold.

He glanced away, his posture rigid. "No. I'm not. I'm worse. Don't fool yourself into thinking otherwise. You haven't seen me— how I am now. You're still seeing who I used to be. When it comes to women, I'm good at two things. Getting them off. And leaving. I try to find the ones who are okay with both."

The words were delivered with sharp, slicing edges. They should've scared her. Instead, she had the urge to move closer to him. "Quite a resume tagline you got there. Is that the line you drop on a woman when you meet her in a bar?"

He looked up at her and smirked. "Not exactly. Leading in with 'I'm an asshole' usually isn't the best tactic."

"You're not an asshole, Donovan. You spend your days counseling people in broken relationships. I'd say your aversion to having one yourself is an occupational hazard not a character failure. As long as you're not lying to women about what it is, it's your prerogative."

"You sound like a wise therapist, Dr. Rush."

She mimed brushing off her shoulder, trying to lighten the mood and that stormy expression on his face. "Well, you know, I'm learning from the best. Hopefully my naive, tender heart can handle the training with that evil bastard Dr. West."

He squared his body with hers and leveled her with a look. Even with a hangover, he looked gorgeous in his pressed suit with his hair mussed and the shadow of stubble on his jaw. This less polished version fit him well. "Don't let Elle get to you. I know you can handle a helluva lot. You already have."

"I have." She smiled and then, acting on instinct, grabbed his lapels to straighten and smooth them. "In fact, you probably should be the one worried. I've raised a teenage boy and lived to tell about it. You have no idea if you can handle *me*." She patted his shoulder and stepped around him to head to the door. "I could be the heartbreaker here. Remember who went looking for whom last time."

But before she could make her escape, a hand grasped her arm from behind and dragged her back. She gasped when she spun and almost collided with Donovan, her hands landing on his chest to stop the momentum. His eyes flared with something new and dangerous, as he peered down at her. "Don't do that, Rush. Don't flirt and sway those hips like that and expect it to roll off me. I'm trying to be good. I *will* be good. But I have my limits. You've got to do your part, too."

Her response got caught high up in her throat, her heartbeat jumping to join it. The teasing comment had slipped past her lips before she could stop it. She'd wanted to flirt a little, wanted to prove to him and herself that she wasn't as sweet and fragile as Dr. McCray had accused. She wasn't experienced in bed. That didn't mean she was some innocent.

But now she'd poked the lion. Everything in her was screaming that she should run, that they were too close, that this was going off the rails quickly. But all the buildup from the night before, her unsatisfying evening, and the feel of him right here with her was just too much.

It was like they were back in that lab again, all alone in the world and looking for something to hold on to if only for a few hot minutes. Her brain fogged, every one of her physical resources zeroing in on the hum in her body, the ache for that connection. She forgot that she was at work. That this was a bad idea. That he'd just told her that he was good at leaving. All she could see was Donovan. His heartbeat thumped beneath her fingertips. Her fingers curled against his shirt.

He hissed out a breath at the touch.

"What are you trying to do?" he asked, his eyes raking over her face, his expression tense. "Tell me what this is."

"I don't know," she whispered.

"Marin." His voice came out gritty, strained.

There was so much in that one simple plea that it completely undid her, ripped the ties holding her good sense together and left them in a tangle on the floor.

She pushed up on her toes, closed her eyes, and kissed him.

Donovan froze, his body going still for a moment under her touch, but then she tightened her hold on his shirt and made this noise. A ridiculous, unstoppable sound that came across way too desperate, way too needy. But it seemed to do something to him. He groaned against her mouth—a dam breaking. His hands went to the sides of her face, cradling her head and angling her just how he wanted her. Hungry. Searching. Hot.

All the control tilted in that one moment as he took over, tasting her lips and dragging her against him. Making noises similar to hers—only sexier, rougher. She melted into it, letting him have whatever he wanted as she succumbed to the sensations rolling through her—the feel of his fingers against her cheeks, the hard heat of his body brushing hers, the bittersweet taste of the coffee on his lips. It was all she remembered about kissing him before but with more urgency, more intensity, more . . . everything.

Marin moaned when he parted her lips to deepen the kiss, and a swift rush of arousal flooded her, making the neglected parts of her throb and ache. His tongue stroked hers, teasing with a rhythm she could only imagine in other places. Her nipples became hard points, straining for touch, and her sex pulsed between her thighs. She wanted to rub herself on him like a cat, find relief. He seemed ready to oblige. Donovan backed her into the wall, his body aligning with hers and his hand sliding down to knead her hip like he was barely restraining himself from tearing off her clothes. Heat against heat, hardness growing against her belly. She was dying. She needed this. God, did she need this.

But a swift knock sounded behind him, shattering the protected moment and blasting through her lust-drunk brain. Marin gasped, and Donovan jumped back and dropped his hands to his sides like she had burned him.

The door swung open, and Ysa poked her head in. "Hey, guys I—" Her words faded as her gaze bounced between them. "Uh, sorry, didn't mean to interrupt."

Poker face. Poker face. Poker face. Marin pushed off the wall and fought hard to look like everything was fine even though her cheeks were burning hot, her lips slick, and her body pulsing in time with her frantic heartbeat. She had a feeling she was failing miserably at pulling it off. They may as well have a neon sign above their heads that read *In Flagrante Delicto.*

Donovan, on the other hand, owner of the world's most impenetrable therapist mask, looked cool and unaffected as he tucked his hands in his pockets, presumably to hide his burgeoning hard-on, and looked at Ysa. "Not interrupting. What's up?"

Ysa glanced between the two of them again but kept her thoughts to herself. "Just wanted to let you know your nine-thirty is here."

Marin gave her a quick, tight smile. "Thanks. We're on our way."

Ysa gave them one last questioning look, then shook her head and disappeared back out into the hallway. When the door shut, Marin put her hands over her face and groaned. "*Son of a bitch.* Now there's more grist for Dr. McCray's rumor mill. I cannot believe I just did that. Here. With you."

Donovan stepped into her space again and took her wrists in his hands, gently tugging them away from her face. "Take a breath. It's okay. Ysa didn't see anything. And even if she figured it out, she would never say anything to anyone. We could be screwing like rabbits in between sessions, and Ysa wouldn't care as long as we were on time for our appointments and taking good care of the clients. You can trust her. She's good people and loyal to me."

But Marin hardly heard any of it with her head spinning and anxiety rushing through her. "God, how could I be so stupid? I don't know what I was thinking. I just—"

"It's not your fault, Marin," he said, his voice gentle. "I crossed the line first." His mouth hitched up. "Plus, I should know not to stand that close to a woman who spent all night watching porn."

A sharp laugh burst out of her, her nerves bubbling up and out. "Right. I'm bound to grab anyone within reach to use for my lecherous purposes."

Donovan looked down at her for a long second, some of that heat from earlier returning, burning her slowly. His hands flexed around her wrists. "I wouldn't mind being used by you, Marin."

Her stomach dipped.

"I didn't make the offer last night because it would've been a selfish move. And a risk. But I want you in my bed. Know that. It's not altruistic. Or professional. And it's out of line." His voice was like water gliding along her skin—smooth, clear, quietly powerful. He lifted her hand and flattened it against his chest over the inner pocket of his jacket. "But if you decide you might want that anyway, know there isn't a thing on this list that I wouldn't love to check off for you. Completely and thoroughly. I could make you shameless, Rush."

She could barely hear him over the roaring sound in her ears. How the hell was she supposed to form words after *that*?

He released her hands and stepped back but kept her pinned beneath that white-hot gaze. "So if you ever need me . . . off the clock, you just have to ask. And if you want me to go to hell and steer clear, that's all you've got to say, too. It's your call."

Everything inside her was buzzing. Her mind had gotten hung up on the words *completely* and *thoroughly*. He wasn't going to pressure her, but the look in his eye said he could rock her celibate world right off its fucking axis. The temptation was like a bright, glittering thing blurring her vision.

But taking that offer would come with a price. Keeping things secret. The risk of being caught. And there would be a time limit. He didn't do relationships. This would just be sex.

Really hot, really intense sex. She had no doubt that was the only brand he subscribed to.

Part of her—okay, all of her—wanted to surrender to the need coursing through her. But they were at work. Her mind was scrambled, and her hormones were staging a coup to take over her executive decision-making faculties. This was neither the time nor the place. She swallowed past the knot in her throat, channeling that part of her she'd honed over the years, the part that kept her from chasing whims like her mother had, the part that knew bright-and-shinies were dangerous, that men like Donovan were dangerous. "We better get going or we're going to be late."

Donovan gave her a long look but then nodded and tucked his hands in his pockets, professional composure sliding back over him like an elegant costume. "Of course. Let's go, Dr. Rush."

16

Donovan's feet pounded against the pavement with quiet thumps as the first pink-gold light of sunrise started to push at the edges of The Grove. He had his earbuds tucked in his ears but no music was on. He'd just worn them to avoid any unnecessary conversation if he came across anyone.

Thump. Thump. Thump. His heartbeat was loud in his ears, keeping time with his feet. He could hear his breath soughing in and out of his chest. It'd been a long damn time since he was out this early, and he'd forgotten how alive and quiet the grounds could be at this time. He should do this more. This felt good. Cleansing. Better than lying in bed awake and letting his mind go to the endless loop of shit it liked to play when his brain got too tired to keep the bad stuff locked in the basement.

Usually he didn't fall asleep until well into the night, insomnia an ever-present companion. He was used to that. Knew that eventually his body would surrender or he'd give in and take a sleeping pill—though he hated those because it often made him sleep through his alarm clock and feel groggy. But the last few nights, even those hard-fought hours of fitful sleep had been elusive. So this morning when the clock had rolled over to five, he'd gotten up and dug out his running gear.

If his thoughts were going to stalk him, he'd just run faster than they could keep up.

But half an hour into his run, his mind continued to drift to Marin. He'd made her the offer to check off her list days ago. That stupid, dangerous offer. He prided himself on his self-control, on moderating his emotions, on making a plan and sticking to it. He'd survived this long sticking to that method. But when Marin had kissed him in the office, every ounce of good sense he possessed had gotten packed up in a box and tossed out the door. He'd wanted her. Everything else, all the potential consequences and catastrophes, had been lost in the sheer velocity of need that had swept over him.

And the suggestion had burst out of him like something else had taken possession of his voice. He needed to take it back. Undo the mess.

But he hadn't been able to bring himself to do it. Every time he attempted, the retraction wouldn't come out. He'd just want to make the offer all over again.

The only thing that had saved him so far was that Marin had the smarts to ignore the offer completely. And to his surprise, they'd had a great week despite the disastrous start. She'd thrown herself fully into the training, her mind like an ever-hungry maw, always wanting more knowledge, always wanting to get it right. When she was like that, so eager and enthusiastic, he could forget about the other stuff for a while. Her thirst for learning set off the psych nerd in him. He liked teaching her.

And she made him laugh—something that felt rusty and foreign to him. He loved his job, but he couldn't remember the last time he'd actually had fun at work. Despite the heavy issues they dealt with in session with clients, Marin was quick to smile and joke around with him and Ysa between appointments. When she'd had success co-leading a couples session with him yesterday, she'd actually done a little victory dance in the hallway after the clients had left. There may have been a Heisman pose involved. Ysa may have broken out a raise-the-roof move. They may have convinced him to join in.

But despite Marin's great attitude and not one word about the kiss, he'd caught her in quieter times looking at him when she thought he wasn't paying attention. He'd caught smoky eyes and pensive stares. He'd seen her blush outside of sessions like she'd been thinking something particularly scandalous. She hadn't forgotten that kiss. But she'd gone on like nothing had happened.

That was good.

He was telling himself it was good.

But it was keeping him awake at night. Stalking him. Temptation whispering in his ear.

He needed to let it lie.

He wanted her so much it fucking hurt.

He ran harder, hard enough to make his lungs burn and the breeze whip his face. Hard enough to quell the surge of desire he got every time he thought of Marin.

And he'd almost outrun the thoughts when the sound of more feet on pavement distracted him. He turned his head to find Ysa only a few steps behind him. Her cheeks were puffing out as she tried to catch up.

Donovan forced himself to not make a face. He adored Ysa. She was one of his few friends at The Grove, but right now he wasn't fit for company.

"Jesus. Freaking. Christ," Ysa said between pants. "Slow. The hell. Down."

Donovan considered telling her he'd chat with her at work, that he was trying to beat some imaginary time for his run, but she'd see right through it. Ysa's bullshit meter was pretty spot-on. Plus, even he couldn't keep up this speed for much longer. His body was about to stage a strike, his muscles threatening to cramp. He pulled out his earbuds and eased back on his sprint.

Ysa caught up and sent him a disbelieving look. "Are you running from a rabid dog or something? Serial killer? Evil clowns?"

Their footsteps synched up as they rounded the corner at the back of the children's building. He feigned innocence. "Was I going that fast?"

She narrowed her eyes. "Don't give me that. I come out here to run every morning, and I may be five seconds from dying right now."

He looked forward, focusing on the path. "You didn't have to catch up."

"And miss the chance to jog next to and annoy my lovely boss? As if I'd pass that up." She flashed a grin in his peripheral vision. "Plus, I should document this occasion. Look how early you're awake!"

Donovan didn't say anything. Ysa had no idea he barely slept, and he sure as hell wasn't going to share that tidbit. "I'm trying to ensure your promotion. I've been on time the last few days."

They took a turn by the pond, and a crane that had been lazily poking at the grass near the water's edge looked up as they passed, apparently annoyed they'd interrupted his private breakfast. Ysa tipped her chin up. "Uh-huh. Of course you are. I'm sure it has *nothing* to do with impressing the new hot doctor you're training."

Donovan's rhythm faltered for a second, but he managed to recover without being too obvious. "Not very professional to call your colleague hot, Ysa."

She let out a laugh, her breath still labored. "Oh, and it's professional to do whatever y'all were doing when I walked in the other day?"

The words made Donovan's muscles tense. He slowed his step, worry moving through him. "Ysa."

She slowed along with him and stopped when he stopped. The crane flapped its wings and flew off with a flourish. Ysa put her hands on her hips, bending over a bit as she caught her breath, but her eyes were on him. "Seriously. Don't freak out. We're good."

Donovan's T-shirt was clinging to him, sweat rolling down his back, but his heart was pounding from something other than exertion now. "Ysa, you can't—"

She lifted a hand. "Dude, I wouldn't. I'd never say anything.

Come on, you know me better than that. I didn't even see anything per se. Y'all just had *caught* written all over you both. And I see how you two look at each other. I've been the victim of lust at first sight before. I get it. Believe me."

Donovan grabbed the edge of his T-shirt and wiped the sweat from his face, his eyes burning from it. He considered lying to Ysa, but that'd only make it worse. She was being upfront with him, so he needed to do the same. She'd keep his secret if he was honest. "It's not exactly that. We knew each other a long time ago. Had a brief thing."

Ysa's dark brow arched. "Whoa. History. Does Suri know?"

"No. No one does. And it needs to stay that way. Nothing's going to happen. What you walked in on was . . . a lapse in judgment. Neither of us wants to mess with our jobs."

Ysa pulled a bottle of water from the belt around her waist and took a long sip, eyeing him. "So don't get caught."

He frowned. "What?"

She shrugged. "Remember that pretty redhead that worked in the teen unit last summer? She was doing an internship?"

"Vaguely," he said, not remembering at all.

"I hooked up with her all summer. No one ever had a clue we were seeing each other. You just have to be smart about it." She sniffed. "And Lord knows, you at least have that going for you."

He smirked. "At least?"

"I mean, I suppose you're also reasonably good-looking if you're into that kind of thing."

"That would've meant more if you hadn't rolled your eyes while you said it," Donovan teased. He fished his own water out of the pack he'd strapped to his back and downed half of it. "But this is a different situation. Getting together with someone in another department is one thing. But I'm working with Dr. Rush every day. I'm training her. It's high risk. Not worth it."

She closed the cap on her water. "If you say so. I'm not the masochistic sort. I'd get that shit out of my system. Otherwise, think how many years of torture it could be working together with all that unfulfilled lusting? That can't be healthy."

Donovan had to fight the grimace. He hadn't thought about it that way. He'd thought about how tortuous it would be to work together after things ended or went bad. Because of course they would. They always did. He made sure of it. But he hadn't considered feeling like he was right now long-term, getting that tug in his gut anytime he was near Marin, thinking thoughts he had no business thinking at work. Not sleeping at night because fantasies of her would drift into his mind and not relent until he put his hands on himself. *Fuck.*

"You're a ray of frigging sunshine, Ysa."

She gave him a sparkling grin. "I know, right?"

He groaned and turned to start running again, needing to move, needing to get these thoughts out of his head. Outrun the temptation. Outrun it all.

Ysa fell into step beside him. Staying quiet for a while but her presence loud.

Donovan gritted his teeth. "Why are you encouraging this? I thought you'd be the first one to tell me to back the hell off and not mess around with our jobs."

Ysa didn't look his way. She just kept pumping her arms and keeping pace. "You're a good boss, doc. And a good guy. But you can be . . . intense. Grim. You've been different since Dr. Rush came around. I like it." She gave him a quick glance. "Everybody deserves something or someone that makes them feel alive every now and then. Even you."

At that, she took a sharp right and veered onto another path, leaving him grinding to a halt and staring after her.

So much for the morning run clearing his head.

He should've run faster.

He had a feeling he'd never be able to run fast enough.

17

During her lunch break on Friday, Marin grabbed a cupcake off the dessert station as a reward for making it through her first two weeks and for managing to keep her hands off Donovan after their kiss in her office that second day. To Donovan's credit, he hadn't brought up anything and had acted like the conversation and kiss hadn't happened. He'd mentored her in sessions, walked her through a few tough cases, and had been generally a helpful, professional trainer. They were developing a good, solid working relationship.

It was driving her mad. Clearly, he hadn't been as affected by that kiss because she definitely hadn't been able to shake it off so easily. How was she supposed to sit in sessions with him, listening to people talk about sex, seeing him wearing those suits, and dishing out brilliant advice in that voice of his, and *not* think about the fact that he'd said he wanted her in his bed? Not think about his erection pressing into her hip or him saying that he'd check off every box on that kinky list for her with enthusiasm?

She'd reverted to being that girl in the back row crushing on the TA. How the hell had she been reduced back to that? So not acceptable.

She slid into a chair at an empty table and set her tray down with more force than necessary, rattling the silverware. Lack of sex was how this had happened. Sex was like sugar. When you cut it out of your diet, you hit a point where you stopped craving it altogether. But as soon as you ate that one little Skittle or licked some icing off a spoon, all you could think about were Skittles and icing. Or naked skin and tangled sheets as the case may be.

She couldn't think about anything else when she was around Donovan now. Even the simplest thing—Donovan twirling a pen between dexterous fingers, Donovan licking an envelope, Donovan chewing his lip when he was thinking hard about a case. All of it would lead to porn-worthy images in her mind. She was like a teenage boy hyped up on testosterone. She needed a goddamned intervention.

She'd tried to take care of things herself this past week, *researching* some of the brands of vibrators they kept stocked. But if anything, the nightly orgasm had only amped her up more, making her want the real thing. She was craving more than a release. She was craving experience. With him.

Oriana slid into the spot across from her and plopped her tray down, breaking Marin from her swirling thoughts. "God, I'm so glad it's lunchtime. Thanks for saving me a spot."

Marin looked up and glanced around the empty table. "Well, it was a lot of work. I did have to give a few band kids the evil eye, and I think I pissed off Brittany from the cheerleading squad."

Ori laughed. "Right? Seriously. This place does feel like high school sometimes—or hell. Though, there's little difference between the two I think."

"Tough morning?"

Ori gave a fuck-my-life groan while she sprinkled red pepper flakes on her pasta. "You have no idea. A-list actress got checked in by her family this morning, and someone tipped off the press. It was a freaking nightmare trying to get her in without anyone getting pictures. And she is *not* a happy camper. My intelligence, my virtue, and my hairdo have all been subjects of her insults this morning. Did you know this color looks terrible on me?"

"Ugh, sorry."

She gave a dismissive flick of her wrist and plunked the pepper shaker down. "Part of the deal. I'm just happy for a brief respite. My impenetrable armor will be back intact once I get some carbs and coffee. And ooh"—she eyeballed the dessert on Marin's tray—"cupcakes. I missed those."

Marin picked up her cupcake, split it to give Ori half, and then went back to poking at her shrimp salad. "Ah, yes, the only food groups of any importance."

"Exactly. So talk to me about something other than how I'm an evil idiot doctor who has no fashion sense and is here to ruin everyone's lives." She licked a dollop of icing off her thumb. "How's week two with the Orgasm Whisperer going?"

Marin's fork slipped from her hand and it hit her plate with a clank. "Uh, we should probably not call him that in public. Plus, I think he hates that name."

Ori gave a cheeky grin and twirled noodles onto her fork. "It's better than some of the other names I've heard people call him around here. And, I bet he secretly loves it. Can you imagine how much play he got out of that nickname?" She inclined her head, taking on a mock serious look. "Hey, baby, I can coax that orgasm right out of you purely with the luscious sound of my voice."

Marin snorted at Ori's imitation. "He so doesn't sound like that. No one would get turned on if he sounded like that."

Ori pointed her fork at Marin, noodles sliding off into her bowl like snakes abandoning ship. "You know what I mean. A guy who could talk you into coming would be hot."

"Well, I doubt anyone can *talk* someone into orgasm. That'd be quite a talent. But the audio is definitely effective at getting you in the right headspace." This was so not what Marin needed to be talking about. She needed to keep Donovan out of her head, not be thinking about how his sin-laced voice used to sound on those recordings or how those fantasies he'd weaved had pushed buttons she hadn't known existed inside her.

"Wait, you've listened to the recordings?"

"What? I—" Marin's lips snapped shut.

"You have, haven't you?" She leaned forward, eyes bright. "I've heard they had that actor James Harlow do the narration. God, his voice is like melted butter. Are they super steamy?"

Marin poked at her salad. "Uh, well, I've never heard the final versions. Donovan and I went to the same university. I heard some of the early recordings from the study."

Ori leaned back in her chair. "Whoa, so like the ones West actually talked on?"

"Yep."

"Were they hot?"

"Yep." She took a bite, chewed viciously.

"Wow, that must be seriously awkward with him being your boss now."

"He's not my boss." Marin said it way too quickly and emphatically, the words just bursting out like a sneeze. Lovely. Stealth she was not. Ninja license revoked.

Ori's eyebrows lifted. "My bad. Your *colleague*. Your very gorgeous *colleague*. Anything you're not telling me, Dr. Rush?"

Marin sent her a withering look.

Ori raised her palm, feigned innocence on her face. "Just sayin'. Dr. West has a reputation for being difficult to work with, but he's very easy to look at. You deny that, and I know you're lying to me."

"He's not that difficult to work with. And I will acknowledge his winning of the genetic lottery but am studiously ignoring his good looks."

She laughed. "Impossible."

Marin pointed to herself. "Girl on probation."

Ori's smile went conspiratorial. "That just means keep it on the down low."

Marin hummed a tune and put her hands over her ears. "Not listening to you and your bad influence. Talk to me after you've jumped that orderly you're lusting over."

"No shot. I'm on lockdown." Ori glanced to the left and tipped her head in that direction. "McCray caught us flirting in the hallway this morning so we're on her radar. Have to lie low for a while."

Marin took a bite of her salad and followed where Ori's gaze had gone. The cafe was humming at this time. Doctors, nurses, and therapists milled around, chatting with each other and choosing from the gourmet options in The Grove's mini food court. Skylights gave the whole place a bright, airy vibe, making it almost feel like an open-air cafe even though it was inside. But one blonde was sitting in a place where the light didn't shine. McCray was flying solo in a far corner, her laptop out and her food untouched, her whole demeanor conveying a don't-bother-me vibe. A bitter taste crossed Marin's tongue. She took a long sip of her iced tea. "It's got to be a nightmare working for her. She seems . . ."

"Scary?"

"Not the word I was thinking but fits."

Ori shrugged. "She *is* scary. Made me cry my first week here when I made a mistake with a client's chart. But I've gotten used to her and have learned how to stay on her good side for the most part. Plus, I've learned a lot from her. She's kind of a badass when you get to see her work. But for my first few weeks here, I thought of her as the Bitch like everyone else."

Marin held up a finger. "There's the word I was thinking."

Ori peered over at McCray again. "Yeah, she comes across that way. She cultivates that image. But one night a few months after I first started, we were both working the graveyard shift, and I had this client . . ." Ori frowned. "The girl was barely nineteen but had lived a fast life. Her parents were famous musicians who were never home, so she'd spent her teen years getting high and getting in trouble with boys. She'd been admitted to rehab when her mom found out that she'd started doing porn. The girl was strung out and beat down and had the self-esteem of a garden pea when she came in.

"A day after we got her through detox, she tried to kill herself with a ballpoint pen she'd gotten ahold of. We found her in time. But after Dr. McCray got the girl's wounds taken care of and the necessities out of the way, she gave this girl a you-are-better-than-this, tough-love talk that I wish I could've recorded. It was like the most kickass, empowering speech I'd ever heard about not letting men use you and about finding your inner strength and worth and . . . God, I wanted to climb on top of the desk and burn my bra or raise the mockingjay sign or something. It was brilliant. It showed me how much McCray cares about her patients. She wasn't giving lip service. She meant every word she said. And it worked. That girl got cleaned up and is doing well now." Ori took a bite and shrugged. "So I've got mad respect for McCray now—even though she can be a nightmare sometimes."

Marin frowned, not wanting to hear anything good about the woman. It made it harder to hate her. "I had a quick chat with her last week when she needed something from our floor. She doesn't like me much."

Ori looked up and made a *meh* face. "Don't take it personally. She kind of hates the X-wing in general. She and West *do not* get along."

"Really?"

"Yeah. She's a stickler about everything—procedures, paperwork, blah blah blah. And Dr. West is . . . well, Dr. West. He does things his way and on his own schedule. Plus, McCray thinks dedicating the resources of a whole floor to sex therapy is a waste. When West came on board, there was only couples therapy. He launched the sex therapy program and wanted his own dedicated floor. That floor had been set aside for an expansion of the rehab unit and then got pulled out from under McCray. She blames him."

"So they hate each other?"

"Pretty much."

Of course they did. It shouldn't surprise her. Donovan stacked the deck to make sure his relationships were doomed from the start. He'd told her as much. But this made her realize that his offer to her meant that he saw her as a safe bet in that regard, too. Maybe not in the same way as McCray, but safe nonetheless.

That annoyed the hell out of her. She wasn't looking for a relationship right now either, especially not one with a co-worker. But being seen as a no-risk prospect for him didn't sit well either. *You can sleep with me but not get to me.* That was the message. Or maybe he just saw her as so wildly inexperienced that she was no real threat for the great Orgasm Whisperer. She was just the sweet, naive therapist who couldn't get through a session without blushing like a schoolgirl. He would be her emotionally detached mentor. Her sexual surrogate.

She shoved her salad aside and grabbed her cupcake, taking a violent chomp out of it.

Yes, she wanted to learn, experience things. And the thought of him being the one to show her turned her on more than it should. She'd been tempted by the offer hourly since he'd made it. But she also didn't want to be someone's pity project. And she'd be damned if she let herself become another McCray to him. Screw that.

She'd left the offer there on the table this long because she hadn't quite been able to close that door. But thinking about it from his point of view, thinking about how he'd gone about things with McCray, about how he must see all this, pissed her the hell off.

Donovan West thought she was safe.

Safe. *Ugh.*

"So what's on your agenda for the afternoon?" Ori asked, oblivious to the storm building in Marin.

Marin swallowed the bite of cake. "Fixing a mistake."

"Already got to that stage today, huh?"

"Nope, I made this one a long time ago."

18

Marin headed back to her building, resolve in her step. This thing with Donovan needed to be staked and turned to dust. She couldn't focus on her job if this thing was hovering over her, whispering temptation in her ear, draining her of her good sense. Sure, she needed to learn some things. Her blushing problem was an ongoing issue, for one. But beyond that, she just really, really needed to get laid. It was time to step into the adult world and break out of this purgatory state she'd been in for all these years.

But she didn't need to do that with Donovan as a training exercise. She wanted someone to want her simply because he was attracted to her, not because she was safe or there was some task list to check off. She didn't need a relationship right now, but she craved something real, something raw. Untempered chemistry. Something like she'd had that first time when it was all desire and attraction and desperation. She didn't want to be someone's student. She wanted to be someone's indulgence. She wanted to be that girl in Donovan's recordings, the woman someone hungered for.

So she would talk to Donovan after the sex addiction group this afternoon and put the whole offer to rest. Cut and dried. Uncomplicated. Smart.

She was good at being smart. Smart had kept her afloat all these years.

She walked down the hallway of the X-wing, her heels clicking sharply against the polished floors. Ysabel and Donovan hadn't returned from lunch yet, so Marin detoured to her office to get some things together for group. But when she stepped inside, she stopped so suddenly she almost turned an ankle.

The room was dark, the curtains drawn. But there was enough light from the doorway to see what was in front of her. A half-naked woman bent over Marin's desk. A man behind her, grunting and pumping his hips hard.

Marin's mouth dropped open at the sight, but no sound came out. So the couple she'd caught in action didn't notice they weren't alone anymore. They just kept at it. The woman was bared from the waist down, her skirt pushed up and her panties around her ankles. The man behind her had only shoved his jeans to his hips and his muscular ass was flexing hard as he thrust into the woman and told her how fucking hot she felt around his cock.

Marin was marble in the doorway—unable to move, unable to look away. She had no idea who these two people were, but the ferocity of their coupling had her in thrall. Her heavy desk was shifting out of place with every violent thrust, the legs scraping against the wood floor. And the woman was begging for more, harder. Her knuckles were white against the edge of the desk like she'd fly apart if she let go. Marin's blood went hot and her mouth dry.

"Marin, I—"

She jolted, the voice like ice water over her head.

Donovan ground to a halt next to her, catching sight of the tableau. "What the hell?"

The man in her office let out a curse but didn't stop the rhythm of his hips. *Slap. Slap. Slap.* Naked skin colliding. "Just give us a sec, doc."

Donovan jostled Marin as he moved past her and flicked on the lights. The woman's hand went up to block her eyes, and sounds of protest came from them both. Yet, their movements didn't abate. The slick, lewd soundtrack of sex filled the room.

"You have ten seconds to put yourselves together or I'm calling security to take you out of here," Donovan said, his tone brooking no argument and his expression revealing nothing.

But the man was already too far gone. His head tilted back, and he groaned long and loud. His shaggy blond hair slid away from his face. Only then did Marin get a good look at him—the hard angles of his jaw, the perfectly executed stubble. All the breath whooshed out of her. Holy shit. She'd seen that face and chiseled jaw before—in movies and on magazines and just about everywhere lately. Eli Harding had become a big deal a few years ago when he'd played a superhero in a summer blockbuster. Now the man that most of the female population would give anything to see naked was in front of Marin with his ass bared and his dick buried in a woman. A woman who had just tipped over into a loud orgasm.

Marin's life had officially entered crazytown.

Donovan peered her way as the couple finished, his jaw tight and something unreadable in his eyes. Their gazes held, neither looking away, and her breathing stalled. Burning blue eyes. The rigid stance of his body. The way his hands flexed. All of it was too much. And not enough at the same time. There was something both wrong and ridiculously intense about sharing a look while two other people were getting off right next to them. Sexy sounds. Sweaty bodies. Naked skin. Something hot and wicked crept along her spine, moved downward, pulsed. Her tongue pressed to the back of her teeth.

Something flickered over Donovan's expression, but he dragged his attention back to the offenders when it was clear they had reached their finish line. His voice was gruff when he spoke. "Go to the restrooms and put yourselves back together. When you're done, I need you both in my office. This kind of behavior is not going to fly here."

Eli pulled out of the woman and drew her skirt down to cover her, offering her some semblance of modesty. He gave her hip a pat. "You can get up now, babe."

He stepped back and slipped off the condom, not making any attempts to hide himself. Of course, Marin's gaze naturally went there. Even going soft, his cock was enormous in that big palm of his. She yanked her attention back upward, but Eli was already smirking her way like he'd enjoyed her checking him out. He tied off the condom and tossed it into her trash can with a flick of the wrist.

"Jesus, Eli," Donovan said, his tone sharp. "Have some respect. This is Dr. Rush's office."

"So I'll buy her a new trash can." He swiped a wet spot from the polished wood surface they'd been sprawled across. "And desk. No big deal."

The woman was up by then, straightening her clothes and setting herself back to rights. She looked more ashamed at being caught, her gaze sliding away from Marin's when she looked her way. "Sorry, Dr. West."

Donovan shook his head. "We'll discuss all of this once you two put yourselves back together. Go."

Eli casually tucked himself into his pants and zipped up, leaving the top button open. The two headed toward the door, and Marin stepped to the side. When Eli passed her, he smiled. "Nice to meet you, Dr. Rush. Sorry about the mess but hope you enjoyed the show."

The smug tone made her teeth clench. Yes, she'd watched. Maybe he'd noticed. But she wasn't going to give this guy the satisfaction of knowing he'd affected her. "The bathroom is down the hall on the right."

He gave her one last lazy smile and led the woman out. Marin shut the door behind them and sagged against the door. "What. The. Hell?"

She hated that her pulse was thumping so hard, hated that even though she wanted to punch that guy, not sleep with him, that her body had gone warm and hyperaware.

Donovan folded his arms and let out a long breath. "I'd like to say I'm surprised, but I'm not. Eli is a new addition to the sex addiction group since he's filming a movie down here and his regular therapist is in L.A. Laura's been in it awhile and has had slipups, but this is a big setback for her. Both have serious exhibitionist streaks, which would be okay if they weren't so reckless and impulsive about it. Laura's lost custody of her daughter over her behavior."

"Wow."

"Yeah. And Eli's on his way to disaster. His publicity team put him in the program because he's almost gotten caught on camera a few times, which could ruin his career. No one wants a guy who has kids' action figures modeled after him to be caught on tape screwing women all over town."

"He seems like a real handful." The words were barely out of her mouth when they registered. She cringed.

Donovan smirked. "Insert: *That's what she said* here."

"Ugh. I can't believe I looked."

"I would've been surprised if you hadn't. He basically held it out on a platter for your perusal. He wanted you to ogle. He's very proud of his superhero penis."

She tapped the back of her head against the door. "I should've been a professional about it though, turned around or something. Not rewarded the bad behavior."

Donovan pressed his hands to the back of her desk chair. "How long *were* you standing there before I showed up?"

She sighed. "I don't know. I think I was too stunned to process what was happening. I wasn't sure who it was or how to handle it. I should've left and found you. But I froze."

He gave a little shrug. "Don't beat yourself up too much about it. Not too many people would look away from catching Hollywood's hottest star doing the deed on their desk. But hey—this is a bit of a victory. You didn't seem embarrassed when it all went down. I'm almost glad that you gave him a good perusal. It's a bolder move than shrinking away. In fact, when he caught you checking out what he had on offer, you gave him this look that seemed to say 'oh, get over yourself.' It was kind of brilliant."

She laughed and pushed up from the door. "Yeah?"

He walked around her desk and tucked his hands in his pockets. "Yeah. And I won't lie. Seeing you knock him down a peg was pretty entertaining. I shouldn't enjoy that. The guy's struggling with all kinds of shit that makes him act the way he does. But"—he lifted his shoulders and stepped closer—"I'm still a guy. And seeing you completely unimpressed with one of *People*'s Sexiest Men Alive feeds my *Geeks Rule! Jocks Drool!* heart."

She crossed her arms over her chest but couldn't help smiling. "Since when are you a geek?"

He gave her a surely-you-can't-be-serious head tilt. "Please. The first time you met me, I had a hard-on while doing psychological research and wore shirts with Freud puns."

"Okay, good point. Maybe I can't recognize geekiness because I'm a member of the same club."

He nodded sagely and reached out to tap her nose. "You definitely are, Rush. It's one of your finer qualities."

She pursed her lips and was about to come out with a teasing comeback but then she paused. This was flirting. They were flirting. *Shit.* This is exactly what she shouldn't be doing. She'd made a decision. She couldn't get sidetracked just because her hormones had kicked in after what she'd witnessed.

She stepped around him to go to her desk and pulled a notepad out of her drawer. "We better head to your office. If we leave them alone too long, they may christen your desk, too."

Donovan frowned. "They better not. If anyone christens my desk, it sure as hell better be me."

Marin sent him the side-eye as she headed toward the door. "Never went there with Dr. McCray?"

She wanted to take it back as soon as it came out, but there was no rewind button. She was stuck with it. Petty jealousy. Out in the open and waving around. *Fantastic*.

He stepped up next to her while they walked. "No, Dr. Rush. I've only taken one girl over a desk, and I've never done it again because I knew it couldn't be topped."

Marin's breath caught and she halted her step. "Donovan, you can't . . . say stuff like that."

He turned to her. "I know. But it's the truth. And if I can't say stuff like that then you can't look at me like you did while Eli and Laura were in here."

She straightened. "And how was that?"

"Like you wished it was us on that desk instead."

She closed her eyes, the words sending her back to their night together all those years ago. Was that how they'd looked? Like Eli and Laura had? She hadn't seen it from that angle back then of course. But her imagination could fill in the blanks. What Donovan must've looked like pumping into her, how wanton and wild they must've seemed. Things tumbling to the floor, bodies joining. She wet her lips and peered up at him.

He stepped closer.

"You're doing it again," he said softly. His gaze skated over her face, her neck, lower. Her body prickled with awareness, her blood pounding through her and desire blotting out everything else. She had no doubt he could read every bit of it on her. She was breathing too fast, and her nipples were hard against her bra. She wanted him to touch her. Needed him to. "Donovan . . ."

The word was a pained plea. He reached up as if to stroke her face but then quickly lowered his arm and stepped back, a grimace tugging at his features and his Adam's apple bobbing before he spoke. "We need to go. Group. Eli and Laura."

The words were jagged in the quiet and ripped right through the haze that had worked its way around Marin. She cleared her throat twice before she could trust herself to speak. "Right. Yes. We should go."

Part of her wished he'd meant go to her house, his bed, the damn janitorial closet down the hall. But instead he stepped out of her way and opened the door.

He wouldn't make a move.

He'd promised her that.

The ball was firmly in her court, spinning around and taunting her. She was supposed to tell him today that this wasn't going to happen. She *needed* to tell him. Losing her self-control like this was proof positive how dangerous this kind of arrangement would be. This man made her go stupid. Despite her best intentions, she'd almost begged Donovan to touch her right here in the office with clients down the hall and a group session about to start. Meanwhile, he could remain calm and detached—barely affected at all.

She needed to end this dance.

She would tell him. Later.

She walked past him, hoping he didn't see the way she wobbled on her feet. This was going to be the longest group ever.

19

This was the longest group ever. Donovan wondered if The Grove still stocked straitjackets because he was losing his fucking mind—slowly and painfully. Group had been going on for half an hour, and he'd barely registered a word of what anyone was saying. Marin was sitting across from him, legs crossed, posture attentive and professional, but all Donovan could think of was how close they'd come to screwing all this up in one ill-advised moment.

They were hitting a breaking point. He'd thought he was the only one. But the way Marin had looked at him. She'd begged for his touch with everything but words. And he'd known with every male instinct he possessed that if he'd put his hands on her, she would've been warm and wet and willing. Her desire had been a palpable thing rolling off her. She'd needed relief. She wanted it from him. And goddamn, did he want to give that to her.

When he'd caught her watching Eli and Laura, he'd only gotten a glimpse of her reaction. Her lips had been parted, her skin rosy, and her breath held. But it'd hit him like a swift punch to the gut.

Dr. Marin Rush had been in a trance seeing Eli fuck Laura fast and hard. And then Donovan had watched her face while the couple found their release. She'd held Donovan's gaze through the ecstatic cries and erotic sounds—a coil of electricity sparking between the two of them. And it'd taken everything he had not to get hard right there. He'd caught clients fooling around before. It didn't hit his sexual radar. It usually just pissed him off because it meant the treatment wasn't working. But being in the same room with Marin with the sounds and fog of sex around them—that had been almost too much to take.

He'd tried to play it off, to make light of the situation. But when Marin had stood in front of him, looking like she could go off at the barest touch, he'd wanted to shove her up against the door, slide his hand up her skirt, and alleviate that problem for her right that moment. He wanted his name on her lips.

It'd taken every damn ounce of his self-control to not say, *Fuck it all*, and give them both exactly what they'd wanted in that moment. But neither of them had been thinking straight and clients had been down the hall. If he touched her, regret would be hot on their heels. Regret and serious consequences. But he was starting to realize how right Ysa had been. This wasn't going to go away simply because they decided it should. They were trying, and it was only getting worse. It was making them reckless.

Something neither of them could afford to be.

He'd promised Marin that he wouldn't push her, and until today, she hadn't shown any sign of accepting the offer he'd made last week. At first he'd been relieved. He'd gotten a get-out-of-jail-free card after the lust-induced, ill-advised suggestion. But now—God, now he'd wished she'd said yes. He could deal with it fine if she wasn't into him. But how was he supposed to handle it when she looked at him like she was fucking starved for him, like he'd landed the starring role in every one of her filthy fantasies?

He'd never obsessed about women like this. A woman was either interested in what he had to offer or not, no big deal. But working with Marin and keeping things professional had become slow, sweet torture. Last night, he'd barely made it into the house before he was hard with thoughts of her and climbing into the shower to stroke his cock. It was like when he'd had to pen the fantasies for the study. The dirtiest, lewdest things badgered his mind, demanding he play out the scenarios in detail. Marin writhing beneath him. Marin spread across his desk. Marin shoved up against a wall, taking his cock, begging for release.

"What would you say is an unhealthy level of masturbation, Dr. West?"

Jane Swenson's question yanked him out of his spiraling thoughts, and he adjusted in his seat, his body becoming way too aware of the road his brain had been cruising down. "Um, I'd say that depends."

That depends was always a good answer when you hadn't been paying attention, though he felt like an asshole for letting his mind drift so much. He prided himself on giving his clients his undivided attention. He'd been an utter failure at that this week.

Jane frowned. "I feel like I've made a lot of progress. I haven't hooked up with anyone in two months, but I'm worried that I'm relying on self-help a little too much. I've been using my vibrator every night, sometimes in the morning, too."

Marin shot a look his way, like she somehow knew he hadn't been paying attention, and then focused on Jane. "Masturbation can be part of the sex addiction, but Dr. West is right. It depends on the level. You need to ask yourself if it's interfering in your daily life—getting in the way of obligations, putting anything at risk, if you're fixating on it."

Jane shrugged. "I don't think so. I mean, I don't think about it while I'm at work or anything. It's not like when I was cruising bars every night. The high for me was always the game of picking

up a guy, not so much the orgasm. I liked feeling desirable, powerful. Masturbation doesn't give me that."

"I jerk off every day. Always have." Dave, another group member, chimed in. "I don't think that's weird. I mean, yeah, if you're
rubbing yourself raw and blowing your salary on porn or something,
probably not good. But otherwise? Meh." He shrugged. "Plus, isn't
it like using a patch when you try to give up smoking? You've
dropped the random hookups. Going cold turkey with no other
outlet could set you up for failure, so maybe it's a bridge for you?"

"That's a great analogy," Donovan said, back up to speed with
the conversation. "It can be a great tool if you're doing it in a
healthy way. If you weren't relieving that tension, it could put you
in a more stressed state, one where you'd be more likely to relapse
and seek a hookup."

"Sex brain," Laura said, not looking up from picking at her
fingernail polish.

"Sex brain?" Marin asked.

Laura's attention drifted briefly to Eli, who hadn't said a word
since group had started. "Yeah, when you get so horny all you can
think about is screwing the nearest guy. It's like starving yourself
for days and then expecting to resist a buffet. You set yourself up
for a fall and make crappy decisions. Then you do something stupid,
and when you come down off that high, you realize you've messed
everything up again. Giving your vibrator a workout has got to be
better than that."

The words were clearly directed at Eli, but he just leaned back in
his chair, knees wide and expression bored. His lip curled in derision.
"A toy or your hand can't substitute for good sex. It's like drinking
diet soda when you want the real thing. I say, just drink the sugar."

"And you do that enough, you get diabetes and die," Laura said
darkly.

Eli snorted.

"My vibrator is way better than a lot of sex I've had," Karina, another group member, offered in an offhanded tone. "Hate to break it to you, boys, but you are very much replaceable."

"Okay," Donovan said, trying to refocus a conversation that was quickly getting off track. "Let's explore this in a different way. We're focusing a lot today on the physical pleasure of sex—which is an important component. But what hookups and masturbation lack is the intimacy you can find in a healthy relationship. The reason many of you are here is because you've leaned too far in the direction of the physical high of it. So how about we discuss some ways to start connecting with others without the physical component at the forefront?"

Different members of the group shared their opinions, and they ended up getting some good things discussed, but by the time the end of the hour was nearing, Donovan was exhausted and his shoulders tight with all the tension he was carrying.

He wrapped up things a few minutes earlier than he normally would have and let everyone file out while he stayed in his chair. He tried to focus on writing down some final notes, but Marin's presence had his gaze straying. After telling everyone good-bye, she walked around the circle of chairs, picking up coffee cups and soda cans that people had left behind. It was a simple thing, but something about the way her skirt swished with each step and the slow click of her heels against the floor was unbearably erotic. He'd like to see her in just those heels.

She caught him watching her. "Good group. Laura's clearly rethinking her behavior from earlier."

Donovan grunted an agreement, trying to reel in the dangerous thoughts. "And Eli is not. But at least he behaved himself in group."

"He did, mostly. And now I have a new term to add to my therapeutic repertoire." She tossed the trash in the bin. *Sex brain.*

"Yeah, that's a new one, but I think it resonated with the other members. We've all experienced that kind of thing at some point—jonesing for something to the point of bad decision-making. For a group fighting addiction, that can be a constant state. And unlike drug or alcohol addiction, lifelong abstinence from sex is not a reasonable goal."

She smirked as she gathered some extra handouts and set them on one of the chairs. "I can attest that it's survivable though."

"Is it?" The question slipped out before he could stop it.

She paused, her smirk falling away, and peered toward the door as if to double-check they were alone. "Donovan, about earlier . . ."

When she didn't continue, he leaned back and waited.

Her lips compressed like she was struggling to find the right words, but he didn't fill in the silence for her. When you filled in for people, you chased off the truth. He needed to hear her truth.

She sighed. "I guess I'm the one suffering from sex brain."

"Oh?" He tried to keep his tone neutral.

"Yes." She walked over to the door, shut it, and then flipped the lock for good measure. When she turned back to him, her arms were crossed and her expression grim. "I'm sorry about earlier. I was caught off guard with Laura and Eli, and after everything I've been exposed to since I've started working here, all the videos and research and just—I don't know. I guess I hit my limit, and it all spilled over. I lost my head for a second, and I—well, my reaction was inappropriate."

"Getting turned on because you saw two people fucking isn't inappropriate, Marin. It's normal."

She winced.

He should've apologized for using the crude term instead of the clinical one. But it was Friday, he was tired, and his ability to keep up propriety with Marin today was wearing thin. "So are we finally going to talk about this thing, then?"

"Thing?"

He braced his forearms on his thighs, keeping his focus on her. "Yeah. The glaring fact that we want each other. That earlier we almost risked both our jobs just to scratch that itch."

She looked away, her lips rolling inward.

"I know you feel it. It's been there since we kissed. Before that even. But I made you an offer and I'm assuming you're not going to take me up on it. So now we're left with this . . . thing. It's distracting us both and it's affecting our work."

"Right. That thing." She curled her fingers around the back of one of the chairs, looking just as weary as he felt. "It's definitely . . . distracting."

"Then why not do something about it?"

She wouldn't look at him.

"I told you I wouldn't pressure you and I won't. But if you're feeling like this, what's stopping you from taking me up on my offer?"

"To check off my list?"

"Yes," he said, maybe a little too emphatically. "To check off the list, to get some experience, to release all that tension you're carrying around. I can help, Marin."

"Right." She finally met his gaze, defiance there. "And that's exactly why I haven't said yes."

He stared at her in confusion. "What is?"

"I didn't take you up on the offer because I don't want to be your project, Donovan."

He frowned. "What are you talking about?"

She groaned and looked to the ceiling before stepping around the chair and sinking into it like her marionette strings had been cut. "I appreciate that you want to help. It's your nature. It's what you do—fix people's sexual problems. Believe me, I'm the practical one, so I see the logic in your offer. But the more I've thought about it, the more I've realized that's not what I want."

She peered at him like he was supposed to understand, but he stayed quiet, mulling over the words, trying to make sense of them.

"I've waited this long, you know? I don't want to sleep with someone because he's helping me check off a to-do list so that I'm better at my job. I don't want it to be a favor. I don't want it to be a training exercise. If I did, I'd just contract Lane for some sessions." She shook her head and stared off toward the window, her voice getting quieter. "I want it to be . . . I want it to be like Eli and Laura today."

"Like *Eli and Laura*?" He couldn't hide the incredulity from his voice.

"I mean, I know it was a bad idea for them, but at least it was real. Raw and dirty and desperate." She glanced his way, her voice fervent. "They were so into it, they couldn't bear to stop when we walked in. It was that intense. Primal, even. I want *that*. Not some sanitized, emotionless version where we check off boxes. Not some nice thing where we cover the basics like a goddamned instruction manual. I've spent years doing controlled experiments. I don't want my sex life to be one, too." She looked down at her lap, her jaw flexing, her fists curling. "And I definitely don't want to be someone's pity project."

A sound of disbelief slipped out of him, the words *raw* and *dirty* and *primal* still knocking around in his head and making bells clang. The word *emotion* scared the fuck out of him, but the others were loud enough to drown that out. "Are you being serious right now? You think I offered what I did because I'm some kind of martyr or that thorough of a mentor or that I fucking *pity* you?"

Her attention flicked upward, her gaze steely. "You sleep with people you think are safe."

"*What?*"

She swung her hand toward the door. "You and McCray hate each other. Yet, that's who you picked to sleep with."

He blinked. "What does that have to do with anything?"

"She was safe. No risk. And it may be for different reasons, but you see me the same way. We can check off a list nice and neat. Build up my sexual experience like a piece of freaking IKEA furniture. And on top of that, you can feel like you're helping me. You can walk away with a clean conscience, feeling like you did me a favor. Yay for Dr. West. Another client helped. Thanks but no thanks."

The words were like sharp little thorns burrowing into his skin. "Jesus, Rush. I don't see it as a fucking favor. I'm not *that* much of a dick. And no risk? Are you kidding me right now?"

She gave a petulant shrug.

He almost laughed. She had no idea! *No. Fucking. Idea.* How she affected him. No clue that the Donovan she'd seen these past two weeks was some alternate universe version of himself. A doppelgänger that showed up on time and laughed and joked and walked around with this *lightness* he didn't even recognize. *She didn't even know.* He stood and put his arms out to his sides. "I almost risked my goddamned job earlier. Like threw away years of building this whole thing for one chance to have you. One damn chance. And I fucking *like* you. Like think-you're-cool-as-shit *like* you. You're nothing but risk, Rush. You're like terror-threat-level risk."

His voice echoed in the room after he was done, but she'd gone still and silent.

He let out a breath and raked a hand through his hair, his seams unraveling. "Look, I've been honest with you. You know you deserve more than what I can offer. Relationships . . . aren't my thing. I've tried. I'm not that guy. So if that's what you're wanting, I'm sorry. I promise I will let you down. But I didn't suggest the list to make things clinical. I suggested it because I thought you'd feel safer knowing what to expect. You don't like going into sessions blind, so I figured you'd be the same when it came to this. But don't think for one second that it was motivated by anything other than the fact that I want you in my bed, that I would kill to be the one to show you those things on that list, and that I haven't been able to think about anything but getting my hands on you since you walked back into my life."

She was staring at him like she'd never seen him before, with this odd wonder. But she still didn't say a word, which sent him rambling on. Once he'd started, he couldn't seem to fucking stop.

"And we already know we have what Eli and Laura had in

spades. Do you really think we're capable of having mediocre, to-do list sex?" He took the chair next to her and spun it so he could sit down facing her. "We kissed last week and our clothes almost caught on fire. We've got chemistry, Rush. And if you think I'm doing this as a favor and that I don't crave exactly that kind of rawness that you're talking about, you haven't been paying attention. I'm happy to take things slow since you're new to so much. But that doesn't mean I don't think about hauling you up against a wall, hiking your skirt up, and fucking you like I own you. I think about it. I think about it. All. The. Fucking. Time."

Her neck had gone rosy red while he was talking, the flush creeping up, her breath quickening. He'd seen her reactions enough to know this time it wasn't embarrassment. She was picturing what he'd said, she was imagining him taking her. Knowing that settled something inside of him, put him back on a playing field he felt more comfortable on instead of feeling stripped down to the studs there in front of her.

He lowered his voice. "So you need to tell me what you want. Do you want to do this or do you want me to leave you alone?"

Her throat worked as she swallowed, but she didn't look away. For a moment, he thought she wasn't going to answer at all, that she was just going to get up and walk out. Leave him hanging again. But finally she said, "I think about it all the time, too. I can't *stop* thinking about it."

The air he'd puffed up with during his declarations sagged out of him in a long exhalation. Thank God. *Thank. God.*

He couldn't stop himself after that. He spread his knees and pulled her legs in between his, her chair dragging loudly against the floor, and then he kissed her. Kissed her like he'd been wanting to since that day in the office, carding his hands through that silky hair and holding her right where he wanted her, drinking from her, all that desire, all that frustration pouring into the connection.

She whimpered into his mouth, a pleading, unraveled sound,

and all he could think of was getting her onto his lap, of her strad-dling him, of tugging away these clothes and getting her to make more of those noises. He wanted to find every thread lacing her up and undo her until she was all feeling and response and sweet need. Until she was his. He gripped her skull, fighting off that blinding need to take more, to take it too far, to take it all. But his body was responding and his heart was pounding and the taste of her on his tongue was driving him over the edge.

His mind playing one message over and over in his head. *This. Yes. This.*

But just when he was about to lose all semblance of his control, she planted her palms against his chest and eased him back. "Don-ovan, wait—"

She was breathless, her nipples pressing hard against her shirt and her lips puffy, but her eyes were focused. That potent hazel stare broke through some of the insanity coursing through him, that single-minded instinct to claim her. He took in a breath and nodded. "Right. We're at work."

She rubbed her lips together. "And I haven't said yes yet."

His heart fell into his shoes. "What?"

"I have conditions."

Relief flashed through him. Okay. Conditions. He could deal with conditions. Conditions weren't a no. "All right."

"I'm going to give you an out," she said simply.

He frowned, the words like a straight pin to his balloon of relief. "What?"

"Thirty days." She shifted against him and her pulse beat fran-tically at her throat, but there was resolve in her voice. "I want to do this, but in thirty days, I will walk away from this and so will you. You've already got your exit strategy in place."

"An exit strategy? I don't need—"

She pressed her fingers to his lips, hushing him. "Listen to me. You already know how this will end. I'm telling you that you've got a guaranteed out. We won't let this get messy. But since I'm giving you that, if we do this, I need you to leave the other stuff behind, those things that keep this neat for you. I deserve more than neat and so do you." Her fingers twitched against his lips but her gaze didn't falter. "I want the Donovan I knew in college, the one who operated on gut and didn't orchestrate everything to make it fit into a certain schematic. The one who showed me that passion isn't just a word in books. And the one who wasn't afraid of being human in front of me. I know he's still there. I see him sometimes. I saw him just now."

The words pinged through him, setting off a cut-and-run reaction. She knew more than he thought, saw more. Right through him, in fact. She wanted *him*. Not the doctor or the trainer or the mythical Orgasm Whisperer. She wanted Donovan West, the geeky kid who lost his parents, wore Freud T-shirts, and used to sleep in a tiny office because he had nightmares about the boogeyman. He didn't know if he was capable of that anymore. He'd been so fucking vulnerable back then. That kid had shored up his life with duct tape and a coat of paint, thought he was managing in the rough winds, and then Mari had set him all off kilter. She was doing it again. This was the girl he remembered. The one who had pushed every one of his buttons, gotten him to talk about things he never had, given him her virginity, and then walked off like a boss. Bold bravery wrapped in a quiet, steel-lined package.

His heart beat loud in his ears as she lowered her hand from his mouth. He drew his tongue over his lips, tasting the salt from her fingertips there.

She leaned back. "Say something."

He didn't know what to say, but honesty won the fight. "I'm not sure I know how to do that anymore. Be that."

Her lips curved into a half-smile. "Then maybe we can both teach each other a thing or two."

A breath coasted out of him. He wanted her more than he could bear. His entire body thrummed with that need. But if she thought she could fix him somehow, put together what was broken, she was only going to be disappointed. His pieces weren't just in a pile on the floor. Many had been lost completely. Even if reassembled, the holes would forever be there. "I'm not going to change, Marin."

Her smile softened. "Not asking you to. Just asking that you be you, not the guy everyone thinks you are, not the guy you were for McCray."

He stared at her, marveling at this woman. Marin was young and inexperienced. And she blushed and got flustered when it came to sex. But hell if she wasn't tougher than any woman he'd ever met. She wasn't afraid to ask for what she wanted—no, she didn't ask, she required. There was a price to be with her and she wasn't going to negotiate.

It was dangerous.

And so fucking sexy—like made-him-hard-just-thinking-about-it sexy—that he found a single word slipping from his lips. "Okay."

Her brows went up. "Yeah?"

He leaned forward and slid his hand along the back of her neck. "Yeah. This is uncharted territory for me, but I want you, Rush. And I'm willing to try it your way."

"Says the man who likes control."

His lip curled. "I never said I was giving that up."

She smoothed her hands over her skirt, the slightest tremble visible, proving that she wasn't quite as steady as she sounded. "I'm okay with that. I know I'm inexperienced, but that doesn't mean I don't remember the recordings. I know your dirty secrets, West."

He wanted to touch her so badly. He could just move his hands up and he'd be at her thighs. He could part her legs and see if this conversation was affecting her as much as it was affecting him, get on his knees and taste her, but he settled for moving his hands to the outside of her knees, rubbing the soft skin there. "You think so, huh?"

"Yeah. I do." She put her hands over his, linking their fingers, and staring down at the connection. "Because I'll let you in on my secret. They're some of mine, too."

"What?"

She wouldn't look up, as if eye contact would be too much. "I kept those recordings. I kept them and I listened to them so much in the year following that I could probably recite them by heart. It was my escape. I wanted to wish them into existence. Sometimes I still do."

His breath zipped out of him, fire lighting his blood. "You want the stuff on the recordings?"

Desire rumbled up through him like a threatening storm, wide and dark and fast-moving. This was so much more than he'd originally imagined with her. He'd thought he could go through Marin's list with her, teach her things, enjoy the basics with her. He liked all kinds of flavors of sex. Simple and sexy with Marin would've been fantastic. But what she was asking for was like offering him his personal heroin with a side of *hell yeah*. She wanted to play the games. She wanted to step into those shadowed places where the rules and niceties went lax.

"You sure know how to knock a man on his ass. That's . . ."

"I mean, unless you've already gone there with . . . other women and that's not exciting for you anymore." Her voice was hesitant for the first time in a while.

He hated that she even had to think of it. Hated that his relationship with Elle had been tossed in her face or that she had to think about other women at all. He took her hand and guided it up his thigh until they reached his very obvious erection. She sucked in a breath.

"This is how non-exciting I find it."

Her eyes widened, and her fingers curled around him. Her warm grip was like fucking heaven even through his slacks. She slid her hand along his length, tentatively mapping him.

He closed his eyes and breathed through the surge of arousal. He fitted his hand against hers when she moved to stroke him again.

After the restraint required over the last two weeks, he didn't trust himself not to go off like a teenager. He lifted her hand to his mouth and pressed a kiss to her knuckles as he met her gaze. "I'm sorry that the Elle thing is here between us, that you have to think about that at all. But hear this. Whatever happens between you and me is not a repeat of that or a substitution or a consolation prize. There's no reason to compare the two situations. They're completely different. I don't hate Elle. But we weren't friends and won't be. We're two workaholics who served a basic need for each other. We didn't have long chats. We didn't hang out. We didn't even hug good-bye."

She looked down at their linked hands. "You don't have to explain yourself. Your past relationships are your business."

"I'm telling you because I need you to know that nothing about you is going to be been-there-done-that for me." He brushed his thumb over the top of her hand. "You make everything new. Have from the start."

She looked up at that.

It was a thought he normally wouldn't have shared. It cut a little too close. But he'd promised her he'd be honest, so he fought past the filters he usually kept in place. "You cut me off at the knees with a kiss. I can't even imagine how hot exploring fantasies with you will be."

The slow smile she gave him was like sunlight breaking through clouds, sending a strange, pleasant warmth moving through him— one that had nothing to do with the iron state of his dick. He liked that he'd put that smile there on her face. He wanted to kiss it off of her. "What are you so pleased about, Rush?"

She leaned forward, smile still in place, and tapped his cheek. "Now look who's blushing."

He straightened. "What? I am definitely not. I don't blush."

Her grin went wide and she slipped her hand from his. "Shall I grab my phone to document this rare occasion?"

He grabbed her wrist before she could reach for the phone she'd left sitting two chairs away. "Don't you dare."

Her gaze sparked at his grip, sexy challenge there.

That's when he knew there was no going back. This was going to happen. Marin wanted him in her bed—to teach, to explore, to show her things she'd only fantasized about. She wanted raw, gritty sex. And she wanted to do it with him. Holy fucking gift from above.

He didn't deserve the luck or that level of trust from her, but he was damn sure going to figure out how to be worthy of it. He let his gaze drift over her. Despite her bold gaze, she was holding her breath. He liked that. No. *Loved* that. Knowing he could affect her, knowing he could turn her on with a simple touch. It wasn't practiced or put on. It was honest and real.

He pulled her closer and let the fingertips of his other hand slide over the nape of her neck. Usually he gravitated toward women with long hair, but Marin's wispy cut had drawn his eye from the moment he'd seen her in the parking lot. He'd since pictured running his tongue along her bared neck and gripping the silky, dark hairs in his fist when she was on her knees for him. He drew a circle with his fingertip on her nape, earning him a shiver. "So we're doing this?"

"Looks like it."

He kept making those circles on her neck, enjoying the way her pupils grew wider, darkened. "Are you making a sex brain decision, Dr. Rush?"

She smoothed her lip gloss. "Probably. I'm not sure how to tell anymore."

He stared down at her. "There's one way to find out."

Her brow wrinkled.

He bent forward, closed his eyes, and brushed his lips against her ear.

"I watch you across the room," he said, sliding into the tone he used to use for the recordings.

She made a noise in the back of her throat.

He loved that sound. Wanted to hear it again. Wanted to imagine her making it when she'd listened to his recordings in the dark of her bedroom. How many times had she touched herself with his voice in her ear, his dark fantasies in her head? The thought pushed so many of his buttons, he lost count.

He hadn't done recordings in ages. The ones that had gotten published were decidedly milder than the versions from college. More vanilla. More commercial. Not him. And he'd never used that style of dirty talk or the scripts in real life. Women had asked. He'd hated when they'd asked—felt like a hired monkey being asked to perform.

But now the words rolled off his lips as if they'd just needed his muse there with him to conjure them. "You're paying attention to the group, but you keep crossing and uncrossing your legs, making me wonder if you're still thinking about what you saw in your office. If you're slippery and hot beneath this neat little skirt, imagining people fucking, imagining being the one getting fucked, imagining people watching you take it. If you're wishing you could get some relief." He pressed a kiss to the spot behind her ear and whispered, "If you want me to be the one to give it to you."

Her breath was a gust of air against his hair. "Shit."

He massaged her neck and pressed his nose to her hair. "Are you wet, Marin?"

He could sense her tense, hesitate, but then her muscles softened beneath his fingertips. "Why are you asking questions you already know the answer to?"

It took everything he had not to drag her to his office, take her right there. But he forced himself to lean back, to look at her. To see the naked lust on her face and not let himself off the leash.

"If we're going to do this, I want to know you're choosing it with a clear head. I don't want to be your Eli." He let his hand slip away from her. "So go home, use one of those toys you're researching. Give yourself that relief. And then if you're still feeling the way you do now, if you still want to do this, meet me at my place at seven tonight. I'll make some dinner and we can . . . hang out."

"Hang out?" she asked, her voice strained, like it was taking everything she had to focus on the conversation. "Is that what the kids are calling it these days?"

"Yes. We'll eat, talk. We don't have to force this. Put us in the same room, and I think we'll be all right."

"You don't hang out with the women you sleep with."

She said it like a statement of fact. He hadn't told her that explicitly. But she said it like she could read the truth about him as easy as picking up a book. And she was right. This was uncharted territory for him. He hadn't had a "date" since he'd broken his engagement. He had roller-coaster stomach just thinking about it. "I hang out with you every day, Rush. I think I can handle it."

"Right. Okay." She scooted her chair back, like she needed to break that touch between them, but he helped her get to her feet before standing up with her. She smoothed her skirt and seemed to regain some of her calm. "You don't have to feed me. I can come over later."

He frowned, not liking that she was setting such a low bar for him already. He reached out and tipped her chin up. "Let's get something straight, Rush. I've agreed to your terms, but here are mine. If you come over, you're putting yourself in my hands. That's the deal. And I will feed you if I want and taste you how I like and make you come in more ways than you can think of before this is all over with. So just be on time, bring your appetite, and I'll worry about the rest, all right?"

The whoosh of her breath was all he needed. He pressed a quick kiss to her mouth and released her. "See you later, Dr. Rush."

He walked out first, ignoring his throbbing erection and his pinging nerves, leaving her standing there in the group room alone.

He had to force himself not to look back.

To not think too hard about the deal he'd just made.

Marin would be in his bed tonight. That's all that mattered. He'd figure out the rest later.

20

Marin was so distracted when she walked into the house after work that she managed to drop the mail, her work file, and her keys before she'd made it into the kitchen. Everything felt off balance, skewed. Like there were no straight lines to count on anymore. She didn't know where the next step would lead. Maybe to someplace amazing. Maybe off a damn cliff. But right now, it was going to lead her right upstairs to put out the fire Donovan had stoked when he'd whispered in her ear with those words, that voice. Her blood was still pumping so hard, it felt like it was going to burst right out of her skin.

"Hey. Need some help?" Nate asked.

Hearing her brother's voice was like a harsh record scratch scraping through her brain. She'd been lost in thinking about Donovan, and Nate's voice ringing through that was like a bucket of ice over her head, making her feel like she'd been caught—like he could tell she'd been thinking about hot kisses and spread thighs.

She fought to find her voice, to keep it even.

"No, I've got it. I thought you'd already left for work. I didn't see your bike." Marin dropped the precariously balanced pile of crap onto the counter and looked up to find Nathan at the table with a pink-haired girl. "Oh, sorry, didn't realize you had company."

Great. Even better. Now she wouldn't be able to escape.

"I parked the bike out back. You okay? You're all red."

Fuck her fair skin. Fuck it and all the ancestors who passed this affliction along. "I'm fine. It's gotten pretty warm outside."

"Oh." Nate jabbed a thumb the girl's way. "This is Blaine. She volunteers in the kids' wing a few days a week. She saw me painting out by the pond and wanted to check out some of my stuff. She's an artist, too—makes jewelry."

Blaine gave a little wave and a smile. "Hiya."

"Blaine, this is my sister, Marin. Or Dr. Rush, I guess, if you see her at work."

Marin's mind was going in ten different directions, and she had the instinct to say, *Blaine? Her name is Blaine?* But she knew the movie quote from *Pretty in Pink* would be lost on these two. "Nice to meet you."

"I don't have to be in until late tonight," Nate said. "Blaine was going to hang out for a while. Are you cooking?"

"Uh . . ." Originally, Marin had planned on fixing pasta tonight, but now she had other things that were more urgent. And a date. Well, no, not a date. Sex. She had sex planned. Sex with Donovan West. *Oh, God.* Or maybe she didn't. She really had no idea how much or how little would happen tonight. She'd thought she'd gotten control of the situation, and then Donovan had shot all that to hell. He'd wrested back the steering wheel with smooth grace and dirty words, taking control over her body and the plan. But either way, she had no idea what to tell Nate. They hadn't gone down this road before.

"Earth to Mar," he said. "You sure you're okay?"

"Um, oh yeah, sorry. There are pizza coupons somewhere in this stack of mail. I'll leave you money, and y'all can order what you want. I . . . I'm going out tonight."

There, that was vague enough.

Nate's eyebrows crept up. "You're going out? Like *out*?"

Marin brushed her bangs out of her eyes. "Yes. Alert the media. Woman goes somewhere other than home or work."

Blaine smiled Nathan's way. "Pizza sounds great. Thanks, Dr. Rush."

But Nate didn't seem to hear her. He was still staring at Marin like she'd announced she was venturing to Mars for the evening. "Is it with a guy?"

Marin rifled through the mail and found the sheet of pizza coupons, pretending not to hear Nate's question. She tugged them out of the stack and set them on the table in front of him. "I've heard this place is good. Local joint. Good prices."

"Ohmigod, their pizza is the best," Blaine said. "They have a seafood pizza with this white sauce that is uh-mazing."

Marin appreciated the girl's attempt at getting Nate out of interrogator mode. Nate was still giving Marin a weird look but didn't ask his question again. "Yeah, thanks. Pizza works."

"Great." Marin left them to it, not wanting to field any more looks from Nate, and went upstairs. Five minutes into her shower, she had her head tipped back against the wall and her body coasting down from the almost instantaneous orgasm. She hadn't needed a toy. Her fingers and Donovan's words replaying in her head had been enough. And though she'd been taken aback that he'd instructed her to do it, this had been a good idea. She was so keyed up that she wouldn't have been able to function tonight. But the quick release was like eating an appetizer when you really wanted a seven-course meal. It curbed the immediate need but in the long run, it'd only made her hungrier.

But as her body came down from the high and she washed her hair, reality started to settle in. Doubts hot on its heels. Her sex brain had cleared, and now she was forced to look at this rationally. She was fooling around with a co-worker. She was about to start a sexual relationship with him—albeit a temporary one. Things could go so very wrong. They could get caught. They could create issues in their working relationship. She could . . . get attached.

No. She rinsed her hair, climbed out of the shower, and toweled off. She was not going to worry about that last one. She'd asked for him to be himself with her, and she was going to grant him the same. Getting a little attached was probably going to be part of the deal for her. That's how she was wired. So what. She'd had feelings for him the last time and had survived walking away. What had made it so intense and real was that she hadn't locked that down. If she wanted to shut off emotion from this, she could've taken his offer of doing the list and let him be Mr. Smooth Playboy with her. That held no appeal.

This would end in a month. She'd set that up. But she wasn't going to focus on the end. You don't go on vacation only to fixate on what it's going to be like when you return to work. You open up and enjoy every moment while you're there.

She'd waited a long time and was damn well going to enjoy this. She wasn't looking for love or a serious relationship. She wanted her feet solidly under her, Nate off to school, and a long-term job before she could even think about looking to date someone in that capacity. Plus, love is what had always gotten her mother in trouble. Men had been the most effective way to derail her mom. Things would be going okay, and then her mom would fall for some guy and lose sight of everything else. It'd be great for a while and then the dude would leave or cheat or some drama, and her mother would completely fall apart. Her mom always bet on forever. The manic side of her full of unchecked hope. Each guy was going to be the answer—The One. Until he wasn't.

Maybe Donovan had been right about the danger of that concept after all. Her mom pinned her hopes on The One and then crashed when it didn't come to fruition. Each time was a fresh tragedy. That's what her mom had been going through before she'd killed herself. She'd snapped over some guy. Some random guy who Marin had never even met.

The thought of losing herself like that over anyone scared the shit out of her. She could see how it could happen. That rush she got today with Donovan was potent—a drug mainlined right into her system. But you can't tie your ship to another floating thing. It could sink and take you down with it. She didn't need that. Wouldn't risk it. But being with someone she enjoyed spending time with, someone who could be a lover and a friend? That was damn appealing. She could share the ocean with him without throwing down anchor.

Her phone buzzed against the bathroom counter as she was finishing up. She grabbed it and wiped steam from the screen, finding a text from Donovan.

Donovan: Take the walking path along the trees instead of the main road. House with black shutters is mine. Knock on the back door. Secret code word will be sent in invisible ink. This text will self-destruct in 5, 4 . . .

She smiled, relieved that he wasn't taking this too seriously, and her thumbs moved over the screen.

Marin: What? No ladder to your window? My Joey is very disappointed in your Dawson.

Donovan: There is also no creek or potential love triangle. #DawsonFail.

Marin: Not sure if I'm impressed or scared that you caught that random pop culture reference.

Donovan: I was in HS when that show was big. What's your excuse?

Marin: Caught a marathon when I had the flu a few yrs ago. Promptly became obsessed.

Donovan: As you do. #TeamPacey

She laughed, the ridiculous exchange easing some of her nerves.

Marin: I was wrong. You are a dork. Need me to bring anything?

Donovan: Spiked heels, head-to-toe vinyl, and a vat of Crisco.

She blinked, and her phone buzzed again.

Donovan: For me, of course. I look great in vinyl and my shoe size is 13.

She snorted and caught her reflection in the mirror, surprised at the bright-eyed, smiling woman looking back at her. This is what Donovan used to do to her—make her forget anything but the moment. That guy was still in there. He was giving her a peek.

Marin: Don't mess with me, doc. That's not playing fair.

Donovan: Who said I played fair?

That sent a little hum through her.

Donovan: Just bring you. That's all I need.

The words were simple, but they had her heart picking up speed. This was going to happen. She and her near-virgin self were going to step into this world with Donovan. That got her nerves working again. And, of course, she couldn't do things halfway. No, she'd been the dumbass who'd been all, *Oh, no, we don't have to go slow and work our way through the basics. We can just go straight to kinky sexy times. Yeah, no problem.* That shit had definitely been her sex brain talking. She wanted those things—in her head at least. But now that the possibilities were staring her in the face, she worried she'd stepped out of the plane without a parachute. Out of her depth didn't even begin to describe it.

But she took a deep, calming breath, reminding herself that she could always say no, that Donovan would respect that, and then she texted that she'd be there on time. But she barely managed to get her makeup on without her hands shaking.

By the time she was knocking on Donovan's back door, her stomach was in knots and she was thanking the universe for the inventors of antiperspirant. She also was working hard to not blush every time she thought about what might happen between them. Despite her rampaging libido, her body's automatic reaction to thinking about all things sexual was still plaguing her.

But when Donovan swung open the door, greeting her with an easy smile and wearing jeans, a soft-looking gray T-shirt, and nothing on his feet, she could feel the heat rising in her already. Sometimes she could trick her mind into seeing him as "just Donovan"—her co-worker, a guy she knew from college, a man she was learning from. But at times like these, it was impossible to ignore the sheer impact of him. The beauty. The maleness. Strong shoulders and lean body, dark blue eyes that saw right into you, and a smile that made things twist inside her. He even had nice-looking feet. Who had that?

"Come on in," he said, pushing the door wide. The smell of oregano and garlic wafted out. "I was just about to grab the pizza out of the oven."

She stepped inside the yummy-smelling kitchen, trying to will down the visceral reaction she'd had to seeing him like this— casually dressed in his own place. She'd never seen him in any setting other than a work one. She tried to focus on the surroundings, anything but the tall sexy doctor next to her. Donovan's place was similar to hers, but had only one story and had been styled with a more modern vibe. More a bachelor feel than cozy cottage. "Smells great in here. Did you order from Gio's? Nate's going to try their pizza tonight."

"Nope. I made my own. Well, I cheated a little. Gio's sells their dough. So I keep some in the freezer. My mom used to make home-made pizza on Friday nights, so I've stuck with the tradition." He hitched a thumb toward the counter. "Want something to drink? I have soda, bottled water, and merlot."

Marin leaned against the counter, warmed by the fact that Donovan had held on to his mom's tradition even when most Friday nights he was probably cooking only for himself. It gave Marin a pang for her own mother. Her mom had been a mess much of the time, but there'd been good times mixed in, times when the three of them had piled onto the couch, eating junk and watching movies, laughing together. Her mom could've been amazing. If she'd had time and money to see the right doctors, find the right medication balance, get the right help. If Marin had been there to stop her that night and put her in a hospital. Marin swallowed past the jolt of grief. "Uh, wine's good."

Donovan frowned as he pulled a bubbling pizza from the oven and set the pan on the stove. "Hey, you okay?"

"Huh? Oh yeah, fine."

"You went somewhere for a second." He tugged off his oven mitt and uncorked the bottle of wine.

"I was just thinking that it's nice that you hold on to some family traditions. I didn't have a lot of those growing up. I've tried to create some with Nate, but it's easy to get too busy and forget about those things."

He handed her a half-full glass. "You raised a kid while you were a kid. I think you get a pass if some minor details got dropped in that kind of juggling act. And I bet you have more traditions than you think. Your brother would probably be able to name a bunch you don't even realize. I remember my dad used to wash his car on Sunday mornings. He'd let me scrub the tires. To me, it was this really cool one-on-one time I'd get with him. But he would've never labeled it a thing. You don't know what's going to imprint on a kid."

She took a sip of the wine. "No, I guess not. Your parents sound like they were pretty great, though. I'm sorry you lost them."

He stepped over to the stove and turned his back to her. He grabbed a pizza cutter and ran it through the pie, his shoulders stiff. "I guess I should be thankful I had them at all. I know many aren't that lucky. It was just hard to accept that two people could be wiped out of existence that easily. Parents seem like this permanent fixture when you're young. But obviously, nothing's permanent. Anything and anyone can disappear at any time."

She frowned. It was a fatalistic way to look at the world even if it was technically true. But she wasn't going to call him out on it. She'd lost a parent, too. She knew how fragile life was. "Did they ever catch the person who did it?"

He put two slices on each plate. "No. The case went cold years ago. I have a private investigator working on it now. The cops tell me I'm wasting my money, but I have to at least try, you know?"

"Of course."

He turned back to her, two plates in hand, and smirked. "So, ready to sample my mad cooking skills and talk about something way less depressing?"

"Definitely. We're not breaking any shrink stereotypes, are we? I'm here five minutes, and we're talking about our childhood tragedies."

He cocked his head toward the small round table in the attached dining nook and she followed him over to it. He sat the plates down and pulled out a chair for her. "I think you're just trying to distract me from the topic we're really supposed to be talking about. Nothing can ruin a sexy mood like dead parents."

She sniffed at his tongue-and-cheek tone. "I'm not avoiding anything."

"Uh-huh." He slid into the spot next to her and opened a bottle of water.

She eyed his drink. "So I drink alone?"

He glanced at the bottle of wine. "I have a feeling you're going to keep me on my toes. I need all my faculties operating at peak levels."

She laughed. "But it's okay if mine aren't?"

"You get one glass of wine because I know you're nervous."

"I am not."

He lifted a brow.

"Okay, fine, a little." She picked up her pizza and took a bite so she didn't have to say any more. It was loaded with veggies, and the sauce had a bit of heat to it. A garbled sound of pleasure slipped out.

He smiled. "You like? I didn't put any meat on it because I didn't know if you were vegetarian or not."

She shook her head and swallowed her bite. "I'm not, but this is fantastic. What's spicy?"

"A shot of Crystal hot sauce. The locals are wearing off on me."

"He shrinks heads *and* cooks, ladies and gentlemen. A man of many talents."

He licked a dollop of sauce off his thumb. "I have a very limited menu with the cooking so don't set those expectations too high. On most days, it's just takeout and sitting in front of the TV, working."

"No play for you?" She had to bite back the cringe when she realized he'd probably been going to Dr. McCray for playtime. But if he thought of that, it didn't show on his face.

"I don't go out all that much. I have a few friends in the city and there are a few people at work who don't think I'm an asshole. But generally, I keep things pretty simple."

"Yeah, what's up with the reputation at work?" she asked. "You pissing in people's Cheerios when I'm not looking? I don't get the aversion to you."

He shrugged. "When I started here, I was in a really shitty place. I wasn't looking to make friends. I wanted to get the X-wing up and running, and I wanted things done a certain way. I pretty much shut anything and anyone else down if it didn't have a direct effect on that goal. So the reputation is well-earned. I've calmed down some since then, now that things are running more smoothly and settled down. But I'm still never going to be the guy heading up the company softball team or going to the after-work mixers. I'm still not here to make friends."

She swallowed her bite and swiped her mouth with a napkin. "What's wrong with friends?"

"Nothing, I guess. But I had a time in my life where it was all about socializing and parties and being seen and who you knew and filling life with all this bullshit stuff. I thought it was good medicine after what I'd been through. But it was just meaningless fluff. Background noise. Nobody was really friends. Not the kind who'd have your back or stand up for you. It was window dressing. I have no desire to have that kind of existence again."

"That was when you were in L.A., right?" She took a sip of wine. "The celebrity fiancée and all that?"

He tilted his head in question. "You know about that?"

She held up her thumb and index finger, indicating a smidge of something. "I may have looked you up once or twice after you graduated to see how things turned out."

"Oh? And what did you think of what you found?"

"Honestly?"

"Give it to me, Rush."

"I didn't recognize that guy. You seemed . . . fake and pretentious and smarmy. I read one interview and couldn't match it up with the guy I'd met. I just figured money had changed you."

He picked a topping off his pizza, thoughtful. "Yeah, well, it wasn't the money. I'd already had a good bit of that from my parents. But fame was its own kind of numbing drug. It was easy to get lost in the glare and just play the role that people expected of me. I didn't have to think too much about anything. Things moved too fast for that. At the time, that seemed like a fucking miracle, to be someone else. But like any drug, it was just killing me quietly."

She heard the wariness hiding behind the bitter tone. "What happened?"

He set down his pizza, something in his expression going shuttered. "The whole thing had been going downhill already but then I caught Selena cheating. Everything kind of went to hell after that. I was . . . not in a good place. Eventually, it was Dr. Paxton who got my head out of my ass. He flew out to meet me and basically told me I was acting like a fucking idiot and wasting my education, my research, and my life."

Marin sensed he'd glossed over something. Tension was there in the set of his shoulders, but she wasn't going to push. "No way Pax said 'fucking.'"

"Oh, I promise he did. He was *pissed*. He made me feel like a dumb shit. But it was what I needed to hear. I *was* acting like an idiot. He strong-armed me into getting my shit together and taking an interview here. I haven't looked back."

"Wow." Marin shook her head. "Guess this is where Pax sends his problem students."

He smiled. "Let's pretend it's where he sends his favorites."

"So, you're happy here?"

He glanced toward the dark window then took a sip of his water, something uneasy filling the silence. "I love what I do here. The job challenges me, and I feel like I'm doing what I'm supposed to be doing. I'd like to work on some research, too, but until I get a director position, there won't be any time for that."

He hadn't answered her question, not exactly, but she let it slide. They ate in silence for a few minutes, letting conversations of the past drift away in their rearview mirrors. The wine started to take effect for Marin—nothing dramatic but a softening of the sharp-edged nerves from earlier. The muscles in her neck and shoulders began to unwind.

"I think I could be happy here once I get more comfortable with everything. The clients definitely will keep me on my toes. I like knowing that each person is a new riddle to figure out." She wiped her hands on her napkin. "And the training is turning out to be very . . . interesting."

Donovan looked her way, amusement lighting some of the darkness that had entered his eyes earlier. He reached out and took a sip from her wineglass. "Yeah? What have you learned so far, Dr. Rush?"

"Well, I've learned that there are sex toys I would've never fathomed existed. And that there are still sexual surrogates. That blushing is a plague upon my house. Oh, and that there is chocolate-flavored lubricant—which I'm still trying to figure out."

Donovan choked a little on the wine and then laughed and set her glass down. "What exactly is there to figure out?"

She gave him a *well-duh* look. "Why the hell would anyone want it to be chocolate flavored?"

He pressed his lips together like he was trying to contain a laugh but mirth danced in his eyes anyway. "You really need to ask? Some people don't like the tastes associated with oral sex."

"Is it that bad?"

"Which side?"

"I'm assuming you've only sampled one side of that equation."

His lips curved, a pirate smile. "Not entirely true. I've never given a guy a blow job, no, but I know what I taste like. I suspect you know what you taste like, too."

The heat that rushed through her hit her face in an instant. Her cheeks burned like she'd been slapped.

"There's the patented Marin blush."

She groaned. "Shut up."

He shifted toward her, his gaze holding hers. "Take off your panties, Marin."

She stilled. "What?"

He got up from his chair and grabbed hers, turning it away from the table. "Your nerves are going to get the best of you if we take things too slow. You can always say no, but I'm asking you to trust me. Do you trust me?"

"Yes." The word popped up automatically.

But before she could say anything else, he lowered himself to his knees in front of her and his lips met hers in a slow, teasing kiss. One that made things melt. One that made the tension in her body unfurl. She gave into it. And as his tongue stroked along hers, he pushed her dress along her thighs in a slow glide, exposing her bare legs. Her heart picked up speed, her stomach tensing. But she didn't stop him. Wouldn't.

He hooked his fingers in the sides of her underwear and broke away from the kiss, his gaze colliding with hers. "I said, take them off."

"Oh." So they were doing this. Now. She tried not to have a panic attack.

Just listen. Let him guide you. This is Donovan. The words whispered through her head, calming some of the nerves. She lifted her hips when he tugged, and she let him slide her underwear down. Shivers chased the fabric down her legs as he dragged them all the way to her feet. He tossed the panties aside and put his hands on her knees.

"Open for me, Marin. I want to see you."

She forgot how to swallow for a moment and couldn't speak, but she didn't offer any resistance when he applied pressure and opened her like a book, a secret book she'd never let anyone else but him read. Self-consciousness swamped her.

But the full, slow inhale he gave at the sight of her spread wide for him sent a rush of hot warmth flooding her. He stared at her bared sex with hungry eyes and drew a fingertip over her crease, earning a soft curse from her.

"So fucking gorgeous." His voice was like water over rough rocks. "You should see how wet and ready you are from just sitting here talking about this."

She closed her eyes, trying to pull in a breath. She felt exposed, vulnerable as all get out, but the earth would've had to shake beneath her to get her to move.

He dipped a gentle finger into her, her body protesting the sudden invasion at first and then another wave of arousal rushing forward and easing the way. Her hands reached out to grip his shoulders, nails digging in. The slippery evidence of how easily she'd gotten turned on made her blush harder.

"How do you think you taste?" His voice was a hypnotic song as he slid his finger from inside her, and then swiped a wet fingertip over her lips. She gasped and he breached her mouth with his finger. The distinct taste of her arousal hit her tongue.

She jolted at the invasion and her eyes popped open, but when she saw the naked desire in his expression, she settled almost instantly. It wasn't the first time she'd tasted herself. They both knew it. They were both scientists at heart. Curiosity their drug. But somehow his looking at her like that made the embarrassment of that fall away like an unneeded layer of skin. Shameless. He challenged her to be shameless. It's how she wanted to be.

He smiled, tugged his finger from her mouth, and then leaned forward and dragged the tip of his tongue over her lips, tasting what he'd painted there. He made a pleased sound and sucked her bottom lip into his mouth, licking it clean. He released her with a slow drag of his teeth over her lip. "I think you taste fucking amazing."

She was breathless. Like she'd just sprinted somewhere. She had to force a response out. "Yeah?"

"Yeah. I need more. Come 'ere."

He got to his feet and put a hand out. She stood, her knees a little weak and the rest of her dinner forgotten. He grabbed the back of her neck and planted a solid kiss on her mouth—like he hadn't planned to do that but couldn't resist. Then he walked her back against the counter. Before she realized what he was doing, he gripped her waist and lifted her onto the kitchen island. He slid the bottle of wine to the side.

"Lie back."

"Why?"

He smiled slow, wholly wicked. "I'm going to have you for dessert."

"Donovan . . ." She didn't know what she was saying. Yes. No. All of her senses were firing at once.

He pressed his finger against her lips. "Let the worries go. I've got you, Rush. All I want is to make you feel good. Tell me if you want something to stop. Okay?"

His eyes were steady on hers, a deep ocean of things played there in his gaze, but the solidness of him, the confidence, made her feel safe. Wanted. She nodded. "Okay."

She shifted to lie back, but he stopped her. "Hold on. One more thing. I want to see you."

He gripped the edge of her sundress and gathered it up her body. Once she adjusted her hips for him, he lifted it over her head and left her bare except for her bra. He quickly unhooked it and did away with that, too. She was left stark naked under the gleaming light of the kitchen with him still fully dressed. Panic welled in her.

But his attention swept over her with undisguised lust, distracting her from her racing thoughts. He reached out to cup her breast, brushing his thumb over her nipple and bringing it to a stiff, aching peak. "You're so goddamned beautiful. I didn't get the chance to take my time the first time we were together, but I plan on making up for that now."

She swallowed past the knot in her throat. "Will I get to see you, too?"

He smiled and stepped between her spread thighs, his fingers gently teasing her nipples, sending hot frissons of need through her. "Later, I'm all yours. You can see and touch and taste whatever you want."

Goose bumps prickled her skin as he kissed the side of her neck. She licked her lips. "I never got to touch you back then. To see you."

He sucked at her collarbone. "I didn't realize that you'd wanted to."

She scoffed, the wine buzz and his hot, wet kisses making her inhibitions blur. "Are you kidding? It's all I thought about for months before."

He lifted his head at that. "Months?"

"Never mind."

He grinned. "Oh no, Rush. Now you've got to tell me. I've got your pretty tits in my hands. You know how easily I could torture you?"

He bent and took one in his mouth, sucking it between his lips and circling his tongue around it. God. *God.* She moaned as the sensation darted straight downward and settled in between her legs. "Oh, fuck . . ."

He pulled off with a soft pop. "See. Tell me. Imagine how long I could suck and tease these without touching anything else and be perfectly content. I could drag out the evening just playing with you and stroking my cock while I do it, never giving you what you need."

He moved to her other breast and she leaned back on her elbows, her thoughts scattering. "Teasing the born-again virgin is not . . . playing . . . fair."

He hummed against her nipple, making the sensation ripple through her. Wetness pooled between her legs.

"Okay, okay." She arched her back as he sucked harder. "*Shit.* I may have had a long-standing crush on you. I may have had completely impure thoughts about my TA for way longer than before that spring break."

He nipped at her flesh and then raised his head to give her a devilish, satisfied smile. "So when you ran into me in the lab and realized who I was, you went about seducing me."

A sharp laugh burst out of her. "I did no such thing."

"You did. Utterly and completely." He cupped her shoulders and lowered her to the island, displaying her like an X-rated feast. "Whether you knew it or not. You're still doing it."

He drew his fingers down her body from collarbone to hip. She closed her eyes, a shiver going through her. She'd never realized in that moment how starved for touch she was. No one touched her like this. No one ever. Her own fingers felt nothing like this. Every stroke of his hands was like a revelation, her nerve endings blooming under the attention. But then the sensation disappeared, leaving her floating without a tether. Her fingers curled around the edges of the island. "Donovan . . ."

"Shh, it's okay." His hands gripped her knees. "I've got you. Every gorgeous part of you."

He spread her open and traced her inner thighs, sending luxurious tingles winding upward. She bit her lip, trying to keep the moan from slipping out. But then there was a gust of warm air against her wet flesh. Breath. She tensed all over. He was right there, up close with her most private spot. Her thighs tried to snap together but he was gripping her, keeping her in place. And before she could fully panic about what she looked like or what he thought or how this would feel, his mouth was on her. Burning hot, confident, and hungry.

"Oh, God." Lightning went through her and then her muscles went lax like they'd forgotten how to work. A puddle. She was going to become a puddle.

Her knees fell fully open now, no resistance. He made a satisfied sound. Then, he licked her full and slow over her outer lips, the roughness of his tongue and softness of his mouth coalescing into some never before felt sensation. Then he found her clit. Her toes arched in her sandals.

"Holy. Shit." Marin couldn't stop the words or the desperate sound that followed from escaping her. He'd put his mouth on her briefly all those years ago. And she'd read about oral sex countless times, had seen it in videos, had educated others on it. But she'd had no idea. No. Fucking. Idea—it could feel like this.

"Agreed," Donovan said, his breath gusting over her. He kissed her there again, openmouthed and deep, his tongue swirling around her clit like he was going to see how many licks it took to get to the center of her Tootsie Pop, for her to just disintegrate into nothing. One. Two. Ten. She lost count how many times.

Her body throbbed with an impending release already, everything tightening to the breaking point. Her nipples were so hard and achy, she almost went for it and rubbed them herself. But instead, she did what she'd been dying to do forever. She reached down and laced her hands in Donovan's hair, feeling the soft strands slide through her fingers.

"You're fucking perfect, Rush." Donovan pushed a finger inside her, pumping slowly while he licked her in between dirty words. "You should see how wet you are, how hot you feel. I'm hard as rock just thinking about what you're going to taste like coming against my mouth."

"Donovan . . . God. I need, I'm . . ."

Despite her garbled speech, he apparently got the point because he moved his finger away, giving her a second to step back from the edge. But before she could really grab ahold of her control again, he slid his hands beneath her ass, cupping her and lifting her higher.

"Open your eyes and look at me," he commanded.

She'd had her eyes squeezed shut the entire time, too overwhelmed by the feeling to take in any additional information. But at his command, her eyes automatically blinked open. And when she looked down her body, her gaze collided with his. He had her held in his palms, his lips slick and puffy, and without breaking contact he lifted her to his mouth and sucked on her clit.

The sight was so obscene, so goddamned decadent that she almost couldn't take it. His gaze held hers like a rope tied between them, anchoring her and challenging her at the same time. *Look at what I'm doing to you. Look at how filthy and sexy and shameless we are.* He lapped at her—slow and sure—and then sucked and nipped at her flesh, bringing her to the edge and then easing her back again. Her brain filled with white noise, emptying of everything except what she was feeling and the man making her feel those things.

Then when she thought she couldn't handle any more, Donovan reached for the wine bottle. While keeping a steady hand beneath her, he tipped it over her, dousing her sex with rich, ruby liquid. The cool splash was a shock against her hot skin, making her cry out, but then he was there licking it off her, dragging his tongue over her thighs and pussy, his lips going red with the stain of the wine.

The plinking drops of the wine dripping off her body onto the island and floor were unbearably erotic as Donovan got a roguish gleam in his eye and lowered the bottle. She didn't have time to process what he was about to do. With his stare holding hers, he dragged the mouth of the bottle along her slit, smooth glass against throbbing flesh. Then he pressed it to her entrance.

Oh. Fuck.

Her arousal was absolute, everything slippery and aching, and the ridged opening of the bottle slid into her without a fight.

Donovan's expression flared with unrepentant desire as he pumped the very tip inside of her with shallow thrusts. "Any way I want. That's how I'm going to fuck you, Rush."

The words rang through her, setting off sparks and making everything catch fire. She'd worried he'd treat her like a sweet, inexperienced virgin. She'd worried that he'd go easy on her. She'd been wrong. So very wrong.

He was going to break her into a million pieces.

And she was going to let him.

He dragged the bottle out of her, leaving her empty and pulsing with the need to be filled, and then he lifted the bottle to his mouth, wrapping his lips around it and draining the last few drops of it. All the while he held her gaze. He licked his lips when he was done. "You're sweeter than the wine."

Her head dropped back to the island with a groan. She could die. That'd be fine.

He pushed the neck of the bottle back into her, a little deeper, and this time she welcomed the invasion. Her body needed that pressure and he knew just how far to go—not too deep but enough to make her hyperaware of every sensation down there. Then he put his mouth back on her, licking, sucking, tasting while he fucked her with the bottle. In and out, in and out. Everything went white in her vision, and her head listed from side to side against the counter. It all felt like too much all of a sudden, too overwhelming. "Oh, God. Oh, God . . . I can't take . . ."

There was no going back. A release like she'd never had in her life busted through the gates, trampling any shred of sanity she had left. Her back arched, her body seized, and all the colors of the rainbow cascaded behind her eyelids in a blinding waterfall. She screamed, an all-out, losing-her-goddamned-mind shriek and then she was rocking and floating and giving in to it all.

She didn't know how long her orgasm went on or what was happening around her. All she knew was that Donovan was there anchoring her, giving her pleasure, bringing her to this place she'd never been. And when she felt like she couldn't handle any more and started tapping the counter with her hand, he eased the bottle away and held her in place on the island while she panted her way back down to earth.

She knew she should do something, say something—move. But before she got enough strength to open her eyes, she was being lifted. Strong arms adjusted beneath her, and she rested her head against a spot that seemed natural. She felt Donovan's stubble, smelled the faint scent of his skin. She inhaled deeply and nuzzled against his neck, mumbling nonsense.

Donovan chuckled softly. "Let's get you in the bath. Then you can attempt speech again."

She lifted her hand with a thumbs-up.

He kissed the top of her head. "Dork."

"Pot and kettle," she murmured.

"Yeah, that's us."

Us. She shouldn't like the sound of that so much.

21

Marin looked ridiculously sexy in his plaid bathrobe when she stepped into his bedroom. He'd bathed her and washed her hair in the tub, giving her time to settle after her orgasm, to process things. But she'd asked for a few minutes to herself at the end. He'd given it to her but worried that she'd needed it because he'd overwhelmed her.

He hadn't planned on letting things go where they had. He'd only wanted to taste her, to give her the pleasure of oral sex. But when he'd gotten her spread and naked across his kitchen island, his baser instincts had kicked in. He'd wanted to not just please her, but to drive her out of her mind, to sully her, to take all that innocence and dirty it up.

He wasn't sure he'd ever seen a more erotic sight than Marin, legs spread, pussy bared, and body dripping with expensive wine and her own arousal. Fuck, every time he saw the picture in his head, he'd had to fight not to stroke himself. He may never be able to drink merlot again without thinking about how it tasted mingling with Marin's flavor. But tonight wasn't about him. He would be patient, give her time to wrap her head around all this, figure out if he'd gone too far too quickly.

Marin rolled up the too long sleeves of his robe and gave him a tentative smile. "So, hey."

With her makeup washed off and her hair damp, he was reminded of just how young she was. Her fierce smarts and all she'd been through made her seem closer to his age, but right now, post orgasm and unsure of herself, their eight-year difference was obvious. Once again, he worried if he was taking advantage. They hadn't talked much during the bath. She'd been quiet, still coming down from all that had happened, but now was going to be the moment of truth. He'd find out if he'd blown it, if he'd scared her. "Hey."

Her gaze skated over him. "You're still dressed."

Something unlocked in his chest at her easy tone. "I like that you sound disappointed."

She gave him a small smile. "I feel like I'm at a disadvantage. You've seen, uh . . . everything there is to see of me."

He patted the bed. "Afraid I'm going to renege on our deal?"

She padded over, her feet quiet on the hardwood, and sat on the bed. "I guess I'm just feeling a little unsure of where to go from here. I didn't . . . well, I didn't expect what happened to happen."

He reached out to grab her hand. "Come 'ere."

She let him tug her closer, and he wrapped his arm around her, letting her settle against his chest. He could feel her quick heartbeat against him. She was far more nervous than she was showing on her face. It was easy to forget that she'd never done this, that it was all new to her. Being with anyone this way. Sharing a bed. Touching. He pressed a kiss to the top of her head. "I told you I'm all yours. But there's no pressure here. We can just sit like this, relax. Talk. Whatever. I know that things went a little far out there. I seem to have trouble taking things slow and easy with you. So I'm sorry if I pushed you past where you wanted to go."

Her fingers traced over his T-shirt almost absently. "You said that the first time, too. I remember you felt bad that you'd been rough."

"Of course I felt bad. You were a virgin. I was afraid I'd hurt you."

"Mmm," she said noncommittally.

She didn't say anything else for a few minutes. The whole thing should've felt weird. He didn't invite women into his bedroom. Any trysts he had happened at the woman's place or a hotel. And tonight he'd planned for things to happen in other parts of the house if they happened. He liked his private space private. He didn't want others in a room where he kept the stack of books his mother had bought him before she'd died. Or for someone to notice the ridiculous dead bolt on his door. Or for anyone to ask him about the photo of San Francisco Bay that filled up most of one wall. This room hid his secrets, the things he didn't know how to fix. But somehow he didn't feel anxious having Marin in there with him. Even though she was a virtual stranger to him, she knew more than most of the people in his life already.

He traced his fingers up and down her arm. "You okay?"

"You like things rough," she said, her tone pensive.

He shifted his hold on her so he could look down at her. "Was I too rough with you? If I was, you just have to tell me."

She chewed her lip and peeked up at him, some of her trademark blush staining her cheeks. "Well, you doused me with wine and fucked me with the bottle."

He winced. "I—"

"But I've never come that hard in my life. And I'm pretty good at making myself do that."

His lips snapped shut.

She scooted over and propped herself up on her hand. "I guess I'm just wondering that if that's Donovan 101, what's the master class?"

The question sent wariness through him. "What do you mean?"

"How far do those desires go? Like, what do you think about

when you're alone and there's nothing to censure your fantasies? Is it like your recordings or more than that?"

He frowned. "Marin—"

"Hey, look, I'm asking you personal questions and not getting embarrassed. You should be proud." She gave him a wry smile. "Plus, you said no judgment for me. I'm offering the same to you. I'm just curious. Not saying I'm willing to go there."

He sighed and let his head fall back on the pillow. "You're asking for my dark corner stuff, doctor? Do you charge by the hour?"

She shoved him in the side. "I do. But you couldn't afford me."

He stared at the ceiling fan going round and round. He should probably edit himself. He'd already set her off balance. If he told her some of his darker fantasies, he'd probably freak her out for good. But he couldn't find it in himself to lie to her. "You're right. I like rough-and-tumble stuff and I like control. Things like giving chase and capturing someone or holding a woman down while I fuck her has a lot of appeal. Enjoying someone fighting back. All with previous consent, of course. Role-play stuff." He wet his lips, trying to tamp back images of him doing those things with Marin, of crossing those boundaries with her. He cleared his throat. "I think because I have to be so stoic and calm at work that the abandon of that kind of thing calls to me."

He peered down at her when she didn't respond, needing to see her reaction. Instead of looking terrified, her forehead was wrinkled in thought. "I can see that. You don't have to be the nice guy then, the ever-understanding therapist, the blank slate."

She got it. Of course she did. The woman was an observer of human nature just like he was. "I like what I do, but you've seen how it is. You always have to be on. You can't have bad days or show too much emotion with clients. It can be exhausting."

"But you liked the rough fantasies before you were a therapist."

He smirked. "Now you *are* trying to give me a session, Dr. Rush.

I was the smart kid in school. Easy target for bullies until my height shot up in high school. I learned early on that people lose interest when you don't give them a reaction. I learned not to show my cards to anyone. He who controls his emotions holds *all zee power.*"

She snorted at his dramatic tone. "And she who blushes loses all the credibility."

He laughed and gathered her against him again, liking the feel of her nestled in the crook of his arm. "We're working on that. Soon your therapist face will be impenetrable."

"Then I guess I'll be the one wanting to break free and have wild, kinky sex." She shifted against him. "Or who knows? Maybe I'm already getting to that point."

He gave in to the urge to stroke his fingers through her hair. He imagined Marin had spent a lot of her life following very strict plans and putting on a brave face—taking care of her mother, becoming a parent to her younger brother, now trying to be a sex therapist when she hadn't been afforded time in her life to experience her own sex life. If anyone had earned some wildness it was her.

"You were beautiful tonight, Marin. The way you gave yourself over to it." He peered down at her, watching his fingers sliding through her dark fine hairs. "You may blush at things at work, but you're sexy as fuck when you push past that initial anxiety. It's part of the reason I couldn't resist taking things beyond what I had planned tonight. I think you might be as filthy and kinky as I am, you just haven't had the opportunity to indulge in it."

"Are you calling me a slut who hasn't lived up to her potential?" she teased.

"If I was, it'd be a compliment." He rolled to his side, shifting her onto her back so he could look down at her. He traced the smooth skin of her chest along the edge of the partially open robe. "All I'm saying is that you're inexperienced, but I doubt you're vanilla. A vanilla woman would've balked at what I just told you

I fantasized about, been scared or turned off or worried. She would've already left."

She rubbed her lips together. "I didn't say I was going to volunteer for those things."

"You didn't say you wouldn't." He gently pushed the robe to the side, exposing the curve of her breast. He drew a finger around her nipple, the tempting bud immediately tightening in response.

She shuddered beneath the gentle attention and closed her eyes. "Maybe it's because I'm not scared that you'd hurt me. And I know if I said no or stop, you would."

He watched her, breathing that in. Marin had no idea how big a fucking deal those simple words were. She trusted him—with her body, with her safety, with her pleasure. It was about the biggest gift she could give him. "Thank you. I'm glad you know you're safe with me. You absolutely are."

She opened her eyes and let her hand drift downward until she was scraping over his denim-clad thigh. "I want to touch you."

The sight of her naked, warm form beneath that robe was calling to him. His cock had already grown hard and urgent against his fly. He wanted to take his time this go-round, explore and nibble and taste every inch of her. But he'd promised her something, and he wasn't going to deny her.

He reached behind him and tugged off his T-shirt, liking the way her eyes roved over him. "I'm all yours, gorgeous."

She pushed up onto an elbow and then flattened a hand against his shoulder, urging him onto his back. She propped herself above him and gave him a long, slow consideration. When her eyes lingered on the outline of his erection, his cock responded, growing even harder and sending a sharp ache through him.

"You really are unfairly beautiful," she declared.

A choked laugh snuck out of him. "Somehow I feel like you're insulting me."

"I totally am." Her hand curved around his erection and stroked. All joking fell aside as his stomach muscles tensed, the light touch ridiculously potent.

When she gave him a squeeze, he hissed. "Fuck."

She mapped him again with teasing fingers. "I want to give you what you gave me."

"Keep doing that and it won't take long."

She moved her hand away and walked her fingers over his abdomen, exploring, dragging her nails through the trail of dark hair there. She paused at the waistband of his jeans. "No, I want you to show me how to do it with my mouth."

He groaned. More perfect words had never been uttered. He wanted to frame those words and gaze upon them daily. "You don't have to return the favor. You don't owe me anything."

She adjusted herself, lifting a knee and straddling his thigh. She was naked beneath the robe and he got a flash of pert breasts and the trimmed dark hair between her thighs as she settled over him. Desire crashed through him.

"I want to know how a man tastes." She leaned down and traced the tip of her tongue around his naval before lifting her head again. "I want to know how *you* taste specifically, Donovan West."

Fucking hell. His head was going to explode. His cock would follow. This woman had no idea how effortlessly erotic she was. He reached out and palmed the back of her head, giving it a squeeze, trying to quell the roar of desire. "Want some chocolate lube on standby?"

Her smile was unhurried, dark amusement there. "I don't like things sugarcoated. I like them real."

Real. That's what she demanded of him. And so far, he found he didn't mind giving her just that. He reached down and unhooked the button on his jeans. When he tugged down the zipper and freed his cock, the change over Marin's expression was enough to fucking undo him right there. She looked . . . fascinated. And hungry for him.

His instincts rumbled to the surface. "Guess it's time you learn how to suck my cock, then."

Marin's breath left her at the sight of Donovan's thick erection in his hand, and her body clenched hard. She'd seen enough penises in her day in books and videos and wherever. But nothing had prepared her for the raw sensuality of seeing this man stiff and ready for her. The tip was flushed and glossy with arousal, and when he ran his thumb over the slit, rubbing the fluid along the head, she almost died. Part of her wished she could just watch him stroke himself, see how he took his pleasure. Did he make noise? Did he slick himself up with lube, making everything shiny and smooth. Did he play with his balls or tease himself?

Goddamn. She was never ever going to be short on masturbation material again. This sight alone could get her off.

She licked her lips as Donovan adjusted her so he could kick his jeans and underwear off. When she was straddling his thigh again, she indulged in the view. The dark thatch of trimmed hair at the base, the heavy sac that looked impossibly masculine, and that proud aroused cock. She wanted to touch and explore, to run her fingers everywhere and follow the path with her tongue.

"Keep looking at me like that and I may come just from that," Donovan said, voice gritty.

She couldn't resist the temptation any longer. She let her fingers encircle his erection, surprised at the silky, taut skin. She wasn't sure what she'd expected but she hadn't expected velvet-encased steel. Her mouth went dry just thinking about what that would feel like inside her. "Show me what you like. Show me how to make you come."

Donovan groaned and gripped the base of his cock, squeezing harder than she would've thought comfortable. His hand tightened in her hair. "Your mouth on me is about all it's going to take, Rush.

I'm already on edge after watching you come earlier and seeing you here now. Hell, I've been on fucking edge since you walked onto the X-wing. Just be careful of teeth and don't try to be too gentle. Anything else, you can explore how you want. I'll tell you when I'm close if you want to pull off."

She positioned herself over him, inhaling the musk of his skin, and looked up. "Why would I want to pull off?"

He closed his eyes as if the question had caused him both pleasure and pain. "Some women don't want to—"

But she didn't wait for an answer. It'd been rhetorical. And she was too turned on, too curious to wait. She slid her lips over the head of his cock and let her tongue sweep around it. She didn't know what she was doing exactly, but her nerves had fallen away the minute he'd opened his jeans. If going down on him felt even a tenth of what she'd felt when he went down on her, she figured she couldn't mess it up too much.

He let out a grinding sound and his hand flexed against her skull, as if it was taking everything he had not to shove her down on his cock and use her how he wanted. Part of her wished he would, but jumping in that deep would sacrifice the chance to savor.

As her mouth closed fully over the head, his taste hit her tongue, and her thighs squeezed together at the rush of desire it sparked. She'd expected salt, the taste of sweat and skin and humanness. And there was that, but God, it was so much more that that. Earthy, musky, and very, very male. She wouldn't have known that was a flavor, but there was no other way to describe it. Donovan tasted like sex and desire and temptation all wrapped around satiny strength. Whoever invented chocolate lube was a fucking idiot.

She'd never want to mask this. It pressed buttons in her she hadn't realized she had, her body knowing just how to react to the feel of him in her mouth, a flood of wet heat going straight to her sex. She inhaled deeply and took another slow suck, earning a tense groan from Donovan.

That was all she needed to hear. She stopped being delicate and slid down his shaft, sucking and licking and working every part of him her tongue could reach.

Donovan cursed and his thigh muscle flexed beneath her, the springy hair of his leg teasing her sex. "That sound you just made . . . *Christ*."

She hadn't realized she'd made a noise, but her response to having him in her mouth was impossible to contain. She could feel his every reaction. Each swipe of her tongue earned her a coiled muscle or a sharp breath or more drops of the slightly bitter pre-come. She loved knowing what she was doing to him. Loved the immediate feedback that she was doing something right.

He clasped her head in his hands and wrested some of the control back, easing her pace. "That's it. Slow it down. I want this to last. You feel fucking amazing."

She groaned and rocked her hips along with the slow motion of her bobbing head.

Donovan shifted his leg beneath her, putting pressure where she needed it most.

"Mmm, I can feel you getting hot and slippery against me. You're making a mess, Marin." His words were low, the sound coasting over her like warm, seeking hands. "You know what that does to me? Knowing that sucking my cock is getting you off? That you need to come so bad again that you're riding my leg?"

Heat flooded her face, an automatic reaction, but he didn't let her pull away or give her time to be embarrassed.

"Oh, no, you don't," he said, sinful intent lacing the words. He shifted his leg fully against her, dragging the hair-roughened surface over her flesh, grinding against her slick lips and clit. "You're going to fuck my leg just like that and suck me hard while you do it. You're going to come for me like I'm going to come for you."

The feel of him grinding against her, the sound of it—all that wet, hot flesh—and the feel of him hard and full in her mouth was too much. All of her systems flipped to go almost immediately, release racing up the line. She whimpered, her hips canting forward despite the snap of shame trying to fight its way in. She was humping his leg like a dog. She couldn't stop if she tried.

His fingers tightened against her head as he pumped her harder against him. He didn't take her all the way down. Her gag reflex had protested the first time she'd tried. But he wasn't taking it easy either. He gripped her hair in his hands, her scalp stinging in a strangely erotic way. Her hold on the moment started to slip, some state of surrender sliding into place. She was a passenger now, her mouth his tool. Her thoughts blurred. She let go of the steering wheel.

"That's right, baby." Donovan's breaths were sawing out of him now, choppy and ragged. "Moan for me. Show me how much you need to come. How much you want to drink me down."

Marin was lost. Her body jerked against his leg, and everything inside her detonated. She made some desperate sound around his cock, her tongue and lips still working, tasting, loving, but sensation spiraling through her and blasting thought from her brain.

"Fuck, yes, oh fuck." Donovan's words were hot rain over already boiling waves.

He swelled in her mouth and pumped into her roughly, spilling his release onto her tongue and down her throat, calling her name and saying sweet, dirty things to her.

She took everything he had to give as she rode the crest of her own orgasm. His taste. Her pulsing clit. The slick feel of her body sliding against his thigh. All of it morphed into one long, drunk-on-pleasure moment. Then he was easing her off of him and rubbing soothing fingers on her scalp.

She blinked back into reality with slow awareness. Her lips were tingling, her jaw a little sore, and her body throbbed with aftershocks as he adjusted on the bed and dragged her into his hold. But she couldn't find it in herself to do much of anything besides let him move her where he wanted her. He cradled her in the crook of his arm, his chest still moving with uneven breaths as he eased down from his release.

His skin was hot against her cheek, the sheen of sweat welcoming. She closed her eyes, sated and sleepy. A lot had happened tonight. She'd probably have thoughts about it. But not now. She'd think about everything later. Right now she just needed this.

"You okay?" he asked after a few minutes.

"Mm-hmm. You?"

"What do you think?"

"Guess I'm a natural at giving head," she murmured sleepily. "Check that off my list."

The dark, quiet laugh rumbled beneath her cheek. "Maybe I'm just a natural at receiving it."

She snorted. "Of that, I have no doubt."

He gathered her closer and brushed his lips over her forehead. "Get some rest, Rush."

She snuggled closer to him, and he pulled the blanket over the both of them, the sweat chilling on her skin. "I can't sleep here."

"I know. But stay for a little while. You went somewhere during that. You need to come down easy from it. Plus, I'm not ready to let you out of my bed yet."

She wasn't sure what he was talking about. But she'd gone somewhere all right. She almost felt drunk with it, her thoughts sticky and her muscles lax. "Okay."

"I'll wake you up before it gets too late," he said softly, but her mind was already halfway to sleep.

She dreamed of it never getting too late. Of staying.

22

Donovan picked at the gravy-soaked fries on his plate, staring at the documents in front of him, the steady flow of conversation around him in the dive restaurant a background hum. He'd driven into Bellemeade to Parrain's Po-Boys for a roast beef sandwich and to go over the most recent report his private investigator had sent him, but he was having trouble making sense of it.

Donovan flipped through a few more pages. Bret had outlined some discrepancies she'd found and some circumstantial stuff. But Donovan couldn't seem to make it line up in his head. He rubbed the spot between his brows. Maybe his late night was catching up with him.

In the early hours of the morning, he'd woken Marin and had made sure she got back to her place. She'd been sleepy and quiet, and he'd been tempted to ask her to stay. But they had to be careful. Beyond risking someone seeing her leave his place, she had her brother to worry about.

But he'd wanted to keep her in bed with him, naked and curled up next to him until the sun came up. Unlike a typical night, he'd actually had to fight off sleep while he lay there with her. After that spectacular blow job and seeing Marin indulging her own pleasure in such a wanton, shameless way, he'd felt sated and sleepy. Content. His mind had been oddly quiet. So much so that he'd had to set an alarm on his phone just to make sure he didn't let her down and sleep past time.

But when he'd rolled over this morning to empty sheets, he'd wished that he'd figured out a way to keep her there. He would've woken her up with his tongue between her thighs, relishing those sweet sounds she made when she got close to orgasm, and then he would've spread her out beneath him and fucked her deep and slow. He'd had erotic dreams all night of sinking into her body, of what she would feel like around him, of her losing herself to the moment. She was so responsive and gorgeous when she surrendered to it.

And that's what it had been—surrender. He'd watched her slip into that in-between place he'd learned about from studying BDSM. Subspace. Marin may not be a dyed-in-the-wool submissive, but when she let go of control, she really let go—willing and pliant, like she would let him take her anywhere. She'd tackled last night like she tackled everything else in her life—all in, no half-assed measures. If she was going to do something, she was going to be the best at it. It was damn erotic.

He adjusted his position in the booth, trying to will himself not to get hard at the table thinking about it. Even though he'd just had her last night, he couldn't get her out of his head. He needed more. Wanted to glut himself on her. They only had thirty days and he felt like they were burning daylight.

But when he'd asked her last night if she wanted to get together for lunch today, she'd said she had plans. He wasn't sure if that was true or if she'd just needed some time and space, so he hadn't pushed. But now he was kicking himself for not setting up another time to meet. Usually he spent Saturdays catching up on work, running errands, or volunteering therapy hours at the kink club in New Orleans—a packed schedule his drug of choice. But he hadn't had the energy or desire to do any of it. All he'd wanted to do was track Marin down and change her mind about today.

God, he hated this shit.

He didn't have sex brain. He had Marin brain. He shoved another fry in his mouth. What the fuck was wrong with him? He didn't do *this*. He didn't spend time worrying about a woman. He needed to get his head together, focus on this report, and get something productive done for the day instead of staring into space and fantasizing like some horny kid.

He tried again to read through Bret's notes as he finished up his lunch, but the sound of laughter broke through his barely there concentration. He glanced toward the door, trying to locate the source and stilled, a fry halfway to his mouth, as he watched Marin step inside the restaurant. She had a parted-lip smile on her face, like she'd been the one who'd just laughed, and she was directing that grin toward the blond man she was with. A familiar man. *Lane.*

Lane pointed toward the line of people waiting to order at the counter and then slid his hand onto Marin's lower back to guide her that way.

Something ugly and sharp rushed up in Donovan, the taste of it bitter on his tongue. He dropped his fry onto his plate, his appetite gone. What. The. Fuck.

Lane was a friend and a colleague. A good dude. But he was also something else, something Donovan had found out by accident one night in the city. And the way his gaze slid over Marin's backside when she stepped in front of him in line was more than co-worker interest. Donovan's fist curled beneath the table. He and Marin had agreed to no one else in their bed during this arrangement, but she hadn't specified not going out with anyone. He thought it'd been implied, but maybe not. Maybe he'd read everything wrong.

Donovan watched as Marin stepped up for her turn. Lane leaned around her, one hand braced on the counter and pointed to the menu board, telling the cashier something. Ordering for Marin? Marin put her hand on his arm and seemed to thank him for whatever it was he'd done. Possessiveness flashed through Donovan—like a whip snapping loud and sharp in his ears.

He watched as they waited for their food, chatting animatedly. He should probably leave. He was done with his food and not having any luck with this report. But he couldn't bring himself to get up. When they grabbed their trays and turned his way, Lane was the first to notice Donovan sitting there. Lane broke into an easy smile and leaned over to Marin to tell her something.

Marin looked up, those big hazel eyes widening when she saw Donovan. He schooled his expression into impassivity. Lane put his hand to Marin's back again and guided her toward Donovan's table.

"Hey, Dr. West. Looks like we weren't the only ones with this idea today," Lane said amicably.

"Seems so." Donovan peered over at Marin. "What are you two up to today?"

Before Marin could answer, Lane jumped in. "I figured I'd show Marin some of the local haunts, introduce her to the best shrimp po-boy, and help her get the lay of the land."

Or the lay of something. Donovan tamped down the thought before it could slip out.

"I also thought it'd be a good chance for me to get to know more about Lane's role," Marin said. "I'm admittedly ignorant about the ins and outs of it."

Despite Donovan's annoyance, he couldn't let that one go.

"The ins and outs?" He lifted his brows and Lane coughed over his laugh.

Marin groaned. "Ugh, you know what I mean. God, the double entendre traps are everywhere in this freaking job."

Donovan smirked. "You get used to it. You two want to join me?"

Lane glanced down at Donovan's mostly empty plate. "Nah, looks like you're wrapping up. We won't bother you with shoptalk on the weekend."

Marin shifted on her feet. "Maybe some other time."

Right. Of course. Some other time when she wasn't on a date with another fucking guy.

He was about to stand up and just get the hell out of there. But then Marin cleared her throat, forcing him to look her way again. Marin held his gaze for a moment, those eyes conveying so much, and something settled inside him.

Okay. This wasn't what he was labeling it as. Lane was definitely interested in Marin—that much was pretty transparent. But Marin . . . well, he was reading something entirely different off of her. And that something had his predatory instinct unfurling.

Donovan cocked his head toward the main part of the dining room. "Why don't you grab a table before they all fill up, Lane? I'm going to steal Dr. Rush for a minute. I've been working on one of our cases today and need to ask her something."

He tapped his report as proof.

Lane smiled and reached out to take Marin's tray. "Sure. I'll go get us set up."

"Thanks." Marin handed over her food.

"See ya, doc," Lane said with a quick nod.

When Lane sauntered off, Marin crossed her arms and gave him a look full of saucy challenge. "Yes, Dr. West? What pressing case may I assist you with?"

He leaned forward on his elbows. "You do realize he thinks this is a date, right? Or at the very least, a prelude to a date."

She made a derisive snort. "Oh, please, he does not. We're here for exactly what I said. Plus, I've heard interoffice relationships are frowned upon at The Grove. He wouldn't ask me to a local place where we could run into anyone."

"Lane is a contractor with us, not a full-time employee. And

I promise you he doesn't give a shit about that rule. In fact, I bet you that before you finish lunch, he asks you to go somewhere tonight." He grabbed his papers and set them in front of her, making it look like they were discussing work.

She braced her hands on the edge of the table, pretending to read the pages and giving him a lovely view down the collar of her shirt. She didn't look up at him when she spoke. "You're on, West. What are we betting?"

Donovan grinned and leaned back in his chair. "If he doesn't ask you out, I will take your next on-call night for you."

"And if he does?"

"If he does, then you're going to say yes."

She straightened. *"What?"*

"You'll say yes, and then you'll text me the time and place of where you're going."

Deep furrows appeared in her brow. "Why?"

"Ah, that is the price of the bet. You don't get to know. You just have to promise you'll say yes, send me the details, and then go on the date."

She frowned. "He's not going to ask me."

He shrugged and gathered the stack of documents in his hands. "Then I guess you have nothing to worry about."

Marin looked like she was going to say more, but Donovan slid out of the booth. He put his back to where Lane had gone and gave Marin a slow, up and down look, making sure he lingered on all the good parts.

She smoothed her lipstick, and her nipples instantly became visible points beneath her shirt. He wanted to bend down and take them between his teeth, mark her skin. He wanted to see that sated look on her face again. He reached out and squeezed her shoulder. From the outside observer, it looked friendly, professional. But no one else could feel how she shuddered beneath his grip.

"You're already thinking about it, aren't you?"

She swallowed, her throat working. "What?"

"How it's going to feel when I finally fuck you."

"I—"

He let go of her. "See you later, Dr. Rush. Enjoy your date."

He strolled off, fighting a hard-on and thrumming with anticipation. There were a lot of things in life he wasn't sure of. But he'd seen how Lane had looked at Marin. He recognized it because Donovan looked at her the same way. And Lane was smart enough not to let her slip by without at least trying.

So when his phone buzzed half an hour later with a text message, he could only smile.

He lifted his phone, laughing at Marin's colorful use of language and angry emoticons, and saved the address she'd sent him.

Game on.

Marin had no idea what she was doing—just that she was doing it. Like Donovan had predicted, Lane had invited her to go with him tonight and see a band at one of the many jazz clubs in New Orleans. She'd made the bet with Donovan. She was supposed to say yes even though she had no intentions of dating Lane.

But she didn't want to lead a guy on. And she didn't want to renege on a bet. So in the end, she'd told Lane that she'd love to go but that they'd be going as friends, that she wasn't ready to date anyone right now. Lane had taken it in stride with his easy charm and laid-back attitude. The guy really did have a talent for making people feel comfortable. She could see how vital that would be in his profession.

But when she peeked through the curtains and saw that he'd pulled up in front of her place in a sleek black sports car, a little flurry of nerves surged. Nate, who'd gotten inexplicably pissy when she'd told him she was going out again, slid into the spot she vacated, openly staring at her visitor. "So this is the dude you went on a date with last night?"

"No."

He looked her way. "*No?* When the hell did you have time to meet two guys to hook up with?"

"I'm a grown woman. I do not *hook up.*"

"Okay, Kelly Clarkson. Whatever you want to call it. But you looked rough this morning."

She made an affronted sound.

"Just speaking the truth, Mar."

Marin frowned. She'd made sure to be back here before Nate had gotten home from his shift, but the kid was too observant for his own good. "I had trouble sleeping."

"Uh-huh." He peered back out the window. "Hard to sleep when you're too busy *hooking up.*"

She groaned. "What's your problem? You were the one wanting me to get my own life."

"I don't have a problem," he said, petulant tone back.

She swatted his shoulder as she toed on her heels. "Stop looking out the window. He's going to see you. And for the record, I'm not going on a date with this guy. It's a friend thing."

"A friend thing that you dressed up for," Nate said without looking her way or moving away from the window. "Whoa."

She searched for her keys in the pile of stuff on the coffee table. "What?"

"He's like seriously hot. Now I get why you're dressed like that."

Marin rolled her eyes. "You've just got a thing for blonds."

"And broad shoulders and messy hair and, damn, that guy works out. Is he bi?"

"I have no idea. Plus, you have a boyfriend, and Lane is way too old for you, so back off."

"Yeah, my boyfriend." Nate sank back down on the couch,

ending his leering routine at the window, but his moody expression unchanged.

Marin sighed. Nate was eighteen but still a teenager in so many ways. The moods were impossible to predict or dissect. It was probably best she was going out tonight. She and Nate would just end up snapping at each other more if he was determined to be like this.

When the doorbell rang, he hopped up. "I'll get it."

"*Nathan.*"

But he was already striding in front of her and swinging open the door. Lane stood on the porch, hands tucked in the pockets of his gray slacks and his shirtsleeves rolled up to his elbows, revealing impressive forearms. He smiled at Nate. "Hi, is this Dr. Rush's house?"

Nate stepped back and swept an arm in front of him. "Yep. Come on in. I'm Marin's brother, Nathan."

Marin tried not to roll her eyes. Despite Nate's apparent irritation with her, he was all swagger and smiles for Lane. Never doubt the power of a good-looking guy to bring out Nate's magnanimous side.

Lane shook Nate's hand. "Lane Cannon. Good to meet you."

Nate raked his fingers through the sideswept hair that hung over his forehead, a sure sign he was trying to look cool. Marin choked down an amused snort.

She stepped forward, and Lane sent a warm smile her way. "Wow, you look great."

"Thanks." She'd chosen a simple black dress and amped it up with a few silver jewelry pieces. She didn't want to look like she was trying too hard, but she also had no idea what to expect tonight. What the club was like. What Donovan had in mind for later. Because she assumed there'd be a later based on how he'd looked at her today. Her body stirred at the thought. She grabbed her purse off the sofa. "You ready to go?"

He offered her his arm. "Always ready to take a beautiful woman out on the town."

Nate sent her an I-told-you-so look and then smiled Lane's way. "Y'all have fun. Remember, curfew's at eleven."

Marin smirked. Nate had probably been waiting to say that one for years. She gave him a look when she passed him. "Be careful at work tonight. And make sure you lock up when you leave."

He slouched against the doorjamb, looking sullen again. "Yeah, yeah. I got it."

She was tempted to prod Nathan more, see what was going on with his attitude, but she let it slide for now. Lane was waiting and she didn't have time for an argument. She gave Nate one last wave, and Lane lead her out to the car. As she settled in the seat, she tried to relax, tried to let the day go and focus on the present. Lane folded himself into the driver's side and sent a smile her way. "Your brother seems like a good kid."

"Don't be fooled. He thinks you're hot. He's nice to hot guys."

Lane chuckled, a deep-in-the-chest, genuine sound. "Well, I'm flattered then. Too bad I don't have the same effect on his sister."

He said it with a light tone, so she responded in kind. "I never said you were a strain to look at."

He turned the key in the ignition and pulled onto the road that led out of The Grove. "True enough. And I absolutely respect this as a friends-only outing. You've got nothing to worry about. I'm happy to have the company."

She clicked her seatbelt into the lock. "I doubt you have trouble finding that."

"Oh, you'd be surprised." The orange streetlights flashed over his profile in an uneven pattern, revealing nothing of his expression. "Women find out what I do for a living and either want to save me, send me to church, or put me in jail. Freaks out pretty much every-one. Even some people at work."

She frowned. "I never thought about it that way. I guess that would be a lot to deal with in a relationship."

"Yep. It is." He shifted gears and sped up as they hit the open road. "Which is why it's probably wise you've decided to just be my friend. Our odds are much better."

She sighed and peered out the window. "Well, I could definitely use one of those."

"Me, too." He drummed his fingers along the steering wheel. "It's one of the things you need to survive with jobs like ours— friends who understand the craziness . . . and/or a steady supply of mood-altering substances."

She laughed. "Yeah, seems the standard welcome gift around The Grove is wine. It's a wonder we don't all end up on the R and R wing."

"Luckily most of us know our limits. Though they do have hurricanes at the place I'm taking you to tonight. Be warned, that drink has taken out more than one employee from The Grove in its day. Tastes sweet and innocent, but before you know it, you're climbing atop the speakers, pulling off your shirt, and singing along to Katy Perry songs." He cleared his throat. "Not that I'm speaking from personal experience, of course."

She laughed. "Katy Perry?"

"It was a bet. I'd had two hurricanes." He gave her a mock serious look. "I really can't be held responsible for my actions."

"Please tell me someone videoed that."

He looked back to the road. "Marin, be careful. I'm a firework."

His deadpan tone set her off again and the laugh bubbled out. "I'll be sure to stick to wine tonight then. You definitely don't want to hear me sing."

"Hey, you never know. It could be fun." He sent her a sideways glance. "And maybe if you get tipsy enough, you'll tell me why West looked at me today like he wanted to challenge me to a duel."

Marin's smile stalled. "What?"

Lane draped his hand over the top of the steering wheel and leaned back, relaxed as you please. "Look, I've known Donovan for a while now. He's a good doctor and smart as hell. But he's a cool customer—not a guy you'd want to play poker against. And I'm telling you, I've never seen him look at a woman like he looked at you today."

Marin forced herself not to react. She could not slip up like this. Had they been that obvious? "Lane—"

He shrugged. "Don't worry. I don't tell people's secrets. And you don't need to say one way or another. It's just, sex is my job. I know heat when I see it. And you two just about burned me down in the crosshairs today. So I wasn't surprised you turned me down for a date if you have that going on."

Marin rolled her lips together, watching the dark road disappear beneath their tires, her heart pounding so loud she was sure Lane could hear it.

"Just be careful." The words were quiet, the message loud.

She peered his way.

He kept his gaze forward, but his hands flexed around the steering wheel. "All that fire can burn you right up, you know? Leave nothing but ashes."

She sensed the warning was coming from personal experience, but the words reverberated through her, making her stomach twist.

"Right," she said lamely.

Lane got quiet after that, and she let him. No need to continue the dangerous conversation. It would lead nowhere good. So she tried to focus on counting the mile markers instead of letting her worried thoughts overtake her. But she didn't get a respite for long.

Her cell phone vibrated in her lap, startling her from the mindless task. She lifted her phone, expecting a message from Nate. But the name on the screen wasn't his.

Your safe word is BLUE. Be ready, Rush.

Little black letters on a white screen. But strung together they changed everything in one quick second. Her lungs deflated, edgy desire stabbing through her, and her muscles went tight.

Donovan. He was out there somewhere tonight and ready to play a game.

She glanced over at Lane.

Don't get burned.

She could already feel the flames licking at her feet.

23

Marin decided to nurse one drink while enjoying the music in the club. She didn't know what Donovan had planned for later, for one. But she also didn't want to risk a loose tongue with Lane. The guy was easy to talk to and though he obviously suspected something was going on with her and Donovan, she didn't want to slip up and confirm it. Let him have his suspicions.

Lane, to his credit, hadn't brought it up again or pushed for any information. Instead, he'd told her about the band, about living in the city, and he'd picked out a few appetizers from the bar menu for them to snack on while they chatted. Marin felt herself relaxing after a while, enjoying the music and the company. She told Lane about her brother and about how she ended up at The Grove. He gave her the inside scoop about some of the people they worked with. And he artfully dodged questions about how he'd ended up in his chosen career when she asked.

It was comfortable and pleasant and . . . fun. She realized how long it'd been since she'd just hung out with a friend. So when he asked her to dance, she didn't feel strange or awkward taking him up on it.

He swept her out onto the floor and pulled her into his hold, settling his hand on her lower back but not dragging her too close. On her first step, she managed to stomp his toes. "Shit. Sorry. I should've warned you that my dancing experience is limited."

He smiled down at her. "Don't worry. I've got tough feet. We'll go slow."

He guided her into a turn, his lead effortless, and she settled into his grip.

"There you go," he said. "The trouble happens when both people try to lead. Your job is just to relax and let me take you where you need to go."

She bit her lip, fighting back a smile.

His brows went up. "What?"

"Nothing. I can just see why you're good at what you do. Why clients let you take them where they need to go. You inspire calm and confidence."

His lips lifted at the corner, his expression openly pleased. "Thanks."

He spun her around with a flourish and then gathered her back into his hold. The music swirled around them, the dance floor filling with couples. "I can't imagine what it must be like."

"What?"

"Your job." She stepped on his toe again and winced, but he waved it off. She adjusted the position of her feet. "I mean, sexual attraction is such a huge, unpredictable thing. How do you work all that out? Keeping things professional with people while still accessing what you need to . . . get the job done? What if you don't find them physically attractive?"

He laughed, the white lights of the disco ball dancing across his face in a polka-dot pattern. "Dr. Rush, are you asking how I keep boundaries yet still get turned on enough to perform, even with people who may not be my type?"

She grimaced. Yep, that had been what she was asking. "Sorry, inappropriate question."

"Maybe. But it's a valid one." His fingers flexed against her back as he moved her a little closer. "I learned a long time ago how to switch modes. I'm either in work mode or personal mode. In work mode, I focus on the tasks, on being a guide. I don't sleep with all—or even most—of my clients. But if the situation calls for it, then I provide that. Getting an erection isn't that monumental of a task. Every woman has something beautiful about them, especially after I've gotten to know them in sessions. But I'm not there to get off anyway. And I find that it's better if I don't take my own release in sessions. It keeps things really clear about why I'm there."

Her steps stuttered a bit, but he caught her before she could stumble and whirled her into another turn. "Wait, you don't orgasm in your sessions?"

"Not usually. Unless a client has a specific need that requires that experience."

"Wow." She shook her head. "That seems like it'd be torture."

Her phone buzzed loudly against her hip, her small purse doing nothing to hide the vibration from her or Lane. She ignored it and they kept dancing. But then it buzzed again.

"Need to get that?" Lane asked, backing up a few inches to give her room.

"No, it's fine, I— Well, no, I probably should check, in case it's Nate."

"Go ahead." He released one of her hands but kept his other on her back, swaying her to the music and keeping them from bumping into others.

She pulled out her phone and slid her finger across it. The message filled the screen.

I spot you across the bar. You look beautiful, and I know you've come here with someone else. I can see him holding you like he wants you in his bed. I bet he's already imagining what you'd feel like beneath him. But he doesn't know. Doesn't know that my eyes are on you, that you're already mine, and that tonight, it's going to be my hands on you, my cock inside you . . .

A gasp slipped out of her, and her feet turned to stone against the floor, halting their movements. They were familiar words. Words from Donovan's recordings. She glanced around, scanning the crowd, looking for him. But the place was dark and crowded, the faces only shapes in the shadows.

Lane looked down at her in concern. "Everything okay?"

She blinked, dragging herself out of her shocked state. "Uh, yeah, sorry. It's . . . yeah, everything's fine."

Lane frowned. "Is it your brother?"

She shook her head and forced her feet to move again after earning an annoyed look from a passing couple. But her blood was pumping hard and her body lighting up with awareness. Was Donovan really here? The thought should've worried her. Stalker behavior, no thanks. But this wasn't that. This was one of the fantasies from college. Your safe word is BLUE. That had been the message earlier.

This was the game. She was now the girl in the recordings.

Her skin prickled with heat.

Lane's gaze was heavy on her. His eyes narrowed slightly. "So it was West."

"Huh?"

Lane kept dancing, but his focus stayed solidly on her. "You're flushed, and I can see your pulse jumping at your throat."

"I really need to stop hanging around with therapist types," she groused. "Y'all are always looking for every little thing. I'm fine."

She moved her hand to drop her phone back into her purse, but in her haste, she fumbled it. The phone clattered to the ground. Before she could make a grab for it, Lane had let her go and swept it out of the way of an oncoming couple. His eyes, of course, skimmed over the screen.

"Lane, don't." She yanked the phone from him.

But when he looked over at her, something new had flared in his green eyes. He guided her back into his hold with ease. "Well, looks like I was right."

She closed her eyes, her face burning. "You cannot breathe a word. Seriously. My job . . ."

"Is perfectly safe. I told you. I'd already figured it out, and I'm not telling anyone's secrets." He leaned closer. "But damn if I'm not jealous as hell."

She looked up at him.

His smile was wry. "I'm a pawn in some scene tonight, aren't I?"

"Scene?"

"Kink." He rolled her out for a spin and then captured her again. "You two are playing."

She let out a breath. How the hell had her near-virgin self gotten into this? Two weeks ago she'd been blushing over talking about masturbation, now she was having a conversation with a co-worker about how she was part of some kinky game. She was flailing around in the deep end, no floaties in sight. But she was caught. There was no getting around it. "You're not a pawn. I didn't know what would happen tonight. And I really do want to be friends and am enjoying tonight. I don't want you to feel like—"

"Don't apologize. I think it's hot as fuck."

"What?" The switch in tone and the frank language startled her.

He shrugged. "I already suspected Donovan was a kinky bastard. I usually recognize my own kind. But I never would've guessed it of you."

Now it was her turn for surprise. "Your own kind?"

The amiable Lane smiled, a wicked glint in his eye. "You know how I said I have work mode and personal mode?"

She nodded.

"Well, personal mode is Master Cannon. After all that patience and tenderness at work, I need another kind of outlet in my off hours."

Her lips parted. "You're a dominant?"

"Now you know my secret. We're even." The music shifted into something slower, and Lane adjusted their movements to accommodate it. "So, you don't know the plan?"

She swallowed past the dryness in her throat. She had no idea why, but somehow it was making her hotter knowing that Lane was now aware of what she was doing with Donovan. "I don't know for sure. But Donovan's recordings—the ones he made for his study in college. There was a scenario like this. A guy watches a woman on a date. You get the sense that they know each other, that maybe she's been teasing him, wants to flaunt her date in front of him, taunt him. And then he . . . calls her bluff. Takes her."

"By force?" Lane asked, no censure in his voice.

Her face heated. "I'd call it strong persuasion."

"Damn," Lane breathed. "It's always the quiet ones. You sure you don't prefer blonds? I'm really, really good in bed. People pay me for it, you know."

She shoved his shoulder, earning a laugh from him.

"All right." Lane tugged her closer. "I'll stop. If you're his, I'm not going to mess with that. But if that's the fantasy, then maybe we should play along."

"Play along?"

His smile turned mischievous, and he leaned forward, brushing his lips over the shell of her ear and sending a shiver down her neck. "Yes, Dr. Rush. You want him to be wild for you, right? If he's here somewhere, let's taunt him."

Marin's breath whooshed out of her. "Lane."

He dragged her to him, his chest hard against hers, all semblance of polite dancing space disappearing. He tipped his head toward her as he rocked his hips in time to the sensual rhythm of the music. "All you have to do is say stop and I stop. But this could be fun.

The more real everything feels, the more exciting it is. Trust me. I know how to play these games, too. Pretend there's no one else in the room but me."

Marin stared up at him in shock. "But what if he thinks we're really into each other?"

"Then he'll be that much more motivated to lure you away from me." He nuzzled her jaw. From a distance, it probably looked like he was kissing her neck. "Imagine the possibilities. He's going to play with your fear. It's only fair that you play with his a little, too."

"I doubt he's that scared," she said dryly. "We've just started this. If I was interested in someone else, he'd just move on."

Lane's hand cupped the back of her head as he gave her a look that anyone watching would've been able to identify. Full-on seduction. He was playing the role to the hilt. "Guess we'll find out."

Before she could respond, he guided her arms around his neck and then palmed her waist, pressing her hips to his. The grind of their bodies against each other was enough to make Marin lose her words. She had another man on her mind, but Lane wasn't easily ignored. Her body was already primed, and having a beautiful man sliding against her fired signals she couldn't have stopped if she tried. But when she closed her eyes to give in to the ruse, all she could think about was Donovan somewhere out there in the darkness watching them. The thought inspired equal doses of desire and tension.

"Hold on, doc," Lane said against her ear.

She opened her eyes just as Lane whirled her to the edge of the dance floor, making the room spin and blur in her view, and then he dipped her low. Lane's hand dragged her knee up to his hip, angling her farther back and holding her there. She felt like she'd stumbled into some scene from *Dirty Dancing*. But with her head upside down, her eyes landed on a man at a table a few yards away. His face was half in shadow, his arms spread wide over the back of the curved booth in a seemingly relaxed pose, but his gaze raked over her with pure hunger. Possession.

Warning.

Fire licked up her spine as an invisible tether between them pulled taut. Suspended animation.

That's when Lane kissed up her throat.

The tether snapped. Donovan's lips thinned, icy cool descending over his expression.

When Lane lifted her back up, the view flipped over in her vision, everything spinning from more than just the dance. It took her a second to clear her head of the dizzy spell. And when she looked over her shoulder, trying to locate Donovan again, needing to say something, to make him understand, he was gone.

The booth was empty, the spot melting back into the darkness without the energy of his presence to light it.

Donovan had left.

He'd believed the act. And he'd left her to it.

Left her to Lane.

Lane had challenged Donovan to make a play for her.

Donovan had decided she wasn't worth the trouble.

Game over.

24

Marin asked Lane for a break after Donovan disappeared, disappointment a heavy rock in her gut. She shouldn't let it get to her. What would she have done if she'd shown up somewhere and saw Donovan dancing like that with some woman? She wouldn't have stuck around to watch either. She'd talk to him about it tomorrow. For now, she'd finish up her night with Lane and get home.

Lane had ordered bottles of water and she'd downed hers, parched after all the dancing. But now her bladder was begging for a break. A different band had taken the stage, and Lane was listening, his arm draped across the back of Marin's chair. She hadn't told him she'd seen Donovan. But she'd told Lane to stop after the kisses to her neck. He hadn't questioned her or seemed bothered.

She leaned over to him. "I'll be right back. Need me to grab anything else from the bar on the way back?"

"Nah, I'm fine. We can head out in a little while if you want."

"Sounds good." She got up from the table and headed toward the back of the club. The line to the ladies' room was impossibly long and she squirmed at the sight. No way was she going to make it that long. The sign for the men's room pointed left at the end of the hall. She hustled that way and turned the corner into another hallway. The men's room was located near the back door. No line. Thank God for men being efficient urinaters. With a quick peek inside the door, she made sure no one was at a urinal and then hurried inside to slip into a stall.

She thought she was home free with her commandeering of the men's room. But after she finished up and headed toward the sinks, two guys walked in. They halted when they saw her there. But she quickly washed and dried her hands and then sent them an awkward flick of the wrist. "Uh, sorry. Just leaving. Carry on."

She strolled past them like she had every right to be there and rushed out the door. She let out a breath when she hit the dark hallway. Victory.

But before she could head back up the hallway toward the club, an arm banded around her from behind and dragged her against a hard body. She let out a yelp, but a hand clamped over her mouth before the sound could fully escape. Fear crashed through her and she tried to jerk away.

"Easy, Rush," the familiar voice said against her ear.

Donovan.

She closed her eyes, her heartbeat thumping wildly and adrenaline making her wobble on her heels.

"You thought I'd forgotten about you, huh?" he said, his voice low and dangerous against her ear. He moved his hand away from her mouth. "You thought I'd watch him put his hands and mouth on you and just walk away."

Her tongue pressed to the roof of her mouth, words sticking in her throat.

"You want to fuck him?" he asked, the calmness in his voice edged with challenge. "Because he certainly wants to fuck you."

It was impossible to tell if his anger was genuine or if this was part of the game. A fine sheen of sweat broke out on her skin, but the nerves didn't stop her desire from spiking like a fever. "No, I—"

"You're mine tonight. Every damn inch of you." His breath was hot against her neck and his arm around her abdomen tight. "Tell me you're mine."

She swallowed past the constriction in her throat. "I'm yours."

"Tell me who'll be fucking you tonight."

She was trembling in his hold, but that initial fight-or-flight response had fallen away. What replaced it was potent and breath-stealing. Flashes of hearing Donovan's words in the hallway that night long ago flitted through her brain. How badly she'd wanted a taste of what that felt like, to be consumed with lust for someone, to break the rules for it. "You."

He nuzzled her neck and her nipples stiffened beneath her dress. "Tell me your safe word."

It took her a second to answer, her body's responses overtaking most of her faculties. "Blue."

He pushed his hips against her, his erection obvious against her backside. "You're going to leave with me. Now's your chance, Rush. What color is the sky?"

She squeezed her eyes shut, goose bumps breaking out over her skin. He was giving her a chance to pull the plug, to let him know if it was too much. She'd told him she wanted the fantasies. But maybe she was jumping in too far too fast. Fear beat a tattoo against her ribs.

His hand splayed out over her belly, sunk lower, pressing on the spot that was starting to throb. "What. Color. Is. The. Sky?"

Her chest rose and fell with a harsh breath. The word was out before she could think too much more about it. "Green."

His hand curved, cupping her sex through the fabric of her dress and applying knee-weakening pressure. "You're going to stay quiet and come with me. If you play nice, I might let your date get home tonight without getting his teeth knocked in for touching you."

"Lane knows about us. He . . . saw your text." She was having trouble stringing together words with his hand stroking her. "He was . . . playing, too. He . . . liked the idea."

"Is that right? Hmm, maybe I should make him watch, then. Show him what he doesn't get to have."

She stiffened, some weird combination of terror and illicit desire braiding through her. "No, we can't—"

He nipped her earlobe. "Don't worry. Tonight, you're only for me. But don't think I didn't feel you clench and catch your breath at the thought of being watched. Filthy thoughts, Rush. You should be blushing. Have you no shame?"

"Fuck you," she ground out but couldn't muster any ire in it.

"That's the idea." He stroked her, arousal clamoring to meet his every move, and her head tipped back against his shoulder.

Voices sounded near the bathroom door, and Donovan dragged her back, farther into the shadowed corner, tucking them between the back door and an empty trash can. His hand shifted and slipped beneath her dress.

She let out a whimper, but bit down on her lip when the two men she'd seen in the restroom exited. If they turned her way, they wouldn't be able to see where Donovan's hand had gone, but she knew everything would show on her face.

Donovan shoved aside her panties and slid two hot fingers along her naked flesh.

"Fuck, yes," he growled. "Feel how soaked you already are. How bad you want this. You know what that does to me?"

She couldn't talk. She was already riding an edge, and his skilled fingers were rocketing her closer to it.

Donovan released his hold on her waist and then a second hand was beneath her dress. He yanked her panties down and she gasped.

"Step out of them," he commanded. "When I walk you out, when you say good-bye to your date, I want to know that all that's beneath this dress is this sexy cunt all slippery and hot for me."

She groaned—the words driving her just as high as his touch. She stepped out of her panties and kicked them to the side. He reached down, swept them off the floor, and tucked them into his suit jacket's inner pocket.

He stepped in front of her, backing her up against the wall and bracketing her with his arms. She'd seen Donovan with desire on his face. But never had she experienced the thunderous lust he was sending her way now. It hit her like an air bag. Boom. Lungs crushed. No breath.

"I wanted you like this from the very first moment I saw you. Back then. And now." He leaned forward, his lips brushing hers. "Tonight. I will fucking have you."

She shuddered, heat tracing over her skin and winding through her. "I want that, too."

He cupped her chin, the scent of her arousal on his fingers, and tipped her face toward him. "Go tell Lane thanks for playing and to have a good night."

She nodded in his grip.

He released her and stepped back. The loss of his body heat was distinct, setting her off balance. But he grabbed her elbow and turned her, guiding her forward on weak knees.

Every step she could feel the cool air drifting up her dress, the slide of her sex as she moved, wet and throbbing with heat. When she stepped back into the club, it felt like everyone would be able to tell just how aroused and naked she was through that thin fabric. But of course, no one paid the girl in the black dress any mind. No one except Lane.

When he spotted her from a few tables away, his gaze slid over her and then hopped to Donovan who'd hung back a few steps. Lane gave an almost imperceptible nod to the man behind her and then swung his attention back to Marin.

She tried to keep her back straight, her walk steady as she made her way to his table.

Lane leaned forward, arms braced on the tabletop, and sent her a sinful smile. "So it worked?"

She tried to speak but had to clear her throat first. "Seems so."

"You're leaving then?"

"Yes. Thank you for tonight. I really did have a nice time." She could feel Donovan somewhere behind her, his gaze burning into her.

Lane stood and pulled her into a gentle hug. "Thank *you*. You two reminded me why it's been far too long since I've played these games for myself. Donovan's a lucky bastard to have the privilege with you."

He let her go and she smiled. "Thanks."

He reached into his pocket and then placed a card in her hand. "I imagine you're very safe with Donovan. But you should have a friend you can trust to check in with when you play. Text me later and let me know you're okay. Doesn't matter what time."

She was touched by the gesture. Lane could've been pissed she'd dragged him into this. Instead, he was offering to be her phone-a-friend. She dropped the card into her purse and then pushed up on her toes and gave him a kiss on the cheek. "You're a good guy, Lane Cannon."

He smirked. "Not that good. Have fun, Dr. Rush."

Donovan stepped up behind her then, placing a proprietary hand on her lower back. "Time to go."

He didn't ask. He told. She found she didn't mind. "Okay."

Donovan looked to Lane and put his other hand out to him. "Lane."

Lane shook Donovan's hand. "Doc."

It was a firm shake, the testosterone high, but Marin didn't sense malice there, only a current of respect. "I trust this stays between the three of us and will not affect any working relationships."

Lane nodded. "Of course."

"Thank you." Donovan released Lane's hand and nodded a good-bye.

With that, he guided Marin forward through the crowded club, his hand warm against her back. To outside eyes, they probably looked like such a proper couple. She in an unassuming black dress, he in a crisp dark suit. Two professionals out for drinks who might go home and have nice, polite sex.

But when they stepped outside into the muggy night air, Donovan's hand slid down to her ass, his grip punishing and his message clear.

She was his tonight.

And he would have his way.

God, did she want to let him.

25

Donovan had to reel himself in as he drove away from the club, Marin next to him, the subtle scent of her arousal perfuming the air. The woman was temptation personified. She had no idea how far to the edge she'd already driven him tonight. Seeing her dancing with Lane, his hands and mouth on her— Donovan had wanted to claim Marin right there like some chest-pounding caveman. But Lane had looked up while he'd mouthed Marin's throat, catching Donovan's attention. Lane had told him all he needed to know with that look. *Come and get her, doc. She's mighty sweet.* Lane had become part of the game.

And though Donovan wasn't on board with sharing Marin with anyone, the interplay had turned him the hell on. Because it meant Marin was all in. She was willing to dance along those boundaries, push the limits, test him. She was a fucking vixen wrapped in the trappings of a virgin. Her responses were so purely sensual, so hungry, that he had to keep himself from wanting to rush into try- ing every damn thing with her. Her shame instinct was there, but once she was turned on, all those shackles broke away. She'd shivered at the thought of Lane watching them fuck. Not fear. Curiosity. She'd spent a life eating white bread and now a lavish feast was spread before her and she wanted a taste of it all.

He wanted to give it to her.

Starting tonight. He reached over and rested his hand on her knee, stroking the delicate skin with his fingertips. "You're quiet over there. You okay?"

She peered over at him. "I'm good. I guess I'm just not sure if we're still in role-playing mode or not."

He kept his eyes on the city streets. "Who said I was playing a role? Everything I said to you in there was one hundred percent true. That was me saying whatever I wanted to say, doing what I wanted to do to you, what I've thought about doing to you all day."

"Oh, well . . . oh."

He glanced over at her with a half-smile. "That make you nervous?"

She considered him, the sharp therapist still there despite the hum of lust. "No. Well, yes, but in a good way."

He let his hand slide toward her inner thigh and pulled gently. "Spread your legs for me."

Her teeth dragged along her lip, but she let him guide her knees apart. He wrapped his fingers around the hem of her dress and eased the fabric up. He couldn't see much in the dark car, but her scent hit his nose and went straight to his cock. "You're still soaked, aren't you? I can smell how turned on you are."

She groaned in what distinctly sounded like embarrassment. "Jesus, West, way to make a girl feel self-conscious."

She tried to clamp her knees back together, but he squeezed her thigh and kept her in place. "Don't you dare. It's sexy as fuck. It's got me hard as iron." He took her hand and placed it on his erection to prove his point. "If I wasn't driving, I'd bury my face between your thighs and lick up every bit of it, wear that scent like goddamned cologne."

A soft expelled breath hit his ears. He moved her hand away from him, worried he wouldn't have the restraint not to pull over to the side of the road and fuck her right there in the car. He placed her hand back on her own thigh, dragging it up and down, making her fingers glide along her own skin. "Lift your dress to your waist and touch yourself for me."

Her arms tensed beneath his fingers. "What?"

He sent her a look. "Recline the seat, keep your legs spread, and show me how you get yourself off."

Anxiety flickered in her gaze, and she glanced at the road before them. He'd taken a back way, gotten them out of the French Quarter and was now heading back out to The Grove on a quiet state highway.

"Donovan, I can't—"

"The windows are tinted and it's nighttime. No one will see you but me. And I want to see." He couldn't tell in the dark, but he had a feeling her blushing problem had returned with a vengeance. "Are you blushing, Marin?"

"You know I am."

"All the more reason to do this." He placed his hand high on her thigh and stroked as he rolled up to a stop sign. "Own it. You are a beautiful woman who knows how to give herself pleasure. That's hot as hell. After I caught you getting yourself off in the lab that night, I couldn't get the image out of my mind. That sight of you so turned on, fingers rubbing between your legs, so needy and desperate to come. I only saw you from the back but man, did I imagine what it might've looked like from other angles. Now I want the privilege of seeing it in person."

Her eyes were wide, but he could tell the nerves weren't going to be a match for the desire swirling there. "Are you going to do the same for me one day then?"

He smiled. "That something you want to see?"

"You have no idea," she said in a rush and then winced like she hadn't meant for that to slip out.

"Sneak over one morning before work, and I'll give you whatever kind of show you want." He reached over and hit the button to recline her seat. "But you're going to show me first."

She bit her lip. "Maybe I should've had that second drink."

He shook his head. "No. You're going to do this for me stonecold sober. Show me how you like to touch yourself."

For a moment, he thought she'd call a time-out or use the safe word. This was past her comfort zone. Hell, she'd hardly been able to talk about masturbation with him that night by the fountain. But after a few long seconds, she leaned back against the seat and lifted her dress the rest of the way.

The dark hair of her mound in the ambient glow of the streetlights was a sharp contrast to the pale skin, giving him more of a view than he'd hoped for, and when she spread her knees, the slick pink lips of her shaved pussy came into view.

Fuck. He'd felt that smooth skin when he'd played with her in the bar, but seeing it was an entirely different thing. She'd shaved for tonight. He didn't have a preference so much on whether a woman went smooth or not. But God, it did something to him to think of her preparing for him. He couldn't resist reaching out and dragging a fingertip over her newly exposed skin. "Trying a new look?"

She closed her eyes, shame clearly still fighting for a hold. "I— I did some research. A lot of women report that they're more sensitive this way, that things . . . feel more intense. I thought I'd try it."

She'd done research. Of course she had. Marin wouldn't go about things any other way. He smiled to himself. He was also happy to hear she'd done it for her own enjoyment. So many women he saw in therapy got hung up on what look would please the guy they were with, never even considering how they personally felt about it. "Well, let's see if it worked. Touch yourself, Marin."

Marin's hand rested on her inner thigh, her fingers twitching ever so slightly. Her anxiety was a flavor on his tongue, an aphrodisiac. Knowing she was willing to push past those fears for him did more to him than it should. He stayed at the stop sign, no one behind them to rush him, and watched as her hand traced closer to the place where she had to be aching. Then as if she were jumping off a cliff, she quickly put her hand on herself and rubbed her fingers over her clit.

The simple touch made her jolt and the sharp sound she made went straight to his cock. She was a vibrating cord of tension, so on edge that the slightest stroke was going to feel like too much. "That's right, baby. Give yourself some relief. It's been such a long night already."

He made sure his voice was quiet, soothing, wanting to add to her experience instead of distract her. And it seemed to work. The tense scrunch of her shoulders eased against the seat and she rubbed herself again, pushing fingertips between her lips and exploring. Any reservations she may have had got swept up in the need for release, for stimulation. He was learning with her that she just had to get to that tipping point and then that secret side of her came out, the one who had dirty fantasies of her own.

Donovan pressed his hand around his erection, needing the pressure but also not granting himself a stroke. He wanted to enjoy the view, savor this. Marin's nipples became visible through the fabric of her dress and her neck curved as she began to softly pant. He wished he could photograph her just like this, show her how fucking gorgeous she was when she let go, but he settled for burning the image into his mind.

"Oh, God." Her plea was soft, breathless.

"It's okay, take what you need," Donovan said, reaching over and brushing his knuckles over her nipple, back and forth, back and forth.

Marin gasped at that, her back arching and her fingers working harder, more focused. The sounds of slick flesh and the scent of arousal filled the car, and Donovan couldn't tear his gaze away as Marin brought herself to a quick, but what looked to be intense, orgasm.

Her chest rose and fell with gulping breaths and her eyes stayed squeezed shut. But after a few last cries of release, she moved her hand away, letting her arm fall to the side.

"Shit," she whispered, almost to herself.

Donovan gave her breast one last stroke. Then he reached down and righted her dress. "Beautiful. Feel better?"

"I can't believe I just did that."

"You're more daring than you think. Your desire's there. You just need a nudge." He finally rolled forward through the stop sign and tried to mentally tamp down his own level of arousal. At this rate, he was going to walk into his place with a monster hard-on leading the way.

She shifted in the seat. "You make me stop thinking. It freaks me out a little."

He smiled and reached for her hand, lacing his fingers with hers and hitting the gas to rocket them down the dark road. "I make you stop thinking, and you wake me up."

The statement slipped out, the private thought hijacking his vocal cords. He almost snapped it right back, said something to undo it. But her fingers simply tightened around his. "Guess we're a pretty good match then."

The words should've scared him.

But with her next to him and the night in front of them, he couldn't access that fear. "Guess we are."

26

Marin kept her hand linked with Donovan's for long, quiet minutes—both of them lost in their own thoughts. She stared out the open window, hair whipping in the humid breeze. The scenery had shifted from civilization to the eerie beauty of the bayous—towering shadows of cypress with low-hanging moss that seemed to grow out of the water, the occasional crane perched on the side of the road, and the dark smell of wet earth drifting in on the air. Another world, really.

It seemed fitting. Since setting foot on the grounds at The Grove, her world had morphed, too. Her feet weren't steady under her yet. Like running on that slippery bayou silt at full speed, she could tumble at any moment. Fall. Get dragged under.

Donovan could drag her under.

They were only playing a game tonight, acting out a fantasy, but her mind was having trouble keeping the lines straight between that and reality. She needed to remember that this was a script, that they were in roles. It felt intense because it was set up to be that way. But the words he'd said, the ones she'd sensed he hadn't meant to let slip out, wound through her head like a drug.

You wake me up.

Four simple words. But they'd crashed into her like a semi-truck, bending and twisting everything inside her.

Why did he have to say things like that? Why do that when he knew this setup had an expiration date? Why try to make her feel something she couldn't risk feeling? Like she was special to him in some way.

How idiotic a thought was that? Donovan was a good guy. She knew he was. But he was also a guy who'd outright told her he was skilled at getting women into his bed and then leaving it. Maybe that's why McCray had been so pissed. He'd made her feel special, too. McCray had thought she was different, that she'd be the one he couldn't walk away from.

But Donovan would walk. That's what he did. That's what he was good at.

Marin needed to keep that at the forefront of her mind. She could give herself over to this affair but not like that. She couldn't plant false hope and let it grow into something that would only die from lack of light when the sun set on this relationship.

"What time is your brother supposed to be home tonight?" Donovan asked, glancing her way.

"He should get in around four."

"Okay." He looked back to the road.

"Why?"

His lips quirked like an afterthought. "Just making my devious plans and I like to know the schedule."

She sniffed. "Is that going to be enough time for all your depravity? I could text him and tell him that he shouldn't expect me until morning." She winced slightly when she realized how presumptuous that sounded. "I mean, not that you'd want me to— Never mind."

His jaw tightened along with his grip on her hand. "I'd love for you to stay the night."

The words sounded genuine, but it cost him something to make the offer. She could tell by the lines that appeared around his mouth, almost like he'd wanted to keep the words in. "You sure? You don't have to feel obligated or whatever."

He looked over at her. When she sent him a no-big-deal shrug, his expression softened around the edges. "Obligated to do unspeakable things to you all night and then sleep in on a Sunday morning with a beautiful, naked you next to me? Yes, sounds horrid. I can't believe you'd suggest such agony."

She looked down, her lips curving on their own volition. "Yeah, sounds awful."

"Text him. We're almost there. You won't have time for your phone after that."

The small warning zipped through her, lighting up things she'd barely dimmed with the relief of her earlier orgasm. She reluctantly slipped her hand from his and fished her phone out of her bag. But when she pulled up the messaging screen, reality wedged its way in.

She'd made the offer because she wanted to spend the night with Donovan, but she hadn't thought through the fact that it would mean telling Nate outright that she was staying overnight with a guy—after only two weeks here. She considered lying. That would be easiest—too tired to drive home, getting a room, whatever. But she'd built her relationship with Nate on being straightforward and honest. She couldn't bring herself to fib.

She sighed and typed out a message.

Marin: Not going to be home til morning. Text me when u get in to let me know ur safe and remember to lock up.

The message went through, and she had a pang of anxiety. It was her brother, but in a lot of ways she felt like she was texting her kid, *Hey there, son, Mom's about to get laid!*

The response took a while to come through since he was probably busy working, but after a few minutes, her phone dinged.

Nate: Srsly? Just friends. Yeah. OK.

Marin grimaced. She could hear Nathan's irritated, judgy tone even through words on a screen. But she had her own surge of irritation to match it. Really? He was going to be angry with her over a night out? How long had she put her own life aside to be the responsible one, to be the grown-up? She never resented Nate or regretted the choice she'd made to raise him, but hadn't she earned a little adventure? She would not let herself feel guilty about this. Would. Not.

Marin: It's not Lane. Old friend. Long story.

The little dots indicating a response being typed seemed to shine on the screen forever. But when the message came up, it was short. Like he'd deleted a whole lot more.

Nate: Whatever. See u tomorrow.

Marin exhaled loudly and didn't bother typing a response. She had no doubt she'd get an earful tomorrow—or more likely, the silent treatment. She tossed her phone back in her purse.

Donovan sent a lifted eyebrow her way. "Everything okay?"

"It's fine. Nate's just in a shit mood. This whole move has been a big transition, and he's taking it out on me. He'll be all right."

"You want to call him?"

She shook her head. "We won't get anywhere. It's best to just let him cool off. I'll talk to him about it when I get home tomorrow. Right now I'll let him think what he wants."

Donovan sniffed. "Which is?"

"That I'm some sex-crazed woman who's jumping in bed with a stranger."

"Hey, I'm not a stranger," he said, as he took the back way into The Grove. "The sex-crazed part is dead-on though."

She laughed. "I will not deny this."

He reached out and cupped her neck. "You should put your head in my lap."

The flip in subject threw her. "What?"

"If you want to be safe, make sure no one sees us."

"Oh." She shook her head, trying to clear her head of other thoughts. "Right."

He guided her down to his thigh, his fingers stroking her hair as he drove the winding road that led to his place. She felt a little ridiculous at the sneaking around, but soon his touch was too distracting to let her think of much else.

"When we get to the house, you're all mine, Rush. Your safe word applies always, but you need to let me know now if you have any qualms about this. We can take things down a notch if you're not ready to continue what we started at the club. It's your call."

His fingertips were gentle against her scalp, but the words were like droplets of ice water against her skin, making everything hyper-aware again. What did she want? What was she ready for?

She closed her eyes, giving the question honest consideration. She was a novice at this. She had no idea what she was doing. Taking the safe route would be smart. They could take things nice and easy, cover the basics. Sex with Donovan was going to be fantastic no matter what. But a little pang of disappointment went through her at the thought of going that way. She wasn't experienced. But some part of her knew instinctually that her wires weren't straight and neat. They were crossed, tangled. That was one of the reasons things had gotten so electric with Donovan so quickly in college. All those vague cravings and fleeting fantasies had been given names when she'd listened to Donovan's recordings.

So all she could muster up at the thought of what might happen if she gave him the green light tonight was anticipation. She'd gotten the painful part out of the way with her virginity, so she wasn't worried about that. And Donovan had told her he liked things rough, but she didn't get the sense he was a sadist who'd bust out whips or knives or anything. Even if he was, he'd listen to her safe word. "I'm ready for this."

His fingers paused for a second, and his thigh tensed beneath her cheek. She worried then that he'd take it back, that he'd decide for her that they'd go easy tonight. But after a moment, she felt him relax. "Me, too, Rush. Me, too."

The sound of a garage door opening and shutting was the last moment before Donovan slipped right back into the place he'd been in the darkened hallway of the club. He palmed the side of her head and lifted her from her spot on his lap. His blue eyes were dark when they landed on her. "Stay put until I get you."

That left her with a shiver as he got out of the car and walked around to her side to open the door. His steps seemed interminable, her heartbeat hopping at the sound of his shoes on the concrete floor. By the time he helped her out of the car, her lungs felt like they weren't capable of expanding. He was so close. So *intent*. He cupped her chin, his gaze coasting over her face and then sliding lower, taking his time and not hiding his open perusal. Her nipples strained against her bra as his attention moved over them. "You ready to play a game, Marin?"

His tone was smooth, dangerously enticing, like a stranger holding the most delicious candy out to her. She could almost taste the sweetness on her tongue. She concentrated, forced her voice to work. "Yes."

His lips ticked up at the corner ever so slightly, something new there in his eyes, a sinister eroticism that drew her in like a winding trail of breadcrumbs. This was the Donovan who'd made the tapes, the private side beneath all those other layers. "You have five minutes. You're going to go in the house and find a good hiding place. You want it to be really good because for each minute it takes me to find you, that's how many times you get to come tonight."

All remaining air left her. *Whoosh.* Gone.

"But also for every minute I can't find you, I'm going to add another item from your list to cover tonight. Items of *my* choosing." His thumb stroked her cheek. "And there are some doozies on there."

Oh, God. The list ran through her mind on fast-forward. Some were things she'd love to try, others she was half-terrified. And she had a feeling he wasn't going to choose the simple ones.

"So you'll have to decide if more pleasure is worth the risk of more boundaries pushed. And the longer it takes me to find you, the more frustrated I'm going to get. I'm not very nice when I'm frustrated, Rush." He leaned forward and brushed his lips over hers, sending hot chills radiating straight downward. "Understand the rules?"

Her tongue swiped over her lip, catching the taste of his kiss lingering there. "Yes."

"Good." He released her and stepped around her to unlock the door to the house and deactivate the alarm. When he turned back to her, his smile was predatory. "Better get going, gorgeous. Your time starts now."

It took her a second for the words to make it through her lusty haze, but when they finally registered, she kicked off her heels and launched herself into the house. Part of her felt ridiculous for joining in some adult version of hide-and-seek, but that small part was drowned out by the sheer thrill of it. How often in her life did she get to have pure, unadulterated fun? To forget that you were supposed to be serious and responsible and practical? She was supposed to be a grown-up, for God's sake. But this, running from Donovan turned all kind of dials for her. Fun ones. Sexy ones. Competitive ones. The edge of anxiety weaving through all of that only added to it. Her senses were heightened already, and they hadn't even made it to the naked stuff yet.

So she didn't care what the stakes were at this point. She was determined to find a good place. She didn't play games to lose. Though, she had a feeling neither of them were going to lose tonight.

She hurried through the house, considering alcoves and behind couches and beneath curtains, but every place seemed too obvious. She tried the door to his bedroom but found it locked. That gave her pause, but she didn't have time to waste. She hustled barefoot into the guest bedroom. She peered under the bed but she wasn't skinny enough to wiggle under there.

"Time's ticking away, Rush." The voice came from the direction of the garage. He hadn't come in yet, but it wouldn't be long.

She yanked open the louvered doors of the guest closet. Donovan's winter wear hung from the rack and the floor had a few pairs of shoes. When her eyes alighted on a pair of black cowboy boots, she paused. Firstly, because Donovan West had cowboy boots. She'd never seen him in such a thing and wanted to rectify that immediately. But secondly, it gave her an idea. She peered over her shoulder to make sure he wasn't already heading down the hallway and then grabbed a black peacoat from the hanger and slipped it on. It was far too big and too long, but that's what she needed. She quickly slipped her feet inside the cowboy boots, happy to see the shoes and coat completely hid her bare legs. She snagged a knit cap from a shelf and pulled it over her head. Then she stepped into the far corner of the closet, shut the doors and turned her back to them.

The bad news was that she wouldn't be able to watch and see if the light changed between the slats on the louvered door. But the good news was that if he opened it, she'd have an outside shot that he wouldn't see her unless he looked closely. There were enough jackets between her and where he'd be and she had everything covered. She closed her eyes, pressed her forehead against the wall of the closet, and strained her ears to listen.

A minute or so later, she heard Donovan call out. "Time's up. Clock's ticking for a new reason now."

She pressed her lips together, trying to calm her breathing. She didn't want to give herself away. But when she heard his shoes hit the hardwoods, her teeth bit into her lip. He walked slow but with purpose. She could hear doors being opened, things being moved around. Her heartbeat thrummed in her ears, and the heat from her body clung to her inside the heavy coat, making everything even warmer.

She swallowed past the constriction in her throat. It was like being in a horror movie, straining to hear any movements, any sign that you were about to be caught. Logically, she knew she was in no danger, but her body interpreted things otherwise. Fight-or-flight was welling up in her and twining with the arousal that had been humming there already, heightening everything. Heart pounding, skin prickling.

"You've earned yourself one orgasm, Rush," Donovan called out from down the hall somewhere. "That's good news. I'd hate for you to go all night without one. The teasing would've been fun though."

She nearly groaned but held it in at the last second. The coat smelled like him. Or what the winter version of Donovan probably smelled like—fresh laundry and charred hickory. Like he'd sat by a fire wearing this coat.

The footsteps moved closer. *Step. Step. Step.* A door nearby opened. Probably his office. His footfalls moved farther away as he explored the room. But then when he called out that she'd earned number two and number three, his voice sounded much, much closer. Oh shit. This room had to be next.

She tucked her hands in the pockets of the coat, her fists curling, and tried to breathe noiselessly. "Last possible room. You're running out of hiding spots, Rush. Are you somewhere imagining what I'm going to do to you when I find you? I'm already hard just thinking about it. Maybe I should just take a break, lie on this bed, and give myself a little respite, a little relief."

The voice was far too close, the words far too tempting. Oh, fuck. He wouldn't, would he? She wanted to turn and look, to bust out of the closet and see if he was teasing or serious. But she forced herself to stay stock-still. She would not break. She would not let him win that easily. She squeezed her eyes tighter.

But then she heard the faint squeak of bedsprings and the clink of a belt being unbuckled. *Oh, Jesus Christ.* He so wasn't playing fair. She'd outright told him how much she wanted to see him touch himself. Now he was going to taunt her with a view she couldn't have unless she gave herself away? Dirty fighting. That's what he was doing.

God, she loved it. Loved that he wasn't going to be a gentleman about this.

When she heard him expel a breath, she broke. She couldn't do it. She had to turn around. With silent feet, she shifted her body, holding herself rigidly so she wouldn't knock any of the metal hangers and then leaned around the edge of the coats. The slats in the closet door wouldn't give her an easy view, but they'd give her something. And when her eyes adjusted to the faint light outside the closet, it gave her more than that. Donovan was stretched out on the bed. He'd taken off his suit coat but the dress shirt was still on, his tie loose and the fly of his slacks open. And his hand, that beautiful hand with the long fingers and strong grip, was wrapped around his cock.

Everything inside her body clenched like a fist. Shameless didn't even begin to describe it. He was taking his time, enjoying long, slow glides over that thick, hard flesh. The tip was glossy in the moonlight that shone through the window, and he casually rubbed a thumb over the top, spreading the fluid around the head.

Guh. That was the sound she made. But she swallowed it down before it could slip out.

"This feels good, baby. So fucking good. I've done this quite a lot lately, thinking about you."

He squeezed and rubbed, squeezed and rubbed. The slick sound alone was going to do her in. The spot between her thighs had become a throbbing, slippery disaster. Freshly shaven and without any panties to contain things, she had gotten embarrassingly wet. At each little movement, her flesh slid against itself with a lewd, sensual glide. She was tempted to find a way to clean things up, make it neater. Hide the fact that she was this affected. But she was more tempted to just tuck her hand beneath her dress and get herself off.

Instead, she did nothing, too afraid to miss a second of the tableau in front of her. Donovan stroked fingers over his sac, teasing himself, teasing her. "This is very good. But I shouldn't have to do this for myself, Marin. It's not very nice of you to hide from me. You're going to have to pay for that. I think it's time you did."

Her heart jumped into her throat as he casually tucked himself back into his boxers and sat up. His pants were still undone, his erection an intimidating outline against the fabric, but the look in his eye was pure promise. She quickly turned, putting her back to the door, knowing he was going to open it in the next breath.

She pressed the front of her body to the wall and the doors opened with a screech. Cool air moved over her. Every muscle in her body froze, all except the incessant pulsing between her legs. He would see her. She'd moved too quick. Something would be showing. But then he sighed and the doors shut again.

All of her breath sagged out of her. She'd done it! She'd won the game. But before she could take her next breath, the doors were jerked open again and a hand ripped the knit cap off her head.

She shrieked as he wrenched the metal hangers aside. Then he was pressed up against her back, crowding her against the wall in the closet. His erection was hard against her, his lips hot against her ear. "I'd say *olly olly oxen free*, but we both know that's a lie. You're far from free, Dr. Rush."

27

Marin had no idea why she did it. She wanted Donovan so much it was physically paining her. But her immediate instinct when he grabbed her was to fight back. Maybe it was because she didn't like losing. Maybe it was because she was startled. Maybe it was because her body had its own ideas. Whatever it was, she thrashed in his grip and tried to break loose.

Donovan lost his hold for a second when the peacoat slipped off. He was probably as surprised as she was by her behavior, but he quickly got an arm around her again, pinning her to the wall. His breath came quick. "Sky color."

She writhed in his hold, still trying to get free. Her body wanted to fight, but her mind held on to what was happening. "Green."

She sensed his relief even if his hold on her didn't ease. "You're not going anywhere. I don't even know why you bother trying. You can't be a cocktease all night, let some other man put his hands on you, then hide from me and expect mercy."

"Get off of me. You can take care of things yourself."

"That's not how this works. I catch you. I keep you. For whatever use I want. And I know just how I want to use you." He let the hand he had on her waist slide lower, his body still pinning her against the wall. He rucked up her dress with a rough pull and then cupped her. All of that warm, wet welcome was evident. She could feel the shame coming on until he hissed out a breath. "Fuck."

She loved that she'd thrown him off his game a little, that she'd surprised him. Suddenly, she wasn't so ashamed at just how much this was working for her. And she wanted to play, too. "Lane really turned me on. I love blonds."

The growl that came from him was full-on possessive and it sent a hot shiver through her. Two fingers plunged into her pussy without warning, rough and oh so sweet. Her heels came off the ground at the sudden sensation. "You're not going to know how to spell the word *blond* once I'm done with you. Lift your hands and hold on to the rod."

She gasped as he curled his fingers inside her but managed to eke out one word. "No."

He cursed under his breath, but she got the sense that it was out of pleasure, not frustration. He hadn't expected her to play along so much, to fight him. He moved his hand away from between her legs and she whimpered at the loss. He clamped one hand around the back of her neck, keeping her against the wall like a criminal getting ready for a pat down and then went about rustling around in the coats with his other.

After a few moments, he adjusted his hold and grabbed her wrists. He lifted her arms to the clothes rod and then wound something soft around her wrists, knotting it tight and securing her to the bar. She still had her back to him, but she guessed it was a scarf. He checked how tight it was and then released her. Now her arms were bound above her head. She gave it a test tug and realized she was secured for real. Her breaths came faster. Whatever he was going to do to her, he was going to do in the closet.

"You think you can fucking tell me no?" he said, his hands

coming around to squeeze her breasts and vicious, seeking fingers finding her nipples.

When he pinched one nipple hard, need shot down through her all the way to her toes. She'd never been handled so roughly, but it was dialing everything up a notch, making it more intense, better. The urbane doctor was gone. This was Donovan unmasked. The Donovan in his and her private fantasies.

"Go to hell." She wrenched out of the touch, which only made the pinch sting harder.

"I like hell. I'd fit in there." She heard the jingling of keys and then the flip of something. She tried to turn her head, but when she did, all she caught was the glint of a silver blade.

Oh, shit. A snap of instinctual panic went through her as cool metal touched the spot between her shoulders. She gasped out his name.

But that didn't stop him. It wasn't her safe word. The switchblade ripped right through the fabric of her dress from shoulder to thighs. She let out a little cry as the dress gaped open in the back, the heat of him hitting her skin. With a few more quick flicks of the small blade, he divested of her straps and bra. Her clothes fell into a tattered heap at their feet.

"Now you can't run." The words were low and dark, coasting over her skin like a coarse caress. "You're tied up, naked, and about to get fucked wearing only my boots. All while your co-workers sleep somewhere nearby never knowing what a very bad girl you are."

The words should've sounded silly. No grown woman wanted to be called a bad girl, right? But goddamn, did everything inside her just light up like a fucking solar flare. She couldn't even summon a faux protest at that. She ached so badly. It was like she hadn't come in a hundred years. "Please."

"Please what?" he goaded as he shifted behind her, belt clinking, clothes rustling.

It took everything she had to muster up the words, but the game only made this better. She wanted all of it. "Please let me go."

"Wrong answer." He nudged her legs wide with a firm tap from his shoe and then when she didn't move quickly enough, he slapped her on the ass, quick and sharp.

She yelped from the shock and then groaned when he rubbed a hot palm over the sting.

"Mmm, that's a better kind of blush. A woman who gets her ass spanked doesn't have room to blush over other things." He gave her another pop on the other cheek. And another until the sounds of the slaps were the only thing she heard, the burn the only thing she could feel.

She was going to die. Just sag against the bindings and die right there. How could the simplest, most basic move set her off like that? It wasn't the sting, though that was tingly and nice. This wasn't about pain. Or even the fact that it was a punishment of sorts. It was the intimacy of the act. The joy of it. That neither of them felt silly or weird or ridiculous. That slaps on skin and heated flesh and playing erotic games could just be fun. It didn't have to be serious or a big deal. They were having a good time and could do whatever they wanted. She imagined him bending her over his lap and just turning everything rosy red and sensation zipped straight to her clit.

"Look at you leaning into it." There was amusement in his voice, pleasure. "I knew you could be shameless, Rush." He stopped the spanking and tucked his fingers between her legs from behind. Her knees almost gave out as his fingers rubbed her, spreading her arousal with purposely sloppy strokes. "Whenever you think about blushing, you think about how fucking dirty you are. You may have not done everything you want to do yet. But just give it time. Give *us* time. You *are* a slut who hasn't lived up to her potential."

She laughed at that, couldn't help it. Her need was almost at a breaking point and it was making her giddy. "Fuck you, West."

"Finally, she admits what she wants." He pumped two fingers

inside her, slow, slow, slow, driving her to the edge of madness. Then when she whimpered and writhed against him, he added a third, increasing the pressure tenfold. "Tell me you need me to fill you up. Tell me you want my cock right now."

She pressed her forehead to the wall, bent at the waist, and openly begging for him with her body, but she wasn't going to blink on the game. "I want you to let me go."

"Oh, look," he said snidely. "She thinks she has a choice. Cute."

His hand moved up to her clit and then something much bigger than fingers nudged her entrance.

She clenched. Oh, God. Part of her had wondered if he'd actually go through with it. He'd seemed so beat up about taking her virginity over a desk. But apparently taking her the second time had no rules. Anxiety over the unknown welled up.

But he didn't give her a chance to fully form those nerves. He plunged into her fast and hard. She cried out, expecting it to hurt like the first time, but of course it didn't. Oh, fuck it didn't. She was so primed and slick, and her body took him in like it'd been waiting for it for a decade. And the sensation. God. Had it felt like this the first time? It felt like everything in that moment. Full and hot and decadent. Her fingers gripped the clothes rod hard as the force of the thrust rocked her onto her toes.

"That's right." Donovan stroked over her clit, playing her like she was a instrument only he knew the music to as he pumped into her again, sinking to the hilt. "You fucking take it. I know that's what you wanted. Nothing sweet for you, Rush. You want real."

She closed her eyes, her vision blurring from the feel of it all and from that sound in his voice, that catch that said he was losing his mind, too. He wasn't in control. He wasn't the stoic therapist. He was right there with her, unsure how they got here but clearly damn happy that they had.

He gripped her hip with his other hand, hard enough to leave marks, and he fucked her. Not nicely, not neatly, not quietly. Their bodies slapped together, damp skin against damp skin, and he made these noises. God. They were the sexiest grunts she'd ever heard. Like he'd turned into a werewolf behind her, huffing and snarling.

And the feel of him inside her was almost enough to send her right over the top. This wasn't her first time, but it felt like it in a lot of ways. She'd used her fingers, she'd used toys, and she had the memory of him. But none of that had been like this. Not this naked, raw sense of being joined with another person. His flesh, a part of him, was inside of her. The man who'd patiently walked her through the computer system at work was currently sheathing his cock in her . . . cunt. The filthy word filled in the blank easily, her mind going to this lovely unfiltered place where no words were off limits. This was fucking. She was fucking. They were *fucking*.

Was she conjugating verbs now? Shit.

Donovan angled deep, grinding against a particular spot and eliciting an altogether new sensation. Oh. *Oh*. A loud moan rattled through her and words tumbled out of her mouth.

It sounded like nonsense to her ears, but Donovan groaned in appreciation. "Fuck yes, I want your cunt. It's all mine tonight. You have no idea what it does to me to hear you talk like that."

Had she said the filthy stuff out loud? She figured she must've because Donovan redoubled his efforts on her clit and thrust high and hard in her. Her ears started to buzz and her breath wheezed out of her like her lungs had lost half their capacity.

"You're so tight and hot around me. You're clenching so hard." He rolled her clit between his fingertips. "Fucking take what you want. Come around my cock."

She didn't have any choice at this point whether he commanded it or not. She was glazed with sweat, her thighs slick with arousal, and her body screaming for release. His cock filling her and his fingers pinching her clit were too much. Everything inside her seemed to explode at once. Her arms jerked above her, rattling the hangers, and she pushed up on her toes, trying both to grab the release and run from it. It felt scary big, almost like she wouldn't be able to take it standing up.

Then it crashed over her in thick, drowning waves. She lost her breath, and her body arched as the force of it rocketed through her. More dirty words tumbled out of her. Prayers. They were dirty prayers. For Donovan to *please, please, please*. To *yes, God, yes*. To help her. That she was falling.

But he held her up and never broke stride as he rode her orgasm with her, his own breaths harsh and strained behind her. Then when she was cresting, flying in the pleasure, he started telling her how beautiful she was, how sexy, how perfect. That's when he fell in with her. He sped up and buried deep, swelling inside her with steel heat, and his noises changed. Donovan falling apart. Then he was coming long and hot inside her, his sounds like balm to her zapped senses.

She closed her eyes, letting her head sag against the wall, and immersed herself in the sensation of him coming, of losing himself to her. He'd used a condom, but in her mind's eye she let herself imagine his release mingling with hers, the evidence of their shared arousal painting her flesh as he slowly eased out of her.

When he'd fully slid out, he wrapped an arm around her waist and pressed his face to her shoulder. "Christ. That was . . . I . . . Damn . . ."

He was panting against her and obviously as blitzed as she was. That made her smile. Mr. Orgasm Whisperer had gone dumb. Not that she could say much more than, "I concur."

He chuckled against her, his breath cool on her heated skin. "Two in two doctors agree."

She smiled at that. "Empirically verified that it was great, then."

He pressed a kiss to her shoulder then untied her from the clothes rod. He rubbed the tingles from her arms and turned her around. When she faced him, she was hit with the impact of him all over again. He'd pulled off the tie and his shirt was hanging open, chest glistening with sweat and slacks unbuttoned. But his eyes, oh, the eyes. He was looking at her like she was the most precious thing in the world. Like she was something to him.

She could get addicted to that look. To him.

No.

She couldn't. Not if she had any good sense.

But before she could pull her gaze away, get herself back together, he kissed her.

And she forgot she was supposed to be careful.

28

"I can't believe I'm up this late on a school night."

Donovan smirked. "I told you I was a bad influence."

"You totally are." Marin was sitting on his kitchen island cross-legged, wearing only his button-down, and eating watermelon in the moonlight. She licked the side of her hand as a particularly juicy piece got the best of her. In some ways, she looked childlike with her messy hair and his oversized shirt. In every other way, she was the sexiest damn thing Donovan had ever seen.

Almost a week of not having her in his bed had been way too long. When she'd left the morning after their role-play in the club, he'd wanted to call her right back inside, had wanted to spend a slow, lazy Sunday with her. But that knee-jerk reaction had scared the hell out of him. That need to simply hang out with her. He didn't *need*. Not like that. So he'd let her go and then had volunteered for on-call duty for most of the week. But it hadn't done any good. The need had only gotten bigger, more insistent, an addiction knocking at his door, calling to him, until every thought had been about her and what had happened Saturday night.

Their interlude in the closet hadn't been planned. Usually he was one to have something in mind before starting, and he had come into the house that night with a plan. Plans were good. Predictable. But then it'd gotten all shot to hell when he'd grabbed her and she'd fought back. He'd never expected her to go there and definitely not to trust him so wholeheartedly.

And he could tell she hadn't been playing along for his benefit. She'd wanted that edge of danger for herself and believed he'd keep her safe. That trust had been a potent aphrodisiac. Then when he'd touched her, he'd nearly lost all composure. She'd been more than turned on. Everything was so slick and hot. Like she was dying for him. And fuck if she hadn't been wearing his boots. He rarely wore the things anymore. He'd left Texas behind in a lot of ways. But he'd never be able to look at them the same way again. Not after seeing Marin wearing them while bare naked and tied to his closet rail. Those boots may get bronzed and put on his mantel.

Or he'd save them for her to wear again.

Because despite how bad of an idea this was, he'd known there would be an again. He'd known it the minute they'd walked into work on Monday morning. His chest had swelled with this foreign sense of joy at just seeing her there. Then, she'd given him this look, this look that said she was happy to see him, that she'd been *waiting* to see him, and that now her day was better because of it. That look thrilled him. And terrified him. Because it was one that made him want to be worthy of it, to be different than he was, to be able to give her more than a few weeks of X-rated role-plays. To be that guy who'd keep that smile on her face. But he knew better than to believe he was capable of that. He didn't know how to keep a smile on his own face much less someone else's.

He'd realized then that the thirty-day limit didn't protect him. It protected her. He wasn't going to be able to quit Marin Rush. When their time was up, he had to trust she'd quit him. Because otherwise, he'd just keep extending it, sucking up all that light from her until he dragged her down when he worked obsessively or hit a rough spot or the darkness washed over him again. She deserved more that that. She'd already been through enough.

But until then, he was going to give her everything he had. He'd learned that joy in life had a very quick expiration date. So he intended to make the most of every second of this time with Marin. He would go in without armor this time. No games. No filters. Just the two of them riding this wave together until it inevitably crashed ashore.

"Feel better?" he asked after eating a few bites of the melon. "I know sex with me requires regular hydration. It's like training for a marathon. Need to get you in fighting shape, Rush."

She narrowed her eyes at him and then spit a watermelon seed at him with impressive velocity. It plinked off his shoulder and he laughed.

"But seriously, you sure you're okay?" he asked. "I know I was . . ."

"If you say too rough, I'm shooting another seed at you."

He lifted a brow. "I was just going to say rushed . . . and intense."

"Sure you were. It's been five days of longing looks at the office. If you hadn't pushed me up against the wall the minute I walked in tonight, I would've been disappointed."

"I might've left bruises." In fact, he knew he had. She'd walked in, and every ounce of his self-control had flown right out of him. As soon as the back door had clicked shut, he'd had her pinned to the wall and his hands and mouth all over her. Once he was inside her, they'd come so fast, it'd almost been embarrassing. Only afterward had he realized how rough he'd been.

She licked juice off her thumb. "You know what word I know?"

"Hmm?"

"Blue," she said simply. "I know how to pronounce it and spell it and everything."

He nodded, loving how direct she could be. Marin played sex games with him. She didn't play any others though. "Point taken."

She set her bowl aside. "I'm not trying to be flippant about it. I appreciate your concern. I just would rather not overthink it, you know? Therapist me would love to pick it apart. Why do I enjoy that? What does it mean? I went through that in college when I first found myself reacting so strongly to the stuff on your recordings. But can't a person just like things a little left of center simply because it's fun and exciting and feels good? I don't have some big dark reason for why I like how rough you are or why it was thrilling to fight back that night in the closet or why I'm not scared. I just know that you do those things and it turns me on and I go with it."

He leaned back against the counter, considering her. "Some people like roller coasters and some don't."

"Exactly. Or skydiving. Or horror movies."

"Did you just compare sex with me to a horror movie?"

Her lips hitched at the corner. "You know what I mean."

He stepped over to her and parked himself between her knees. "I have to say. You're sounding pretty shameless there, Rush. I wonder how that happened."

She hooked her legs behind his back and fed him a piece of watermelon. "Be careful, West. Gloating is not attractive."

He sucked the fruit juice from her fingers, nipping at her fingertip. "Liar. You love that I'm a know-it-all. You recognize your kind."

She snorted. "I am no such thing."

He took her hand and kissed her wrist, tasting sticky sweet watermelon there. "And a messy eater."

"Shut up. That was an exceptionally ripe melon."

"Mmm-hmm." He pressed his teeth into the tender flesh of her arm, feeling her pulse against his lips. "And a girl who's owed more than a quick fuck against the wall."

"Don't underestimate the power of a good wall bang. You don't owe me anything."

He smiled against her skin and looked up. "*Good?* Just good? Well, clearly I need to up my game. You're not allowed to leave with just *good*. My entire reputation is at stake now. Things must be proven. Egos stroked." He ran his thumb down the center of her palm. "Other things stroked."

She licked her lips, giving herself away despite her protests. "We've got work tomorrow."

"Sleep is overrated." He leaned forward and kissed her neck, marking a path along her throat.

She closed her eyes and made a breathy noise that went straight to his dick. "Maybe so."

"Plus, I have something in the bedroom for you."

She lifted her head at that, playfulness in her gaze. "Is that something the hard thing that's pressing against my leg?"

"Not quite. Though that will be heavily involved as well."

"Now you've got me curious."

"Hmm. We've done spanking and light bondage and role-play so far, a little voyeurism, a little exhibitionism. I've been thinking all week about what else we can check off that list."

Her pupils were already going dark with desire, but she managed to stay focused on him. "Oh?"

He straightened and unwound her legs from around his hips, his own nerves trying to make an appearance now at what he had planned. She kept her gaze on him, but once she'd scooted to the edge of the island, he lifted her up and set her on her feet. "Come with me."

He grabbed her hand and guided her toward the hallway.

She cleared her throat as she followed. "If there's some massive sex swing or something in there, West, I'm out."

He chuckled under his breath. "Come on, give me some credit. I save that for at least the fourth date. Plus, you'd have to do stretches before that. I wouldn't send you in cold."

She smirked. "Okay, so defiling via wine bottle is date one. Tied-up sex in the closet is date two. Third date is wall sex. And fourth will require yoga warm-ups. Got it. You should write a dating guide."

"Totally. I'll do that." When they reached his locked bedroom door, he lifted his arm to feel around for the key on the top of the doorframe and then unlocked the door without opening it.

She frowned as the lock turned over. "I meant to ask you last time. Why the dead bolt on your door?"

"I'm that kinky."

She tilted her head and gave him a not-buying-his-bullshit look.

"You're giving me the therapist look?"

Her eyebrow lifted.

He sighed. "Fine. Remember how I slept in my office at school?"

She nodded.

"I used to have nightmares that my parents' killer came back for me. It kept me from sleeping at home and when I did, it was pretty ugly. So Dr. Paxton suggested I get a dead bolt for my bedroom to make me feel safer. It's become kind of a touchstone wherever I live." He ran a hand over the back of his head. "Stupid, I know."

Her fingers tightened around his. "Not stupid at all. I didn't drink a drop of alcohol until last year because I was convinced if I did, I'd instantly transform into my mom and not be able to stop. We do what we need to do to keep moving forward."

He released a breath. The complete acceptance and lack of judgment did more for him than he would've expected. He hated looking weak or scared, but she didn't see it like that. She saw it as just another thing, a part of him. He leaned down and kissed her because he had to. There was nothing else he could do in that moment but that.

When he finally pulled back, he grabbed the handle of the door. What lay behind it made his hand tremble. But now more than ever, he wanted to give this to her, wanted to show her that despite their thirty-day agreement, she was not just another notch in his bedpost. Not a hookup. Not back then and not now. She'd always been something more. He swung it open. *Here goes nothing.* Inside, his bedroom was just as he'd left it. Filled with flickering candles, the bed covered with rose petals, and the scent of vanilla in the air.

Marin blinked as if she couldn't quite make sense of what she saw. Then, she slowly turned to him, big question marks in her eyes. Questions and something else altogether—wonder. "What's all this?"

Her voice was soft, like she was almost afraid to ask.

He cupped her chin and traced her bottom lip with his thumb. "There's one thing I wish I could've given you back then. One thing that's always bothered me. I like you dirty. And I like you kinky. But everybody deserves a little romance for their first time. I didn't give you that. I thought we could have a do-over."

She simply stared at him, leaving him feeling far too vulnerable as he braced for her reaction. He could feel his defenses rising, a smart-aleck comment poised on his lips to downplay things.

But then the smile that broke over her face stole the words right from him. She pushed up on her toes, wrapped her arms around his neck, and kissed him. Everything that was knotted inside him unwound at that, and he dragged her against him. When she leaned back from the kiss, her eyes gleamed in the reflection of the candles. "You've had this planned the whole time?"

"I'm a planner, Rush. I can't help that someone has no patience and assaulted me as soon as she walked in the door."

She grinned wider. "Oh, is that how you see it?"

"I was a mere passenger on the train."

"Uh-huh. So do you have a plan for what happens next?"

He reached for the buttons on her shirt, unfastened them, and then pushed the fabric off, revealing all that smooth, fair skin. "Just this. You and me. Naked. On that bed, doing what feels good."

She shivered at the trace of his fingertips over her shoulders, her nipples stiffening to tempting points. "I can work with that."

"So can I, Rush."

So can I.

Marin didn't know what was showing on her face, but she hoped she didn't look as flayed open as she felt. She hadn't known what to expect when Donovan said he had something in the bedroom for her, but the last thing she'd expected was this. The man who didn't believe in The One, who seemed to see romance as a silly illusion we fed ourselves, had set up the most romantic thing she could imagine. He wanted to give her the fantasy first time, the storybook one. And though she had zero regrets about how her first time had gone with him, she couldn't deny that this nudged that secret part inside her that still got swept away by happily-ever-afters and sappy movies.

This guy was going to freaking kill her. She'd told him she wanted him to be himself, to not put on any masks, but maybe that had been a dangerous thing. She could deal with the Donovan who got her body revving, the one who'd fuck her in a closet or do naughty role-plays. But she wasn't sure she could handle this version. This version could hurt. Slice her right open and get to the tender parts.

But before she could finish her silent panic attack, Donovan lifted her and brought her over to the bed. The sheets and flower petals were cool beneath her back as he laid her out. He straightened by the side of the bed, looming in the candlelight, shirtless with just his pair of slacks on, and this intent, almost pained, look on his face. He brushed the back of his hand over her breast, making her shiver and sending heat blooming there. "You're beautiful, Marin. You look like art right now. I wish I had my camera out."

She licked her lips. She'd noticed the photographs hanging on the walls of his place the first time she'd been here. Mostly black-and-white landscapes and city skylines. The same type of photos that hung in the therapy office. Things captured from a distance, never close up. Behind him was a stunning one of what looked to be San Francisco Bay.

Now she realized why they'd drawn her attention. All those photos were his. The world seen through Donovan's eyes. "You do photography."

"Not anymore, but you're making me regret that now."

Goose bumps appeared at his full-length perusal. A few seconds ago, if someone had suggested she take nude photos, she would've laughed them right out of the room. Incriminating pictures that showed every flaw possible? Yeah, no thanks. But the way Donovan was looking at her made her skin pull tight and everything warm. "How would you photograph me?"

His gaze slid to hers, something fiery and dangerous there. He trailed his fingertips over her breast and down her belly, circling her navel. "Just like this. All spread out and bared for me. Willing and wanting. Trusting."

Her toes curled at the teasing touch, her back arching. "Yeah?"

He walked around the foot of the bed, leaving his hand on her but trailing it along with him. He pinched her left nipple with erotic precision, sending fire through her. "Then maybe a close-up shot of just these pretty pink nipples, straining for a touch or my tongue. Then a shot of them swollen and wet from my mouth."

She closed her eyes and could almost feel his lips on her. But all he did was map the edges of her areola, making everything hypersensitive.

"The possibilities are endless." His voice had taken on a hypnotic quality, one that was lulling her into this suspended state of being aware of every inch of her body. He walked his fingers over her collarbone. "I could stroke myself just thinking about every way I'd want to photograph you." He let his touch glide down her arm. "Maybe tied up for me. Maybe touching yourself. Maybe covered with my come because I just couldn't resist rubbing my cock while I took pictures."

She bit her lip and a little moan escaped her at that image. It was explicit and dirty, pornographic. But she couldn't drum up shame about that. Being tied up and having Donovan masturbate over her—goddamn. Yes. Please. Could she put in an order for that?

Donovan made a pleased sound in the back of his throat, his fingers finding her hair. "You're getting all pink, baby, and I have a feeling that's not a blush. You like the idea of that, huh? Of me seeing you through a lens or documenting just how shamelessly sexual you can be."

She fought to find her voice. "And give you blackmail material? No way."

He laughed and traced his hand down from her neck, over her sternum and down, down, down until he was cupping her sex. She jolted at the touch. She felt hot and heavy there already, but his palm seared her. He slid his fingers over her. "Yeah, you seem really concerned."

Her knees bent and she whimpered at the need building there. How could he stoke her fire so easily after what had already happened tonight? Surely, she had a limit. Or maybe her body had some storehouse of missed orgasmic opportunities from all these years and was ready to make up for lost time.

He slid two fingers inside her. "What's your safe word?"

Her teeth dragged over her bottom lip. "Blue."

"Grab hold of the headboard and keep your legs open like this. Don't move unless I tell you."

Her eyes snapped open at that. "Donovan."

He gave her one last maddening stroke. "Trust me for now. You have your word if you need it."

Anxiety rippled through her, but something in his gaze smoothed the edges of it. She found herself lifting her arms and reaching for the headboard. Donovan gave her a nod, clearly pleased if the look on his face and the obvious erection in his pants were any indication. Then, he walked over to his closet, opened the doors, and pulled something from a high shelf. She knew what it had to be, but when he turned around and pulled a fancy camera from a bag, her belly dipped.

He kept his eyes on her and set the bag aside. "This camera is not connected to the Internet. Pictures are stored on a little card inside. You can have the card when we're done or break it in two. But right now, I want to see you through my lens, naked on my bed, wearing only candlelight."

Her heart had crawled up into her throat, but her body was starting a one-woman band of pounding beats. Everything felt electrified. Her fingers curled around the rails of the headboard.

He waited for a long moment, watching her, then finally asked. "What color is the sky, Marin?"

She closed her eyes, took a deep breath, and let her head fall back against the pillow. "Green."

That was when she heard the first click.

It was like a blast in her ears in the silent room. But a wash of heat went over her like the camera had hands, touching every naked part of her. *Click. Click. Click.* There was nowhere she could hide, but she wasn't sure she wanted to. Knowing Donovan was there behind the lens, caressing her with his eyes, seeing her in a way no other had, making art out of her body had desire winding through her like thick smoke.

What was he photographing? The hard pebbles her nipples had become? Her goose-bumped skin? The way her thighs were parted for him? Or maybe the slick, wet place at her center? Just imagining Donovan photographing her there had her clit throbbing and her arousal creeping into the near unbearable state.

This shouldn't be doing it for her. She didn't even recognize this version of herself. But that soft click of the camera might as well have been a kiss against her skin from him.

She heard the metal sound of a zipper opening. She didn't dare look yet, afraid she'd lose her nerve if she stared into the camera's eye, but her ears were tuned to high. And the rustle of Donovan's clothing had her pressing her tongue to the roof of her mouth. He was taking her picture, but he was getting naked. Maybe this was driving him just as out of his mind as it was driving her.

She swallowed hard. "Are you touching yourself?"

Another click. "I've got my cock in my hand, but don't worry. I'm just teasing myself. I'm saving the real thing for you. You have no idea how fucking sexy you look. I could take a whole series of pictures of just the way your teeth keep digging into your lip or how your belly's rising and falling or how slippery and flushed your cunt is getting. You look like you could come and I haven't touched you."

Her mouth was a desert, words a former ability.

"But this. This is my favorite." *Click. Click.* "This I can't get enough of."

Marin couldn't stop herself. She ventured a peek and something tight squeezed her chest. Donovan was on the side of the bed, naked as she'd ever seen him, cock in one hand and camera to his eye. And the lens was focused in one very specific place. Right on her face.

He snapped another picture. And then lowered the camera, turning the screen her way. On the bright little square was a woman she didn't recognize. Hooded eyes, puffy lips, and ransacked hair, the candlelight hitting her just so, making her sexy in a way she'd never have assigned to herself. This was what wanting him looked like on her. This is what he saw.

"What do you think?" he asked softly.

"I think your camera is kind."

His lips curved as he set the camera aside and bent to brush his lips over hers. "I think it doesn't capture even one percent of what I see."

She inhaled deeply, trying to center herself. She'd joked earlier about sex with him being like skydiving, but now that was proving true. She felt like she was falling, falling and there was no parachute cord to pull. He wasn't playing fair. She reached out for him, feeling the ground rushing up toward her. "Donovan. I need you."

"I've got you." He climbed onto the bed and pressed a line a kisses along the curve of her neck. She writhed under the touch, and he put a hand on her hip to anchor her. "I need you right back."

He took his time, using his mouth on every square inch of her, teasing her nipples and pressing hot wet kisses along her ribs. Then he was stroking between her thighs with maddening precision until she thought she might cry from all the pent-up . . . everything. Fear. Desire. Emotion. It had all weaved into a glowing, knotted ball of sparking energy in her gut. She called his name, not sure what she wanted him to do. But then he was rolling on the condom and he gave her the answer. He braced himself over her, settled in between her thighs, and pushed deep inside her in a long, slow glide.

Yes. That. That was what she needed.

And when she opened her eyes, finding him watching her, his deep blue gaze capturing her and holding her there, she felt all of those swirling things settle. He was skydiving with her. They were on this ride together. They'd either float safely to the bottom or crash alongside each other.

But at least she knew one thing: He was as lost to it as she was.

She wrapped her arms around him, her nails digging into the hard muscles of his back, and she took him deep inside her body, never breaking the eye contact.

They'd never made love face-to-face. She'd never seen him this stripped down. So naked. So human. And she couldn't get enough.

She'd asked for the boy she used to know. But she'd gotten a man who was so much more than that. He was fire. Brash and bold and dangerous. But he was also rain. She could see it there in his eyes, like he could drown if he let some of the stuff inside him come to the surface. Like he was always saying good-bye. Deep, deep waters.

It was beautiful.

It was terrifying.

But when they both fell over the edge of the cliff together a few minutes later, all she could do was fly with him and hope they landed in one piece.

Twenty-three more days.

It would be too much.

It would never be enough.

29

"She's a whore," Lawrence declared. "All women are in the end. Fucking selfish whores."

Donovan glanced up from his notes, lips parted and poised to interject, but Marin sent him a quick look that was as effective as holding up her hand. He hid his smirk. Rush was getting confident. He'd be sure to let her know how happy he was to see her progress when she came over later tonight.

For the past few weeks, they'd made it an almost nightly occurrence. They'd work together all day, pretend that there was nothing between them, be professional, and then after her brother left for his nightly shift, she'd sneak over to Donovan's place for a little nightcap.

Of course, a little nightcap often turned into the all-night kind. They were both sleep-deprived as hell. And Marin had twice gotten home after her brother because they'd gotten carried away and lost track of time. But goddamn, he'd never been happier to be an experienced insomniac. And on the nights she couldn't make it over, he found himself missing not just her presence in his bed, but her company.

Last night, he'd given in to the urge and had called her. They'd ended up talking on the phone for over an hour and co-watching some silly thriller movie from the eighties. They'd put it on mute and inserted their own dialogue. It'd been ridiculous.

She made him ridiculous.

And she was about to tell him good-bye.

Three days. They had three days left, and he had no doubt that she was going to stick to her word and end things. He needed to let her.

But just the thought of letting her go had sent those old demons snapping at his ankles again. He could feel them there in the shadows, breathing, waiting, reminding him that he could run but never hide. Letting her go would be best for them both. But even knowing that, he found himself considering things he shouldn't. Scary things. Selfish things. Like getting rid of the time limit. Like asking to meet her brother. Like telling her that he thought she was the most amazing woman and that maybe he'd changed his mind about that whole concept of The One.

But she still had no idea that he was a version of her worst nightmare, the thing she'd feared most all her life. There was so much he hadn't told her about his past. About his present. Things that would frighten her. Things she shouldn't have to deal with. But he was getting more and more tempted every day to come clean anyway, to lay it all out there and brace for the consequences. But even if she could get past those things, what were they supposed to do? Continue to hide and sneak around? Keep risking their jobs?

Plus, she might not even feel the same way. What if this really was all about sex and experience for her? What if *she* was ready to walk away?

The thought punched him in the gut. *Fuck*. He was in so much goddamned trouble with this woman. So much trouble.

He couldn't let his mind go there right now. No time for panic attacks while trying to help clients. He forced his focus back to the session, waiting to see how Marin was going to handle Lawrence.

She stayed tall in her chair and didn't flinch away from Lawrence's tirade or harsh language. "Why don't you tell us what happened to change your mind about Rebecca?"

Lawrence's leg bounced up and down like he was barely able to keep himself sitting down. "I wrote her again and she sent me the same email about the sex toy. It's a fucking form email."

To her credit, Marin didn't visibly react or do what Donovan really wanted to do—say, *No shit, genius*. Instead she nodded. "I see. So you're angry because you feel like she tricked you?"

"She just wants to make money and make people buy her shit. I mean, I don't care that she probably gets a pile of fan mail. Don't make it sound personalized when it's just a damn sales pitch. I feel like . . . I dunno. Like a fucking chump. Like she's laughing at all of us dudes who watch her movies."

Marin managed a sympathetic expression. "No one likes to feel like that. But maybe it would help to think about it from her perspective. Just like any other person who performs a role, she's playing at something she's not. She's an actress. On screen, she's the girl who wants every guy and who can orgasm a thousand times and is sex personified. She's the fantasy girl. But no one is that in real life. She's doing that job because she has bills to pay and her own goals to meet. It's a means to an end. I doubt she's laughing at her fans, but I think she probably sees you as customers. That's what you are."

Lawrence looked ready to fight back, to disagree for the sake of disagreeing because he didn't like what Marin represented—the truth. But finally he let out a breath. "You think I'm an idiot, don't you?"

Ah, the unintentional trap so many people were good at setting in therapy. *Come here, doctor. Just step right here. Confirm what*

I think about myself. Tell me these horrible things I think are true so I can redirect this anger at you.

Marin adeptly sidestepped the quagmire. "I think you're good at keeping yourself safe."

Donovan smiled behind the fingers he'd steepled in front of his mouth. *Three points, Dr. Rush. Nailed it.*

Lawrence's hackles went up. "What the fuck is that supposed to be mean?"

Marin set her notepad aside and took off her glasses. Donovan had learned she'd do that when she wanted to have a let's-just-talk-you-and-me vibe with the clients. He found it unbearably sexy.

Better yet, it was effective. Lawrence sagged a bit in his chair, his fighter's pose softening.

"Hear me out," Marin said. "It's smart to want to be safe. It's a natural instinct. If we protect ourselves—our bodies, our minds, our hearts—we can avoid all these messy things. Being embarrassed. Making mistakes. Looking dumb. Getting our hearts broken. But there's a huge price to pay for that safety. And usually that price is being alone or being stuck. Whether that's stuck in a job or a relationship or in a place you don't want to be. Everything has a price. For whatever reason, something in you wants to be safe. Girls in movies are safe."

Lawrence's expression didn't change, but he was obviously listening.

"We've met for a number of weeks now, Lawrence. I *know* you're smart. I know you know that Rebecca Bling was not a real possibility, that it was a fantasy. That email may have brought that home, but it didn't tell you something you didn't already know on some level. So what we really need to focus on is figuring out why you have this need to feel that safe, what price you're paying for it, and if that price is worth it."

Donovan leaned back in his chair, impressed with Marin's approach. She'd managed to call out Lawrence's flaws and get past

his hair-trigger defenses by framing it in a compliment and focusing on the positives—*you're smart, you're good at staying safe.*

Lawrence chewed on a thumbnail, considering her. "It sucks
being alone all the time. I mean, who wants that? But women
don't . . . get me."

Triumph flared in Marin's eyes, and Donovan wanted to stand
up and cheer for all three of them. They were finally getting somewhere with Lawrence.

But Marin kept her expression as smooth as water on a windless
day. "Okay, let's talk about that. What do you think women don't
get about you?"

The rest of the session went quickly, and both of them were able
to get some things out of Lawrence—one being that the guy had
been humiliated during an early sexual experience and had anxiety
about that. It was a victory all around. The guy was talking, actually getting to the heart of things, and Marin had been the one to
do it. Not a blushing cheek in sight.

When they finally wrapped up the session and walked Lawrence
out, it took everything Donovan had not to sweep Marin up in his
arms and twirl her around. Tell her everything, let it all spill out.
Instead, he shut the door and leaned against it, smiling wide. "Is it
bad that you rocking the hell out of that session kind of turned
me on?"

She laughed and let out a little squeal, which was uncharacter-
istically girly for her. "Oh my God, that was such a rush. I feel like
I actually got somewhere. Like I may be able to help him after all."

He stepped closer to her, a moth to flame, and put his hands on
her shoulders. "Of course you'll be able to help him. You're a brilliant therapist. I never doubted you for a second."

She narrowed her eyes. "Bullshit, West. After that first session
with him, you were expecting I was going to be the next victim of
the X-wing gauntlet. You were probably already chiseling my pro-
verbial headstone."

"Never. I'm too good of a trainer to let that happen."

She smirked. "So this is all you, then? You're taking credit."

"Totally."

She shoved him playfully. "Egomaniac."

He grabbed her wrist and brought her hand to his mouth, brushing his lips over her knuckles. "Seriously. I'm so damn proud of you. This is all you. You're a natural."

He gathered her closer, and she let her head fall to his shoulder with a sigh. "God. It feels really, really good."

He could smell her hair, the sweet scent that lingered on his pillows, in his head. "What does?"

She took a second to respond but when she did, her voice had gone soft. "Figuring out where you're meant to be."

He ran his hand along the back of her head, a spike of something potent going through him. He knew her words were about finding her place at work, but they weaved through him, too, holding a whole other kind of meaning. He held her tighter.

Let her go.

The command whispered through his head, but he couldn't heed it. The words were surging up in his throat. He wasn't strong enough to let her walk without at least saying it. He needed to tell her how he felt. Tell her about his past. He couldn't keep pretending.

He lifted her face to him. "Marin . . . there's something I need to talk—"

But before he could get out the rest, the door swung open behind him, and voices hit him like a two-by-four to the back. He and Marin both leapt back from each other, unable to play it off, and spun toward the intruders. So much of him was hoping it was just Ysa or even a client, but no. Of course the universe couldn't be so kind. Elle McCray had walked in . . . with Dr. Suri.

Elle's face lit with feigned surprise. "Oh my, I am *so sorry.*"

Donovan hated Elle in that moment. Hated himself for ever getting involved with her. Yes, he deserved her wrath, but bringing

Marin into it was taking it too far. People's fucking careers were on the line, and she was putting on some stupid performance.

Dr. Suri looked honestly stunned, her dark eyes darting from him to Marin then back. "Dr. West, what exactly is going on here? Didn't I just see a client leave this office?"

Marin stepped forward. "Dr. Suri, I'm so sorry. It was—"

"My fault," Donovan supplied. Marin's head whipped around to gawk at him. "Dr. Rush was excited about a breakthrough with a client, and I . . . I hugged her and got carried away."

Dr. Suri went ramrod straight, her demure height seeming to grow two feet. "Dr. Rush, has Dr. West been putting you in an uncomfortable situation? This institute does not tolerate any form of sexual harassment and—"

Marin put her hands up. "No. God, no. It's nothing like that," she said in a rush. "I—Donovan—well, we used to have a relationship. In college. And—"

"Weren't you a *freshman* when he was a graduate student?" Elle asked, all innocence and faux shock.

Dr. Suri's expression switched to full-out appalled.

"Wait, no, that's not what it was like. And—"

Dr. Suri cut her off with a lifted palm. "Dr. Rush, we'll talk about this separately. You shouldn't have to feel pressured by your trainer to do . . . anything."

"I don't! I'm a grown woman, we're—"

"Dr. West," Suri said, her tone like a hacksaw. "In my office. Now. I'm not going to discuss this here."

He didn't react, didn't show the devastation crashing through him. He knew where this would go. This job—it once meant everything. It was his life. But losing his job would be the least of it now. He'd never forgive himself if Marin lost her spot, too. "Of course."

Elle's eyes burned into him from behind Suri's back. *Checkmate.* That's what this was. But she didn't seem triumphant about it anymore. Her expression had shifted into what almost looked like regret. Like maybe she'd just realized how far she'd taken this.

It didn't fucking matter. Elle had fired the shot, but this was his fault. He'd promised Marin he wouldn't risk her. She'd trusted him and he'd let her down. He'd ruined everything because he had no goddamned self-control.

Marin stared at him like she was going to protest more, throw herself on a sword or something, but he gave a little headshake. This was not her fight.

He'd broken his word. This is what happened to the things he touched. His shrapnel had flown her way, drawn blood, damaged things. But he wouldn't let this hurt her any further. The best way to keep safe from shrapnel was to remove the bomb.

He walked past her without saying another word.

30

Marin paced Donovan's living room. She'd let herself in with the key he hid outside for her, and she'd been wearing a track in his wood floors since. She'd tried to text him, but apparently, he was still in with Suri because she hadn't heard a word. And this was taking way too long for it not to be bad.

Everything looked so awful from the outside looking in. He was her trainer. She was younger. They'd been at work, embraced, almost kissing right after a client had left. God, they'd been so stupid. But when he'd looked at her the way he had today, all logic had gone out the window. She'd felt like he was going to tell her something important. Like maybe things had changed for him, too. Like maybe this experiment was turning into so much more than that.

But then everything had blown up in their faces like an atom bomb. One second—great. The next—annihilation. Fucking Elle McCray. She'd apparently been biding her time and waiting for an opportunity to catch them off guard. She spent a lot of time stopping by the X-wing, presumably to consult about clients they shared, but Ysabel had commented that it was odd she was over there so much. And many times it'd been with Suri. But all it'd been was surveillance. She'd been setting this up all along, hoping to catch them. She'd probably seen Lawrence leave and then realized she and Donovan had never come out.

Marin squeezed her temples, a headache pounding behind her eyes. She would not cry. Would. Not. They would fix this. She couldn't lose this job. Donovan couldn't lose his. But shit, she couldn't see Suri letting them work together so closely anymore. She probably thought they were getting it on in between sessions or something. *God.*

The stabbing sensation in Marin's head increased and little dots of light danced in her vision. *No, not now.* She took a detour from her pacing and went to Donovan's room. She needed something for her head or it was going to turn into a full-blown migraine. She couldn't be laid up in bed with a migraine while all of this was going on.

She made her way to his bathroom and opened his medicine cabinet. His razor was in there along with a number of bottles. Some over-the-counter, some prescription. She skimmed over the orange ones, looking for ibuprofen or aspirin, but then her attention got hung up on one of the prescription labels. The drug name all too familiar. Not just from work but because it was one her mom had been on at some point. An antidepressant.

She stared, a record scratch sounding in her head, and picked up the bottle, hoping the name would morph into something different. The name of an antibiotic or allergy medication. But no, there it was. Donovan was taking antidepressants. And right next to that bottle were prescription sleeping pills and an antianxiety med.

She swallowed hard. It shouldn't bother her. Hell, she shouldn't even be seeing it. This was his private space. His own business. These medicines helped people. If he needed that kind of help, she should be glad he was getting it. Her mom's disorder had claimed her life because she *hadn't* received the right medications or treatment that could've stabilized her. This didn't have to be a big deal. But Marin couldn't help her heartbeat from ticking up.

Donovan was depressed? It was hard to wrap her head around. The guy she knew had so much light in him. That smile of his was like a freaking sunrise. But even as she had the thought, she knew that wasn't the whole story. She'd only let herself read part of those pages. There were times, quiet moments, when she'd seen glimpses of the darkness, too, the sadness. It'd been there from the start. From the very first week she'd met him when she'd found him drinking and lost to grief. She'd ignored it, edited out those parts.

Her hand went sweaty against the bottle.

"You need something, Marin?"

Marin jumped and the pill bottle went tumbling to the floor. She spun around, finding Donovan looking completely blank. Not mad. Not upset. Just *nothing.* He reached down and picked up the bottle from the floor.

"Oh, God, I'm sorry. I had a headache and—"

He stepped past her and set the prescription on the shelf and then grabbed another bottle. He tossed it to her. Aspirin.

She caught it but couldn't take her eyes off him.

He braced his hands on the sink behind him, looking at her with an unreadable expression. "Need something else?"

Her lips parted. Shut. She forced words out that had nothing to do with the meds. "What did Suri say?"

His gaze shifted away to some spot on the wall. "I'm suspended until she can do a full investigation. She'll want to talk with you tomorrow, but as long as you tell her I made the first move, your job will be safe."

Marin's heart sunk. "I'm not going to tell her that."

His jaw flexed. "You should. It's the truth."

"*I* kissed *you* that first time. I wanted this as much as you did. You didn't take advantage of me, Donovan. You know that."

"Do I? You were my responsibility to train, to get you set up for success at work. But I wanted you in my bed from the moment you walked back into my life, and I made sure that happened."

"And it sure as hell wouldn't have happened if I hadn't wanted it to. You think you have some kind of magical seduction powers that tricked me into your bed? Come on. Be serious."

He raked a hand through his hair, anger bubbling to the surface. "You were nearly a virgin, Marin. Getting you keyed up and wanting me was like shooting fish in a fucking barrel."

The words landed like acid on her. "*What?* Did you just call me *easy?*"

His eyes met hers, hardness there. "It is what it is. So tomorrow, tell her the truth. Keep your job."

She stared at him, refusing to look away despite what a fucking cold bastard he was being. He was trying to hurt her. She just couldn't figure out why. But she could feel the bite of it, the intent to harm. "What were you going to say before they walked in on us?"

His gaze flickered with something else for a moment but then the blank wall snapped back in place. "What?"

"You said you wanted to tell me something. What were you going to say?"

His fingers were white against the sink. "I was going to remind you that the time limit was almost done, that it was time to start wrapping this up."

She stepped forward and poked a hard finger to his chest at that. "Bullshit. That is *bullshit*, West." Her words fired like bullets, her finger punctuating them. "You don't look at a woman like that because you're about to break it off. Why are you being such a fucking coward right now?"

She could feel the tightness in her throat, the angry tears that wanted to spring forth, but he barely flinched. That goddamned therapist mask. She wanted to rip it off him.

His Adam's apple bobbed, the only indication that she'd gotten something through, that somewhere in there, he heard her. "You need to go, Marin. It's not going to look good for us to be seen together."

She stared at him, so furious and hurt she could barely string words together. "So just like that? This is done, we're done?"

"I'll be fired within the week. This job, this house won't be mine anymore. Those were the only things holding me here." He took her wrist, moving her hand away from his chest and eased her back. "I told you what I was good at, Rush. Here's me doing it."

Her hands balled into fists. "That is such a shit thing to say. A shit thing. Don't be that guy. You are *not* that guy. I told Lawrence he was paying a high price to keep himself safe. Well, his fucking bill is nominal compared to the costs you're racking up." She pressed her hand to her chest. "This. This is the price, West. Look at me. Look at this woman who was falling in love with you and keep telling her to go to hell. Ruin something that could be great. Put that bill on top of the stack."

He finally reacted, flinching like she'd slapped him hard. Good. She was not going to let him push her away this easily. He may not love her. But she'd be damned if he was going to stand here and act like he felt nothing. Fuck him for that. Fuck. Him.

He stepped forward and grabbed her arm. "Come here."

She stiffened at the touch and the rough hold but couldn't do anything but go with his momentum. For the first time in her life, she wanted to throw down and fight, to shake some sense into him. To wrestle him to the ground and freaking *hit* him. But when he ground to a halt, he spun them both to face the beautiful cityscape of San Francisco.

"Look at that picture, Marin."

She blinked, thrown off her angry tirade for a second by the non sequitur. "What? Why?"

"You know where I took that from?"

The bay was stretched out in front of the city, the hilly streets dotted with colorful buildings. "From a bridge."

"Yes. From the Golden Gate." His grip on her arm tightened. "After I caught Selena cheating, I left L.A. and just drove, not knowing where I was going, not having anywhere *to* go. I ended up in San Francisco. And when I took that photo, with that bay rolling beneath me, I had one glaring thought running through my head. That if I jumped, no one would care. That *I* wouldn't care."

The words hit her like a blow to the chest. "Donovan . . ."

"Yeah. *That's* what guy I am. The broken kind. The kind you can't count on. I told you that from the start."

Her stomach was knotted, her emotions curling in on themselves. Donovan had thought about suicide. Donovan kept a picture of the moment in his room. "Why did you hang it on your wall?"

It was easier than asking why he'd wanted to die. It was the only thing she could get out.

"Because some days I'm still on that bridge. Me up there alone and the world going on across the water, doing just fine without me. I walk past this photo every day to remind myself to keep moving forward. Not to stop and risk taking the photo. It can't catch me if I don't stop moving."

She closed her eyes, pain seeping into her. Is that what it had felt like for her mom? She'd gone a hundred miles an hour until she couldn't. Until all got still and quiet and dark. Until the monster she was running from won. "What happened that night?"

He let out a tired breath, a weary one. "I stood on the bridge and almost jumped. I'd like to say my education stopped me, that I recognized the signs that I was in trouble. But it wasn't that. Someone saw me and called nine-one-one. Paxton was still my emergency contact, so when he got the call, he flew in to help me get my head straight. I spent thirty days at a facility just like The Grove. Then Pax sent me here to bury myself in work." He turned her toward him, his eyes sad, some of the Donovan she knew coming back. "You told Lawrence today that he had pinned his hopes on a fantasy woman who didn't really exist. Well, this guy you think you're falling in love with isn't real either. I'm still messed up, Marin. I don't sleep well. I get bouts of depression. I keep the meds around because I go through rough patches. This needed to be temporary because *I'm* temporary. This version of me is temporary."

Tears burned her eyes now. "It doesn't have to be that way."

"It is that way. And you don't need that. You've already spent way too much time taking care of the people in your life. Too much time worrying. I don't need you worrying about me, too. And I don't want you to see that side of me. I like how you see me. What we've had here has been great. Like that week in college. Perfection immortalized in time because we didn't let it go long enough to mess it up. Let's keep it that way. Let it stand on its own, and we can call on that memory when we need it."

She shook her head, tears tracking silently over her cheeks but fierce determination welling in her. "I don't want a trophy on my mantel, Donovan. I don't want a memory of happiness. I want happiness. And when we're together we have that. I'm not saying your depression isn't real or that I can fix it." She swiped at her cheeks. "Believe me, if anyone knows about the power of brain chemicals, it's me. But that disease preys on loneliness and you're feeding it. You're feeding it by pushing me and everyone else away and not fighting harder to keep this job or what we have going. What if opening yourself up to someone helps? What if when the darkness hits, you have me here to chase it with you?"

"I don't need a nurse," he said, the words sharp.

"That's not what I'm saying." She threw her hands out to her sides. "Hell, you act like I'd be signing up to be with some ticking time bomb, but have you thought about me? The risk label that comes along with *my* history? I have no idea if one day my mom's disorder is going to sneak up and wrap its arms around me. My mom wasn't diagnosed until her twenties. The docs think having a baby set off the imbalance. What if that happens to me?"

She'd never voiced that blinding fear out loud, but there it was.

She wasn't in the clear. She could have to face those demons, too. It kept her up at night sometimes. And hearing the words ringing in her ears, made her feel chilled all over.

"But it's not going to stop me from living my life. How many people come through the doors of The Grove who are managing just fine despite their challenges? These things don't doom us. We fight. Everybody fights. Every single person out there in the world has something to deal with. And people still find happiness and success and love and live full lives. That's the whole point of our job. If it were hopeless, why would we go into work every day and try to help our clients? What would be the point? And what if we're just what each other needs? Have you ever thought of that? I know it hasn't been long, but what if the universe is giving us our shot and we're turning our backs on it? What if this could really be something?"

He stared at her a long time, his gaze holding so much, but then he shook his head and stepped back with a smirk. "I can't believe you're going there. The One, Marin? I told you there's no such thing. And if there is, I'm not it. You've only slept with one guy. You're attaching to what's familiar. Once I leave, you'll see that. You've just got sex brain. This isn't love and was never going to be."

The words splashed over her like icy-cold water. She wanted to get through to him, knew this was his defense mode, but she'd be damned if she was going to stand here and be insulted, her feelings belittled. "So that's it, huh? I lie about what happened. You get fired. And see ya in another life?"

He crossed his arms, that steel gate sliding back in place. "I never lied to you, Marin. I told you what this was from the start."

She gritted her teeth and tossed the bottle of aspirin onto the bed with a rattle. "You didn't lie to me. But you're certainly good at lying to yourself." She stabbed him with a look. "Watch me walk away, Donovan, and know that you're not doing this for my own good. You're not the martyr here. You're doing it because you're fucking scared."

She turned on her heel and strode out. Past the guest room where he'd surprised her in the closet. Past the island he'd spread her out on. Past the table where they'd shared so many nights, laughing and being the one thing Donovan claimed he couldn't be . . . happy.

She didn't look back. She wouldn't allow herself to.

But when she made it to her front door, she fell the fuck apart.

31

Marin took a minute at her door, trying to regain her composure and not walk in a sniveling mess in front of Nate. She wiped her face and evened out her breathing and prayed that he was in his room or the kitchen so she could sneak by. But when she walked in, she saw immediately that there was no shot of going unnoticed. Because not only was Nate there but so was the pink-haired girl, Blaine. But they weren't discussing art this time or choosing which pizza to order. There'd be no room for discussion with the way they were all twisted up on the couch, Nate with a big handful of boob and his tongue in Blaine's mouth.

What. The. Fuck? Marin thought the words were in her head, but apparently they'd slipped out because the two teens immediately jumped away from each other, Nate's hand getting tangled in Blaine's shirt liked it'd turned into a Venus flytrap.

"Shit." Nate yanked his hand back and looked to Marin with wide eyes.

Blaine tugged down her shirt and scrambled up from the couch, panic on her face. "Uh, hi, yeah, I've gotta go."

"Wait." Nate reached for her, but Blaine was already grabbing her flip-flops and hauling ass toward the back door. Face as pink as her hair.

The screen door slapped the backside of the house and the reverb of silence was deafening. Nate looked back to Marin, surprise morphing into full out annoyance. "Jesus, Mar. What the hell are you doing home so early?"

The sharpness in his tone had her drawing up. *He* was going to come at *her*. Oh, hell no. "What are you doing feeling up a *girl* on my couch when you're dating Henry? What are you doing feeling up a girl at all?"

Nate grimaced and tugged a hand through his hair. "I don't want to talk about it."

"You don't—" She shook her head. "What about Henry?"

Nate sneered as he stood. "You mean Henry who broke up with me *weeks ago* because he didn't want a long-distance relationship?"

She blinked. "Weeks ago?"

"Yeah, if you ever bothered to, you know, speak to me lately, I might've had a chance to tell you. But no, you've freaking lost your mind. Drinking. Going out every night. Screwing your boss."

Her lips fell open.

He scoffed. "Like I didn't know. I've heard you talking to him on the phone. Blaine told me who Donovan is."

"He's not my boss."

"Whatever he is. You barely sleep anymore. You come home at all hours."

She couldn't believe she was getting berated by a teenager. "I've been seeing someone. Sue me."

"Sue you?" His jaw clenched. "God, you don't even see it. But then, I guess you wouldn't."

His dismissive tone pushed all of her bitch buttons. Her emotions were too raw, too exposed for this right now. "See *what*? That my little brother is jealous that I'm dating someone?"

"Jealous? I don't care if you're seeing someone. I care that you're turning into our fucking mother."

The accusation stabbed right through her, ripped downward. "Nate."

"How long before you lose your job? Or go nuts because he breaks your heart? Or—"

"Come at you with a kitchen knife?" she asked, unable to stop herself. "Is that what you think?"

He stretched his arms out to his sides. "How the hell am I supposed to know, Mar? Maybe. You're scaring the shit out of me. You used to be able to tell if I had a bad day just by looking at me. I couldn't hide anything from you. But this last month, I've gone through the worst breakup of my life, have barely been able to deal with this move, and then I freaking started up something *with a girl*. I could be bi. I have no clue what to do with *that*. I don't want to *be* that. And the one person who could maybe help me piece all this shit together has forgotten I exist. And I could be losing her like I lost Mom. I could be watching it happen right before my eyes and not be able to do a damn thing about it."

Every word was like a cut to Marin's skin. But when Nate's eyes filled with tears, she bled full-out. Her brother was terrified. She'd been so wrapped up in her own thing that she'd failed to see the person most important to her in the world waving his arms for help. She'd met Donovan and sent Nate to the back of the line.

Nate crossed his arms, holding his elbows tight, and the tears finally fell.

Her feet moved forward on their own, every bit of anger inside her slipping away. Nate flinched when she touched him, but then he let her wrap her arms around him. The tall eighteen-year-old kid folded in her hold, sagging into it and crying. Nate was one of the toughest people she knew. He'd handled so much. But sometimes she forgot how vulnerable he was, how young. He was in this world alone except for her. She was the anchor, and she'd let herself become unmoored, leaving him to float away. She'd become unmoored by a guy. By a relationship that guy didn't even want.

She knew she wasn't her mother. But this part, this part seemed all too familiar. She'd fallen headlong into something and had lost sight of everything else. And Nate's words rang all too clear. *Next you'll be losing your job.*

That was a painfully real possibility. She'd planned to go in to Dr. Suri's office and tell the truth, that she'd been as much an instigator of the relationship as Donovan had been. But what if that meant she'd be let go, too? In all this, she'd forgotten why she was here. This job meant Nate's schooling. This job meant security for them both. Without it, they were back to scraping by, Nate's dreams would drift past without him and so would hers. If she told the truth, she was risking everything. She was risking Nate.

She tightened her arms around him. "I'm so sorry, honey. So sorry. But you don't need to be scared. I promise I'm okay. It's all okay. I'm just dealing with the oldest mistake in the book—falling in love too quick and too hard."

Nate lifted his head at that, surprise all over his tearstained face. "You're *in love* with the guy?"

She wiped at his tears with the back of her hand and shook her head. "Doesn't matter, kid. He doesn't feel the same way. It's done."

He frowned, his eyes searching her face as if just noticing her disastrous state. "I'm sorry, Mar."

"Yeah, me, too." She gave him a sad smile. "And I'm sorry about Henry."

Nate pressed his lips together like the pain was almost too much to voice. "He didn't just break up with me. We waited for each other all that time. But the second week I'm gone, he went to a party and slept with someone. I know you think I'm young, but I thought he was it for me."

"The One," Marin said softly.

Nate's shoulders sagged. "Yeah."

She put her hands to his cheeks, her own heart breaking in her chest. "Don't worry. He wasn't The One."

Nate's eyes lifted to hers. "How do you know?"

She pulled him back into a hug, needing her brother as much as he needed her. "Because there's no such thing."

After a long night of lying awake, Marin walked into Dr. Suri's office first thing the next morning with her goals in mind. She would not lose this job she'd come to love. She would not jeopardize her brother's dream.

But she also couldn't lie.

As much as she needed to keep this position, she wouldn't hold on to it by throwing Donovan to the wolves. He may have hurt her. He may have broken her heart. But professionally he'd done nothing wrong. She wasn't going to say otherwise.

Women were harassed and taken advantage of at jobs every day. She had the utmost respect for Dr. Suri handling this with a swift and strict hand. Marin would've killed to have that kind of person on her side at her first waitressing job when her supervisor kept telling her how nicely she filled out the uniform. But with Donovan, this had been both of their faults. Two combustibles had been put into the same tank. Things were bound to ignite.

So when she sat down in Suri's office, she was armed and ready to handle the questions she knew would be thrown at her.

Dr. Suri settled into the spot behind her desk and offered Marin a kind smile. "I'm sure you know why I asked you here today, Dr. Rush."

"I do."

"Do you feel comfortable with me being the person you speak with about it?"

"Yes." Marin felt like she'd been put on the stand.

Suri nodded and folded her hands atop her blotter. "Dr. Rush,

I have a list of formal questions I'm supposed to ask you. But I'd rather we just talk about this straight. Why don't you tell me what happened?"

Marin cleared her throat and linked her fingers, trying to keep them from trembling. "First, I need you to understand that this was in no way harassment or coercion or anything like that. Donovan and I had a brief relationship back when I was eighteen. He didn't know at the time that I was so young. I lied about my age."

Suri's brow quirked up almost imperceptibly.

"And I didn't realize when I accepted the interview here that I'd be working with him. We hadn't kept in touch. But when I found out he'd be my trainer, we talked it out on day one and agreed to let the past be the past and forget it happened."

"I'm assuming that didn't work out."

Marin shook her head. She wanted to come up with a professional way of explaining it, make this less awkward, but the words wouldn't fall together right. So the truth came out of her instead. "You ever had a person in your life who just sparks something for you? Like if he's in the same room, even if you don't see him, you somehow sense he's there? Like your brain and body are somehow attuned to that particular frequency?"

Suri didn't answer but something in her eyes told Marin that maybe she had had that experience at some point.

Marin sighed. "That's Donovan for me. It's my fault that I didn't see the risk in taking the job. I thought I'd be able to block out that attraction. I'm a rule follower by nature. And this job means everything to me. Coming into this, I would've told you that nothing could tempt me to put this position at risk. Nothing. I would've bet everything I had on it."

"Then Donovan West happened."

Marin laughed, no humor there, but the sound blurting out. It just fit so perfectly. Donovan happened. Like he was an earthquake or a lightning strike or some world-altering event. He had been *her* world-altering event. "Yes. And I promise you that nothing ever happened that compromised my training or our clients' care. Our relationship was off the clock and private. What you walked in on yesterday wouldn't have gone further than that. We just got caught up in a moment because I was excited about a breakthrough with a particularly difficult client. Yes, we were reckless to start up this kind of thing because off-hours relationships can cause tension at work when things go badly, but neither of us would ever compromise care. That was never a question. When we were at work, we were working. I'm sure if you talk to any of the clients, they would say they were receiving professional, top-notch treatment."

Suri sat back in her chair. "I have talked to some of your and Donovan's clients as well as your colleagues as part of your probationary period. All have had good things to say about you. Well, mostly all."

Marin released a breath. "Let me guess, Dr. McCray isn't a fan."

Dr. Suri smirked. "I'm well aware that Dr. McCray has personal feelings that are clouding her judgment. She and Dr. West have bad blood over political matters at the institute."

If only it were just that. But Marin kept the thought to herself.

"And I'm glad to hear that this wasn't a harassment situation. Though being in a relationship with someone who is training you is less than ideal."

Marin looked down. "I know. I'm sorry."

Dr. Suri sighed. "There are no rules against fraternization outside of work here. It's not my favorite thing, but it's not grounds for termination. And I'm aware that we work long hours and many of us live on campus. Entanglements are bound to happen."

Marin's heartbeat pounded against her ribs and her palms were sweaty, but she liked how this was sounding. "So I'm not getting let go?"

"No, Dr. Rush. Your job is safe. Though, you will continue on your probation period."

Marin nodded, relief like a waterfall through her. "Of course. Thank you so much. I can't tell you how much I appreciate another chance."

"I'm impressed with your work. Keep that up and you should be fine."

The thrill of knowing her job was safe quickly crashed when she thought about the rest of the equation. "What about Donovan?"

Suri shifted, her chair squeaking. "That's up to him."

Marin frowned. "What do you mean?"

She tilted her head. "Dr. West came in here yesterday and said he'd crossed a line he shouldn't have in his position, and he tendered his resignation. He made me promise I wouldn't dismiss you from your job for his mistake."

"*What?* He told me you put him on suspension."

"Did he now? Interesting." Suri adjusted her glasses and her lips twitched into a sardonic half-smile. "I probably shouldn't say this. If you repeat it, I will deny every word."

Marin stilled, not sure what to brace for. "Okay."

"Despite what Dr. West believes, I don't have it out for him. I wouldn't suspend him without solid evidence that there was wrongdoing. Donovan is one of the most brilliant doctors I've ever met. He's one of the best we've ever had or will ever have. The way he connects with the clients is something to behold. He could go all the way to the top here. But he is a man obsessed. Work is everything to him, his clients his only focus. Nothing stands between that. Which could be a good thing in many situations but bad in others. And he has driven me up a wall and back with his continuous refusal to compromise with others. My job here is often as referee, making sure everyone is getting along so that this place can run like one team with a common goal. But all Donovan's focused on is his department and how he wants to run it. He couldn't manage to have a partner on his wing because he chased everyone off. The X-wing is his baby and that's just how it was going to be.

"But yesterday, that man who would never let anyone or anything come between him and his work, who has been fighting like a pit bull for a promotion since last year, lied to me and gave up the one thing he cared the most about—his job. He gave it all up without hesitation in order to protect you." She shook her head. "And then you came in here, knowing you could secure your job by throwing him under the bus and you didn't."

Marin couldn't even register the words. They weren't assembling in the right order in her head.

"So though I don't approve of what I walked in on yesterday, I at least can see that it's more than a fly-by-night dalliance." She gave Marin a sage look. "Love is a powerful thing. Even the strongest of us can have a hard time resisting the pull of it. So don't be too hard on yourself, Dr. Rush. And don't be too hard on him. I've never seen that cocky man so wholeheartedly undone." Her smile went wide. "I have to say, I thoroughly enjoyed it."

Marin had to laugh at the pure joy on the older woman's face even though her heart was splintering inside her chest. Donovan had given up what he loved most to save her. Then he'd torn her to pieces to make sure she didn't hook her lifeboat to what he saw as his sinking ship.

"So, if you can convince Dr. West to take back his resignation and you plan to continue this relationship, all I ask is that there is full disclosure. Scandal is in the secrets. I don't like scandal at my institute," she said, her tone leaving no space for argument. "So if you're going to date, you be open about it. You make sure it does not interfere with your work. And though you can still shadow Donovan for training, someone from the couples wing will be assigned as your official mentor."

Marin looked down at her hands, all of the information whirling around, slashing through her. "Thank you, doctor, for your understanding. But I don't think it's going to be an issue. Donovan ended things yesterday."

Suri was quiet for a moment and then let out a beleaguered sigh. "Oh, men."

Marin looked up at that.

"Go talk to him. I bet you can make him see things in a different light." Dr. Suri sniffed. "I don't know why men get it in their heads that they need to rescue us. We do just fine handling things ourselves. And you, Dr. Rush, are no damsel in distress who needs saving. Tell him to get over his martyr complex and that if he doesn't take back that resignation, I'm giving the X-wing to Dr. Rhodes. That'll get his attention."

Marin smoothed her hands over her skirt and nodded. She was glad Suri had a positive outlook about all this, but all she felt was dread inside. Maybe Donovan had tossed himself into the fire to save her. But the way they'd left things . . . she wasn't sure if there was any getting through to him.

He'd already written his life sentence and he was determined to live it. Alone.

But she wasn't one to walk away easily or give up. She'd give it one more shot. That's about all her pride had left.

But when she made her way across campus and knocked on Donovan's door, there was no answer. No car. And no sign of him.

She knocked again, not even sure why she was bothering, why she was going to leave herself exposed like this again, when a voice came from behind her. "He already left."

The familiar voice sent a rush of anger right through her. Marin spun around, clashing gazes with Elle McCray. "Stalking him now?"

McCray tucked her hands in her lab coat and glanced toward the horizon, lips in a thin line. "I came to apologize actually."

"A little late for an *I'm sorry*, don't you think?" Marin spat out.

"Yes," Elle said, no sarcasm in her tone. "But I was taught that when you screw up, you take responsibility for it. I screwed up. I owe an apology to you, too."

Marin walked down the front steps of Donovan's porch, not

wanting to air their dirty laundry for anyone who might pass by. "Not interested."

Elle released a breath and faced Marin. "Yeah. I imagine you're not. I'm sure you don't want to hear anything from me at all. But maybe one day you'll end up thanking me."

This woman was fucking unbelievable. "Oh, is that right? What? For almost getting me fired?"

"Suri was never going to fire you. Not for that." Lines appeared around her eyes, like the dappled sunlight was too much. "But you're young. You have your whole career in front of you. Your whole damn life. Don't screw that up chasing some guy who's incapable of real emotion. He'll just drain you dry."

"Incapable of emotion?" Marin scoffed, her disbelief too big to hold in. "Have you *met* Donovan? He's not incapable. He's got too much of it."

She made a sound like that was the most ridiculous statement she'd ever heard. "Yeah, well that guy who's so full of emotion just packed a suitcase and headed out of here without so much as a good-bye. I'd say he looked broken up about it, but he seemed just fine to me."

Marin's heart dropped into her stomach. "He left?"

McCray's brief smile held no triumph, no malice, just a deep weariness. Sadness. "Take it from someone who already made this mistake. Cut bait and run, Dr. Rush. We both deserve someone who wouldn't be able to walk away that easily."

And with that, she turned around and headed back up the walking path, her heels kicking up the gravel, leaving only dust, an empty house, and Marin behind.

Donovan had left. Without a word. Just like that.

He'd already dipped their time in bronze and put it on a shelf.

She was just another trophy now. Nestled in between McCray and the spot for the next woman who'd warm his bed but not get through the fortress around his heart.

She'd told herself early on she was prepared for this to end. That she'd put protections in place. She'd set a date, for God's sake.

But turns out, she wasn't prepared at all.

Heartbreak was like a tornado. Even when you saw it coming, you never knew how much it could tear everything apart until it was upon you.

And falling for Donovan West was an EF5.

32

The bottles behind the bar weren't blurring yet. This was an unacceptable set of circumstances. Donovan motioned the bartender for another Jack and Coke. The guy poured him another drink and set a bowl of peanuts next to it.

"That's bartender code for *pace yourself*, doc," Lane said as he slid into the seat next to Donovan. He looked to the bartender. "Can I get a Miller Lite?"

Donovan kicked back his drink. "What's the good of calling a ride if you pace yourself?"

Lane smirked. "Because if you vomit in my new Corvette, I'm going to forget I like you and kick your ass."

"Noted."

"So why are we getting drunk on a random Thursday night?" Lane lifted the beer the bartender had plunked in front him and drank, eyeing Donovan. "And why'd you call me? I thought you were pissed at me for taking your girl out."

"Maybe she should've stayed on that date with you. God knows she would've been better off," Donovan muttered.

Lane frowned and set his bottle down. "Not that I'm going to disagree that I'm a catch. Because let's face it, I totally am."

Donovan snorted.

"But you know I never had a shot with Marin. She was great to hang out with, but she was with you that whole night. Even when she was in my arms dancing, she was with you."

Donovan stared into his drink, the words like acid on open wounds. "It was just a fantasy role-play. She was caught up in it."

"Mmm. That's how you see it, huh?" Lane put his elbows to the bar top, not looking Donovan's way as if sensing Donovan couldn't deal with a face-to-face chat right now.

It was the truth. He couldn't. It'd been hard enough to even call someone. He didn't call people. Not for favors. Not to talk. He wasn't sure what had possessed him to do it this time.

"You know," Lane said, his tone suspiciously conversational. "At the club I belong to, we have ways of identifying which submissives and dominants are spoken for and which are available. Sometimes it's obvious things, like collars or colored wristbands. I'm sure you've seen it. You volunteer at my club, right? That's how you knew about me?"

Donovan shrugged. "I was there one night when you were doing a demo."

"Right. So you know what I'm talking about. The markers."

Donovan stared at the bottles again. Now the edges were getting fuzzy, the colors of the bottles blending. Good. "Yeah, sure."

"Right. So those are the obvious ones. But then there's another type that doesn't have any physical markers, but they're taken nonetheless. In my head, I call them imprinted. They're not collared or in a committed relationship, but they've been marked somehow. Some dominant or some submissive has figured out their unique code and has punched those numbers. No one else is going to get in that door." Lane peered over. "When I saw you and Marin together that night, that was my first thought. *They've imprinted.*

It's why I didn't put up a fight for Marin's attention. There's no competing with that. I wouldn't want to."

Donovan closed his eyes, the wash of grief moving through him complete and crushing.

"That's something special, doc. Worth protecting. Worth fighting for."

Donovan's fingers dug hard into his glass. "She imprinted on the wrong guy. I fucked it all up."

"Then un-fuck it," Lane said.

Heh. Like it was that simple. Like he could just say *I'm sorry* and make it better.

He'd lain in bed last night staring at her photo like he could rewind time. It'd been the only picture he hadn't deleted from that night with the camera. Honest hazel eyes staring up at him with lust on her face . . . no, more than that. The first bloom of something real. Marin had looked at him that night like he mattered, like he was more than a lover in her bed, like she'd been searching for something and maybe had found it.

But he'd been the one who'd found it that night. He'd fallen hard and fast. Already gone before he even knew what was happening. He'd known then that he was getting in too deep, that he should back off, that he should be totally honest with her. But he hadn't been able to bring himself to do it. Marin Rush had given him the most insidious disease of all—hope. It'd been planted and had grown and festered until he was so encased in it that he'd almost told her he was falling in love with her there in that office before Dr. Suri and Elle walked in.

He'd almost blurted out something about wanting a relationship. He'd been ready to take the leap. To risk it all. To see where this thing led.

But then everything had gone to hell. He'd walked into his house after talking to Suri and had found Marin in front of his medicine cabinet. He'd seen the look on her face when she hadn't known he was watching. The utter fear. The shock. She'd held that bottle of antidepressants and had looked terrified. All the color had drained from her face, and her hands had been shaking. She could deny it until she was out of ways to say it, but he'd seen the truth. And he didn't blame her. No one wanted to fall in love with a broken man. With a time bomb. Especially not someone who had spent her life picking up the pieces after mental illness decimated her family. So instead of admitting how he felt about her, he'd done what he knew how to do. He'd been cruel, tried to make her hate him.

And she'd called him on his bullshit. Hadn't let him use anything as an excuse. *You're not a martyr. You're a coward.*

She'd been dead-on right.

She'd seen past the hateful words, past the cocky smart-ass, past the smarmy doctor, past it all. She'd seen him and had nailed his ass to the spot.

He was a coward. A bully. Pushing everyone away so that they'd leave before they mattered to him.

But she'd mattered to him from the start.

And pushing her away had done something to him that he hadn't felt since that morning he'd found his parents.

Sadness. Devastation. Loss.

He'd gone through many rounds of depression in his adult life. He knew what to expect. They'd all felt the same. This numbness edged with anxiety. This free-floating sense of nothing mattering, of his place in this world being insignificant. Of being without purpose. He didn't cry. He didn't feel down. He'd feel nothing.

Walking away from Marin hadn't made him feel nothing. It'd made him feel everything.

And the pain fucking sucked.

But he could almost hear Marin whispering in his ear, *At least it's real.*

Maybe the first real thing he'd had in years.

"I can't just undo it." He pressed the heels of his hands to his brow, his head starting to pound. "I keep thinking, what would I tell her if she was a client in my office and she was telling me about this guy—about me?"

"And?" Lane said quietly.

He closed his eyes. "I'd tell her to run. That the guy would end up hurting her, letting her down. That he didn't know how to not destroy good things or be happy. That she deserved better than that."

Lane didn't say anything for a while and then he blew out a long breath. "Come on, doc. That's a lie. You would never make that decision for a client. I've seen you work. You would tell her to get that guy in therapy and make him work through whatever makes him fight so hard to be alone." His voice got quiet. "What makes you fight so hard, Donovan?"

The statement was like a sharp blade in his side.

"You don't have to tell me." The sound of a beer label slowly ripping filled in the background. "But I've known you for two years, and this is the first time we've had a conversation that wasn't about work. You needed a ride tonight, and I'm the closest friend you had to call. It's something to think about."

Donovan couldn't lift his head or look at Lane. Everything felt too heavy, too . . . much. But the words sunk in just the same. Since that day he'd found his parents, watched his safe world burn to the ground, he'd locked himself inside the panic room. The person he'd been had curled into a ball and gone to sleep, hidden away from anything that could hurt too bad. And what was left had been this hollow version of himself, the man who'd gotten on the hamster wheel and gone full tilt, afraid to stop, afraid to feel anything at all.

This is what waking up felt like. Marin had ignored the man on the wheel and had broken the code on the door to get to the real guy. Now he had to figure out how to step outside the room without brandishing weapons and tearing her apart.

He didn't know how to do that. He could feel machetes and

machine guns within his reach. He'd used some of them on her yesterday.

Donovan shoved his drink to the side and managed to look at Lane. "Got any plans tonight?"

Lane lifted a brow. "What'd you have in mind?"

Donovan dropped bills on the bar. "Leaving."

33

The letter came the next morning. Hand-delivered by Lane and bearing handwriting that was written on her memory like sweet, painful scars. Handwriting she used to run her fingers over when she'd read through his fantasies in college. And all of her bravado and righteous anger from the day before, the stuff that was keeping her upright, shattered at her feet, leaving nothing but the soft, vulnerable stuff behind.

She took the note from Lane, the envelope warm between her suddenly cold fingers. "Why isn't he giving me this himself?"

"Because he's gone."

She closed her eyes, the words ripping through her, making it hurt all over again.

Lane reached out and cupped her shoulder, the touch grounding and kind. "He wanted me to give this to you. And I know this is hard, and I'm here for whatever you need, Marin. But I'm going to walk away now because this note is for you alone. So you're going to read it and then you're going to go to work. And then after the day's done, you're going to meet me for dinner."

She looked up, still stricken at the finality of the word *gone* and thrown off by Lane's declaration. "Lane, I can't—"

He lowered his hand and leveled her with a look. "You will. Catfish and beer are good balm for shitty days. You said you needed a friend. Well, now you've got one. And I'm a relentless sonofabitch. I'll pick you up at six thirty."

She wanted to protest further, but the look on his face was enough to shut her up. A friend. Yeah, she could use that right now. "Okay."

He nodded and leaned over to kiss her cheek. "See ya, doc."

Marin watched him jog down her steps and then he was gone around the path that headed up to the main building. She almost couldn't make herself open the note. Part of her had been convinced that Donovan would come to his senses, that he'd show up and apologize and they would fix this.

But this letter wasn't going to be that. He was gone. *Gone.*

She stepped inside, shut the door, and then leaned against it as she pulled the note from the envelope. Her throat was already tightening as she began to read.

Marin,

I'm so very sorry. I need you to know that. For what I said. For how I acted. For everything, really. I wish I could've told you these things in person. But I know if I see you again, I'll be too selfish to let you go a second time.

The words blurred in her vision, and she had to swipe at her eyes to keep going.

You were right. I lied to you, to myself. I've lied for a long time now. If anyone could make me believe in the possibility of love or The One, it's you. You are amazing and smart and beautiful and so sexy it makes me hurt to think I might not ever touch you again.

The time we've spent together has made me want things I've never wanted before. Things that thrill me. Things that scare me. Things that are so real it makes me bleed. But you deserve someone who can be equally amazing with you. I'm not that guy.

Not yet.

But I want to be.

She slid to the floor, the words reverberating in her head like a never-ending echo. *I want to be. I want to be.* Tears dripped onto the page, raising lumps in the paper, making the blue ink smudge.

I've contacted Dr. Suri and rescinded my resignation, but I've asked for a summer sabbatical instead and told her to take me out of the running for the promotion. There are things I need to do. Things that are long overdue. I don't expect you to wait for me. I expect you to kick ass on the X-wing and make friends and find your place at The Grove.

But I'll wait for you. Because I can't not. You've gotten to me, Rush. You're in here with me, maybe have been since that very first night in Harker Hall, and I don't want to shake it anymore. So if you ever want to call, talk, share completely inappropriate fantasies, I will always take your call.

Always.

D

Marin didn't know how long she sat on the floor in her foyer. Or how many times she read the letter. But she made it to her appointments. And she made it to catfish and beer.

And when she went to bed that night, she made her first call.

34

Donovan rolled down the windows, letting the summer breeze smack him in the face. He'd forgotten how beautiful this place was. Or maybe he'd never really seen how beautiful it was. Last time he'd been here, he'd only focused on the fog, the gray skies. But today, the sun sparkled over the bay and the russet-colored bridge stood out proud against the hills behind it. He could see why the Golden Gate was such a popular place to die. If you wanted your last memory to be of something majestic, this was it.

But he had a different view that kept drawing him. Taped to the dashboard of his rental car was a photo he'd received a few days ago. As soon as it'd popped up on his phone, he'd stopped at a copy shop to get a color print of it. Marin was at a table in the po-boy shop with a group of co-workers around her. Everyone was smiling, probably a few beers into the night, and Lane had his arm draped over the back of her chair, giving Marin bunny ears.

They all looked happy.

She looked happy. Without him.

Something tight clenched in Donovan's chest.

He parked the car, lucky to snag a spot in the small lot, and climbed out. He could remember doing this the last time, going through the same motions. Taking deep breaths, feeling the wind whipping off the water, seeing the tourists strolling over to walk the bridge. Having one purpose in mind.

This is where he needed to be. He'd been a lot of places these past few weeks, but it all came back to this. He grabbed the picture of Marin, put it in his pocket and then walked toward the bridge. He could smell the sea air mixing with the fumes of the cars whizzing by, hear the roar of waves crashing against rocks in the distance. Everything was so much the same from last time.

Comforting and terrifying all at once.

He stepped onto the walkway and grabbed the railing, feeling disoriented for a second. Heights had never been his favorite thing. But when he got his bearings, he made his way to the center of the bridge to find the spot he'd taken the photo from. To find the spot where he'd almost climbed over the railing. Crisis-counseling signs were posted on the bridge. *There is hope. Make the call.* He hadn't seen those the last time. He'd seen nothing but churning water.

A few people glanced his way as they moved past him, just another guy blending in with the tourists. But he wasn't here to be a tourist. Like last time, he was here for one reason.

He neared the center of the bridge. The water looked calm and deadly as it stretched out beneath him. The city of San Francisco hummed along across the bay. Alcatraz stood watch in between. The world went on, indifferent as always.

It didn't take him long to pinpoint the spot he wanted, knowing the details of the view by heart. He blinked in the bright sunlight as his steps slowed. The photo on his wall was in full color now, stretching along his right as far as he could see. A stunning post-card. A painful memory.

Then, he did the thing he'd promised himself he'd never do

again. A thing he'd gotten good at over the last few weeks. He turned toward the view and stopped moving. He stopped moving and looked down at the water and didn't try to block anything out.

The same questions he'd posed to himself all those years ago drifted into his head now.

If I jumped, would someone care?

If I jumped, would I care?

Donovan gripped the rail and closed his eyes, breathing in the air, feeling the precariousness of his position above the water. Then he smiled—big and broad and full. He opened his eyes, peered over his shoulder, and stopped a young couple who was strolling by. He held up his phone. "Would you mind? I suck at the selfie thing."

The girl smiled and adjusted the camera she had hanging around her neck, her ponytail swinging. "Sure. Would you mind getting one of us after? We're on our honeymoon and have managed to get, like, no pictures of us together."

"Of course."

She took Donovan's phone and snapped a picture of him. Then they switched places. Seeing the smiling couple through the camera lens, giddily cuddled against each other in front of the view that Donovan had looked at on his wall every day with dread, jarred him for a second. So much happiness. Hope. This view would have a new memory now.

He thanked the couple and wished them a good honeymoon. And as they walked away hand in hand, instead of Donovan feeling cynical about what lay before them, he felt something altogether different. Envy. The best kind. The kind that stoked that burgeoning fire in his gut.

He checked the shot the girl had taken of him, pressed a few buttons, and sent the photo.

The response that came was immediate.

Marin: Things that are not fair—You looking at a beautiful view and being ridiculously handsome while I'm stuck here about to counsel

Karina about forgetting to wear a bra to group AGAIN. Double D's need support, West.

Donovan chuckled, the sound getting lost in the wind. Marin knew exactly what that picture signified, knew this was different than all the ones they'd exchanged since he'd left, but he loved that she didn't go there. She went with making him laugh. And despite the view, he wished with everything he had that he was there with Marin, dealing with the antics in group. He missed his life at The Grove. His clients. His job. *Marin.*

Miss wasn't a strong enough verb for that last one. *Pine* was more accurate. He pressed his hand over the place where her picture was in his shirt pocket, a heavy ache there. But he'd needed to do this. He'd needed to step off the hamster wheel and sit still. Be with all that ugly stuff he'd been sprinting from. Get real help this time instead of just throwing himself into a relentless work schedule to block out the bad. Grieve his parents, the losses in his life. Breathe through it all. Feel it. Take the advice he would've given a client who was in this position.

But all this time away felt like an eternity now. He'd checked himself in for a thirty-day intensive therapy program, finally facing the demons head-on. And then he'd traveled, taking his first break from work in his life and putting his head back together. So he could be that guy. He wanted to be that guy. Not just for Marin but for himself. His parents wouldn't have wanted him to be some miserable workaholic asshole. It wasn't who they'd raised him to be.

Donovan's fingers moved over the screen of his phone.

Donovan: Maybe she was trying to help everyone overcome distraction. Unsupported double D's could be a powerful teaching moment.

Marin: *rolls eyes* They have the power to derail a group therapy session, for sure. Two guys took really long bathroom breaks. But srsly, u good?

He'd talked to her last night, told her where he'd be today. He'd talked to her every night since he'd left. About nothing. About everything. They had long phone dates every night doing all the things he should've done with her instead of just jumping straight into sex. Though their talk had slipped into the erotic zone on more than one occasion. She got him sexually. Understood and connected in a way he'd never experienced before. But it was so much more than that. She got *him*. He fell in love with her a little more each time they talked. And he loved that it wasn't always serious. They had *fun*. A concept that had eluded him for most of his adult life. Last night they'd caught a rerun of *Dawson's Creek*. They'd sent each other selfies of their best Dawson ugly cry face. He'd totally won that contest—and had gloated. Obnoxiously. She was still making him ridiculous.

He loved being ridiculous.

And once upon a time that question—*you good?*—would've stirred up all kinds of complicated answers. But this one was an easy one.

Donovan: I'm good, Rush. But I miss you.

Marin: I know.

He laughed.

Donovan: You going Han Solo on me now?

Her response was a long time coming this go-round, the little dots indicating her reply seeming endless. Then her response popped up.

Marin: Joking is easier than telling you the truth. That your photo kind of wrecked me. That I miss you every goddamned minute.

The simple words reached inside him and gripped, making everything yearn. He'd already known it was time, but now he wished he had a teleporter, that he could just snap his fingers and have her there in front of him. Wrap his arms around her.

Donovan: I'm ready to come home. Ready to have me?

More dots. More waiting. More held breath.

Marin: Is this a sext?

Donovan smiled. He could picture her there in her office, grinning through the tears and being the strong woman he knew her to be. One who would always keep him on his toes.

Donovan: Yes. Obviously.

Marin: Then yes. Obviously.

Donovan ran his finger over her name on the screen. When he added it all up, he'd only known Marin for a short time. But in some ways, he'd felt like he'd known her his whole life. They'd missed that first opportunity, and the universe was giving him his second chance.

Another text dinged.

Marin: Come home, West. We all miss you.

We. Not just Marin. But the people who'd kept in touch with him on this trip. Lane. Ysa. A few of his clients who had emailed him wishing him a relaxing vacation. Even Dr. Suri had sent him well wishes, though no one but Marin and Lane knew about where he'd gone and why. He had people. It'd been a long damn time since he'd had people. Too long.

Donovan: OK

He didn't say anything more after that. There was nothing left to say. He'd finally figured out where home was. And the answer to both those questions the water always asked when he was here was an easy one now: *Yes.*

He walked back down the path and to the car.

Yes, he cared.

And yes, someone cared for him.

That was all he needed.

35

Marin didn't know when he was coming. Or if he'd changed his mind. Or if it'd be weird and awkward when he came back. Things had been so easy and comfortable on the phone these past few weeks that now it had her nerves gathering. They'd talked until all hours of the morning, opening up every door they had inside them, stripping things bare. Being honest. Being real. Being dorks.

And even though he'd been the one going through therapy, they'd tackled a lot of her fears, too. The fear of her genetics. Her fear that she wouldn't be enough for Nate as he got older. Her worries about doing a good job at The Grove. They'd laid it all out there.

But she didn't know if that would translate to real life, how that would feel when they saw each other again.

If they saw each other again. She hadn't had another text in the two days since his photo on the bridge and he hadn't called. It was driving her to goddamned distraction. So when she finished up dinner with Nate and saw him off to work, she went back to the

X-wing to work late, anything to keep her mind off what might or might not be.

Ysa and the social worker who'd been helping out while Donovan was gone had long left for the night. All the hallways were dark and quiet except for the humming *Exit* signs and occasional safety light. She'd gotten used to this dead version of the X-wing. The first few nights she'd found it a little spooky, but now she found it peaceful. She could get a lot done, and it felt better than sitting in her empty house. This made her feel like she was doing something productive.

She studied case files, read the books they recommended to clients, researched the toys and devices they had on hand—though, some of that research she, of course, had to save for home. But tonight, she planned on going through some of the videos they prescribed to clients. She'd made it through a list of instructional ones for couples. Now she was on to the ones they recommended for straight-up arousal issues. It probably wasn't the best plan of action, considering how pent up she was lately. Even light flirting on the phone with Donovan could key her up like nothing else. But she'd had a client today who'd needed one of the videos, and Marin hadn't known which would be the best fit. She hated not knowing.

So after making herself a cup of coffee and getting a pack of powdered donuts from the vending machine, she'd settled onto the couch in her office and cued up a video on the tablet. This one Donovan had marked as a top five in effectiveness for female clients based on feedback. She hit play and took a long sip of her coffee as the movie started.

In an instant, she could see why this one had made the favorites list. The actor in it was very easy to look at, which she'd found was a rarity in most of the porn out there. He wasn't overly tan or too muscle-bound. He looked like a hot guy next door. In fact, that was the role he was playing. The quiet guy next door who caught his pretty neighbor sneaking into his pool for naked late night-swims.

The plot was ridiculous, of course, but the way he reacted to this transgression was pretty captivating.

Marin found her skin warming as the guy bent the woman over his knee for a good, hard spanking by the side of the pool. Her memories infiltrated the image. She could almost feel the sting of Donovan's hand the night he'd done that to her, could remember how her body reacted.

Damn, this had been a stupid, stupid idea. Her body was already pulsing with deprivation, and there was no way she'd scratch that itch at work, even if no one was here. She'd learned that lesson in the sleep lab all those years ago.

But right as she was about to hit stop on the movie, she heard something out in the hallway. A little *tap, tap.* Footsteps? Something falling off a desk? She couldn't tell but it'd made her heart jump into her throat. She tried to hit stop again on the video, but the screen wasn't responding and the movie kept playing.

"Shit."

She tossed the tablet to the other side of the couch and got to her feet. If someone was out there, she needed to know. Last time this had happened, she'd found a mop in the middle of the hallway, victim of a strong gust of the air-conditioning and a cleaning-supply closet door left ajar. She expected as much this time.

But when she stuck her head out of her office, she saw nothing amiss. "Hello?"

Her voice echoed down the hallway, and she had the brief thought that she was acting like a too-stupid-to-live horror movie heroine, calling out for the bad guy so he knew exactly where she was. *Here I am! Come and get me, crazed serial killer!*

But of course, that was ridiculous. The Grove was like Fort Knox with all the high-profile clients they had here. There was a guard at the entrance and pass codes to get into the buildings. High walls. No press was getting in and no guy with a hockey mask and a knife either. Still, she had to rub chill bumps from her arms. Nate's penchant for scary movies had given her imagination way too much fodder. She gave one last listen, trying to pick out anything that sounded off.

The film was still playing low behind her from the tablet and the cry of an orgasm filled in the quiet. No sound came from the hallway.

Okay. Nothing to worry about. She could finish the movie or maybe give up on that and work on some case files.

She turned and headed back in the office. But before she could take more than a few steps, an arm was wrapping around her waist and another clamped over her mouth. She screamed into the hand.

"Shh, Rush. Don't want to let anyone know what you're up to in here."

The sound of the familiar voice crashed through her, the scent of him registering a second later and slicing through her instinctual fear. *Donovan.* She wanted to cry. She wanted to cheer. She wanted to see his face and kiss it all over.

"I can't believe I leave you on your own for just a few weeks and this is what I find you doing, watching dirty movies at work." His voice was low against her ear, playfully accusatory. "Were you going to touch yourself? Were you checking the hallway to make sure you were alone?"

She shook her head in his grip, her heartbeat ticking up.

He pressed his nose to the curve of her neck and inhaled. "God, I've missed you, Rush. Missed you like fucking air."

The longing in his voice nearly undid her. She closed her eyes and let all that feeling move through her. All that ache.

He brushed his lips against her shoulder. "I love hearing your voice on the phone. But it doesn't give me this. The scent of you. How your skin flushes when I touch you. How it feels when I taste you."

Marin swallowed hard, heat pooling in her. She'd worried it would be awkward. She'd worried that time would change things.

She'd pictured stilted conversations over coffee when he came back. Uncomfortable questions about how therapy was, how he was feeling, where things stood. Slow, plodding steps. She'd been dreading that part so hard her stomach had hurt every time she thought about it. But she should've known better. Even from thousands of miles away, Donovan could read her.

He wasn't going to give her a chance to be awkward, to overthink things, to undo what they'd forged over the phone. He was going to do exactly what she needed to shut her mind off and turn her body on. He would make her shameless.

His hand slipped away from her mouth, his quickening breath tickling her neck. "Tell me now, Rush. I want you more than I can put into words, but you know I'll listen. I'll always listen. What color is the sky?"

She sucked in a breath. So much time had passed. So much had happened. But suddenly it felt like nothing, like a blink, a flash. He was gone. But now he was here. Here. Everything that had been askew shifted and locked into this new place, this perfect place. Like everything inside her had been waiting for this one moment all her life. She'd fallen for Donovan a long damn time ago. But it'd never been the right time. Or the right place. Sometimes she'd wondered if it'd been the right life. Now it was. And she was done talking.

"Trapezoid."

She felt him smile against the curve of her neck. "That isn't a color."

"That's how much I care about the sky right now."

"Mmm. Be careful." His grip on her tightened, the edge is his voice sharpening. "The doors to this floor are locked, and I have Lane standing guard. He won't come in no matter what he hears."

She could feel him growing hard against her, sending hot desire racing up her spine.

"I'm feeling pretty crazed for you right now. You could be putting yourself in a lot of danger, Rush."

Everything had gone liquid inside her, and her heart had decided to set up camp in her throat. But there was no fear. Only pounding, urgent need. "Playing it safe is overrated."

Donovan spun her around at that, his blue gaze colliding with hers and breaking her open inside. God, she'd missed him. More than she'd wanted to admit to herself. So much so it almost hurt to look at him. He brushed his lips over hers in a slow, reverent glide. "Yes. It is."

And she knew then he wasn't talking about sex games or role-plays in that moment. She heard it in his voice and saw it in the naked expression on his face. She'd spent her whole life playing it safe, but so had he. No more. Neither of them knew what the future would hold. They all had ghosts and demons and challenges. Everyone did. But there'd be no more running. They'd take each other's hand and plunge into the unknown together. That's what life was. That was living.

That was love.

He cupped her face, tracing her cheekbones with her thumbs. "Guess it's time for us to be amazing."

She smiled, the slow, sweet rush almost too much to hold all at once. "I think we already are. Always have been."

He lowered his head, putting his mouth to hers, and poured all the longing from the time apart into the kiss. Lips clashing, tongues twining, breath mingling. Their hands moved everywhere, mapping each other like they'd worried they'd forgotten each peak and valley. Like they were afraid one of them would dissolve into an apparition. Like they would wake up. How many times over the last few weeks had she dreamed of this and woken up? But none of that happened. Just hungry, breathless kissing and whispered, desperate words. He was back. They were good. They were amazing.

And they couldn't wait any longer.

When Donovan couldn't get his hand successfully up her shirt, he grabbed the collar of her blouse and yanked. Buttons went flying and plinked onto the wood floors. All of her breath whooshed out of her, the glimmer of violence like a heat flare to her system. He cupped her breast with a hot hand, panting his words as he kissed her neck. "Don't think I can be gentle."

She tilted her head back and moaned as he bit her shoulder. "Good."

Whatever he wanted he could take. She wanted him to take it. Donovan growled and divested her of her bra, making her nipples go taut in the cool air, and then his mouth was on her, sucking and nipping and making shocks of electricity move straight downward. She gripped his hair in her hands, tugging hard and losing her own hold on control.

"Fuck yes," he said against her skin. "Hurt me, Rush. Show me how much you need this right now."

He guided her against the wall and kissed down her stomach, making her belly jump and flutter. She didn't let go of his hair. It'd been so long since she'd been touched and the adrenaline was making everything weak. She could dissolve into a puddle any second. "Please. *Please.*"

"I know, sweetheart, I know." He fumbled with the button on her shorts and then yanked them, along with her underwear, down and off. His thumbs grazed her over her crease, and they both groaned at how obviously turned on she was. "Every night that I stroked myself, I thought about you like this. So hot and sweet and open for me."

The back of her head tapped against the wall, the need to come like a hammer pounding at every one of her senses. She was burning up from the inside out.

Then his mouth was on her and fingers plunged deep and streaks of light moved behind her eyelids, everything going multihued and blurry. *Oh, God.* She held on to his hair like it was her only rope over a ravine. His tongue lashed her, teeth grazing her, everything imprecise and messy. Ravenous. He was off leash and devouring her, like he couldn't help but glut himself on her. He grabbed her thigh and lifted one of her legs over his shoulder, spreading her open even wider and his tongue moved at her entrance. Licking her around his fingers, the sound of her arousal and his wet mouth the lewdest, sexiest soundtrack she'd ever heard.

"You're gushing, baby," he said in between kisses and licks. "I could eat you all night like fucking candy."

She dug her heel into his back, shameless now, riding his face and putting him where she needed him. She gasped out her response. "As long as there's cock involved somewhere on the menu."

He laughed, a surprised bark of a thing, and he stroked his fingers against her swollen flesh. "I fucking love that about you, Rush. You blush so pretty, but you're so goddamned dirty beneath that." He tucked two fingers inside her. "And I promise. Cock will be heavily involved in tonight's activities."

"Excellent."

"But right now you're going to come for me. You're going to come hard on my face and then I'm going to fuck you over that desk. It's been far too long since I've seen you bent over for me."

She didn't have time to respond because then his mouth was on her again and his fingers were pumping and any thought she'd ever had in her life drained out of her brain. All that was left was sensation and need and the *pulse, pulse, pulse* of her clit beneath his lips and her pussy around his fingers.

Her gaze locked on the bookcase across from her. All her textbooks, her bound research studies, all her academic awards. It was the bookcase of a studious, diligent woman. A woman who had stayed on the smart, safe path. But reflected in one plaque she could see herself and Donovan, her leg thrown wantonly over his shoulder, that dark head between her thighs like she was the most decadent meal of his life. And the two things seemed to merge into one. The respected doctor. The sensual woman. She could be both. She would be.

Her eyes fell shut as Donovan hit her sweet spot and everything fell away. His hair turned to hot silk between her fingers and every nerve ending on her body lit up. She came with a loud cry and rocked her hips against him, unashamed to take. And he gave her every bit she needed, sending her flying, and holding her up when she started to coast down.

But he didn't give her long to stop spinning. Before she'd caught her breath, he stood and lifted her into his arms. He hadn't taken off his button-down or even unfastened his pants and she was a naked, wet mess in his arms. She couldn't find it in herself to worry about it. She reached up and touched his stubbled jaw. "You're good at that."

He smiled, his lips still shiny from the pleasure he'd given her. "You look drunk. You going to fall asleep on me, Rush?"

She dragged her nails along the edge of his jaw. "No, you promised me something, doctor. I expect to get it. I've been waiting a long time."

Possessiveness flared in his eyes. "I've been waiting my whole life."

Warmth spread through her, and Donovan set her on her feet and gave her a soft kiss. Then he turned her around. The desk loomed in her view. It was a new one. Eli had replaced the other as promised. But all of her mundane office things were on it. Files. Papers. Supplies.

Donovan shoved it all to the far end and then stepped behind her. The sound of his belt being undone sent a hard shiver through her. He grabbed her hands and drew her arms behind her back. The belt wrapped around her wrists as he secured her arms. The feel of the leather against her, the snugness of the restraint sent her blood fizzing.

He brushed the tip of his nose along that sensitive spot behind her ear. "Every time you sit at this desk from now on, you're going to think about what I'm about to do to you. You're going to get warm and wet while trying to do your work. You're going to want to touch yourself. It's going to be torture. And I'm going to love it."

He pressed a hand to her back and guided her down. Her naked skin pressed to the cool surface and everything went extra sensitive. She closed her eyes, a fresh wave of arousal going through her. He checked the tightness of the belt and then went over to the cabinet.

"What are you doing?" Her breaths were coming sharp and fast by the time he returned.

"I think I left you with an unfinished list." She jolted when he gripped her thighs, spreading her stance wide. "Easy now."

One careful finger brushed over her back opening. Her entire body tried to clench. "Oh. *Oh.*"

He teased her oh-so-gently, activating sensations that made her toes curl in her sandals. "I seem to remember a particular fantasy I wrote for the study that you left copious notes on once upon a time. The handwriting was so messy on a certain part that I knew your hands hand been shaking. And the ink had been smudged. Like wet fingers had touched it."

She squeezed her eyes shut, trying to focus on not making a sound, on not letting him know how he was affecting her.

Donovan's blunt nails raked over her ass cheek. "Oh, how many times did I stroke my cock with thoughts of that? The quiet girl down the hall had taken my fantasy about a woman getting held down for anal sex and had touched herself over it? Do you know what that did to me? Thinking about what you might have done to yourself?" He pushed his erection against the seam of her ass, the denim of his jeans coarse against her and making everything even more sensitive. "Did you try a finger here? To see what it might feel like?"

Marin bit her lip so hard she worried she'd cut it. She knew exactly which scenario he was talking about. She'd been shocked and appalled and ridiculously turned on by it. At eighteen, she hadn't even realized women did that. But God, it'd put ideas in her head. And she had touched herself, had learned how sensitive that part of her could be. She would've never admitted that out loud.

Until now. "Yes."

The sound Donovan made in the back of his throat—like pain and pleasure and everything sexy and wonderful rolled into one—made her admission worth it. "Shameless. Who could've imagined?"

"You made me that way."

He shifted and something nudged against her sex. Something smooth and cool. "Tell me again the color of the sky."

His voice sounded strained now, tense. He was riding an edge.

"It's green, Donovan. It's always green with you."

He let out a breath and then pushed whatever he'd been teasing her sex with forward. It was small, slid in easily, and partially curved around the outside to press against her clit. She groaned when the vibration started.

She screwed her eyes shut, breathing hard. She felt too keyed up already and a vibrator was going to send her over again quickly, but then cool liquid slid along the crack of her ass. The unusual sensation had her brain honing in on that one spot, forgetting the pleasure the vibrator was stirring.

She shifted restlessly against the desk, the ticklish feeling both sensual and maddening. The overwhelming ache to be penetrated everywhere at once was new but desperate. Her senses had been dialed to eleven and now they wanted to be at fifteen. She wanted Donovan to have everything she had to offer. She'd given him her virginity. Now she wanted to give him another of her firsts. She wanted him to be all her firsts.

His fingers coasted down the backs of her thighs and he spread her open. She'd thought she'd been vulnerable to him that first time over a desk, but this was so much more. Every secret place of hers was there for the taking.

He smoothed the lubricant over her, massaging her, and making everything crave touch as the vibrator did its work against her clit.

The need for release beat at her like crashing waves but she would need more. This wouldn't be enough. She needed the edge. Her teeth clenched. "Donovan. Please."

"You don't want me to rush this, gorgeous. I don't want to hurt you."

He pushed a finger inside and she moaned, the pressure and sensation making her ears ring. But she rocked back against him. He thought she knew all her secrets but he didn't. He didn't know that she'd made good use of that toy cabinet. He wouldn't hurt her. She'd felt what her body could accommodate already.

"Fuck me, Donovan," she panted, her hands flexing in the bindings. "I can handle you."

He gripped her hip, and she could sense how hard it was for him to be acting with restraint. She didn't want that restraint. She wanted the chains cut. She wanted to go into that sexy, dark place together.

"I read that fantasy. I know what happens next," she said, the words coming hot and fast now. "I'm not scared of you. Take me like that. I crave it, too."

She thought he would balk again. But then his fingers were gone and the sound of a condom packet being ripped open filled the room. She could feel his heat behind her as he stripped out of his clothes.

And then he was spreading her open and the head of his cock pushed against her opening. It felt impossibly big, too much. But she trusted her body and she trusted him, breathing and forcing her muscles to relax.

He thrust forward, slow but unyielding and after one fierce show of resistance, her body gave, opening to him and lighting her up from the inside out. They both made desperate sounds. Hers sharp, his belly-deep and gravel-laced.

"That's what you crave, Rush. To be fucked hard in the ass? To be forced?" The words were like bullets. His thrusts sliding long and deep.

"I crave *you*."

He grabbed her hips with hard fingers and dragged her back onto him, seating himself to the hilt. Her eyes wanted to roll back in her head. But everything felt aware, alive, amazing.

She let out a long groan. *"Fuck."*

That's all he needed. The green light. He went for it then. Like the fantasy. Hard and rough and so goddamned wonderful she didn't even recognize the sounds she was making. She didn't know what to focus on, everything felt so lit up. But it was all good. So very good. Her skin went slick and slid along the desk, the vibrator humming, and his cock filling her.

The girl who had once turned red even thinking about these things now was begging for it, feeling every bit of it, loving it.

And when they each came a few minutes later, their sounds echoing off the walls of her office, she knew then why she'd waited all those years. Somehow her subconscious had known all along. She hadn't waited because she was too shy or too busy or too innocent. She'd waited because a regular guy wouldn't have been able to keep up with her. She'd waited for this. For him.

She'd waited for the real thing.

And now she had it.

They didn't talk much as they got themselves and the office back together or while they walked back to his place. But they didn't need to. She felt content and calm and right.

And when they curled up in bed later that night, the photo of San Francisco gone from the wall, Donovan put his lips to her ear, his arm wrapping around her. *"I hear her in the hall. I don't know who she is or where she's from. I didn't know she was listening. I didn't know she could hear my secrets. But I see how she's looking at me. I know she sees how turned on I am. And she thinks it's from my work. She thinks it's from what she heard. She thinks it's for something else. And maybe it was at first. But it's not now."* He gathered her against his chest, his words soft against her senses.

"Because I've never seen a more beautiful girl. And I've never been looked at the way she's looking at me. Like she sees who I really am. And when I talk to her night after night, it's over. I'm done. I know in that moment that even though I don't know how it can ever be, how I could ever be right for her, I want her to be mine. I want to believe in fate and fairy tales and happy endings."

Tears gathered behind Marin's lids.

"I want to believe in The One." He kissed her hair and breathed her in. "I believe."

The bigness of feeling moved through her like tremors. She turned in his arms and looked into those blue eyes and felt that love resonate in her bones. And she knew then that whatever life threw their way, they had it. They would be okay.

No.

They would be amazing.

EPILOGUE

Four months later

Parrain's Po-Boys was empty tonight except for the raucous table in the middle of the restaurant. Marin's colleagues had reserved the place for the evening and were in high spirits as they ordered everything on the menu—fried things landing on their table like delicious flavor bombs and drinks flowing freely.

Marin hadn't wanted any big thing made over her probation turning into an official position, but Ori had looked at her like she'd said she wanted to wear black to her wedding. So Marin had been made passenger on the party ship, and Ori had sent the word out. But now that Marin was surrounded by the group, she was glad Ori had gone through the trouble.

Though Oriana had made one gaffe on the guest list. Not knowing the history, Ori had invited Elle McCray to the festivities. Marin had been shocked to see her walk in. They'd managed to forge a professional relationship at work, but they were never going to be friends. However, McCray had shown up and had even brought a little congratulations gift of expensive wine. Maybe she was trying to build bridges. Because, God knows, she didn't look comfortable being there.

Marin actually had a pang of sympathy for her, realizing for the first time that maybe Elle wasn't lonely by choice. Maybe she didn't know how to be with other people like this. So before the party got going, Marin pulled Lane aside and asked if he'd try to put McCray at ease.

Lane's brows had gone high. "You want me to hang out with Dr. Ice? She hates me. I once overheard her call me a hooker to someone."

"She doesn't hate you. Who could hate you?"

His gaze slid over to McCray. "Lots of people, doc."

Marin handed him an extra glass of wine to bring over. "Look, you're the best I know at making women feel comfortable. Just . . . chat with her. Bring her a drink."

Lane sighed and then leaned down to kiss her cheek. "Only for you, doc. But when she scratches my eyes out, you're paying the medical bills."

She smirked and patted his arm. "Oh, Master Cannon, I think you can handle one hardass doctor just fine."

"Can I bring cuffs, maybe a ball gag?" He looked over again, wary, but something else flickering over his expression.

"Play nice."

"Never." But he strode off and carried the wine over.

Arms wrapped around her from behind and Donovan gave her a squeeze. "Poisoned her wine, right?"

Marin laughed and turned in his arms. "Do I look that vindictive?"

He nodded sagely. "Yes."

"Shut up. I was actually doing something nice." She pushed up on her toes and kissed him. "I told Lane to keep her company."

Donovan looked over, his eyes narrowing, a calculating look on his face. "Hmm, that could be . . . interesting."

"What do you mean?"

He turned back to her and smiled. "Never mind, gorgeous. I came over here to tell you a) how proud I am of you, b) how hard it is for me not to drag you back to our place with this dress you're wearing, and c) that your party is requesting you back at the table."

She looped her arms around his waist. "Thank you on all accounts. And you can drag me back home later. But we're going to have to be quiet. Nate and Kai are staying the night."

He groaned. "Hmm, well maybe their loud monkey sex will drown out ours."

"I'm going to pretend I didn't hear that first part. I don't want to know if they're doing that yet."

"Oh, they so are. Look at them together."

Marin glanced over. Nate's and Kai's chairs were so close they may as well have been sitting on the same one, and they kept looking at each other like no one else was in the room. And truly, she couldn't find it in herself to be stressed by it. Nate had worked through so much over the summer. Moving. Losing his first real boyfriend. And then having a temporary moment of insanity—his words—with a girl. She was happy to see that he'd started school and had found a guy to light him up like that.

Which did not mean she wouldn't be pulling him aside before the night was done to reaffirm her stance on safe sex. Old habits die hard.

Marin looked up at Donovan. "How you doing, West? It's been a long week."

He'd gone back to Texas this week. There'd been a break in his parents' case earlier this month. A new arrest had been made—a career criminal known for break-ins. Marin had worried that the news would derail Donovan. But he'd handled it well—taking a few days to absorb the information, to process it, but getting comfort from having some sort of closure, some justice.

Donovan brushed her hair away from her face. "I'm good, Rush. I'm really good."

"Good." She smiled and kissed him again. She never got tired of doing that. "I love you."

"I know."

She rolled her eyes.

"Don't give me that look. *Love* isn't a strong enough word for what I feel for you, woman. New words need to be invented. Maybe whole languages."

Warmth moved through her. "You can be devastatingly romantic when you want to be, you know that?"

He nuzzled his nose against hers. "Don't let the word get out."

"Stop making out and get your asses over here. There are toasts to be made," Oriana called out. "Drinks to be had. Drunken mistakes to commit."

Marin and Donovan laughed, and he let her go so they could take their seats at the table.

Once they were settled, Ori raised her mug high and the rest of the people at the table followed suit. "To Dr. Rush, the newest official member of our crazy-ass team. May she facilitate many happy relationships and many successful orgasms during her illustrious career."

"Ori!" Marin shot her a disbelieving look.

"Well, she *is* excellent at facilitating them," Donovan offered from the spot next to her, an unrepentant grin on his face. "Exceptional, really."

"Oh my God. Shut up." She smacked Donovan's arm, making his drink slosh.

And her little brother, who apparently everyone had forgotten had been invited to this soiree, put his face in his hands and groaned. "Dear God, please let a lightning bolt hit me. Please erase this memory from my head."

Everybody laughed and Kai put a hand on Nate's knee as he grinned. "Your family's parties are the best, dude."

Nate glanced up, a long-suffering look on his face, but when his eyes met Marin's, she saw the glimmer there, the quirk of a smile. *Family.* Yeah, that was nice.

They'd always had each other. They always would. But looking at the faces around the table—Lane and Ori and Ysabel. *Donovan.* She could feel her heart swell big in her chest. She hadn't just found a job. Or her passion. Or love.

She'd found their place.

Nate lifted his Coke, his cheeks red. "To orgasms then!"

Everyone clinked their mugs, and the resounding chorus rang out in the restaurant. "To orgasms!"

Then they drank and laughed and ate. They made fun of each other and walked each other home. They did what friends and family do. And when she fell into bed next to Donovan later that night and felt his arms go around her, his naked body pressing against hers, all she could do was smile.

He rolled her beneath him and stared down at her with one of his wicked looks. "What's on that mind of yours, Rush?"

She let her hands slide down his back, loving the heat of him, the hard muscle, the way he felt against her. "Really, really dirty things. Scandalous, even."

"I was hoping you'd say that." He grabbed her hands and pinned them above her head, his grip hard as he aligned himself along her body "Tell me *all* about it, Dr. Rush."

She did.

In illicit detail.

And she never once blushed.

ONE NIGHT ONLY

1

Bianca had never been particularly prone to violence, but right now, sitting in this five-star restaurant, she wished she knew how to throw a solid right hook. She let her sip of iced tea slide down her throat, keeping her glass steady in her hand, as she watched Cal's expression morph into an apologetic one. That probably worked on most people. He had that kind of generically handsome, nice-guy face that you wanted to trust. *Hey, we're all friends here. We all make mistakes, right? You understand.*

No, she didn't. Fuck that apology and that nice-guy mask.

The man was a liar. He'd talked to her for *six goddamned months* online without mentioning this? Had taken her on two dates. Hell, she'd gone to freaking therapy and worked with a sex surrogate for God's sake. And *this* is what Cal had failed to mention in all that time? Forget a right hook. This deserved a swift kick to the balls with a pointy-toed shoe.

"Please say something," he said, his voice gentle, like she was a skittish horse or like *she* was the one who was being unreasonable with her lack of response.

Bianca set her glass down, smoothed her napkin in her lap. "You're married."

"Yes. But it's not like . . ." He frowned and folded his hands on the table. "It's not a good marriage."

Thank you, Captain Obvious. "Are you getting divorced?"

He rubbed one thumb along the other, his gaze watching the movement. "Not exactly. It's complicated. We have kids and—"

Kids?

"All righty," Bianca said, her tone clipped and her voice tight in her throat. "So, I'll be going now."

Cal reached out and clamped a hand over hers before she could get up. "Please, don't. I know this is a surprise, but . . ."

A surprise? No, a surprise was an unexpected visitor on your doorstep. Or finding out your favorite TV show had been canceled. Finding out the guy you'd been sort of dating for half a year was married with kids was more like a guerrilla attack.

"But what, Cal? What the hell do you expect me to say? Oh, no problem. I don't mind the whole *wife thing.* Or the kids. Minor issue."

"I've just never had a connection like this with someone before. And I thought that maybe you'd be open to, you know, an alternative arrangement. I rarely sleep with her anymore and—"

Bianca yanked her hand from beneath his and held up her palm. "Hold on. Rewind that. *Why* exactly would you assume I'd be open to some alternative arrangement? Which is called cheating, by the way, in case you needed a more accurate word. I didn't have anything like that in my profile."

Then it happened. It was as brief as a blink, but his gaze jumped to the scarred side of her face and neck. And she had her answer. All the air rushed out of her, and a cold, trembly feeling replaced it. It was a familiar sensation, one she'd had time and again in her life when she'd catch someone staring or someone would tease her. But she steeled herself before the vulnerability could show. No way would she let this asshole see that he'd stung her. "Never mind. I got it. You thought I'd be open to being some guy's thing on the side because obviously, a woman who looks like me must be desperate for any attention a man such as yourself would be willing to throw my way."

He flinched. "Bianca, no, of course not—you're . . . lovely."

Lovely. Yeah. Okay. She sent him a vicious smile because it was better than crying and grabbed her purse. Her chair scraped the floor loudly as she stood. "Well, enjoy your meal, Cal. And afterward, feel free to go to hell."

He jumped up from his seat. "Bianca—"

But she was already turning on her heel to go. Six months. Six freaking months of going to therapy, of fighting those demons, of battling that instinct to stay hidden away, and this was the guy she'd wasted that effort on? She wanted to punch things. Him. She'd thought Cal would be her real first. She'd lost her virginity with Lane, the surrogate from The Grove, a few weeks ago, but it had all been preparing for Cal. This was going to be her stepping out into the real world of adult relationships.

Instead, she'd gotten a lying, cheating bastard with bad taste in neckties.

Fantastic. And it's not like she'd been holding on to some big hope for epic love. She'd kept her expectations at a reasonable level. She just wanted to find a fun, sexy partner to go on some dates and have a good time with. To practice. She was in her thirties now and tired of hiding, of feeling like an outcast. She'd wanted someone with whom she could feel comfortable in her own skin, who'd make her feel desired, who'd take her to bed and let her see what all the fuss was about.

She thought that person was going to be Cal. They'd gotten along so well in their chats and on the previous two dates. The lying shit had *kissed* her the last time she'd seen him. *God.* She'd been catfished.

Her stomach flipped over. She was a fucking cliché. Lonely girl gets duped by creep online. She'd thought she'd protected herself with video chats. But there were more things to lie about than your face and your name.

Married. *Ugh.*

The host at the front of the restaurant opened the door for Bianca and wished her a good day as she stepped out into the steamy noontime air of the French Quarter. Good day. Right. It was just peachy so far.

The narrow sidewalks were packed with people, the ever-present tourists weaving in with the locals who were hunting for lunch. Tempting scents laced with garlic and cayenne drifted out of the restaurant doorways as Bianca walked with purposeful steps down the uneven sidewalks. People streamed past her, most preoccupied with their own destinations. But she didn't miss the double takes a few gave her. She'd grown used to it.

Since the car accident she'd been in at twelve, she'd learned that it was hard for people to look away from the burn scars that marred her left jaw and the side of her neck. Usually, she wore high-necked clothing to minimize it, but today had been date three and she'd been feeling more confident—brave, even. So she'd worn one of her favorite pieces from her spring collection—a flowered wrap dress with deep aubergine trim and a plunging neckline. It was a dress she'd designed but had never imagined wearing herself. Then she'd seen it hanging in her store earlier today and it had called to her. She'd taken a leap and decided to give it a go for her lunch and art museum date with Cal. It was going to be her I'm-getting-laid outfit.

Now the beautiful dress simply made her feel exposed and raw in the blinding sunlight. And though she was used to people's eyes on her, right now they felt extra heavy, like everyone was critiquing her. She knew that wasn't the case. She'd learned in life people were way more concerned about themselves than others. But after Cal's assumptions about what a girl like her would be willing to do, she couldn't help but feel oversensitive. She found herself glaring back at the people who looked too long.

And by the time she made it to her car, she was shaking—with anger, frustration, embarrassment—she wasn't exactly sure. Maybe all of them. She unlocked her sleek, black Mercedes, ready for the safety its tinted windows offered and sank into the driver's seat, tipping her head back and closing her eyes despite the stifling heat inside.

Maybe her mother had been right. She should never have put herself out on the dating market. *You'll get hurt, Bee. Men will take advantage of you for your money and success. You should stick to people who are already in our circle and know you.*

Her mother meant well and had spent much of Bianca's life hovering and protecting. But what Bianca heard in her mother's words was, *No one would want to date you for real. They'd only use you because you're wealthy.*

Or maybe because they think you're so desperate that you wouldn't mind all that much if they were, you know, MARRIED.

Bianca pinched the bridge of her nose and tried to stave off the tears. If she was thinking, *Maybe Mom was right*, she'd taken a wrong turn somewhere. She wouldn't do this. She needed to pull it together. But all she wanted to do was go home, park herself in front of her worktable, and forget she'd ever tried this. Go back to the security of her predictable life.

No.

If she drove home right now, she would tumble backward. She could already feel herself wanting to crawl into that shell. She'd fought too hard to get to this point. She didn't want to go back to staying in the house all the time, working nonstop, and ignoring the fact that she had no personal life.

She took a deep breath, turned on the car to get the AC going, and dug her phone out of her clutch purse. They'd told her she could call anytime. She'd thought that a little bit of overkill when she'd first started seeing Dr. West at The Grove. Sure, some of their departments dealt with serious mental illness. But were there really sex therapy emergencies? Come on. But right now, she was thankful the doctor went above and beyond for his clients. She hit the number.

Ysabel, Dr. West's assistant, answered, and once Bianca had assured her that it wasn't a life or death emergency, she said Dr. West or the new doctor, Dr. Rush, would get back to her as soon as possible.

Bianca didn't want to hang around in the parking lot, since she had no idea how long a callback would take, but right as she was pulling out of the narrow streets of the city and onto the interstate, her phone rang. She activated the speakerphone.

"Bianca? Are you okay?" Dr. West's voice was like a warm blanket to her nerves—calm and reassuring, familiar. "Tell me what's going on."

She rubbed her lips together, trying to find some still place in her mind as her hands gripped the steering wheel tightly. She could do this. She was an expert at tucking away her emotions. She ran an entire company, goddammit. No one ever saw her lose it. But as soon as she tried to speak, it was like some sobbing monster of doom burst out of her. "I . . . Cal . . . wife!"

The words were broken, the tears finally charging past the fortress she'd tried to put up. The road blurred in her vision.

"Bianca, take a breath." Dr. West's voice was gentle but firm. A command, not a request. "Are you driving? It sounds like you're in a car."

She nodded. But when she remembered he couldn't see her, she managed to say, "Mmm-hmm."

"Okay. You sound very upset. If you're crying, you shouldn't be driving. Is there somewhere you can pull over?"

She sniffed and swiped at her tears, clearing her vision. "I'm . . . okay. Can drive. Just . . . needed to talk. But I—"

Her voice broke again and more tears threatened to spill out.

"Okay, Bianca. Are you anywhere close? It might be better to talk in person. Dr. Rush and I have a full schedule today, but if you can come by, we'll work you in."

She swallowed past the knot in her throat. She was at least forty-five minutes out from The Grove. But her house was halfway to it, so it wouldn't be too far out of the way. And having a session sounded like a better idea than falling apart alone at home. Dr. West and Dr. Rush could help her regain perspective, help her rein in all the shit that was tumbling around her brain right now. "I can . . . be there. An hour."

"Perfect. Do you want us to send a car for you or are you really okay to drive? Be honest with me."

"I can drive."

She could almost hear him nodding. "Okay, Bianca. Drive safe and I'll see you soon. Call the line if you need anything before then."

"Thank you."

She ended the call and took another deep breath. She'd gone from I'm-getting-laid hopefulness to I'm-getting-emergency-therapy patheticness. Wonderful.

Banner day, Bianca Marsh.

2

Bianca's scattered emotions settled a bit as she walked onto the campus of The Grove. There was something about the towering oak trees, the historic buildings, and all that green space that soothed her. The place had once been an asylum, so she assumed that serenity was the intended effect. Peacefulness in the surroundings when people were fighting chaos in their head.

She headed inside the building Dr. West was located in and made her way to his floor, taking one quick detour to clean up her tear-smudged eye makeup. She was a wreck inside but that didn't mean she needed to look like one walking in. Ysabel gave her a friendly smile and told her the doctors were in a session but that she'd let them know she was here when they got out.

Bianca thanked her and made her way to the posh waiting room. Usually she was the only one in there—just her and the bubbling wall fountain—but when she stepped inside today, a broad-shouldered man was sitting wide-kneed in one of the cushy chairs, his eyes on his phone and a scowl twisting his mouth. His gaze flicked up at her entrance, and her breath caught in her throat. Pale jade eyes, blond messy-on-purpose hair, and a very, very familiar face. She'd last seen it on a movie poster.

Eli Harding.

She couldn't seem to move forward. Some men were good-looking; others were handsome. Then there were ones like Eli, men so ruggedly beautiful you wondered whether they actually existed, if maybe they were just some creation of CGI or Photoshop. Well, there was no technical enhancement here, and if anything, Eli was even more of a stunner in person. So much so that it took a second for her to process the sight of him. But when she realized she was staring, reality quickly snapped her back into motion.

One, they were in a therapy waiting room. Ogling was rude any day but particularly here. And two, she had a weakness for entertainment gossip since celebrities were some of her best customers, and she knew Eli had a reputation for being a jerk and a hothead. No, thanks. She didn't need any more drama today. So she managed to kick-start her muscles from their paused state, gave Eli a polite nod, and took a seat on the other side of the small room. She reached for a magazine and blindly flipped through it. *Flip. Flip. Flip. Nothing to see here. Totally wasn't staring at you, Mr. Beautiful Man.*

But before long, her skin got that tingly feeling like she was being watched. *Don't look. Don't look.* But the temptation was too much to resist. She lifted her head and caught Eli looking, this time sans scowl. The impact of having his attention on her stirred something in her blood, but then his gaze caressed the injured side of her face in an unhurried sweep.

Oh, right. Of course that's what he was looking at. Great. Just what she needed. Hollywood's hottest gawking at her scars. She sent him a quelling look, and he quirked a brow but didn't bother turning away. How fucking rude. Her earlier knee-jerk infatuation cooled immediately. *Go to hell, pretty boy.* She forced her focus back to the magazine. But of course, the page she'd paused on had

Eli on it, cozied up to some *Playboy* centerfold type. Perfect. She turned the page so hard it ripped at the edge.

In her periphery, she could see he was still watching her. She let out a breath and looked up again. "Have you catalogued each scar yet or would you like me to turn to the side so you can get a better look?"

His mouth twitched, mild amusement there. "I wasn't looking at your scars."

"Right."

He shrugged as if to say, *Believe what you want.*

She pressed her lips together and dragged her attention back to the magazine she wasn't reading. But after a long few seconds of awkward silence, she slapped it shut. "So what were you staring at, then?"

He peered her way again, no doubt caught off guard by her hostile tone. She knew she was being a bitch for no good reason, but she couldn't seem to turn it off.

He lowered his phone and met her gaze. "I was looking at a beautiful woman. It's been known to happen."

Her lips parted, the words absolutely not what she'd expected to hear, but then her spine snapped straight. This was a game. "Okay. Whatever."

He sat up from his slouch and braced his forearms on his knees, his eyes never leaving hers. "You find that so hard to believe?"

Her fingers curled around the arm of the chair. "Please don't patronize me. I've had an exceptionally shitty day, and I don't think I can deal with one more lying jerk."

He stared at her for a long moment and then said, "Your mouth."

"What?"

"You asked me what I was staring at, and you don't want me to lie. So specifically, I was staring at your mouth."

"My mouth," she said, deadpan despite the fact that hearing him say the word *mouth* made something warm prickle her skin.

"Yeah, when you walked in, you looked like you were holding back saying something. You kept pursing your lips. I liked it. So yes, I was staring. Not at the scars. Though, I did notice them on the way down to checking out the rest of you in that dress."

Heat flooded her as his gaze traced over her again—slow and lingering, the guy somehow managing to be shameless without it coming across as a leer. She frowned. "I can't tell if you're messing with me or if you have zero filter."

He smirked, a deep dimple appearing. Damn, he was gorgeous.

"Choice two. You apparently ran into a lying asshole today. I figured I'd change the pattern and be an honest asshole instead."

She blinked, unsure what to make of him. "Well, then . . . thanks, I guess."

He shrugged and leaned back again, returning his attention to his phone, effectively dismissing her.

But she wasn't ready to let the conversation go just yet. She wet her lips. "So are you really an asshole?"

He sniffed and didn't look up. "Yep."

Now it was her turn to watch him. At first glance, he'd seemed intimidating over there in the corner, his big, broad body making the chair look like a child's seat and his movie star looks almost too much to take in all at once. But now that she really looked, she could see the tense hold of his shoulders, the furrow in his brow. He was in defense mode. She knew what that mode was like. She lived there half the time. "You don't seem like one."

His gaze slid her way, wary now. "You don't know me."

"That's true." And Lord knows she'd been a shitty judge of character lately. She should shut her mouth and read her magazine and leave him be. Words spilled out anyway. "I guess I just figured if you were really an asshole, you wouldn't say so."

Lines appeared around his mouth. "Well, why don't you be the judge? Want to know what I'm doing right now?"

The question wasn't a question. It was a dare. A challenge. He was trying to scare her off. She straightened and tipped up her chin. "What?"

He pinned her with those wicked green eyes. "Fine. Right now, I'm sitting over here playing poker on my phone because if I don't distract myself, I'm going to turn on the charm and flirt with you until I can convince you out of that dress. I've already thought about what I want to do to you and how I'd do it, all the different ways I'd make you come. And I know that I'd walk away right after and never call because that's what I do. All that and I haven't even asked your name yet."

Every cell in her body jerked to attention, and any words she might've said dissolved into the ether. "I . . ."

He punched a finger against the screen on his phone, focusing on it again. "So now you know, and I'm going to stop talking now."

Oh, the hell he was. A man couldn't say something like that to a woman and expect her to just let it drop. She'd heard his warning. He was a hit-and-run kind of guy. She'd also heard the other stuff. And the other stuff sent a hot shiver rippling through her. "My name's Bianca."

His jaw flexed, but he didn't look up.

"And since we're doing the honesty thing, I'm sitting here right now because the guy I've been seeing informed me today he's married with kids and hoped I'd be cool being his mistress. He figured, you know, with the scars and all, I'd be happy for whatever crumbs he threw my way. So for what you just said, thank you. It was entirely inappropriate. But I fucking needed that."

Eli's head lifted, something flaring in his eyes. "What a dick."

"Yep. He's a real winner." She couldn't believe she'd said all of that out loud, but it felt good to just lay it out there. She smoothed the hem of her dress. "I know how to pick 'em."

"You didn't pick him. He targeted you. Guys like that know how to do it."

Yeah, well, apparently, I'm an easy target. But she kept those words to herself.

Eli flipped his phone in his hand, considering her, the hard lines around his mouth softening a little. "I'm here because tomorrow I'm checking myself into rehab for sex addiction."

Her brows shot up. "Oh."

"Yeah."

She gave him a chagrined smile, the earlier boost of confidence taking a little tumble. "Well, I guess that at least explains it."

He frowned. "What?"

"Why you wanted to flirt with me."

"Why I— Wait, you think . . ." His expression darkened, a thundercloud moving over it. "That has nothing to do with it. My addiction makes me want sex and gets me into trouble. It doesn't make me want a woman I wouldn't be interested in otherwise. I said what I said and was thinking about you that way because you're hot. Don't let whoever that lying fucker was screw with your head. I don't know anything about you personally. But I can tell you one thing for sure. You're easy to look at, Bianca."

She swallowed past the dryness in her throat, surprised and secretly touched by his fervor. Yes, he was only commenting on her outer shell. He didn't know her as a person. But she already knew she was a decent person, a good friend, daughter, boss, all that important stuff. For once, it was nice to hear the shallow side directed at her. *You're hot.*

She cleared her throat, trying to find words other than, *Oh my God, you're so hot, too.* "So how does the addiction get you in trouble? I mean, sex is sex, right? If you're being safe about it and not lying to anyone, what's the harm?"

He let out the breath and ran a hand over the back of his head. "I would've agreed with you not that long ago. I didn't think it was that big a deal even when Dr. West pointed out the negatives. But last month, I missed visiting Trenton, a kid who has cancer and is one of my biggest fans, because I was hooking up with a co-star. When I called my assistant to reschedule, I found out Trenton had just passed away. He was buried two days ago in the Captain Blaze superhero suit I was supposed to sign. So status confirmed. I'm the worst kind of asshole."

Bianca's lips parted, the story punching the starch right out of her and bringing tears to her eyes. Eli looked away then, his jaw tight, and his posture rigid.

"God, I'm so sorry." Her heart broke for that child and his family and a little for Eli, too. He'd done a horribly selfish thing, but it was obviously eating him up inside. She wanted to go to him, lay a hand on his arm, comfort him in some way.

"And the shittiest part is," he said, sarcasm lacing his words, "despite being fucking gutted over it, all I've wanted to do since I found out is go out and forget. Get laid and go numb inside. Drown myself in the forgetting."

"But you're not doing that," she said quietly. "You're here instead, getting help."

He smirked and glanced up. "No, I'm here, thinking about getting you into bed. Let's not pretend that didn't happen. If you would've given me any sign you were interested, I'd have lost my resolve to stay in this waiting room."

"I don't believe that."

He made a sound of derision. "You should. When people tell you they're fucked up, believe them. If you said yes, I'd be out of here."

She did believe him about his addiction. But she had a feeling that the boy who'd died had impacted Eli far more than he realized. There was no going back after a thing like that. She was seeing Eli at his bottom point. He was here for help and wouldn't leave until he got it. She also believed that he was being honest when he said he wanted her.

And she probably should be appalled that he wanted to numb his grief with meaningless sex, but on some level, she understood.

The mind can only handle so much guilt and pain before it seeks relief. Living in the guilt can feel like there are hands tugging you down under a churning ocean. She'd gone through that after the accident. She'd survived, but not everyone in her family had. Sometimes you just had to escape. To forget. To feel good and smile for a minute.

Maybe she could offer that to Eli. She would never stand in the way of him getting help. But maybe there was a way for him to have both, at least for today.

"What if I were to say yes with conditions?" she blurted out, the words tumbling into the space between them.

Surprise flickered across his face. "What are you talking about?"

She took her breath, shoring up her nerve. "I never said I wasn't interested."

The wariness on his face was absolute and she thought he was going to shut her down, but after he stared at her for a long second, something hot and dangerous flared in its place. "Be careful, Bianca."

The warning raised goose bumps on her skin.

She leaned forward, lacing her hands around crossed legs and letting some untapped side of herself bubble to the surface. "Maybe I'm tired of being careful."

He inhaled slow and silent, his gaze never leaving hers, the look burning her into a pile of ash.

She shifted in her chair, trying to find her voice again. "If you really want this—*me*, I'll make you a deal. Go in your session and commit yourself to your rehab plans. Make sure there's no getting out of it. Then afterward, if you want to have one last ill-advised hookup before you go on a ninety-day fast, you come find me at the Morning Cup, the coffee shop right outside the gates."

He didn't speak for a long moment but his attention never left her. It was as if he expected her to suddenly laugh and say—*ha ha, just kidding*. But finally, that deep, rumbly voice hit her ears.

"You're serious? I just told you all that ugly shit about myself and you're offering to sleep with me?"

"Yes. You've been honest. I'm being honest, too. I want this. You. I could use an escape as much as you can. Is it smart? Probably not. Right now, I don't really care."

At her declaration, his whole demeanor shifted. The hunger that she'd only seen glimmers of was there in full force now, all over his expression and the tilt of his posture, like it'd just been hovering beneath the surface, waiting for permission to show itself.

If she'd had any doubts earlier about his attraction to her, she didn't now. She'd never seen a man look at her like that. Never felt the sheer impact of that kind of lust. Like she was the sexiest, most desirable woman alive and he was going to devour her whole. And maybe it *was* because she was the last meal for him. Maybe she could be any woman. And maybe she was offering this to him because she needed her own medicine, that fat dose of confidence that came from how Eli Harding looked at her. But sometimes you needed to use and be used. At least they'd be making an even exchange, neither expecting anything more than the simple forbidden solace they could offer each other in the moment.

Eli got up then and crossed the room in two smooth strides, his towering size shrinking the space and making her feel like she was a gazelle who'd just provoked the lion. He sank into the chair next to her and turned her way. His green-eyed gaze was like slow, hot fingers over her skin as he let his attention drift over her face and downward. He took her hand, his thumb stroking over the top. "I want you, Bianca. You have no idea what your offer is doing to me. But I need you to be sure about this. I'm the guy I said I was. Not a nice one."

"I know, and I'm sure. But you need to be sure, too. These scars travel down my arm and partly on my chest and side. It's not pretty."

His eyes met hers and he lifted his other hand to gently stroke the roughened part of her jaw. "Scars don't scare me. We all have them. Some we can just see more than others. I think you're beautiful."

The simple words tightened her throat but she swallowed past it. "And I'm not very experienced—sexually. It's part of the reason I come here. You should know that, too."

His expression shifted at that, surprise there, but he didn't pry. "I don't mind taking the lead."

She gave a curt nod, trying to look put together even though his gentle strokes against her skin were awakening things in her body and making her blood pump. Her nipples pushed against the fabric of her bra and pulsing warmth gathered between her thighs.

He cupped her jaw and mapped her bottom lip with his thumb, apparently truly fascinated by her mouth. "And here's my honesty. I want you. And I want to make you feel good, want to feel you beneath me and watch you lose yourself to the pleasure of it. But I really am leaving tomorrow and there won't be anything after this. I don't . . . I'm never with anyone more than one night."

She closed her eyes, already overwhelmed by his nearness, the sinful promise in his voice. "No expectations, Eli. Just one night."

"Okay." The word was soft, almost a whisper.

Deal made. Fate set.

The thrill of that rippled through her. She was jumping into a world she'd never visited before. Scary. Exciting. Daring. Who was this woman?

And before she could open her eyes, his lips brushed against hers. The shock of it jolted her at first, but then the sensation rushed through her like wildfire. Warm lips and cool mint and Eli's hand sliding to cup the back of her neck as his mouth touched hers a second time, gently coaxing a kiss from her. There was no resisting, no help for the way her body clamored to meet him halfway. She groaned into the easy connection and reached out, bracing a hand on his knee as she returned the kiss. He'd probably been going for something quick and simple, a taste, but she couldn't help herself. All the practice with Lane had been slow and gentle and friendly. Neat. She didn't want that. She wanted the passion, the blurred edges, the abandon. Her lips parted and she invited Eli in.

He groaned and eagerly accepted the invitation, taking them both deeper and making her body hum and heat. His hand slid into her hair as their tongues twined, the connection urgent, hungry. Like they'd die if they didn't get another taste. She slid her palm to his thigh to steady herself, the thick muscle barely giving when she squeezed it, and he grunted his approval with this sexy, chest-deep sound. Yes. This. So much this. Her heart beat like a hummingbird's wings and her brain screamed at her—*more, more, more.* She wanted to climb over the arm of her chair and straddle the guy. This is what she'd been after.

No, it wasn't a relationship and never would be. And it probably was a dumb idea in the grand scheme of things. They were both hurting and damaged right now. But God, *God*, this was good in the most basic and primal way. The need to connect with someone physically, to feel alive and sexy and shivery in all the right places.

"Fuck." Eli groaned into her mouth between kisses. "So. Good. Want to touch. Everywhere. But we're . . . in . . . the shrink's . . . office."

The words sunk in, drifting through her lusty haze, and she broke away from the kissing on a laugh. She pressed her fingers over her mouth, trying to hold back an embarrassing guffaw.

Eli grinned, the smile lighting up his face and turning beautiful into Roman god status. "This is beyond fucked up, right? There's a *Psychology Today* on the coffee table and someone pouring their guts out on the other side of that door. We are very, very bad people."

A snort came out despite her best efforts. "So very."

He shook his head and tucked her hair behind her ear. "So worth it, though."

She found herself biting her lip like some schoolgirl and forced herself to quit doing it. "Agreed. But you're right. We should stop."

"Of course. We should stop." His gaze coasted over her, unhurried and full of illicit promise, and then he leaned close to her ear, his hand going to the back of her head. "But how the hell am I supposed to make it through a therapy session knowing you're out here somewhere, lips puffy, skin flushed, and pussy wet?"

Her breath left her at that. Normally, she'd be put off by the crude language, but rolling off his tongue it sounded like a prayer of worship. *Flushed. Wet.* She licked her lips. "Same way I'm going to make it through a cup of coffee knowing you're fighting a hard-on."

He groaned and tugged her earlobe with his teeth before leaning back into his chair. "It's going to be a *looong* hour."

He had that right. She felt like she'd been waiting her whole life for this. Now another hour stared her in the face. So feeling decadent and high on the lust buzz, she let her attention drift down to Eli's spread thighs. She and Eli couldn't touch right now, but she could damn well look. And from what she could tell, boy, did he have something to look at. She wanted to reach out . . .

A door creaked behind her, and she spun around with an involuntary yelp. Dr. West stood in the doorway, gaze jumping from Eli to her. "Sorry to startle you. Everything okay?"

Shit. She tried to school her face into something other than hand-in-cookie-jar status. Or imagining-her-hand-on-Eli's-cock status. "Uh . . ."

But Eli saved her.

"Doc, isn't asking two therapy patients if everything's okay kind of pointless? If the answer was yes, we wouldn't be here. That's what we pay you the big bucks for. To make us A-OK."

The sarcasm rolled off him easily, his whole demeanor slipping into that smug persona he was known for. But now Bianca could see it—it was a persona. Another role to play. That was his armor.

Dr. West sniffed, endlessly unruffled, and tucked his hands in his pockets. "Eli, why don't you go on in. Dr. Rush is already in there. Tell her I'll be there in a minute."

"You got it, doc." Eli pushed himself up from the chair, surreptitiously adjusting himself, and didn't give Bianca another glance.

Thank God, because she would've blushed and given herself away.

Once Eli was gone, Dr. West took the spot across from her, his brow creased in concern. "I'm so glad you made it out here, Bianca. Was Eli bothering you?"

"No, not at all. We were just . . . talking."

Dr. West's eyebrow arched but he let her statement lie. "Okay, well, I only have a minute right now, but I'll be able to work you in after Eli's done."

Oh. Right. Therapy. Why she'd been sitting in this room. Suddenly, she had zero interest in rehashing the Cal date. She sat up straighter and tried to look poised. "Actually, you know, I think I'm feeling better now. Today, I . . . I found out Cal is married."

Dr. West stared at her a second, registering the news, and then grimaced. "Wow, that's . . . what a shit."

She smiled. That's what she liked about Dr. West. He was a good doctor but not so formal that she couldn't relax around him. He cursed and he didn't pull punches in his opinions or advice. "Yeah, he is. And I was really upset at first, but I think I just needed to get out of the situation, get over the shock. The drive over and the wait in here has helped clear my head."

Dr. West frowned. "But you came all the way out here. You sure you don't want to talk it out? That's a lot to process."

"It is. But I can wait until our scheduled session next week."

Dr. West didn't look totally convinced. "Are you sure? It's really no problem to work you in."

"Yep. Positive."

Because she'd figured out a better way to erase the ugly day.

One smoking-hot actor, a no-strings-attached hookup, and no worries about tomorrow.

Bianca Marsh was about to get spectacularly laid.

3

Eli walked out of the session with the doctors feeling flayed open and altogether freaked out. West and Rush had heaped praise on him for opening up about Trenton's death and for wanting to check into rehab. They'd been shocked, too. He could tell. But being the well-trained therapists that they were, they'd mostly covered their surprise. Eli knew neither of them were fans of his after some of the shit he'd pulled in sessions and in group.

Up until this point, he'd been treating therapy like a joke. His agent and the studio had insisted he go while he was here in New Orleans filming his next movie. They'd made it part of the contract, so he'd had to attend. And he'd stuck to that. But he hadn't really participated or done any of the work. He'd shown up to therapy sessions and to group like he was above it all and had wreaked havoc, acting like some smarmy spoiled child. He'd figured it was better than actually having to talk about real shit.

But now he realized the joke was on him. He'd fucked things up to the nth degree and had been pissing on the people who were trying to help. He was no better than his junkie father. Eli had thought never touching alcohol or drugs would keep him safe from that particular family legacy, but he'd just substituted one type of addiction for another. He fed off the high of sex, that thrill of losing himself to the moment with someone. The escape of reality.

But inevitably, the sex would end and he'd lose interest in the person he'd been desperate to have just moments before and all the bullshit would come rushing back. The regret. The consequences. The hurt he caused when he walked away from women, making them feel used up and discarded.

He hadn't been lying to Bianca. He was an asshole.

He should stay far away from her.

She was beautiful and sexy and some intriguing combination of toughness and innocence. She deserved better than him.

When he'd told her why he'd been looking at her, she hadn't believed him. It hadn't been the false modesty he so often saw with the actresses he hooked up with. Bianca truly didn't think she was worth the attention. Someone had told her those scars made her ugly. And then some married, cheating douche-canoe had confirmed her fears.

He could only imagine what she'd been through. People were cruel and scared of things that were different. But when Bianca had walked into the waiting room today, he'd seen long dark hair, bright brown eyes, and a body that made his mouth water. And the scars, though they'd drawn his attention at first, were just another part of her. He'd grown up on comic books and now made a living in superhero movies. The scars were what made the characters interesting and often what gave them their powers. He hated that Bianca had suffered that pain in her life, but if she thought that how she looked would turn him off, she was wrong.

And when he'd kissed her. Damn. He couldn't remember the last time he'd wanted to make out with someone just for the pleasure of it. Usually kissing was a means to an end, a step while the clothes were coming off. But kissing Bianca had reminded him what things had been like when he was young and when kissing a girl had still been new, when each little nuance was a discovery, a thrill to explore. If they hadn't been in the waiting room, he would've been happy to make out like teenagers for an hour.

But that's not what he was heading to that coffee shop to do. Bianca had shocked the hell out of him by making the offer to meet. And she'd outright admitted that she didn't have much experience, which meant she wasn't in the habit of setting up one-night stands. So how was this even happening? For the first time in years, he'd been flat-out honest with someone about who he was, and she hadn't run screaming. Instead, she'd offered herself to him without fine print. One time. No drama.

He didn't deserve it.

Didn't mean he would walk away.

He parked the rental car outside the coffee shop, grabbed a baseball cap and sunglasses to avoid anyone recognizing him, and headed inside the Morning Cup. Quirky indie music drifted through the shop and the line snaked toward the door. Almost all the tables were taken, but Eli didn't have any trouble spotting Bianca. There was this elegance about her that stood out—proud spine, long legs crossed at the knee, and broad sunglasses perched on her head as she gazed out the side window and sipped her coffee. She looked like royalty.

Some foreign emotion invaded him and he pulled up short from striding over there. He was *intimidated*. For the first time in as long as he could remember, he felt totally and completely out of his league. Beautiful women were a constant part of his life. He'd slept with some of the biggest stars out there. He never walked into those situations with anything but utter confidence. And if he got rejected, so what. There'd always be another woman looking his way the next day. But now he felt his heart picking up speed. He'd shown Bianca a real piece of himself. He'd given her something he never gave anyone—honesty. Now if she turned him away, the rejection would be real. Personal.

But before he could deal with that unexpected worry, Bianca turned her head and caught sight of him. The warmth in her smile was enough to let him exhale. Okay. She wasn't running. He returned the smile and made his way over to her. "Need a refill on your coffee, gorgeous?"

She set her cup down. "I'm good. All done, actually. I was just waiting for someone."

He braced his hands on the back of the empty chair next to her. "Yeah? Who's the lucky guy?"

She shrugged. "Just some dude I met at the shrink's office. I forgot his name. Something biblical."

He laughed. "Sounds ominous."

"Indeed. Everything go okay with your meeting?"

He nodded, something tightening in his gut. Tomorrow, he'd no longer be a free man. Ninety days. Ninety fucking days. He couldn't think about it. "Yep. No going back now."

Empathy flashed through her eyes and she put out her hand. "Good. Ready to get out of here, then?"

He lifted a brow, surprised she didn't want to chat for a while first, but took her hand and helped her up from her chair. He was more than on board with getting out of here sooner rather than later. The last thing he wanted to do was rehash anything about his therapy session. Plus, the longer he hung around, the more he risked someone recognizing him. He led Bianca outside into the thick warmth of the late afternoon. "I'm staying in the city. You want to go—"

"There's a small bed-and-breakfast a few miles from here. I called and rented the private guesthouse. It sits right on the bayou. Quiet. I've stayed there before, and the owners will leave the key under the mat so that you don't have to worry about anyone knowing who you are."

He paused on the sidewalk and turned to her, frowning. "You didn't have to do that. I don't want you paying—"

She held up a hand and gave him a brief smirk. "If you're protesting because of money, please don't. It's . . . not an issue. I just thought it'd be easier to have some place private and close by, especially since you'd be heading back this way in the morning."

He took her chin in his hand and brushed his lips over hers. "I'm paying. I don't care if you're heir to the British throne. But thank you for thinking of my privacy." He kissed her again when she didn't move away. Her lips tasted like coffee and something sweet. "You aren't, right? Heir to the British throne?"

She smiled against his mouth. "No."

He leaned back and looked down at her, cocking his head. "What do you do, Bianca?"

For some reason, he suddenly wanted to know everything about her. Another weird impulse he wasn't used to.

"Ever heard of B.B. Marsh?"

"The fashion designer? Yeah, sure. I was a model before I was an actor. You work for them?"

"I am them." She gave a little shrug. "Bianca Baylor Marsh."

"Wait, you're *the* B.B. Marsh?" His lips parted. "Wow. That's . . . wow."

She smiled. "That's the same thing I thought when I first saw you."

"I thought B.B. was a dude."

"That's my COO. I let him handle the public stuff for me."

"Oh." He frowned. "Why?"

She didn't answer. Instead, she kissed him again and then pushed on her toes to get close to his ear. "We should probably get out of here. Making out on the sidewalk is not exactly discreet, Mr. Movie Star."

She didn't want to talk. He knew that game, had played it many times, and though it stung him a little to be shut out, he'd be a hypocrite if he called her out on it. This wasn't a date. She didn't owe him anything.

"Good point." He took her hand and tugged. "Come on, mysterious lady who wants more kissing and less talking."

She laughed as she let him lead her to the parking lot. But when they stopped at his rental, she let go of his hand. "We should take both cars."

He looked back at her. "What? Why?"

Her gaze shifted away. "They'll probably tow us otherwise."

That wasn't the reason. He could see it on her face. She was giving them both an out. If things went wrong or someone wanted to bail, they each had their own ride. It was practical. He'd been looking forward to sharing the drive over, getting to know her more. But he wasn't going to push. If she wanted an escape route, she had the right to have one. He was a stranger to her. A big, flashing risk. If this made her feel more safe with him, he was all for it. "Yeah, sure. That's cool. I can follow you."

She nodded and jabbed her thumb to the left. Her hand trembled slightly. "I'm right over there. The black car. The place isn't too far."

He glanced over at the sporty little Mercedes, but he could hear the nerves making her voice shake, sense the shift in her. Things were getting real for her now. She was getting scared. She took a step to head to her car, but before she could get out of his reach, he grabbed her hand. "Hey."

She looked back to him, her lips rolling inward.

He pulled her closer until he was leaning against the side of his car and had her in front of him. He put his hands on her shoulders. "Listen, there's no rush or pressure here, all right? We can still go somewhere and talk first. Get to know each other a little more. Or you can change your mind altogether. You can always change your mind. At any moment. Just say the word."

She glanced down and smiled. "My nerves are that obvious, huh?"

He stroked his thumb along her shoulder. "It's fine. We can do whatever you want to do. Including stop things right here if that's what you need."

She lifted her head and met his gaze at that. "Is that what you want?"

A bark of disbelief escaped him. She thought *he* was backing out? "Ha. No. That is exactly the opposite of what I want. But I'm not that big of a jerk. I don't do pressure. If we do this, both of us need to be all in or it's a no-go."

She rubbed her lips together. "I'm all in, Eli. But I'm nervous as hell."

Relief made his breath sag out of him. She still wanted this—him. He slid his hands down and looped his arms around her waist, gathering her close. "Tell me what you need."

She braced her palms against his chest and even that touch made warmth ripple through him. She was staring straight ahead where her hands were but he could feel the tension in her body, almost sense the wheels turning in her mind.

"Tell me," he said softly.

Her fingers curled against him. "When we get there, I don't want to talk. The more we talk, the more I think, which means the more nervous I get. I just want you to . . . take over."

Take over. Hot, wicked lust zipped through him. "Take over, huh?"

She nodded quickly. "Yes. Please."

The heat of her body was seeping into him, and her words were firing thoughts he shouldn't be having in a public place. But he couldn't resist. He leaned down close to her ear. "So you want me to follow you to some out-of-the-way cabin in the bayou, pull you inside without a word, and fuck you until neither of us can remember our names? Do I have that straight?"

She shuddered hard in his hold and that was all he needed. Bianca was anxious but she wanted this. He could taste her desire in the air, hear it in the catch of her breath. This was a woman who'd been denied, a woman whom other men hadn't been smart enough to notice. She craved passion.

He craved her.

He kissed the spot behind her ear. "Get in your car, Bianca. I'm not going to say another word to you until we're inside that cabin. And once we walk through those doors, you're mine. The only thing that makes it stop is if you tell me no. Got it?"

Her sharp, quick breaths were like sweet heaven against his senses. "Yes."

He leaned back and brushed the back of his knuckles over her cheek. "Go."

Bianca held his gaze for a beat longer, apprehension still there but something far more potent winning out.

Want.

Need.

A plea for him to unravel her, to *take* her.

And goddamn did he want to answer that call.

4

This was not happening. She was so not doing this. She was not going with a perfect stranger to a secluded cabin for a no-holds-barred, one-night stand. Nope. This was some hot dream she'd conjured up. She was dozing on her couch after watching an Eli Harding movie and weaving her own tale.

Bianca's hands were sweaty against the steering wheel as she took the turn onto the road that led to the bed-and-breakfast and checked her rearview mirror. Eli was right behind her, looking intimidating and hot as hell in his ball cap and aviators. This man was going to take her over as soon as they got inside. Somehow in her addled state of lust, she'd basically handed over all the power. Yes, she could say no. And yes, she believed he'd honor that. But the thought of handing over that responsibility and just holding on for the ride was terrifying—and ridiculously enticing. She didn't have to know what she was doing. He would tell her. He would lead her.

That's the part that had helped her work with Lane. Lane had been her guide. There'd been no pressure to be the expert. But with

Lane, it was therapy. This was something altogether different. Wild. Daring. All the things she'd never considered part of her personality.

But when she pulled into the driveway of the cabin and parked under the canopy of cypress trees, she knew she wouldn't pull the plug on the whole plan despite how insane it was. She didn't feel fear. Nerves, yes. But not fear. This was what she needed. And she hoped it was what Eli needed, too.

She shut off her engine, took a deep breath, finding some steady place inside herself, and then climbed out of the car. She could do this. She *would* do this.

She didn't look back. Didn't check for him. All she did was tilt her chin up and stride toward the door, feigning a haughty confidence she didn't quite feel. Her mother had taught her that. Never let anyone see you break poise. Always keep your head up. And maybe she put a little extra sway in her walk for Eli's benefit as she made her way to the door.

She bent down and grabbed the key from beneath the mat, fumbling it once, and then unlocked the door. The cool air inside was a sharp contrast to the heat outside and her skin instantly prickled, making her more aware of how thin the fabric of her dress was, how very sensitive each part of her had become since Eli had kissed her.

She stepped inside and didn't bother flipping on the lights. The afternoon sunlight created a hazy yellow glow through the gauzy curtains at the front and two broad windows at the back of the cabin had been left bare and looked out onto the screened-in porch and the dark waters of the bayou. The cabin was well appointed with a big king bed and crisp white sheets on one side and the few rustic furniture pieces on the other. She'd stayed here once before and had found it endlessly peaceful and solitary. Electricity almost seemed out of place in the secret little cabin. They were in the wilds of Louisiana. She wanted to lose herself in that mind-set. The real world didn't exist here.

She left a crack in the door behind her and kept her breathing calm and even as she made her way to the back windows. A soft breeze kissed the top of the nearly still water, and a gray crane that had perched at the edge of the marsh was her only company.

But she wasn't alone long.

Slow, heavy footsteps sounded behind her. *Clomp. Clomp. Clomp.* Thick-soled boots on worn wood. She rolled her lips inward and closed her eyes. This was it. Her last chance to back out.

Big hands closed over her shoulders. "Still with me, gorgeous?"

Her body shuddered under the simple touch, the sheer size of his hands and heat of his palms making her thoughts scatter like leaves in a hurricane. She swallowed hard. "Still here."

His breath tickled the back of her neck, and his hands coasted down her arms. "I like you just like this, standing here looking out at the water. Waiting for my touch."

The scent of him drifted over her—something clean and edged with mint. She smiled. "Who says I'm waiting for you? Maybe I'm just fascinated with the view."

"Mmm, the view is mighty nice." He pressed his lips at the sensitive spot where neck met shoulder and dragged his tongue along her flesh.

Shivers chased across her skin, and her abdomen pulled tight as a ping of sensation went straight downward. She tilted her head back. "I meant the view of the bayou wildlife."

"I didn't. And I think it's cute that the more nervous you get, the more you give me a hard time." He nipped the curve of her shoulder and then soothed it with a sweep of his tongue. "But you don't have anything to worry about. I promise I'm going to take good care of you. Gonna touch. Taste. Find all those places that make you moan like that."

Had she moaned? God, she had. Just a few barely there touches of his tongue, and her body was ready to hold a ticker tape parade in his honor. She shifted in her heels, her now-damp panties slipping against her skin and teasing her.

Without sarcasm as a defense, she didn't know what to do next, how to respond. She was on a new playing field and didn't know the rules of the game. Was she supposed to turn around and kiss him? Do something else? How was she supposed to think straight when her body was revving like an engine at the start of a drag race?

"It's okay. I've got you," he said softly, somehow reading her thoughts without her voicing him.

He took her by the wrists, drawing her hands behind her back, and clasped them in one hand. Then, he pulled her hair to the side with the other, wrapping the locks in his fingers, and kissed her neck again—this time with hot, wet strokes of his tongue, teeth grazing and lips sucking along the way. The sound of his mouth on her skin alone would've been enough to make her moan, but the feel of it . . .

Damn. She'd never thought of her neck as particularly erogenous, but she kept it covered so much that it felt like he'd found this forbidden and private place on her. *No one* touched her here. So with every stroke of his tongue, her body surged with need, every sensitive cell waking up. Each different part of her wanted his tongue on it, envied the attention her neck was getting. Her nipples strained against her bra. Her clit throbbed and ached. Even her thighs tensed as she imagined him licking his way up the inside of her legs.

Instinctually, she tried to reach out for the side of the window to steady herself now that she was on quivery legs, but Eli had her bound in his grip, her wrists secured behind her. That only stoked the fires. She whimpered as he tightened his grip on her hair to angle her head differently and then his lips and tongue were on her scarred skin. The sensation was different, less sensitive in some ways and acutely intense in others. But it didn't matter because all she could register was that he was kissing what she most tried to hide, kissing it like he was totally into it. Something twisted in her gut.

"Eli . . . you don't have to . . . I know they're not . . ."

"No, I don't think you do know," he interrupted. He dragged his tongue along her ravaged skin. "You're sexy everywhere, baby. I want to taste you everywhere."

She closed her eyes. She wanted to believe him. God, she did. But it was so hard to wrap her mind around. "Eli . . ."

The hand he had around her wrists shifted backward. "Unclench your hands."

"What?"

"Unclench, Bianca."

The command in his voice made her belly tumble. She did as he asked, and he guided her bound wrists farther back. Her fingertips grazed something hard and hot and . . . *huge*. He let her hands track over it, mapping the outline of his cock through his jeans, marveling at how very aroused he was. Jesus. Every muscle in her body tightened.

He pressed her hand fully against his erection and brushed his lips over her ear. "This is what kissing you does to me. My mouth could lie. My body won't. I wanted you from the moment I saw you."

She closed her eyes and inhaled a shaky breath, her heartbeat like a bass drum in her ears. She turned him on. *All* of her turned him on.

Something ugly and tangled unfurled inside her, opening up, loosening, lightening. And she found herself falling into the moment, the self-consciousness slipping off her like an itchy, unwanted coat. She was doing this to him. That gave her the push she needed to let go, to enjoy, to own it. "You didn't tell me you were carrying a weapon down there. That's . . . a little scary."

He chuckled, the sound soft and dark against her ears. He released the grip on her wrists and slid his hand to her hip, pulling her backside against his cock. His fingers roamed over her belly.

"Don't worry, gorgeous. I'm going to take my time with you. Kiss you all over, taste you, touch you, lick that sweet cunt until you can't think about anything else but how much you want me inside you. Then when you're slick and aching and begging me for it, you'll take every last bit of me and love it."

Fuuuck. They were only words but her sex clenched like a fist and a rush of fresh heat surged through her. She felt on the verge of coming already. A few strokes to her clit and she'd go off. "Taking your time might kill me."

She could feel him smile against her skin, but he didn't answer. Instead he released her hair and gathered her dress up her thighs.

Anxiety tried to claim her again. Naked was the scariest part of this whole thing.

But when Eli cursed, obviously catching sight of what she was wearing beneath, it distracted her from the automatic response trying to overtake her. "Damn, woman. Now who's trying to kill who?"

She bit her lip, fighting a pleased smile. She'd gone all out in anticipation of her date with Cal and had bought a black panty-and-bra set from La Perla that had a beautiful pattern of strategically placed lace flowers. It'd been an indulgence, but now she was so glad she'd gone all out.

He ran a hand over her backside and gave her ass a squeeze. "I should probably care that these were meant for some other guy, but fuck. All I can think of is what a dumbass he is to have let you slip by and what a lucky shit I am."

She laughed and peered over her shoulder. "I didn't wear them for him. I wore them for me. The bra matches."

"And . . . the dress is coming off." He shot a devastating smile her way and then untied the piece holding the wrap dress together. The expensive material fell to the floor, and that instinct to cover herself rushed through her. She'd never been this exposed to anyone but Lane, and he'd been paid not to judge. And she certainly hadn't stood in front of Lane naked in heels in the sunlight.

But as soon as Eli turned her around, the undeniable lust in his eyes turned that old worry from a roaring lion to a retreating mouse. His gaze swept over her with hungry eyes, lingering on her breasts, which were barely covered by the sheer slip of material. "You should always wear this. Just walk around the house, doing what you do, wearing just this. It was made for you."

She laughed, the sound coming out lilting and giddy. She didn't recognize that girlish laugh, that ease. But she liked it. "Might get kind of cold."

Eli stepped closer and palmed her hip. "I could keep you warm."

"Yeah, well maybe I'll invite you over next time I wear it." The words slipped out before she could stop them and she winced. "Sorry, I didn't—"

"Shh," he said, gently squeezing her hip, but shadows flitting over his expression. "It's okay. I wish I could be there the next time you wear it, too. I don't want to think of some other guy seeing you like this."

The little admission tugged at something in her chest, something she couldn't let get tugged. They were just strangers caught up in a moment. Stray impulses like that didn't mean anything. She pressed her lips against his. "Too much talking, not enough touching."

He smirked, a little of that trademark Eli Harding smugness sliding into place, and moved his hand to her ass. "You're right. Definitely not enough touching."

"And not enough nudity. You're still dressed."

He lifted a brow. "Then why don't you fix that."

Her pulse kicked up. Eli Harding naked? Yes, please. She liked that he was leading her without going into total control mode. She didn't feel like a passenger. He was making her a participant. She reached out and dragged the hem of his shirt upward.

He helped her along since he was so much taller than she was but as their hands moved up together, the blinding force that was Eli shirtless came into view. Of course, she'd seem him shirtless before. He spent half the movie that way sometimes. But Christ in Heaven, the movie screen didn't do it justice. The man's body was perfection. Muscular and broad and honed. That vee above the waistband of his jeans—deadly. She wanted to trace it with her tongue and bury her face in him.

He smiled down at her as he tossed his shirt to the side. "Be careful with that look you're giving me. My ego is inflated enough. You'll only make me more unbearable. Things will be flexed. Poses struck. It will be embarrassing for us both."

She rolled her lips over the grin she couldn't stop. "I'm trying to play it cool, but I'm not gonna lie. Every female chromosome in my body just had a mild heart attack." She traced her fingers down the bumps of his abdomen. "Just give me a second, it will pass, and then I'll make sure to knock you down a peg so your ego doesn't shift into supernova status."

"Just wait until you take off my pants."

She snorted at that and looked up to find his eyes twinkling with amusement. She shoved his shoulder. "Well, supernova status has been reached already apparently."

"Clearly." He grabbed her hand and kissed the inside of her wrist, sending a shiver up her arm. But when he looked at her again, his gaze had gone serious. "At the end of the day, it's just a costume, though. Part of my job. A nice surface distraction to hide the ugly stuff beneath."

She moved closer to him and let her fingertips tease at the button of his jeans. "I'm not so sure the inside is so ugly."

Frown lines appeared, but she didn't give him time to comment. The real world wasn't supposed to invade. Frowns weren't allowed. So she stuck with what had worked so far, less talking, more touching. She unfastened his jeans and boldly dipped her hand inside. He hissed out a breath, and before she could register that he wasn't wearing any underwear, his massive erection filled her hand with smooth, searing heat. Something altogether primal and wholly feminine jolted inside her.

She'd felt him through his jeans earlier but nothing compared to being skin to skin, his arousal literally in the palm of her hand. There was just so much of him and she wanted to explore every bit. She stroked him, loving the instant groan he gave her.

That was all the encouragement she needed. He said he wanted to make her feel good, but she wanted to offer the same. She wanted to feel that thrill of knowing she was giving him pleasure, too. She lowered herself to her knees and helped him tug off his boots and socks, and then she was dragging down his jeans. When she lifted her head, his cock was there before her in all its masculine glory—flushed and smooth and glistening at the tip. Lord. He was pretty everywhere. She let her gaze travel upward, finding him watching her.

He looked almost pained as he cupped a hand over the back of her head. "Get up, baby. I didn't come here to take from you."

But she didn't move. Her attention traveled back down, over the planes of his chest, down the deep vee and the faint trail of hair, and then to the proud erection jutting from between his thighs. She'd never given a blow job. It's not something she'd gone over with Lane. It had felt too intimate to consider. But right now, she wanted nothing more than to taste Eli.

She dragged her teeth over her lip. "I want to . . . I've never . . ."

Eli's grip on her head tightened a bit. "Bianca . . ."

It wasn't a yes. But it wasn't a no either. She steeled her nerve, met his gaze, and then without a word, moved her head forward and wrapped her lips around him. Eli closed his eyes and cursed on a breath.

The taste of him hit her tongue, and his scent filled her senses as he slid farther in—salt and musk and a hint of bitter. She hadn't known what to expect, had been braced for not liking the experience, but oh—oh, the things it did to her when he rocked into her mouth and his moan hit her ears. Her clit pulsed and her heart sped up, the power of knowing she was making him feel good an erotic rush.

She slid a hand to his thigh, bracing herself, and with her other hand, explored as she sucked him. There was no way she'd be able to take all of him into her mouth, but she used her hand to stroke him to the base. This apparently was the right move because his hands clamped her head, almost like he needed grounding or he'd lift off. She hummed at the positive reaction and then ventured farther back with her hand, palming his balls and feeling the weight of him in her hands. He was so goddamned beastly. Everywhere she touched was overwhelming. His body could crush hers. His hands could break her. It was intimidating and thrilling and the hottest experience of her life.

She could spend all afternoon exploring, learning. But when she swiped her tongue over the slit at the tip of his cock, Eli growled and tugged her head back. The move was so sudden, her vision swam for a second. She looked up. "Did I do something wrong?"

He reached down to grasp her elbow and helped her to her feet. His hands cradled her face and he brushed a thumb over her bottom lip, his green eyes almost black now. "No, too right. Your mouth is too good. It's going to send me over before I get my turn with you. And I need my turn. In fact, if I don't get my tongue between your thighs within the next minute I might fucking explode."

Her throat worked, the declaration rippling through her system. "Oh."

She couldn't say much more than that before he was lifting her off her feet and into his arms. She cried out in surprise and held on to him as he headed toward the bed. He tossed her onto the thick mattress and the air left her. The man looked like a stalking wildcat as he climbed onto the bed with her, yanked off her panties, and removed her bra. A predator with one single mission. To devour.

She was a happy victim.

After tossing the lingerie to the floor, he braced a hand on each side of her, his voice low and gravel-filled. "Hold on to the headboard and spread those long legs for me. Show me how wet you are for me, how much you want me to taste your cunt."

Her head fell back against a pillow. Good God. The dirty talk was going to kill her. It's not like she'd never heard any before. She'd seen porn. The talk was what always made her snort and roll her eyes, but coming from Eli, it was as good as a hand against her skin. Filth sounded good rolling off his tongue.

She reached above her and locked her hands around the slats of the headboard and slowly parted her legs.

"Fuck, yes," he said, the words a rumble from his chest as he looked down at her, his gaze shamelessly lingering on her bared, freshly waxed pussy. "You're sexy everywhere, Bianca." He traced a gentle finger over her labia, making her toes curl. "Pretty and pink and soaking wet for me. I can't wait to feel you around me."

He slid a finger inside her and she gasped, then groaned. Her body gripped him like it'd been waiting all its life for a single touch from this man.

"Mmm," he said, leaning down over her and working his finger slowly in and out. "You feel so hot, baby. So ready for me. But not yet."

She whimpered when he eased his finger out, but she didn't have long to complain because as soon as he shifted on the bed, he bent down and sucked a nipple into his mouth, laving at it with brutal precision and then nipping her with his teeth.

Her back arched and a dart of need went straight downward, as if her clit was connected to her breasts by electric current. "Oh, God."

His hand reached for her other breast and swiped the juices he'd gathered on his finger over her nipple, slicking it up and rolling the sensitive bud in his fingertips to match the movements of his mouth on the other.

Never in her life had she thought she could come from that kind of stimulation but she felt on the verge of breaking apart. *"Eli."*

His name was a gasp on her lips.

"Not yet, baby," he said against her skin. "Ride the feeling but don't go over."

She had no idea if she could do that. She'd become an expert on taking care of her own orgasms, but she didn't tease or deny herself. Patience wasn't her virtue. When she needed to come, she came. But right now, she forced herself to breathe through the sensations moving through her, to relish them, to enjoy the dance on the edge.

Eli lavished her breasts with attention for so long and so effectively that her brain began to buzz, her thoughts going blurry. The man was a genius with his mouth. But as soon as she got to the point where she didn't think she could take any more, he moved off that spot and showed he was true to his word. He would take his time. He kissed her everywhere, licking and tasting. Her belly, the underside of her breasts, the curve of her pelvis, her collarbone, the crease where hip met leg. He even licked the sensitive spaces between her fingers, giving her a preview of what his mouth would feel like between her thighs. He was worshiping and savoring and all the while that thick cock of his was brushing along her skin in all kinds of different places, leaving trails of pre-come and teasing her with how hard and turned on he was, forcing her to imagine what he'd feel like inside her.

But when he started kissing and sucking his way up her thighs, she nearly lost it. Her back arched like she was possessed and her heels dug into the mattress. "Eli!"

That's when it happened. That full, luscious mouth of his was next to her knee one minute and then it was flush on her clit the next. The flat of his tongue glided over her swollen, slick flesh and she saw stars behind her eyelids.

She'd never had a man go down on her. She'd imagined it, but never could she have imagined the intensity of it, how absolutely fucking amazing it felt. Hot, hungry mouth and tongue against her—shameless and messy and perfect.

She couldn't help it. She let go of the headboard and laced her fingers in those blond locks of his, gripping tight and doing everything she could to hold on. He made a sound of rumbling pleasure, and the vibration of it nearly undid her. "Eli . . . please."

He licked her hard and hot and then slid two fingers inside her, curving them, scissoring them, making her aware of every movement. Her body tensed around the sweet invasion. He pumped them inside her, slow and easy at first and then quicker when she started to rock her hips and chase the movement.

"Please!" Her voice had gone desperate now. "I can't—"

"You taste so fucking good," he said, the words panted against her skin. "Come for me, gorgeous. Let me have it."

That's all it took. All the tethers she'd put on herself broke free and her control shattered. She cried out long and loud, the orgasm sweeping over her like a steamroller. The bed squeaked beneath her as she rode his mouth and fingers and took everything he was offering. He didn't back off. If anything, the louder she got, the more he gave her.

Then, when she felt like she couldn't bear any more, like pleasure would overwhelm her and turn into pain, he pulled back. She collapsed onto the bed in a panting, sweating heap, blindly reaching for the sheets to ground her while she came down from the high.

But the comedown didn't happen like normal. She expected to feel sated, content, mellowed out like she did after masturbating. But this time, her body continued to pulse despite the orgasm, begging for something Eli hadn't given her yet. She felt . . . empty.

"I need . . ." She knew what she needed but her words wouldn't come. She sent Eli a pleading look.

He smiled. Wicked. Pleased. The man looked like the god of thunder as he rose up on his knees, lips slick and puffy with her arousal.

"I'll take care of you, baby. Stay just like that. Spread open and ready for me."

Eli climbed off the bed and went to his discarded jeans. She wondered what the hell he was doing, but then he pulled out a wallet and the condom inside.

Oh. Right. Somewhere between nipple worship and the orgasm of her life, she'd forgotten they would need that.

He was back on the bed in a second, looking down at her with a gaze that lit her on fire. "You ready for me, Bianca? Because there's nothing more I want right now in the world than to be inside you."

She swallowed past the dryness in her throat, searching for her voice. "Please. Need you."

His jaw flexed, determination filling his face. He stroked his cock, his big hand gliding up and down in an erotic show before rolling on the condom. "You need to tell me if I hurt you. We can take this as slow as you like."

Her belly was rising and falling with quick breaths still, and she couldn't take her gaze away from his hand stroking himself.

She knew she should probably be scared or worried. She was inexperienced. This could hurt. But somehow she couldn't drum up that emotion. Eli had been gentle and generous with her. He wouldn't hurt her. And the way he was looking at her flipped all these switches she didn't know she had. He made her feel wanton and desired and sexual. Feminine. She hadn't thought about her scars once since he'd tossed her on this bed.

The impact of that made her chest constrict.

"You weren't lying, were you?" she said softly.

He tilted his head and brushed her hair away from her face. "About what?"

"The way you're looking at me . . . I can see how you see me in your eyes. You think I'm sexy."

The smile that tipped his lips up was like sunshine against her bare skin—blinding in its stripped-down honesty. He ran a fingertip over her cheek. "I lie for a living, but I haven't lied to you once, Bianca. You're not just sexy, you're beautiful. And I have a feeling you're even more gorgeous underneath all that."

That sunk in. Really settled into her bones. He wasn't playing a game. He would leave her tonight, but he had given her a gift nonetheless. He saw her as beautiful. And for the first time since her accident, seeing that reflected in someone else's eyes, she finally believed it could be true. Finally realized that it wasn't her problem to fix if others didn't see her that way. This was who she was. And that was good.

Fuck men like Cal or people who would dismiss her out of hand. She may be different, but so were most of the clothes she designed. No piece was perfect, no stitch exact. That would be boring. Why did she expect it of herself? Who needed to look like every other glossy girl in a magazine? She was beautiful because she was who she was—scars and all. She could own that. She didn't want to hide anymore.

She lifted her gaze to Eli's. There were questions there in his eyes. Maybe he was thinking she was going to halt things or slow them down. But that was the last thing she wanted to do right now. Instead, she held his gaze and did what her surrogate, Lane, had once asked her to try in a mirror but that she'd never been able to do. She put her hands on her body, the body she'd spent her life hiding, and now, finding some new shameless part of herself, she let her fingers travel over the scars on her neck and down her collarbone, presenting herself without self-consciousness and highlighting every part of her. Over her breasts, down her belly. The touch felt sensual, but the way Eli's focus zeroed in, the way his tongue touched his bottom lip, made goose bumps rise on her skin.

"God, Bianca, you're driving me crazy."

She smiled and traced her fingers over her hips and down her thighs, taking her time, enjoying the sheer freedom of not having to hide. Then she teased her fingers over her labia and spread the lips, stroking herself just enough to make electricity move up her spine.

Eli groaned and gripped his cock at the base like he was going to explode just from watching her. The sight was so breathtakingly sexy that any remaining patience she had burned to ash.

She slid her hands to her thighs and spread her legs, showing him exactly how aroused she was. "I'm all yours, Eli. Show me how bad you want to fuck me."

Eli growled and crawled up her body, that predatory side surging to the surface. "Don't tempt me like that, baby. I'm supposed to be taking my time, and now you're making me think dirty thoughts of taking you hard and fast, making you take all of me right this very second."

She licked her lips and looped her arms around his neck. "Do it. I'll tell you to stop if I can't take it. But I'm tougher than I look."

A grinding sound escaped his throat and his hand gripped her behind the knee, lifting her leg and spreading her wider than she thought she could go. He pushed the tip of his cock against her entrance, teasing her. "You're going to wreck me."

"Only if you wreck me first."

That was all it took. His lips were on hers in the next instant, claiming her in a desperate clashing of lips that stole her breath. His tongue plunged into her mouth, and all she could think of was to beg for more. He'd snapped his leash. She could feel the control slipping. And she liked it. She grabbed his ass and dug her nails in.

"Please." The begging word burst out of her between the frantic kissing. "Now."

Eli didn't resist this time. He rocked his hips and pushed inside her as he kissed down her throat. The sensation of her body working to take him made her bite her tongue but *God. Oh, God.* Her head tipped back and overwhelming need filled her. She cried out for him.

"Am I hurting you?" He broke the kissing long enough to get the words out, his gaze searching.

"Fuck me, Eli. I didn't say to stop."

He grinned at that. "Look who's getting bossy."

But before she could give a smug reply, he tucked a hand between them, finding her clit, and slid farther inside her. She was so slick and hungry for him, so keyed up, that her body took him in without much fight, his fingers on her clit, making her rock her hips and seat him even deeper.

A loud groan came from Eli. "Yes. Fuck. *Fuck.*"

No more words were needed after that. Neither had to worry anymore about pain. She grappled for him, urging him on, *faster, more, deeper,* and he went for it. That long, thick cock making her feel full and stretched and used in the best way, and those dexterous fingers making her forget her name.

The bed protested beneath him and sweat slicked both their bodies. It was urgent and messy and the opposite of all that nicely choreographed romantic sex she'd watched in movies. It was perfect. And all the while, he kissed and kissed and kissed her. His cock plunging deep and his tongue stroking hers and her mind swimming in the pleasure of it all.

Eli broke away from the kiss and looked down at her, his gaze catching hers as his pace picked up, thrusting into her with abandon now. She wrapped her legs around his hips and held the eye contact, the connection between them sizzling in its silence, the intensity in the look burning into her like a brand.

"Come with me, beautiful." His voice was all command and strength. "I want to watch the pleasure on your face."

Watch her. It was something she would've panicked over before. She didn't like anyone looking at her for too long. But right now she felt like a goddamned sex goddess beneath him. So she tilted her hips where she needed, grinding her clit against his fingers and taking him deep. One, two, three times and that was all she needed. That spinning ball of sensation that had been building from the moment he'd entered her collapsed on itself and then burst open like an exploding star, light and colors dancing in her peripheral vision.

A long, aching cry dragged out of her, and she had to close her eyes to field the whopping impact of the orgasm. But as soon as she could, she fought to open her eyes again so she could watch Eli, fought so she could see the moment he lost himself to it.

It didn't take long. He'd watched her come and now his eyes were hooded and the muscles in his neck straining. He looked like a vengeful god. And soon he was crying out along with her. The deep sound vibrated through him as he sunk his cock to the hilt. Then, he grabbed her hip and held her there, making the sexiest grunts and groans she'd ever heard as he spent himself inside her.

It was glorious to watch and even better to feel.

This. This is what she'd prepared herself for with the therapy, what she'd earned. Passion. A stolen afternoon. A beautiful man who wanted her so badly that they'd torn the sheets off the bed and made the floors beneath them creak.

This wasn't love. Or long term. Or even potential for that. This was lust. Pure and simple. Two people grabbing on to each other in a storm and riding it out together.

And that was okay.

In fact, it was perfect.

EPILOGUE

One year later

Bianca straightened the neckline of her simple black dress, taking a few deep breaths, her nerves humming with the knowledge that her name would be called soon. She'd been to Fashion Week countless times, but had always hovered behind the scenes and pretended to be staff instead of the designer. But for the last few months, she'd been slowly stepping out into the spotlight, doing interviews and being seen at events. Now she was going to have to walk the runway as soon as the last models finished showing off her new line.

She stepped into a pair of to-die-for red heels a designer friend had given her for the occasion. They were glorious. But they were high. "I should've worn flats. What if I trip?"

Bianca's assistant, Helen, rolled her eyes. "Girl, you walk in heels better than most people walk barefoot. You'll be just fine. Do your strut and wave. You've earned this. The new line kicks ass."

"I may vomit."

Helen laughed. "This isn't your first rodeo, lady. You've got this."

"Right. Yes. Got this." But despite her recent experience with this type of thing, the other shows hadn't been as big as this one. Every media outlet she could think of was on the other side of that curtain. And the crowd was full of celebrities and VIPs. So many freaking eyes on her.

"Go out, do your thing, and then have that new man of yours take you out for a night in good ol' Paris to celebrate." She said it like *Paree* and did a little flourish with her hand. "That's what you need."

Bianca adjusted her neckline again and sighed. "That sounds great. But that man's not here. I broke things off before the trip."

Helen's eyebrows lifted. "Seriously? You let that baseball player go? Lord, I would've kept him around just to admire his backside a few times a day."

Bianca smirked at Helen's wistful tone. Yeah, Dirk had been nice to look at and a decent enough guy. But something hadn't clicked.

"What happened?"

Bianca shrugged. "I wasn't feeling the chemistry."

Helen groaned and took over the adjustment of Bianca's dress, handling her like she was one of the models and revealing more of Bianca's cleavage. "That's always your excuse. You've ditched the last three for the same reason. I'm not judging, but what's up?"

"I don't know. I'll know the right one when I find him, I guess. In the meantime, I'm just enjoying the hunt." She said the comment offhandedly, but the reality sent a pang through her. Truth was, she'd set the bar too damn high out of the gate. Eli had marked her psyche without trying and now every other man seemed to pale in comparison. Every guy she dated got held up to this mythical person, this guy whom she'd been with all of once in very unique circumstances. It was completely unfair and unrealistic. To the guys. And to her.

She'd tried to reason with herself. She didn't even know Eli. They'd had a smoking-hot physical connection, end of story. She didn't know anything else about him but what he'd told her, really. And those things hadn't been pretty. But still, he hovered there in the back of her mind, always ready to infiltrate her dreams or her drifting thoughts.

She hadn't let herself mourn or pine over him. Since that day with him, she'd been dating, getting out there, living her life in a way she hadn't done before. She'd even talked through the whole incident in therapy. But some bone-deep part of her still hung on to Eli.

She'd watched the gossip columns about him going into rehab. She'd read the interviews after he'd gotten out. He seemed to be doing well and the rehab had, at least from the outside looking in, helped him. He was getting great roles and good reviews. A part of her had hoped she'd run into him in Dr. West's office again but he wasn't local. The doctor had just been a temporary therapist while Eli was in New Orleans. Now Eli would be back in the glitzy world of Hollywood.

They had been two ships passing in the night. And that night was done. She needed to let it go. She needed to stop holding up new guys to some imaginary standard.

"Let's hear it for designer B.B. Marsh!" the announcer called, the sound echoing through the backstage area.

Cheers sounded from the other side of the curtain, and Helen gave her a beaming smile. "You're on!"

Bianca groaned but gave Helen a smile. "If I fall, it will be your fault."

Helen gave her a little shove, and Bianca headed toward the runway. The flashing of the cameras blinded her as she took a few steps down the catwalk and gave a little wave to the audience. The faces all blurred and the sound blended into white noise, but she could feel the love, sense the genuine enthusiasm of the crowd, and that made the moment in the spotlight worth it. They'd liked her designs. That's what was most important.

The models came onto the stage to surround her and she gave a little bow. After a bit more applause and another quick wave, she headed back behind the stage without wobbling on the heels. Yay. But by the time she cleared the busy area, the exhaustion hit her. All the buildup and planning and sleepless nights piled onto her. But at least it'd been a success. She sagged against a wall in a darkened corner, relieved that the night was done and had gone off with only a few minor glitches.

She closed her eyes and breathed, enjoying the harried sounds that came along with being backstage at a fashion show. Her schedule flipped through her head. The rest of the night was booked with parties, and she had been planning to peek in on a few other shows, but right now, the bathtub in her hotel sounded mighty nice. Maybe she could sneak out.

She opened her eyes and glanced toward her models and crew, wondering if she could make it past them unnoticed. If she could sneak past Helen and . . .

"Planning an escape?"

The deep, familiar voice zipped down her spine and sent goose bumps along her skin. She spun around, almost toppling in the heels this time, and put a hand to the wall to steady herself. "What?"

Eli stepped out of the shadows, hands tucked in the pockets of his gray slacks and gave her a small smile. The impact of him was no less than the first time she'd seen him. No, it was worse. Now she knew what he tasted like, how he felt inside her. Plus, he was wearing her version of man lingerie. A perfectly tailored suit that highlighted every delicious bit of him. Eli as James Bond. "Eli Harding."

He nodded. "B.B. Marsh."

Her heart fluttered in her chest. Maybe she was hallucinating. It'd been so long since she'd seen him that her mind had conjured him up. "What are you doing here?"

He gave her a half-smile. "Your show was a hit tonight. Not a surprise. You're a talented woman. I think it was even better than your winter show in New York."

Her lips parted. "You were at my New York show?"

"I sat in the back. I wanted to see your stuff." He tipped his head to the side. "And I wanted to see you. But you didn't go out onstage that night. I had to settle for a glimpse at an after-party."

Now she knew she was staring at him like a crazy person. He'd gone to her show? He'd wanted to see her? "Why didn't you come back and say hi like you're doing tonight?"

He shrugged, all nonchalance, but his gaze shifted away. "You had a guy with you. I— It wasn't my place to interrupt. You looked . . . happy."

She frowned, trying to think back to whom she was with that night. Whoever it was, he hadn't lasted long. "Oh. He's . . . not in the picture anymore."

"Oh." His attention swung back to her, his expression shuttered. "Well, either way, it was probably for the best I didn't say anything. I wasn't in the right place yet."

"Right place?"

He stepped closer, his hands still in his pockets, but even that little move into her space made the room feel ten times smaller, her skin feel tighter. "Yeah. I thought maybe I was. I wanted to see you. Had thought about you more than I should. But then I saw you and that guy, and I realized, I'd only complicate shit for you. You didn't need some recovering addict hanging around, even as a friend. I needed to leave you alone, focus on my recovery, and get my career going back in the right direction."

She wet her lips, his words sinking in and spinning like dervishes in her head. "From what I've seen, you're doing great."

He lifted a brow, some of that trademark smugness playing over his face. "So you've looked me up?"

Only a thousand times. She tilted her head and gave a little shrug. "I might have checked a few websites. I'm the curious type, you know."

"You know, I don't know," he said, playful tone going serious. "But I'd like to."

She looked up, her heartbeat quick against her ribs. "What?"

"In rehab, they encouraged us to write letters to our families or friends, build support networks, mend fences. And I did. But I also wrote letters to you. I never sent them because we'd agreed to let that night be the end of it, but I felt this intense need to talk to you. Something inside me changed when I met you. I wanted to tell you about what I was going through, get to know who you are beneath that beautiful exterior, to do all the things I'd never had the desire to do with a woman before. Be with you. Really *be* with you.

"And I thought when I got out, I'd just come find you, ask for a chance to see where things would go. But I realized that was fucking selfish. I wasn't worthy of that yet. You didn't need my drama in your life. You didn't deserve a dude who was a goddamned project. So when I saw you with that guy, I thought maybe it was for the best. But the wanting didn't go away. I wanted to be that guy making you smile. And I started to wonder, what if this really could be something, what if in that one night, somehow the universe got it just right, and we missed the message. I couldn't stop thinking about you. I still haven't, Bianca."

He lifted his gaze to hers, and her breath caught.

"Eli . . ."

He reached out and took her hand between his. "I know I probably sound like some stalker or crazy person. Or some woo-woo guy spouting off about fate and soul mates. We don't really know each other. I don't know if you prefer the Beatles or the Rolling Stones. I don't know how you take your coffee. And I don't know what dreams you have for yourself. But I do know how I felt when I was with you. And I don't think I can move on until I ask."

She couldn't move. Couldn't breathe. "Ask me what?"

"Bianca Baylor Marsh, I've never met anyone else like you, and I haven't touched another woman in the year since I've touched you. You don't owe me a damn thing, and feel free to tell me I'm crazy. But if any part of you thinks there could be something here, something real that might be worth exploring, then I'd like to take you out to dinner tonight and talk. Nothing else. Just me and you getting to know each other and starting things the way normal people start."

Bianca stared at him, her hand trembling in his. The words were too much to process. He had wanted her since he'd left. The guy who'd been addicted to sex had been celibate for a year. And now he was here, asking her on a date.

It *was* crazy.

But something that had laid dormant inside her since she'd seen him last perked up and bloomed bright inside her. A lot had happened since that afternoon with him. She'd gotten her confidence back. She'd put herself out on the dating market. She'd slept with two other men since Eli. But nothing had felt like those few hours with this man. And nothing felt like this moment right now.

She didn't know why Eli had this effect on her.

And she couldn't know where it would lead.

But she did know one thing.

She couldn't wait to find out.

She wrapped her fingers around his and smiled. "I prefer the Stones, one sugar no cream, and I've got a lot of dreams. One of which just walked through that door. I haven't stopped thinking about you either. It's damn annoying."

The smile that broke over his face nearly melted her. "Yeah?"

"Yeah." She stepped closer. "Now let's go see Paris, Eli Harding."

He gathered her to him and touched his forehead to hers. "No, let's see the world, gorgeous."

She wasn't sure who met whom first. But somewhere in the

middle, their lips found each other, and they kissed so long that the noise around them went silent. And the restless place inside her went still.

The girl who'd hidden from sight all her life now had the attention of every eye in the room. And she'd never felt more beautiful.

Don't miss the next novel in Roni Loren's
Loving on the Edge series

Loving You Easy

Cora has an amazing sex life. She's beautiful,
daring, and the most popular submissive in Hayven.
Too bad none of it's real . . .

IT specialist Cora Benning has figured out the key to her formerly disastrous love life: make it virtual. In the online world of Hayven, she's free of her geek girl image and can indulge her most private fantasies with a sexy, mysterious master without anyone in her life discovering her secrets. That is until her information is hacked and she finds herself working to fix the breach under two very powerful men—one who seems all too familiar . . .

Best friends and business partners Ren Muroya and Hayes Fox were once revered dominants. Then Hayes was wrongfully sent to prison and everything changed. Ren wants to get back to who they were. Hayes can't risk it. But when they discover the new IT specialist is their online fascination, and that she's never felt a dominant's touch, the temptation to turn virtual into reality becomes all too great . . .

Coming soon from Berkley Books

Roni Loren wrote her first romance novel at age fifteen when she discovered writing about boys was way easier than actually talking to them. Since then, her flirting skills haven't improved, but she likes to think her storytelling ability has. Though she'll forever be a New Orleans girl at heart, she now lives in Dallas with her husband and son. If she's not working on her latest sexy story, you can find her reading, watching reality television, or indulging in her unhealthy addiction to rock stars, er, rock concerts. Yeah, that's it. Visit her website, roniloren.com.

Printed in the United States
by Baker & Taylor Publisher Services